THE IMPERIAL ALCHEMIST

A. H. WANG

FOR MY HUSBAND…

THE MUSE.

AUTHOR'S NOTE ON PRONUNCIATION

Here is a brief guide on how to pronounce some of the names of the characters and locations:

QIN, QI: The letter *q* is pronounced as *ch* in English. Hence, Qin is pronounced as *Chin*.

HSU FU, LU HSING: In Chinese, *hs* is pronounced much like *sh* in English.

SUN QUAN: Again, *q* is pronounced as *ch*, and *Sun* here is pronounced as *soon*.

XI'AN, XIANYANG: Like *hs*, the letter *x* is pronounced much like *sh* in English.

WANG JIAN: *Wang* as in English *father*. The *ian* sounds like the currency *yen*.

ZHIFU: *Zh* is similar to the *j* sound in English.

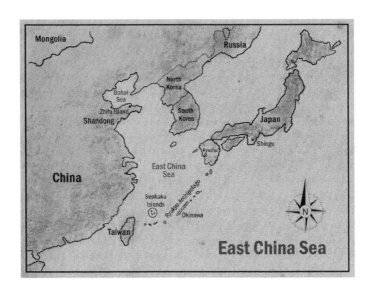

F A C T:

221 BCE, China. *After two centuries of war and turmoil between the Seven Warring States, a man named Qin Shi Huang conquered all others and unified China for the first time. The new Chinese empire was born, and this man proclaimed himself as its First Emperor.*

Keen to prolong his reign, Emperor Qin made many attempts at acquiring the elixir of life, of which the most well-known is the Voyage of Hsu Fu. In 210 BCE, Hsu Fu was sent to sail east with a fleet carrying hundreds of young men and women, in search of the mystical Penglai Mountain: the fabled home of the Eight Immortals.

They never returned.

PROLOGUE

211 BCE, China

HE WAS RUNNING *out of time.*

Panic erupted in his chest as this realisation sank in. As if on cue, the emperor launched into another spasmodic coughing fit. His whole body quaked, the sound of his outburst echoing through the cavernous chamber. When the coughing finally ceased, he withdrew the golden silk handkerchief from his lips, and saw that it was stained red with blood.

His hands trembled.

The emperor looked about him, as if to check whether anyone else had noticed that the tremors were becoming more frequent. The imperial guards stood stock-still at their stations, looking dead ahead, as they had been trained to do. The court sorcerer, a decrepit hunchback, leaned over the sacrificial vessel, his face a picture of concentration on the task at hand. The entire imperial ancestral temple was silent, apart from the crackle of the fire burning steadily in the bronze vessel, throwing elongated shadows of the sorcerer onto the distant wall and ceiling.

Emperor Qin shifted in his throne, watching as the sorcerer performed the pyromancy ritual, anxious for the whole thing to be

I

finished. He needed answers. All of his hard work over the years—and for what? Who would look after all that he had achieved? His sons were imbeciles, weaklings who had no concept of how to rule a people. And he had too many enemies, men who would leap upon any signs of weakness. No doubt the vast land he had united would crumble back into war and chaos if he were to relinquish his reign.

There was so much left to do. He had such a grand vision for the empire that he had just managed to amass.

No, he was not about to give it all up now.

He must live on.

He watched as the sorcerer finished carving texts on a tortoise shell, anointing it with blood. The old man carefully placed it in the sacrificial vessel and stood back, his shadows dancing with the movement of the flames.

Moments passed, and Emperor Qin grew impatient, shifting restlessly on his throne. After what seemed to be forever, a loud crack finally sounded from the vessel. With great fanfare the sorcerer stepped forward to retrieve the shell, picking it out of the flames with long pieces of bamboo. Qin leaned forward, expectant and anxious. He watched as the sorcerer placed the heated object on a platter, studying the cracks on its surface. The old man's face was etched with the lines of time, all of which deepened as a crooked smile began to slowly spread across his lips.

Qin felt a cold shiver rise up his spine.

"Your Majesty," said the sorcerer, now bowing before the emperor, his voice the hoarse whisper that Qin had always found chillingly disconcerting. The old man extended his arms, offering the cooled shell in his splayed palms. "The gods have granted an answer to your query."

2015, China

GEORGIA LEE WATCHES in agitated silence as the four men grunt with exertion, using a long steel rod to lever a large rock away from the entrance. The round stone holds stubbornly at first, then shifts ever so slightly, gaining momentum, and rolls a few paces before stopping again. A narrow hole about a metre in height is revealed, exhaling a sigh of thick, stale air.

The entire excavation team draws in an audible breath, the anticipation amongst them palpable.

"That's great," Georgia calls out, and the men with the long rod throw relieved glances at her, releasing the apparatus with a loud clang.

She hands a torch to the man beside her. Professor Chang, a solemn and looming figure from Peking University, has been working by her side since the first day of excavation. Georgia has hoped that by now they'd have developed a more affable relationship, yet despite her Chinese lineage and fluency in the language, the professor still treats her as a foreign outsider.

Without uttering a word, Chang knits his brows, giving her a terse nod.

Then, turning to her PhD students, Kate and Michael, Georgia instructs: "Stay up here, I'll head down with Professor Chang first."

Georgia peeks through the entrance to the tomb with her torch and sees polished stone steps leading down into a gaping void of darkness. She smiles to herself, feeling the rush of adrenaline as she squeezes through the gap. With Professor Chang following closely behind her, she slowly descends the stairs. As she approaches the landing, Georgia sees an elaborate archway sentineled with a pair of Chinese guardian lions, each almost as tall as her.

"Are they—are they carved out of jade?" Professor Chang says in Chinese, gasping with surprise.

"Looks like it," Georgia confirms in the same language,

and she sweeps her torchlight over the two statues, watching as the light glints and shimmers from the translucent emerald surfaces.

Her heart drums forcibly in her chest. Guardian lions are traditionally carved from stone, and the more extravagant ones in front of imperial palaces may be carved out of marble. But rarely has she seen these sentries made from solid pieces of jade—especially jade of this quality.

The tomb, whoever it belonged to, must be the resting place of someone very important and powerful.

She feels the full force of excitement hit her, and she steps through the threshold, wondering what she will find beyond.

LONG AFTER, when she finally re-emerges from the tomb into the frigid air, she sees that the sky has darkened into a deep purple hue. Glancing at her watch, she raises her eyebrows in surprise. She realises that the whole day has passed as she explored in the underground palace.

Michael walks towards her as she brushes dust and cobwebs from her braided hair. He hands her the mobile phone, explaining, "It's Sarah, calling from Sydney."

She smiles. After all these years of working side-by-side, her assistant has developed a knack for reading her mind, even when they are continents apart. She thanks Michael and takes the phone, wedging it between her cheek and shoulder as she sits on a nearby rock, unrolling her sleeves against the chill of the evening air. "Hey! Good timing, you won't believe what we found today."

"Yeah, Michael said that the dig is going well." Sarah's voice rings down the line.

"*Well* doesn't even begin to describe it. It's a full treasure trove down there—I wish you could see it. The tomb hasn't been touched since it was sealed. It was like a scene straight out of the movies—bronze vessels, jade combs and bracelets, silk robes and paintings, and an entire library of manuscripts." She's talking fast, a swell of emotion rising in her chest as she delivers her next revelation: "We found *seafaring* maps, Sarah."

There's a long pause before the older woman replies. "But I thought you dated the tomb to be around 200 BCE?"

Georgia nods enthusiastically even though Sarah can't see her, a laugh bubbling out of her throat: "I know, right? Think about it, Sarah, this proves *everything*. All our hard work—what, five years of research? Years of trying to get people to take us seriously for funding and now excavation—it's all come to this point."

She exhales, thinking about the impact this finding will have on her work: it is central to proving her theory that the ancient Chinese had possessed seafaring abilities far surpassing the conclusions of all contemporary historians and archaeologists. Sure, popular theory recognises the Chinese as the inventors of the magnetic compass around 210 BCE, but most believe it was used solely for the purpose of divination and feng shui, and was only adopted for navigation during the eleventh century. Finding seafaring maps in a tomb dated around the 200 BCE period proves the Chinese were widely navigating the seas much earlier than most people thought.

She flexes her fist by her side at the triumph of the moment. Over the past decade, many of her writings and lectures have promoted her belief in this hypothesis, and it's one she has been criticised and sometimes ridiculed for. Today is the day she will prove all of those sceptics wrong.

"Wow," Sarah says, yet her voice lacks her usual enthusiasm. "That's fantastic, Georgia."

Georgia frowns. "What's wrong?"

She hears Sarah exhale a long sigh, and the back of her neck prickles in anticipation of the bad news.

"Listen, Georgia. I think you better get your arse back here. We've got a problem."

1

Two months later, Sydney

GEORGIA HAS no idea why she is here. Really, she should be back at her office, catching up on the mounting paperwork.

Driving her car through the gates of Lambert Estate, she takes a deep breath as she absorbs the sheer immensity of the property. Sprawling grass plains stretch as far as the eye can see, and beyond the horizon a blazing scarlet sun is about to set over the majestic Blue Mountains. A two-storey mansion looms some hundred metres ahead, brooding and ominous with its dark grey masonry walls. It's a hot day, unseasonably so for April, and it's been warmer still because the air conditioning in her ailing Ford Festiva decided to fail during her two-hour drive from Sydney.

After receiving Sarah's call on the day they opened the tomb in China, Georgia dropped everything at the dig, reluctantly leaving Kate and Michael to document the findings with the Peking University team, their joint venture partner in the excavation project. Two days later, she arrived back in Sydney to find out she'd lost all of her project grants for the next year.

The newly elected government has been making major cuts to education, especially in areas they deem less essential to the economy. As devastating as it is, everyone at the university has seen this coming. But to have lost all of her private grants too? Georgia can hardly believe that within two months of making one of the most significant archaeological discoveries in the past decade, she and Sarah are now scrambling around, searching for all possible avenues of funding.

So far, they've come up with nothing. Who knows, she'll probably be out of a job at the university too by the time her department decides how to allocate what dismally little money there is left.

As her car advances towards the mansion, Georgia wonders about the host who has invited her to dinner tonight. A self-made man, the English-born, fifty-two year old billionaire first made his fortune in the pharmaceutical industry in England and the United States, later expanding his investments to a broad range of other business ventures.

Sarah had a glint in her eyes after receiving the phone call from Lambert's personal assistant the previous week. "Did you know," she gushed in her accented English, "he was listed as one of the most eligible bachelors in *TIME* magazine?"

Georgia rolled her eyes at the celebrity gossip. "But he isn't even on our list of sponsors, and we didn't call them... Did you ask what the meeting is for?"

"Nope." Sarah shrugged. "But after all the bad luck we've been having, this could be the break we need!"

"I don't know." Georgia shook her head, not liking the idea at all. "I really have better things to do right now than entertain some rich—"

"Georgia." Sarah lowered her tone, folding her arms across her chest, and Georgia swallowed her argument. "What can you possibly achieve over one night in the office?

We've submitted every grant application, called all the funding bodies in the country. It's likely we'll be forced to pull out of the China dig in two months. And I'll probably have to look for a new job soon! Even if Lambert's not interested in giving us money for the project, at least get a decent meal in your belly before we're all thrown out on the streets begging for work. You are going to meet this man, and I don't want to hear any more about it."

Georgia sighs in aggravation at the memory of their conversation. Sometimes she really doesn't know who the boss is in their relationship. These kinds of social engagements are a pet peeve of Georgia's, and Sarah once pointed out that it's precisely this kind of attitude which ensures that Georgia will always remain a lowly research professor, and never have a shot at climbing the bureaucratic ladders of university administration.

At this, Georgia scoffed in reply: That was a future she'd happily settle on.

Now, crawling to a stop before the enormous house, the little Ford splutters and complains audibly as she shuts off the engine. She exits her car, its door protesting with a groan as she pushes it shut. At the foot of the over-sized double doors, she takes a fortifying breath before pressing the doorbell.

Within seconds, a portly middle-aged man in an austere three-piece suit opens the heavy doors, and she instantly feels under-dressed in her simple black shift.

"Good evening. You must be Professor Lee," he says with a pompous English accent, his posture so erect she wonders if there are stiffeners hidden in that black suit.

"Yes, hello. I'm here to see Mr. Lambert?"

"Of course, please come in. I am Joseph, Mr. Lambert's butler."

Joseph leads her through the cavernous marble foyer with a sprawling staircase, into an exquisite drawing room adorned with antique European furnishings. The air has a mixed aroma of tobacco and rich coffee.

"Mr. Lambert shall be down shortly. Would you like a drink while you wait, Professor? Tea? Coffee? Some wine perhaps?" Joseph offers.

"I could do with a glass of red after that drive," she says with a weary smile.

The butler proceeds to rattle off a long list of vintages that Georgia doesn't recognise. She shrugs, giving him a perplexed smile. "Whatever is easiest for you, Joseph."

"Of course. I'll be back shortly with your drink." He makes a slight bow of his head, exiting the room.

Georgia lets out a soft whistle as she surveys the lushly appointed space, admiring the various masterpieces on the wall, including one by her own favourite artist, O'Keeffe. Her eyes are drawn to the table beneath the large mirror on the wall, cluttered with picture frames boasting images of Mark Lambert with prominent figures. It is clear the man has no shortage of powerful and famous friends: there are photos of him playing golf with eminent leaders of the world, partying with Hollywood celebrities, and even one of him shaking hands with the Dalai Lama.

"Professor Lee, sorry to keep you waiting," a deep voice booms from behind her. She turns to see a tall, commanding man standing at the doorway. Dressed in a black polo shirt and grey slacks, his silvering hair is immaculately trimmed, his face tanned from the Australian sun, and he wears a relaxed, confident smile that Georgia is sure he's used to beguile countless women of her age—or younger.

She resists the temptation to roll her eyes. Sarah has warned her to play nice.

Evidently sensing that she is unmoved by his charms, he crosses the distance between them in a few strides, offering his hand. "I'm Mark," he says, now donning an amused smile and assessing her anew with his steely grey eyes.

Up close, she can see why this man is a highly coveted bachelor, and why Sarah was giddy as a schoolgirl at the thought of Georgia having dinner with him. The man is handsome, in the conventional sense, and does not look a day over forty-five. With his chiselled jaw, expensive haircut, and his intense, smouldering gaze, he looks like he has just walked out of a *GQ* photo shoot.

She shakes his outstretched hand with a firm grip. "Mr. Lambert—"

"Please, call me Mark. We're in Australia and that puts us immediately on a first name basis." He winks, and Georgia catches a subtle whiff of a cockney accent which hints at his more humble upbringing.

"Mark," she says, "thank you for the invitation tonight."

"You're very welcome. I'm so glad you could make it. I've been a fan of your work for a long time."

She narrows her eyes. "I'm sorry, Mr. Lambert—"

"Mark," he corrects as he gestures to a couple of lounge chairs by the fireplace, sitting down in one and crossing his legs. Joseph reappears with their drinks, placing two glasses of wine on the coffee table, before silently disappearing again.

"Mark," Georgia says, joining him by the fireplace as she watches him sip his drink. "I'm surprised that a man of your standing knows of my existence, let alone my work."

Mark holds her gaze, taciturn and thoughtful. After a long awkward silence, Georgia feels her usual confidence wane under his piercing gaze, and for a brief moment she regrets the biting tone of her remark.

When he finally speaks again, it is with a sincerity that makes her icy resolve thaw. "I think you undervalue your work, Georgia. I know you probably despise people like me— hedonistic dilettantes with poor taste and too much wealth for their own good. But I assure you, some of us *do* read and have interests outside of money." He smiles with mirth, taking the edge off his observation.

She draws in a breath, heat creeping up her face. Unsure of what to say in response, she stutters, "I—I'm sorry."

Mark holds up his hands, letting out a short chuckle. "No, that's fine. I guess I *am* guilty of liking beautiful things. I'm a collector, and I like to buy rare and exquisite objects from the past. I think the past can teach us a lot of things, wouldn't you agree?"

She nods, feeling oddly chastised.

"Take O'Keeffe, for example." He gestures to the large artwork above the mantelpiece, one of the artist's famed floral paintings. "We can all learn from her resolve to remain independent from the shifting trends of her time, and to stay true to her own vision. Without vision, and the resolve to see it through, not much can be achieved. It's not surprising, then, that O'Keeffe became one of the first female American artists to be recognised by her male peers."

Georgia murmurs her agreement, looking over at the painting to hide her now scarlet face.

"You know, I've read all of the books you've published over the years," he says, now focusing his gaze back on her.

"You have?"

He nods. "Your most recent, *The First Emperor*, is my favourite. It offers a different perspective on the Qin Dynasty. Emperor Qin's methods of uniting China were inspirational—they gave me an insight into my own business strategies."

Georgia raises her brows in surprise. *The First Emperor* is the fruit of years of research and too many sleepless nights. It takes an in-depth look at the infamous ruler, whose totalitarian regime embittered the oppressed people of his reign and gave him a most notorious reputation. His cruel methods of dictatorship also led to numerous assassination attempts, which he somehow managed to thwart.

But in a different light, Qin was also the man who—at long last—united China, which until then had been a myriad of small warring states battling ceaselessly against each other for over two centuries. In addition, Qin also unified China's currency, measuring units, and its written language. The terracotta warriors, one of the most important archaeological discoveries of the twentieth century, were also the creations of Qin; as, of course, was the Great Wall.

Most people condemn Qin as a brutal tyrant, yet Georgia sees the invaluable contributions he also made, which helped to shape China into the country it is today. If Qin had not defeated the Warring States, it is likely the country would have gone through many more centuries of internecine bloodshed, war, and turmoil. A new Chinese empire was born, and its civilisation eventually prospered into one of the great powers of the world.

Georgia has received countless criticisms of her book and her opinions, but it appears Lambert is in agreement with her. Quite frankly, she's glad to have another person take her side. She realises, with some relief, that tonight may really just be dinner with someone who genuinely understands and appreciates her work.

"Pardon me, sir," Joseph appears by the door way. "Dinner is ready to be served."

"Shall we?" Mark stands, leading her out of the drawing room. "I hope you're hungry, Georgia. I had my kitchen prepare a feast for our meeting tonight."

DINNER IS A SUMPTUOUS SEVEN-COURSE MEAL, starting with freshly shucked oysters for appetisers and finishing with the most delicious homemade ice cream she has ever tasted: salted butter caramel, wild fig, and malted syrup topped with crunchy honeycomb. In spite of herself, Georgia sits back after her last bite of the dessert and lets out a sigh of contentment. She has always been a sucker for good food.

She takes another sip of the Bordeaux the butler keeps

pouring for her, feeling glad she isn't driving all the way back to Sydney tonight. Sarah, bless her, has booked a motel nearby.

Dinner conversation has roamed over a wide range of subjects, from politics and Asian art to the latest discovery of water on Mars. Georgia is unexpectedly impressed at her host's interest and extensive knowledge in numerous artistic, scientific, and intellectual pursuits. She finds herself speaking at length about her current excavation project in China, and Mark's eyes gleam with enthusiasm as she describes with great detail the uncovering of the ancient tomb a mere two months ago. When she tells him about her university's loss of funding, and their imminent withdrawal from the project, he grows quiet, seemingly contemplating the issue.

"Do you know who the tomb belongs to?" Mark asks as he leads her to the library with his after-dinner cognac in hand.

"We've narrowed it down to a shortlist of three possible candidates," replies Georgia. "We'll know for sure as the team examines the artefacts and manuscripts in there."

She stops short upon entering the library, gaping at the sublime space before her. The walls are lined with shelves full of books reaching to the five-metre high ceiling. Ladders lean against the shelves, providing access to the volumes. The place smells of both old books and new. The last time Georgia saw a library as beautiful as this was at the Strahov Abbey in Prague.

Mark chuckles at the expression on her face. "As you can see, Georgia, I do like to read. And no, they aren't just for decoration."

Georgia surveys the room, noticing it is also a cabinet of curiosities adorned with Asian art and relics. Scrolls of Chinese ink paintings hang on what little wall space there is between the bookshelves. A full samurai suit stands in one corner, encased in glass. A series of museum display cases are scattered about the room, and she spies in one some ancient Chinese swords, and in another, bronze vessels.

"It's beautiful," she says in awe as she settles down in a leather arm chair beside Mark's, basking in the warm scent of old, worn leather bindings as she sips her tea.

"Well," Mark says, "I suppose now is a good time to talk about why I've invited you here tonight."

She tenses.

"We spoke before about your book on Emperor Qin," Mark begins. "In it, you describe at length his search for immortality."

Georgia nods slowly. The Emperor's prolonged quest for the elixir of life is notorious. It became one of his many obsessions later in life. He dispatched several eastward expeditions to find the magical potion for eternal youth, and when they were unsuccessful, he roamed the northern shore of Shandong Province to hunt down the evil spirit he believed was keeping him from contacting the Immortals who supposedly possessed the elixir. Qin visited the Zhifu Island of Shandong three times, hoping to find immortality there. Ironically, all of his futile attempts to avoid death actually became the cause of his demise. The First Emperor died at the age of forty-nine, having consumed mercury pills prescribed by his alchemists as a means to build up his resistance to death.

"I was interested in your description of Qin sending the imperial alchemist, Hsu Fu, to search for Penglai Mountain," Mark continues. "This mythical island was rumoured to be where the Eight Immortals lived."

Georgia sips her tea, pensive. This is a tale familiar to her since she was a little girl. Hsu Fu requested a fortune for the voyage, which he claimed was a gift for the Immortals. It is believed that his fleet included sixty barques, some hundreds of virgin boys and girls, and craftsmen of different fields. The mission failed, of course, and they were never seen again. To this day, no one knows for sure what happened to the expedition.

"Anyway," Mark says, "all of this was just mere interest, pure myth to me. Until recently."

Georgia looks up, cocking an eyebrow. "Recently?"

"Yes." He pauses to take a drink from his glass tumbler. "You know, I heard another story that wasn't in your book. This version explains that the quest didn't just end there. It tells of Hsu Fu's journey as he sailed east. What Emperor Qin didn't know was that Hsu Fu had his own reasons for making the trip. His son was born with an incurable disease, and his condition was worsening. Even Hsu Fu, a renowned alchemist and healer, couldn't help his only child.

"Qin's generous offer was an opportunity that came at a perfect time. Hsu Fu didn't really believe in the elixir, but he hoped to find other herbs in some distant land to experiment with, so that he could cure his son."

"Yes." Georgia frowns. "I've heard of this legend as well, but really there's no proof—"

"Humour me, Professor, please. Allow me to finish." Mark smiles, and she falls quiet again. "The story goes on to say, that even though Qin had believed the elixir was on Zhifu Island, Hsu Fu thought otherwise and kept sailing east. He sent messages back to court regularly to inform the emperor of his progress. But after a month, the messages stopped.

"Qin grew impatient, and ordered the court diviner to communicate with the gods. They carved the emperor's questions on a tortoise shell, then performed a pyromancy ritual which had only existed back in the Shang Dynasty—"

"Okay, I'm sorry, but I'm going to have to stop you there," Georgia interjects again, feeling growing irritation with the hocus-pocus direction of the story. It annoys her when people mix fiction with history. She is a woman of science, after all. "My grandmother used to tell this story to me as a bedtime fairytale. Please don't tell me that a man of your education has fallen prey to myths and fantasies."

Mark takes a deep breath, and Georgia can see the muscles of his jaw working. Rising from his chair, he says, "Let me show you something."

He walks over to a display cabinet in the centre of the room. Opening the lid, he carefully lifts out a small object, then returns to show her the item in his outstretched hands.

She looks down at the relic, seeing it is displayed on a tray lined with soft black cloth. Frowning, she leans in to study it further. Then, as recognition sinks in, her eyes grow round and she jerks her head up to meet his gaze.

"Where did you get this?"

2

MARK LAMBERT SMILES, satisfied that he finally has the professor's undivided attention.

"This piece came into my collection several months ago," he explains. "The man I got it from said it was dug up by a farmer outside of Xi'an. That was all I could get out of him."

He sets the small tray on the table before Georgia and offers her a magnifying glass. She murmurs her thanks as she takes it, her eyes never leaving the object. Like a true archaeologist, she is now completely captivated by the relic.

Mark watches as she leans over it, examining every inch of its surface. It's the belly side of a small tortoise shell, slightly larger than the professor's hand. Fragments that have broken off are set in the grooves of the custom-built tray, securing them in place. On the surface of the shell are faint carvings of texts, forming vertical lines down the centre and also along cracks in the shell.

"It's an oracle bone," she murmurs in awe, more to herself than to him. Her eyes are still fixated on the prize before her.

Mark nods. Oracle bones were one of the more difficult relics to track down for his collection. When they were first discovered in the early twentieth century by local villagers, they were used as 'dragon bones' in Chinese medicine, ground up and ingested by patients to cure various ailments. By the time an antique dealer had realised their true origins, news spread quickly and the market of oracle bones exploded amongst foreign collectors. Decades of uncontrolled digs in China meant that many of these pieces quickly disappeared into private collections in the West before archaeologists even had a chance to study them. Mark guesses Georgia has not seen many of these intact.

He watches as she scrutinises it, a slight crease at the centre of her forehead emerging. A stray strand of hair falls in her eyes, and she absentmindedly flips it back, her long, jet-black hair cascading down her slim shoulders.

The professor is a beautiful woman, more stunning in person than in photographs. Yet she carries herself as if she is completely oblivious to this fact, and Mark finds this fascinating. He studies Georgia as he leans back in his chair. She is wearing hardly any makeup, which is a positive compared to the heavily powdered women he is used to dining with. Her chosen attire for the night, however, is the exact kind that he hates: a black A-line shift dress. Simple, elegant, conservative, and boring. Lambert is accustomed to women garbed with an ostentatious and seductive flare in his presence, and he can tell Georgia has not dressed with the intention to impress tonight.

She is so understated. And yet surprising in so many ways.

With her petite frame, big, almond-shaped eyes, and near-perfect Asian complexion, she can easily pass as a kid just out of college. On appearance, it's hard to imagine this gorgeous woman is half as accomplished as her resume describes. The only thing that hints at her true age and maturity are the few strands of grey around her temples, the glint of sharp intelligence in her eyes, and the ever-so-subtle air of melancholy in her gait. She walks as if she is a woman burdened by the experiences of life. Even so, Mark finds it hard to believe she is now well into her thirties.

Things are not always as they seem. He, of all people, should know that.

"This oracle bone—it's not like any other I've seen before," Georgia concludes, almost breathless. She looks up to meet his gaze, her dark brown eyes now shimmering with excitement.

"How so?"

"Oracle bones were used for a method of divination during the Shang Dynasty, which dates back to around 1000 BCE," she explains in the authoritative voice of a professor, and Mark can instantly picture her at a university lectern with hundreds of students before her. "They bear the earliest known significant corpus of ancient Chinese writing: the Oracle Bone Script. But the words carved on this shell are in Seal Script, which was only adopted as the formal system of writing during the Qin Dynasty. And the Qin Dynasty began much, much later—in 221 BCE.

"Now as far as we know, this form of plastromancy stopped being practised after 700 BCE. That's 500 years before the Qin Dynasty. These rituals were only ever carried out for the Shang kings: a turtle shell or a piece of ox bone was anointed with blood, and questions were carved into the surface. Then the shell was heated in a pit until it cracked, and the diviner would read the cracks to interpret the answers."

"Which begs the question: who did this oracle bone belong to, and what were they asking?" Mark says, his lips curling into a knowing smile.

Georgia dips her head, squinting and slowly reading one of the faint inscriptions aloud in Chinese.

She points to a group of texts on the surface. "This is the date the divination was performed." She translates the words for him, her voice laced with disbelief. "*The eleventh year of*

Emperor Qin's reign, the month of Yin." She pauses briefly. "That's the year 210 BCE, around February."

Reading the next line of text, she utters, *"Li Zhen*—I assume this is the name of the Diviner who performed the ceremony. And this bit," she continues, tracing her finger down the centre of the shell, "this is the question they were asking the gods: *Location of Hsu Fu… voyage progress?"*

Georgia inhales sharply, looking up at Mark. He sees in her face a mixture of incredulity and wonder. Then, without speaking, she turns her attention back to the oracle bone, reading the text along the cracks: *"The man with the green eyes resides in… Wo. Quest successful."*

The professor leans back in her chair in stunned silence. Mark sees a storm brewing within her, the struggle of scepticism against intrigue. When she finally speaks again, her voice is almost a whisper. "Have you had this authenticated?"

"Of course. Carbon dating places it between 250 BCE and 180 BCE, which validates the date written on there."

"Wo was the oldest recorded name for Japan in China," Georgia explains. "This oracle bone could very well explain why many people believe that Hsu Fu actually defected. The popular legend is that he was scared of being executed by the Emperor if he went back to China empty-handed. So he fled. Some say his fleet eventually ended up in Japan, that they colonised it, and began what is known as the Japanese civilisation. The country was still in its stone age when Hsu Fu supposedly arrived. There's even a rumour that he became Japan's first emperor.

"But," she continues, a deep frown appearing between her brows as she looks at the oracle bone again, "I don't understand this bit about *the man with the green eyes.* There's no mention in any historical records that Hsu Fu had such an uncommon characteristic. And *quest successful?* What the hell is that supposed to mean?"

"I had the same incredulous look on my face, I believe." Mark watches her, amused. "May I continue my story now?"

Her muted consent gives him a sense of triumph, and he resumes the tale. "As I was saying, this story goes on to say that Qin had his court diviner perform a plastromancy ritual to find the whereabouts of Hsu Fu, the result of which lies before you. Hsu Fu was said to have landed in Japan, his mission a success.

"The Emperor was furious, of course, and anxious to have the elixir for himself. His health was pretty dire by then. He sent his most trusted general to retrieve Hsu Fu, but the general was also never seen or heard from again. Emperor Qin followed him shortly afterwards, travelling east himself, and it was on this journey that he died. After this, the country was thrown into chaos with many rivalling for power, and the quest was not pursued again."

He pauses, and they sit in a silence swelling with a torrent of unanswered questions. He can tell that the professor's mind is working at a breakneck pace.

"You know," he muses, "I've been pondering this subject more and more lately. From time immemorial, there's been a desire to prolong life, to cheat death. Human beings are inherently scared of their mortality. That's why we invent stories of vampires, immortals, deities and demigods. But we've also always known that eternal life is not possible, and so instead we comfort ourselves against the horrors of our impending death by trying to leave some sort of legacy behind. If our bodies cannot last through time, surely our legacies will. Some people find this through their work: artists, writers, and musicians live on in their creations after their deaths, and that immortalises them. Most people have children, and in a way, a part of themselves lives on in their offspring. Still more turn to religion, which assures you that you'll at least have a life after death."

He pauses, cocking his head as he looks at her. "What

about you, Georgia? What is your legacy? How have you decided to live forever in this world?"

Looking a little confounded by the sudden and personal question, Georgia gives a self-conscious laugh. "Uh, well, I have no children," she says, and he catches a brief glint of sadness flashing across her dark eyes. "And I'm definitely sceptical about God. So I guess I'd have to go with my work."

"And your work does you great justice in immortalising your name," he replies, nodding in agreement. "Indeed it does."

"And you, Mark?" She turns the question on him. "I'm sure there're countless achievements you must be proud of. Look at the empire you've amassed in your lifetime, not to mention all the charities you've supported, and institutions you've been a benefactor of."

He shakes his head, giving a dismissive wave of his hand. "No. These things mean little to me now. And I have no interest in child rearing this late in my life, and certainly none in religion."

At her dubious look, he explains, "See, Georgia, I started in the pharmaceutical business. In all of my years in the industry, I've seen drugs save countless lives. But I've also seen them fail many more." He sighs as images of his late sister come to mind: the dramatic weight loss, the frustrations as she slowly lost control of her body and her brilliant mind, and the many bouts of pneumonia she'd suffered as she neared the end of her life.

Georgia clears her throat, looking uncertain. "I'm not really sure what all this has to do with the oracle bone. Surely you don't believe there's actually an elixir that could give everlasting life?"

"Well, Professor." He smiles. "This is where you come in."

She raises her eyebrows. "Me?"

"I've followed your career closely, Georgia. You were considered a child prodigy, entering university at fifteen, and becoming one of the youngest professors in the world at only twenty-two. Your long list of accolades is truly impressive, especially for someone your age. The contribution you've made to the field of archaeology is something to be envied. What's more, you've got an excellent instinct when it comes to hypotheses that contradict popular beliefs, and you've also got a habit of proving to everyone else that you're right. It's what makes you outperform others in the same field. This project needs someone who has those sharp instincts, a nose for the extraordinary that most people don't have."

"What project?" she asks, now staring at him as if he has gone mad.

"I'd like you to go to Japan and find out what happened to Hsu Fu. I have someone there who can show you some very interesting—not to mention revealing—information."

"Information on—?"

"On the possibility that—two thousand years after his expedition left China—Hsu Fu may still be alive."

3

"WELL! Looks like someone had a big night last night." Sarah pulls up a chair beside Georgia, grinning as if she is privy to some conspiracy.

Georgia nurses her sore head with a steaming cup of coffee, trying her best to ignore the older woman. She did enjoy the superb wine at Lambert's place, but she was definitely sober and alert by the time she left the estate last night. The alcohol is not to blame for her headache. Rather, it is the fact that she hasn't had a wink of sleep since examining the oracle bone. And the horrendous drive back to Sydney this morning certainly did her no favours, either. She has stumbled out of her car and straight into the university cafeteria for her fourth coffee of the day, hoping to get some peace and quiet before the inevitable interrogation by her nosy assistant.

No such luck. It appears Sarah has read her mind yet again, prancing into the café not long after and deftly spotting Georgia at the far corner table only minutes after she has sat down.

"Soooooo, how was it? I want to hear all about it—Every. Single. Gory. Detail." Sarah effuses, flicking an eyebrow up at every word.

Georgia groans inwardly, knowing the impending interrogation is inevitable. Bit by bit, question by question, Sarah manages to draw out the entire story: asking Georgia to describe the house, the food, the wine, the conversation, and in great detail the man himself and what he was wearing. When Sarah is finally satisfied, she mouths a silent *wow*, and they sit in a vacuum of stillness within the bustling background of the cafeteria.

From the corner of her eye Georgia studies her assistant, hoping to read her mind. The afternoon sun filters through the wooden venetian blinds, highlighting the silver in Sarah's short-cropped hair, her high cheekbones, and the faint pockmarks left behind from acne scars of a distant youth. It is in one of these very rare moments of quietness that Georgia sees Sarah for the handsome woman she really is. Despite being a Chinese woman in her late fifties, Sarah often behaves like a gossiping teenage girl, and it's not common for her to remain silent or sit still for even a few seconds. But in their years of friendship, notwithstanding the frequently exasperating, confronting, and intrusive behaviour of the woman, Sarah has on numerous occasions demonstrated her depth of insight and wisdom on matters demanding sincerity of thought and action.

Georgia doesn't like to admit it, but more often than not, she looks to her assistant for advice. Simply put, she is the closest thing to a tiger mum Georgia has ever had.

Sarah prides herself in the role, often explaining at length to those unaware why Asian mothers are far superior and adept at producing chess prodigies and mathematical geniuses. It is simply because, she proclaims, they enforce a strictly totalitarian regime when it comes to children. She's boasted with pride that she has raised her own kids this way, getting her own hands dirty and personally conducting long arduous hours of tuition, inquisition and cross-examination, and—of course—the occasional bout of espionage.

Georgia's own parents, on the other hand, have the philosophy of minimal involvement when it comes to child-rearing. They have raised their only daughter with a large degree of freedom and independence, sometimes bordering on questionable neglect. To this day, Georgia is undecided on which parenting method is more effective.

A long moment passes before Sarah clears her throat, visibly weighing her next words. When she finally speaks, her voice is uncharacteristically gentle. "Does Lambert know about Jacqui?"

Georgia feels the usual, unwelcome squeeze of her heart at the subject. "No. Well, at least I don't think so."

"But what he's said has you interested, even if you don't want to be," Sarah points out.

Georgia doesn't reply, and they lapse into silence again.

"And he's offering you full funding for the next three years if you agree to do it?" Sarah confirms again.

"Yeah."

Drawing a deep breath, Sarah claps her hands together as if in a Japanese Shinto ritual, declaring: "Well, you've just got to take on the job, there's no other ways about it."

Georgia jerks her head at the sudden decision made for her. "What about the dig in China? What about my work here?"

"Details to be sorted out." Sarah waves her hand dismissively. "And anyway, the dig will only continue if you take on this project. Three years of full funding is more than enough for us to finish the dig in China, and for you to finish your research paper, and the book you're writing now. Not to mention all the brownie points you're gonna earn with the department for securing such a prominent benefactor. You simply can't turn it down: you get to keep your job, I get to keep my job."

Georgia shakes her head, her pride waging war against Sarah's logic. Despite her initial intrigue concerning the oracle bone and what it revealed, she is now sceptical of its authenticity. The concept of an elixir of life is so ludicrous she refuses to entertain even a modicum of belief in its possibility. Georgia's had plenty of job offers from collectors of Lambert's type, wealthy hobbyists who've watched too many adventure films and are drunk on fantasies unrelated to facts. Frankly, she finds it a little demeaning to her occupation. She loathes to stoop that low just to get a bit of money—she is a scientist, not a tomb raider.

"The man is mad," Georgia argues. "He thinks the elixir actually *exists*—"

"Of course he does." Sarah shrugs, giving her a wry smile. "It's exactly what a fifty-something megalomaniac does when he's contemplating his own mortality. As did Hitler, as did Emperor Qin."

"—and I don't get this oracle bone business, and this idea that Hsu Fu had green eyes. It just adds to how ludicrous the whole thing is—"

"Not necessarily," Sarah points out calmly. "What about the Manchus, and the village of Liqian? There're plenty of examples throughout history where minority groups of China had Caucasian features, especially those that lived on the northern borders. Hell, just the other day I read an article on the theory that the Terracotta Warriors could have been influenced by Greek art. Invaders of all races galloped back and forth across those borders, you know that. Hsu Fu was from —what—the state of Qi? That was right up there too."

Georgia is quiet, knowing Sarah is correct. Liqian is a small village in northern China, on the edge of the Gobi desert. Its people are well-known for their fair skin, aquiline noses, light-coloured hair, and blue eyes. Only recently, tests have shown the DNA of some of these villagers is fifty-six percent Caucasian. The current prevailing theory is that they may be the descendants of Roman legionaries.

"Look, Georgia," Sarah continues, "we've had our fair

share of absurd job offers. And I'll admit, this one seems to top them all on the scale of crazy. But think of it this way: what have you got to lose? Just humour him—go to Japan, get the funding, everyone is happy."

"But—"

"Yes, it's a massive waste of your time." Sarah rolls her eyes, mimicking Georgia's tone as she accurately predicts what she's about to say. "Yes, you hate prancing around like a dancing monkey for billionaires who think they can buy anything, and anyone's time. I get it. But you know I'm right."

Georgia stares at her in exasperation, and is about to launch into another string of arguments when she sees the unexpected weary look on Sarah's face. Georgia suddenly realises that the past many weeks of sleepless nights in the office have taken more of a toll on Sarah than she would likely admit.

The bottom line is, she knows Sarah is right. And it irritates the hell out of her.

"Think of it as a holiday," Sarah cajoles now, "an all-expenses-paid holiday. Isn't it cherry blossom season now? Ooh, maybe you can take your assistant with you?" She grins, wiggling her eyebrows and nodding enthusiastically at Georgia.

Georgia lets out an unexpected laugh, feeling her heart suddenly lighten despite herself. "Absolutely not!"

4

One week later, Osaka

Professor Georgia Lee.

Georgia walks towards the uniformed man holding the hand-written sign and identifies herself. He bows to her deeply, introducing himself as Yamamoto-san with a thick Japanese accent.

"I am driver," he explains, "our trip to Shingu, about... three and half hour."

She smiles with relief. Exhausted from a long flight and transit from Sydney to Tokyo and now Osaka, she's looking forward to a little snooze in the car on the way to their destination. Yamamoto-san promptly takes her bag and guides her out of the Osaka International Airport, navigating through the car park, and opens the door for her to a stately black Toyota Crown. She settles into the leather seat of the car and lets out a yawn of contentment. She must admit that despite her reluctance to come on this trip, she's glad Lambert has made sure she travels comfortably. His assistant, Hank Law, has seen to it that Georgia travels first class on all of the flights, and the car she is now in is luxurious compared to her own little Ford at home. Christ, it even has a TV screen at the back of the passenger seat to make sure she's entertained all the way to Shingu.

As if on cue, her phone starts to ring beside her, the screen showing Hank as the caller. She answers it as Yamamoto-san pulls the car out of the parking lot.

"Georgia, I hope you had a nice flight?" he says in his pleasant London accent. His soft-spoken voice travels to her ears and she envisages him as a skinny, pale young gentleman with a clipboard in his hand, doing his boss' bidding. As soon as she accepted the contract, Lambert palmed her off to Hank, asking her to give all reports and updates to him instead. Evidently, Lambert has an empire he needs to tend to.

This arrangement is all fine with her. Even though she's never met Hank in person, she finds him much more approachable than the billionaire.

"Yeah, great. Thank you." She smiles. "How is Muffin?"

Muffin is Hank's ten-year-old Rottweiler. Early on in their conversations it became apparent that Hank and Georgia share a love for dogs. Muffin, sadly, has been frequenting the vet's clinic for diabetes of late.

"She's in good spirits. Vet isn't so optimistic though—he tells me to prepare myself. I'll be sad to see her go." Hank's voice drops.

"I'm so sorry to hear that, Hank," Georgia says. She knows what it's like to lose a pet, especially one that's been part of your life for over a decade.

"Yeah. She's been a good friend. We've had good times together."

Georgia hears Hank muffle the phone as he speaks to someone in the background. When he returns, his tone has taken on an edge she has not heard before. "I'm sorry Georgia, I'm being called away. I just wanted to let you know I've booked your hotel in Shingu and sent the address to Yamamoto-san. He'll take care of everything. Let me know if there's anything you need—anything at all. Mr. Lambert wants your complete focus on the project."

"Sure. Thank you, Hank," she says, then adds: "Give Muffin a cuddle for me."

"I will," Hank replies, and Georgia can hear the smile return to his voice. "She'll like that."

They say their goodbyes and she looks out the window, watching the cars flash past them on the highway. Shingu is the long-fabled location of where Hsu Fu had landed in Japan. In fact, in many areas of Japan he's worshipped as a deity known as Jofuku: the god of farming, medicine, and silk. There's a tombstone in town which commemorates him, and a Jofuku Park where you can buy tea from the medicinal plant he supposedly discovered. You can even dress up in hired Chinese costumes and get your picture taken in the park's Chinese garden.

At the thought of this, she rolls her eyes. The fact that Lambert has her chasing after clues in Shingu is testament to his specious reasoning. She is pretty certain this errand he's sent her on will yield no useful information. Annoyed as she may be about the expedition, however, she has promised Sarah she'll at least try and enjoy herself in Japan. What's more, the person Lambert has organised for her to meet today is none other than Akiko Hata: the last remaining heir of the prominent Hata family, owners of the famed Hata Collection. This fact alone will be worth the tiresome trip.

As they drive away from Osaka, the trees blur into a mass of green, and her eyelids begin to feel heavy as her mind drifts back to the night of her dinner with the billionaire.

"THINK ABOUT THE POSSIBILITIES, *Georgia. If it's true that Hsu Fu found something, anything, it could be the single most important discovery in the history of mankind. If he's still alive, this could mean the end of illness, of cancer, of HIV."* Lambert paused, then added: *"It could bring an end to child mortality."*

Georgia felt as if he'd punched her in the gut. Winded, she searched his face, trying to detect any signs of knowledge about Jacqui. She could not find any, for he was now moving on to his next point.

"As I've said before: in all of my years in business, I've seen the potential as well as the shortfalls of pharmaceuticals. Wouldn't it be a worthwhile cause to bring an end to suffering for everyone who is sick, and also for the loved ones around them? Now that, professor, is something I'd like to have as part of my legacy."

She looked at him, and found herself at a loss for words.

"I know you have your doubts. But really, what is there to lose? If you're right, then the world will stay as it has always been. If I'm right, well—then mankind would have much to thank you for." *Mark leaned forward, holding her gaze with his silvery eyes. "So my proposal to you is this, Georgia. Go to Japan for me. See what you can find, and bring it back to my scientists and biochemists. This could very well be humanity's greatest quest."*

AKIKO HATA GATHERS her silver hair, pulling it into a bun at the back of her head. She examines her reflection in the mirror, satisfied with the result. Glancing at her watch, she notes that her guest should be arriving any time now. She settles herself at the low, antique table with her knees tucked under her and rests her hands in her lap, impatient for the visit.

Akiko has reluctantly agreed to this meeting at the request of Mr. Lambert, and she wishes her late father had never put her in this position. In fact, over the past week she has debated fervently with herself over whether or not to go through with it. In the end, however, she decided she is bound by honour and duty to carry out her father's wishes, regardless of any reservations she may have.

That being decided, she is now anxious to get the whole affair over and done with, as quickly and smoothly as possible.

Hearing the crunch of gravel beneath the tyres of an approaching car, she rises from her seat and walks out of the house, watching patiently as the black vehicle slows to a stop. A young, attractive Chinese woman exits the car, smiling warmly at her.

Akiko makes the customary greeting for the Japanese, bowing to her visitor. "Hello. Professor Lee, my name is Akiko Hata. Welcome to my home."

The young professor returns the deep bow, uttering a greeting in Japanese. "*Hajimemashite*. Thank you for having me," she says in a gentle voice. "Please, call me Georgia."

Akiko smiles in response. She watches as Georgia's bright eyes roam appreciatively over the exterior of the two-storey house, and Akiko feels a surge of pride as she follows her gaze. The traditional Japanese architecture is a rarity nowadays, with its wooden frame and dark grey tiled roof, and perfectly manicured pine trees in the front yard. Sometimes Akiko forgets just how beautiful her family home really is. She has lived here all of her life, and it is easy to take it for granted until a new guest makes you see it again with fresh eyes. Sadly, it is also a rarity to have a visitor at the Hata estate these days.

The driver opens the trunk of the car to retrieve a couple of large black cases, and Georgia smiles almost apologetically at Akiko. "I hope you don't mind," she explains, "I came prepared with some equipment in case I needed it. I know how precious your time is and I just want to make sure I get all the information I can."

Akiko gives a slight nod of her head. "Of course."

She leads Georgia into the house, pulling open a sliding *shoji*, a traditional Japanese door made of translucent paper over a frame of wooden lattice. Beyond the shoji is a world from another time. The drawing room is of traditional Japanese design with tatami straw mat flooring and sparse, elegant furniture. Across the room from them, beyond another set of open shoji reveals an enclosed Zen stone garden: a simple yet sophisticated composition of rocks and raked sand to represent ripples in water. The faint scent of incense fills the room.

At Akiko's prompting, Georgia sits down at the low table at the centre of the room, tucking her legs underneath her. "You have a beautiful home," she compliments.

"Thank you." Akiko beams. "My great-grandfather built it, around the turn of the century. A lot of the furniture you see here was made by him too."

Georgia nods, clearly impressed, running her hands over the smooth, varnished surface of the table.

Akiko asks of Georgia's journey as she pours green tea and serves her guest some *wagashi*, a traditional Japanese sweet beautifully sculpted into the shape of flowers and fruits. They fall into easy conversation, and she takes an instant liking to the young woman as they chat cheerfully about the upcoming cherry blossom festival in Japan. Georgia's knowledge of Japan is impressive, and she even speaks a little of the language. Akiko is surprised at how pleasant this young woman is, for she is nothing like any of Lambert's other associates she has met.

"So I gather from Mr. Lambert," Georgia asks as Akiko sips her tea, "that you are close family friends?"

Akiko purses her lips, feeling a stone lodged in the deep seat of her stomach. "Well, my late father was a passionate collector of ancient relics. He and Mr. Lambert met at an auction and became instant friends. They did a lot of business together."

Georgia nods, her gaze lingering on Akiko's face, and the older woman gets the odd feeling that the professor is reading everything she has left out of that response from her expressions. But she doesn't elaborate. It is not her place to speak ill of her father's friend. Instead, she clears her throat and says, "I guess we'd better get to the reason why you are here. Mr. Lambert has asked me to show you this."

Akiko makes room on the low table, bringing out a length of soft cloth and spreading it across the surface. Reaching her hand under the table, she finds the small protruding peg and pushes against it, hearing the familiar soft click. A secret drawer to the side pops open. Reaching inside, Akiko lifts out the black lacquered box, setting it on the tabletop. She undoes its golden clasp to open the box, revealing its contents to Georgia.

She hears Georgia draw in a breath of anticipation, and unease fizzles in her stomach. Akiko gets the uncanny sense her very actions are setting something in motion, a series of events that may have far-reaching consequences. She wonders if Georgia understands the full extent of what she is getting herself involved in.

Akiko slips on a pair of white gloves, and with both hands, carefully lifts the ancient scroll out of the box, placing it gently on the length of soft cloth.

"This scroll has been in my family for many, many centuries—much longer than this house has been around. My father first showed it to me when I turned twenty-one," Akiko declares. "The preservation of history and relics has always been a strong culture in my family, you see, and throughout the generations the Hata family has acquired a significant collection of artefacts. After my father died last year, we donated a big portion of it to the Tokyo National Museum. Our collection was getting too significant for me to handle on my own, so I thought it best to share it with the rest of the world."

Georgia nods, remaining quiet, though Akiko assumes from Georgia's knowing smile she is aware of the Hata collection and her family's reputation.

"But this particular piece," Akiko continues, looking at the scroll before her, "I decided it was best to remain with us."

"Why is that?"

Akiko takes a deep breath, weighing her next words. "My family believes it may lead to the proof of our people's origins, and that it would ultimately refute the lineage of some of the most powerful families here in Shingu."

She unties the red string holding the scroll together, and begins the slow and cautious unravelling of the fragile document. Long, narrow strips of bamboo, each carrying a single column of faded brush-written text, are bound by thread into the scroll format. In its entirety, the scroll is roughly twenty-five by seventy centimetres in size.

Before the invention of paper, these bamboo slip scrolls were one of the main media for written text in ancient China, the earliest surviving examples dating from as early as the fifth century BCE. The scroll before them is obviously very old, but there is also clear evidence of restoration to keep it intact. It is in excellent condition for its age, despite the fragments that have broken off the slips. There are also large sections where the writing has faded so much it is impossible to make out the text.

Georgia scrutinises the document before them, surprise evident on her face as she raises her brows. "This is written in the Seal script of the Qin Dynasty."

"Yes," Akiko confirms. "This is why we don't believe it should be made public. As you know, the Japanese people are very proud, and many would still like to believe we as a people are descendants of the sun. Or at least, we'd like to believe our origins are very independent from our neighbouring countries. My family feels this letter would suggest otherwise, and that would cause a great uproar in our community."

Georgia nods, turning her attention back to the scroll, squinting to make out the faded texts. "It's a letter... to Emperor Qin," she says softly, almost to herself, "...from Wang Jian?"

Georgia looks up with surprise, gazing at Akiko's face as if searching for confirmation, who nods solemnly. Akiko is well versed in ancient Chinese history herself; the knowledge comes from years of managing the Hata collection on behalf of her father. She knows Wang Jian is considered one of the four greatest generals of the Warring States period, and a key player during the unification of China. Under his command, Qin's army conquered the states of Zhao, Yan, and Chu. He was one of Qin's most trusted advisors, and it has also been rumoured that he was sent to Japan when the imperial alchemist defected during the quest for an elixir.

"Has anyone else—any other scientists—examined this?"

"No." Akiko shakes her head. "You have to understand, professor, this piece is very precious to us and we almost never show it to anyone outside of the family. It's only at Mr. Lambert's request that I have agreed to do this today. I haven't been able to decipher much of the contents myself, but throughout the generations of my family, it has been passed from parent to child, an heirloom that is part of our legacy. When my father mentioned it to Mr. Lambert, he took a special interest."

When Lambert called Akiko, he at first besought her to send the scroll to his scientists for examination. At her polite refusal, he suggested the professor make a personal visit instead. This, Akiko had to grudgingly oblige. To decline the request a second time would have been considered rude in her culture and brought shame upon her family, especially given the close friendship between Mr. Lambert and her father. Nonetheless, she made it clear she would allow only this one visit.

Georgia points to the badly faded sections of the document. "These areas," she says, "I may be able to recover them using a technique called multispectral imaging. The process is non-invasive. I'll need to take a series of photos of the scroll using different lights and filters. Will that be okay with you?" She gestures to the cases of equipment she has brought with her.

Akiko hesitates briefly, then gives her consent with a slight nod of her head.

It takes Georgia a while to set up her imaging system, but slowly and painstakingly, she photographs every detail of the scroll. She goes through the whole process with Akiko as she works, and explains she will later analyse the images using various algorithms to recover the missing texts.

When she is finished, she turns to Akiko. "Is there anything else you can tell me about it?"

"Not much, I'm afraid." The older woman shakes her head. "The secrets of the scroll were lost long ago when all those words faded."

Perhaps for the best, Akiko thinks.

She wonders what the young scientist will find, and if she has any inkling of the kind of person she is working for. Looking at Georgia intently, Akiko says, "I must emphasise our wish for your discretion on this, Georgia. Whatever information you find in this document, please remember to use it wisely, and keep it to yourself. As far as the world is concerned, this document does not exist."

5

BACK AT HER hotel in Shingu, Georgia spends many long hours tweaking her algorithms and analysing the photographs of the scroll. The anticipation to know what secrets it holds is almost impossible for her to contain. She works tirelessly and persistently, examining every section of the document with careful scrutiny.

Some parts of the text were so badly damaged that she had to extrapolate the content, but when she finally sees the faded script and drawings appear on her screen, her breath is taken away by what it reveals.

Your Majesty, Son of Heaven and Lord of Ten Thousand Years:

At last, I have captured the traitorous Hsu Fu at Your Holy Highness' orders.

Wo remains a place for primitives, it has none of the comforts of our newly united China. Since our arrival, my men have scoured much of its lands over many months with no fruit to bear, and they grew weary and sick for […]

[...] gods were on our side the night we heard a man of Wo speak of a legendary healer living on the southern coast. The rumour was, that his magic could banish any ailments, and that he had extraordinary jade-coloured eyes.

It was not long after that when we located the knave. Wo has changed him, but those treacherous green eyes are undeniably his.

We tortured him. Of course, he denied me any answers at first. Yet I have come prepared with an expert in interrogations, Lu Hsing. Lu Hsing possesses a wealth of wisdom on the art of torture, and he performed one of his own invention on Hsu Fu. He named it Lingchi: death by ten thousand cuts.

Your majesty may find it of great interest, for it is a long, drawn-out, lingering death that dismembers the victim piece by piece while he still lives. It consists of a slow slicing of the arms, legs, and chest—taking care, of course, to avoid severing any major veins, which may kill the victim immediately. Then, the limbs are amputated, followed by decapitation or a stab to the heart.

Lu Hsing had boasted that no man would last beyond two or three cuts without begging for mercy, for the excruciating pain was often too much to bear and the fear of not being whole in the afterlife would sway most into submission. Yet, Hsu Fu was a stubborn man, refusing to speak even after Lu Hsing had spent hours with him. His screams echoed through the valley, it left the horses perturbed and restless. Upon nightfall, Lu Hsing left the loathsome toad bleeding and unconscious, promising of more by daybreak.

I awoke early morning to find Hsu Fu unconscious, still bound against the tree. He was plenty bloody from the interrogations of the day prior; yet, the wounds had vanished. The flesh which had been cut from his body was once again replenished. I ordered men to bring water to wash him and, indeed, there was no longer a mark left on his body.

I took Hsu Fu by the throat, demanding to know how this was possible. With those accursed eyes he bore into mine, and a most blood-curdling laughter erupted from him. Upon seeing this some of my men very well lost their minds. They disappeared with several craven others [...]

Lu Hsing explained that this was an advantage: if the alchemist could heal overnight, then it was possible to inflict even more pain without killing him. Though his body could sustain the torture, certainly he still felt the pain of a mortal man. No doubt, his mind would soon yield to us.

[...] and the screams continued day and night [...]

Three days passed. Each night, Hsu Fu's wounds magically healed by daylight, and the next day Lu Hsing would continue Lingchi on him. Yet the haggard fiend was silent save the grunts, moans, and occasional screams. By now my men were truly unnerved, and more deserted during the night. A weariness had even overcome Lu Hsing's usual *[...]*

[...] the alchemist to acquiesce. I threatened to write to my emperor at once, to beseech your majesty to grant Nine Familial Exterminations on the Hsu family. My men in China would hunt down every last of his relations and each of them would suffer Lingchi, and the Hsu lineage would be forever forgotten from the earthly realm.

"I suspect they would not heal like you," I spat at the vile scum. "But if they could, then my emperor would have surely found his elixir. He could feast on their flesh, and immortality would finally be his."

I saw fear for the first time in Hsu Fu's eyes, and he acceded at last, telling me thus:

The elixir is real, [...]

Hsu Fu's fleet had sailed south from Shandong, in search of Penglai Mountain. On the tenth day, a fierce storm struck. The heavens and the ocean blended into one towering mass of fury, pounding and tossing the ships until they all capsized and sank to the bottom of the sea. Hsu Fu suffered a deep wound on his leg, but luck was on his side. A wooden barrel floated by and he grasped on, soon losing consciousness.

When he awoke, he saw he had landed on a beach. His wound

was still oozing, the flesh now white from the brine; he thought he would surely die by nightfall. He welcomed death, for he had watched his wife and son drown in the wreckage and he could not save [...]

Yet Hsu Fu woke again, and this time found himself in a cave. A fire burned bright nearby, and a dark figure hovered beside the hearth. Hsu Fu lost consciousness, awoke again, and fainted again many times over [...]

[...] conjured the strength to fully awaken, he saw that the figure was a woman with long, silver hair, though her face was of a youthful beauty. Her name was Naaya. She had saved him from the beach. He looked to his injured leg, and found that the gaping wound was gone. He could not find a trace of it on his skin.

Naaya spoke of the gods, and of how they had given him a second chance to live; and at this, he knew that she was an Immortal. He knew he had at last found Penglai Mountain.

He spent many months on the isle, learning from the Immortal many healing methods. She taught him endless techniques of medicine, and yet denied him the skill to cure mortal wounds like the one he had suffered from the shipwreck.

I questioned him on the location of this isle, but he knew not its place. He had been unconscious when the tides swept him onto the beach, and when he left it was on a ship navigated by the Immortal's servants. Naaya had besought him to go to Wo, for his destiny lay there, and he was to bring the gift of medicine [...]

Hsu Fu may know not its location, but he knew that Naaya's servants had sailed north towards Wo, reaching land after two weeks' journey. He said that the legends are true: Penglai is but one of the isles on which the Immortals live. There are also two others, Yingzhou and Fanzhang. Penglai is the largest, filled with medicinal trees and herbs. The other two isles are smaller, rockier, and abundant in beautiful, giant caves for the Immortals' residence.

Ire frothed in my veins, for this told me not the way to the isles, nor the means to identify them. Finally, he drew a picture and told me thus: the island of Yingzhou is the smallest, and the most peculiar. It has two peaks on either side of the isle, and flatness in between, as if the gods had gouged a hollow in the mountain. On top of the smaller peak stands a vertical rock, a pinnacle seemingly placed there with intent. The larger peak slopes upwards from the west, with a sharp and crescent descent from the apex to the east.

This, he said, was the way to identify Penglai Mountain.

I trust this is pleasing news for your majesty. By your leave I shall take Hsu Fu and what is left of my troops to sail for the isles. The green-eyed alchemist warns me of fire-spewing sea monsters, but we have come prepared with archers. On the morrow I shall travel south and find the elixir that my emperor longs for.

Your most loyal and undeserving servant,
Wang Jian

6

GEORGIA FROWNS at the elaborate Chinese archway towering over her, taking in its gaudy yellow tiles complemented with painted decorations of bright blue, red, and green. Across the top of the archway, a large sign with yellow kanji characters reads: JOFUKU PARK.

She's not entirely sure how, or why, she has decided to come here.

Earlier this morning, after deciphering the Hata scroll and reading through Wang Jian's description of Hsu Fu's capture and interrogation, she felt so bewildered she needed to get out of the hotel room for some fresh air. The scientist in her in revolt, she desperately needed space to think. So she put on her running shoes and jogged aimlessly through the suburban streets at a leisurely pace, enjoying the cherry blossoms whilst turning the puzzle over in her mind again and again. By the time she ended up here at the Jofuku Park, the running app on her phone showed that she'd traversed over six kilometres.

Walking through the archway, she sees that Jofuku Park is really no more than a quaint little garden with a souvenir and ice-cream shop to the right, and a small toilet block beyond that. The 'park' consists of little more than a fish pond, a few trees and well-kept bushes, and a concrete sculpture of a plump, smiley Hsu Fu dressed in full-length robe with his hands clasped before him, greeting all visitors to the park.

Not exactly awe-inspiring, but Georgia finds herself wandering in and sitting down on the bench facing the statue of the man who has plagued her mind since she left Sydney.

There is a sign beside Hsu Fu, describing the legend of how he may have come to Japan, and how he'd allegedly discovered the *tendaiuyaku* tree. Even though the plant does not grant eternal life, locals believe it aids kidney diseases and rheumatism, and the city of Shingu has planted several of the bushes in the park.

Her phone buzzes in her pocket, the ringtone breaking through the tranquillity of the garden. She picks it up when she sees the caller ID.

"Hello, Hank."

"Hi, Georgia," Hank says, excitement lacing his soft voice. "I've just read your email." He pauses to let the words sink in.

"Yeah." She draws a deep breath, tugging at the end of her long braid. "I've managed to recover most of the missing text. It took a while, but it worked. Some sections are very badly damaged, but what I've salvaged is still pretty revealing. As you can see in the translated version I sent you, what Akiko's got there is just about mind-blowing. And to tell the truth— it's a little hard to digest." She swallows. "Do you know if Mark has tried to persuade her for an authentication process?"

"He has, but she wouldn't agree to it. You have to understand that the Hata family is very private about this, and they've only agreed to show it to you as a personal favour to Mr. Lambert. We've been told that under no circumstances is the scroll to leave the possession of the Hata family," Hank explains.

Georgia already suspects this is the case, and from what

she can gather, the artefact appears to be genuine. Even so, there is so much more she could find out if only the scroll could be properly examined in the laboratory at her university. She can't think of any reason why the Hata, a well-known and respected aristocratic family, would want to fabricate something like this. It doesn't serve them at all. Besides, Akiko Hata has already dropped the subtle hint that she would deny the existence of the document if Georgia were to make her findings public.

"This is an amazing breakthrough, Georgia." Hank continues, "Mr. Lambert is very pleased with your progress. He'd like to know what your next steps are?"

"Well, I—" she falters. She hasn't yet thought that far, she's still processing her own disbelief and shock from the discovery. "I guess the drawing of the island is about all we've got to go on—which, to be honest, is not much at all. I can run a search on known islands south of Japan, and see if we come up with anything."

"Great. Let me know if you make any headway with it," Hank says. "As Mr. Lambert has said, anything you need will be at your disposal." He pauses. "Oh, and Georgia?"

"Yes?"

"Be careful with the information you've got. I wouldn't go around showing it to just anyone," he warns.

"Yeah... Sure."

She stares at her phone for a moment after she hangs up, dumbfounded by the absurdity of it all. It appears she is now truly on a hunt for Emperor Qin's elixir. Before she visited Akiko Hata, she was sure that by today she'd be on the plane heading home, having discovered nothing worthy of investigation. Instead, she has found herself searching for the mythical Penglai Mountain.

She brings up the photos of the Hata scroll again on her phone, frowning down at the drawing Hsu Fu made. Geographically, the smaller island certainly is a peculiar formation, and something about the crescent descent from the apex seems familiar to her. She's sure she has seen that shape somewhere else before, but conjuring up the memory is like grasping for an elusive, fleeting scent that is just beyond her reach.

According to Chinese folklore, Penglai Mountain was on an island in the eastern region of the Bohai Sea, where the Eight Immortals lived. Each of the Immortals possessed a special divine power, and a talisman that could give life or destroy evil. In the legends, everything on Penglai was white. It was a land of happiness and pleasure; the plates were always filled with food and the glasses with wine, and there were also special fruits growing in the trees that could heal any disease and grant eternal life.

An enticing description, especially for an emperor who was on the brink of death.

She has already previously checked on the maps and deduced that there is nothing due south of Shingu: just the vast expanse of the Pacific Ocean and the Ryukyu Islands to the south west. But it would have taken much longer than a mere two-week sail to get to Ryukyu, especially for a boat from the days of rudimentary seafaring techniques.

She ruffles her hair, unsure of what to make of all of this.

Something is not right.

She feels as if someone is playing a trick on her.

THE SHORT, stocky man stands behind the archway, watching the professor as she looks at something on her phone with great concentration. She is sitting on the bench with her back turned to him, her long black hair in a braid down the length of her spine.

She seems perplexed. Frustrated. It appears this little treasure hunt that Lambert has given her has now fully captured her interest. Not an easy task, for the eminent professor is one sharp woman, and it takes a complex puzzle to entice her.

The man smiles, scratching his goatee out of habit, feeling the deep scar that extends from his right ear down to the chin, partially hidden by the facial hair. A warm sense of joy fills the cavity of his chest, and he almost chuckles with elation.

The wheels have been set in motion, and now it's only a matter of time. Like the good hunter he is, all he has to do now is wait. And after years of training, patience is something he has plenty of.

He rubs his bare scalp, feeling the stubble of regrowth from the closely shaved head. He wonders how long it'll take before she figures out the location of the islands.

Not long, most likely. With her photographic memory and an impressive track record, it can't possibly take much longer.

7

GEORGIA OPENED HER EYES, *feeling utterly exhausted. Blinking slowly, she felt as if something was grating against the surface of her eyeballs. She fought against the urge to go back to sleep, pushing herself up from the hospital bed to stretch out her stiff back.*

She let out a silent yawn and looked over to the bed, seeing that Jacqui was still asleep, her little chest moving rapidly under the thin blanket. Georgia's heart clenched at the sight of her daughter's pale blue lips.

"How's our little girl doing?" Lucas whispered as he walked into the room, holding two disposable cups in his hands.

"Okay, I think. Same," replied Georgia, accepting one of the drinks gratefully.

They sipped the bitter cafeteria coffee, a cavity of silence between them. Her mind drifted back to their conversation with Dr. Rennard, and a torrent of emotions swelled in her chest.

Eisenmenger Syndrome, he'd called it. A condition created by a congenital heart defect that causes pulmonary hypertension.

In layman's terms, she had given her baby girl an incomplete heart, a heart with a hole in it. Now the poor little organ was struggling to deliver enough oxygen to Jacqui's blood, causing her skin to appear pale and greyish all over.

Georgia's eyes began to water.

Even before Dr. Rennard had given his verdict, she'd known the prognosis was not good. Still, it was the very last thing Georgia had wanted to hear. It had taken her and Lucas so many years of trying, of praying and wishing for this child, and they were overjoyed when she'd finally arrived. Jacqui was their miracle baby. But their happiness was short-lived: Jacqui had barely turned two when the doctors gave them the bad news.

Two years was not enough. It just wasn't. Little Jacqui was meant to grow up to become a beautiful woman, have a life of her own, and watch her parents grow old and grey together. She was meant to outlive them, not the other way around.

Georgia dropped her head in her hands, taking slow, deep breaths to will away the tears. She couldn't break down: not here, not now. Sensing that Lucas had moved closer, she straightened before he had a chance to touch her.

"I'm fine," she said, almost in defiance—not intended towards him but at the suffocating despair that threatened to overcome her. The chill in her voice surprised even herself, and she regretted it as soon as the words were uttered, for Lucas flinched as if she'd slapped him. Retrieving his outstretched hand, he stepped back and repositioned himself in his chair. Georgia thought to apologise, but could not find the words.

A silence, awkward and strained, stretched between them.

"I've spoken with the doctor," Lucas finally said. "They're looking into organ transplant options."

She nodded, numb. She wasn't sure if she was grateful, or irritated, at his attempt to give her hope despite the direness of the situation.

"Momma." Jacqui's eyes opened suddenly, and their attention both zeroed in on her. Georgia reached out, grasping her little girl's hand, instantly appalled at how cold it was.

"Yes, sweetie, Mummy is here."

"Momma." Jacqui repeated as if she hadn't heard Georgia, and

then she began to cough violently. Her eyes wide with panic, she gripped harder.

"Momma!" She spluttered as blood appeared on her lips, tiny sprays of red staining the white hospital sheets.

SHE WAKES WITH A START, her breath short and rasping. Finally realising it was a dream, Georgia closes her eyes again and lets out a deep sigh.

Images of Jacqui linger, at all ages and moods, shifting in and out of the darkness. Her eyes well up, the emotions like a wild beast gnawing at her, threatening to burst through the gates. She draws a few deep, tremulous breaths, wrestling the creature back into the deep recesses of her heart.

It takes Georgia a moment to remember where she is. The dark hotel room is bathed in a flashing blue and red glow, the sound of the morning news channel droning on in the background.

The phone next to her suddenly shrieks, piercing her ears. Georgia groans, suppressing a need to hurl it against the wall. She answers it instead when she sees the caller ID.

"Hello." Her voice comes out as a hoarse whisper.

"Georgia? Are you okay?" Sarah asks, already knowing that something is amiss.

"Yeah." Georgia clears her throat. "You woke me up is all."

There is an audible pause on the other end of the phone. Then, Sarah says, "You were having the same dreams again, weren't you?"

Georgia sighs and flops a forearm over her closed eyes, thinking that Sarah's kids would probably make excellent spies if they've ever managed to keep any secrets from her.

"Sorry. Want me to call back later?" Sarah offers.

"No. It's fine," replies Georgia. She could use a second

opinion on everything she has uncovered so far.

Sitting up, she starts chatting to her assistant, catching up on Kate and Michael's progress in China and her other students' projects at home. Of course, Sarah also slips in a bit of departmental gossip, office politics, and the latest rumours of who will be keeping their jobs despite the funding cut, and others who may not be so lucky.

"So, I told you my lot, now you tell me yours," Sarah says after her lengthy report. "How is Japan? Did you see any cherry blossoms?"

"Well… it's not what I expected," Georgia replies. Her eyes trail to photographs of the scroll scattered over the bed, evidence of her obsessions last night. Wang Jian's drawing of the island lies before her, taunting her with the fleeting sense of recognition. That shape… she knows she's seen it somewhere, and yet the memory evades her.

With Sarah as a rapt audience, Georgia begins to describe in detail her meeting with Akiko Hata, the scroll that was shown to her, and everything it revealed. A long silence ensues when Georgia finishes her tale.

"Fuck me," Sarah mutters. "So Wang Jian *did* find Hsu Fu in Japan."

Georgia smiles at the expletive. For someone of Sarah's generation, she's got an extremely filthy mouth. Sarah attributes it to her love of American movies, especially the Tarantino kind. If she's not at work, she is generally glued to Netflix at home.

"That's what it said in the letter, yes," replies Georgia.

"Do you think the letter ever reached Qin?" Sarah asks.

"It was dated in the month of Hai, which was around November in 210 BCE. Qin had died by then—two months prior," she replies.

"And Wang Jian wouldn't have known about Qin's death then," Sarah points out. "No one did."

Georgia murmurs her agreement. In September 210 BCE,

Emperor Qin died during his travels to Eastern China, about two months away by road from the capital, Xianyang. The prime minister who accompanied him, Li Si, was worried Qin's death would start an uprising in the empire, so he decided to conceal the news until they returned to the capital. It is said most of the imperial entourage had been ignorant of the emperor's demise. Li Si had ordered two carts of rotten fish to be carried before and after Qin's wagon, to hide the foul smell emanating from the decomposing body. Eventually, after returning to Xianyang months later, news of the emperor's death was finally announced.

Sarah mumbles, almost to herself, "Wang Jian would have found out about Qin's death eventually, and he would probably have returned to China straight away."

"Not necessarily," Georgia counters after a pause. "Remember that the general was a known supporter of Qin's first son, Fusu, who was the rightful heir to the throne. But Li Si had conspired against Fusu, forcing him to commit suicide, and also had all of his supporters killed."

She pauses, reiterating the historical details in her head. The prime minister had wanted power for himself, and plotted an elaborate plan for Qin's eighteenth son to be crowned instead as a puppet ruler. Revolts quickly erupted, however, and a scramble for power ensued. The empire Qin had worked so hard to amass began to crumble, and within four years, the puppet emperor was also dead.

"So it's likely that Wang Jian never returned to China if he found out what was going on," Sarah hypothesises, "because he would have been hunted down and killed by Li Si's men. This happened to the other generals who supported Fusu too. Wang Jian could possibly have stayed in Japan instead."

"Maybe." Georgia chews on her lip. "I think the Hata family probably came to the same conclusion, and that's why they think making the letter public would not be a good idea. It would fortify the theory that the Chinese colonized Japan."

"Then it's also possible Wang Jian ended up sailing south with Hsu Fu to find this island." Sarah pauses, then whispers, "Holy shit, do you think it was really Penglai Mountain? Do you think they *found* it?"

"I don't know." Georgia exhales audibly, still chewing on her bottom lip. "I don't know what to think right now. All this stuff—it's beyond absurd. I can't wrap my head around it. From what I can tell, the scroll itself looks legitimate. And I really can't imagine the Hata family making something like this up. But Penglai Mountain? An elixir? *Really?*" She rubs her forehead in frustration.

Sarah lets out a wordless grunt, falling silent. After a long pause she finally says, "What does your gut tell you, Georgia?"

She takes a deep breath. "My gut says that I'm interested," she admits reluctantly. "It says that I've not been this interested in a long time."

"Well, there you go. You have to go with that." Sarah makes her customary conclusion on Georgia's behalf. "I know you'll find something from this. And it's probably come at the right time to keep your mind off things, too."

She remains quiet, knowing that Sarah is referring to her impending divorce. It's been over five years since Jacqui's death, and after two years of separation, she and Lucas are finalising their divorce next week.

"You know what?" Sarah pipes up, interrupting her thoughts. "Even if there wasn't an island and Hsu Fu was lying through his teeth, this letter alone may be one of your most significant findings! It proves Hsu Fu ended up in Japan. Not that the Hata family will ever let you make it public or allow an authentication process, but anyway. It's still a bloody amazing discovery."

They say their goodbyes and Georgia hangs up, hopping off the bed and heading straight into the bathroom. Her morning breath is starting to seriously bother her. She looks at her image in the mirror and a corner of her mouth slants down with dismay. Dark circles have begun to form under her eyes from the restless nights of late. She realises her age is beginning to show in the grey springing up around her temples.

Georgia shakes her head, reminding herself that this is a good thing. All her life, people have been dismissive of her capabilities because of how young she looks.

As she brushes her teeth, her attention drifts to the TV that's still on in the background. CNN news is on, and she pays half-attention to the voice of the news reporter as he announces various world happenings with solemnity.

"Tensions rise, as China's coastguard ships confronted Japanese vessels last week in the waters surrounding the East China Sea islands that are claimed by both sides…"

She frowns, walking back into the bedroom with the toothbrush in her mouth.

"…Japan's defence minister recommended substantial upgrades in its military power in defence of what it deems to be its territory."

She stares at the TV, her frown deepening. Her attention is not focused on the naval ships traversing the waters in a military standoff, but on the satellite image of the three little islands in the top right corner of the screen. The camera angle shifts to view one of the islands from sea level, and her mouth gapes open, her toothbrush tumbling to the floor.

The words of Wang Jian's letter resurface with clarity in her mind:

…It has two peaks on either side of the isle, and flatness in between, as if the gods had gouged a hollow in the mountain… The larger peak slopes upwards from the west, with a sharp and crescent descent from the apex to the east.

8

"THE SENKAKU ISLANDS?" Hank exclaims, barely able to contain his excitement.

Georgia juggles the phone between her shoulder and ear as she surveys the photographs of the scroll spread out over her hotel bed.

"Yeah," she confirms. "The drawings and the description in Wang's Jian's letter match these islands exactly. I thought the peculiar shape of the island looked familiar, but I couldn't remember where I'd seen it before. In actual fact, the Senkaku have been all over the world news recently. There's been some dispute between China, Japan, and Taiwan about the sovereignty over the territory."

"This is remarkable, Georgia," Hank says. "Mr. Lambert will be pleased. He's right—you're the perfect person for the job."

"It was a stroke of luck," she says. In her experience, luck usually has a lot to do with many archaeological findings. "As far as I can tell, the islands have been uninhabited since the fifteenth century, which was the date of the earliest records I can find. It might be worthwhile to visit the island that Hsu

Fu referred to as Penglai. It's the biggest of the three, now known as Uotsuri Island."

"Great," he agrees, "I'll organise your trip straight away."

She frowns, adding, "I'm not sure how we can possibly access it, Hank. Especially with all the political tension going on in the area at the moment."

"Leave that to me," Hank says, and Georgia can tell in his voice that he's confident it won't be an insurmountable obstacle. "You'll hear from me later today. Just be packed and ready to leave for Okinawa."

———

HIS PERSONAL PHONE vibrates silently on the table beside him. Casting a quick glance at the caller ID, Mark Lambert pushes his chair back to stand.

"Ladies, gentlemen," he addresses the board of directors sitting at the table. "My apologies, but I must take this. I believe we've covered everything we need to today. Shall we continue in the morning?"

Murmurs and nods of general agreement are exchanged around the room, and Mark shakes several hands as participants of the meeting file out of the conference room.

He picks up his phone as soon as he is alone. "Hank—talk to me."

"I've sent a draft of the new security plan to you, sir. Please have a look and we can implement it as soon as you approve it." Hank's smooth voice travels to his ears. "I have all the men in position, ready to be deployed."

Mark grunts his approval, bringing up the documents on his laptop.

"And, sir," Hank continues, "there is good news."

Mark's grip tightens on the phone.

"Professor Lee believes she's found the location of the islands in the East China Sea. I'm organising her trip to

Senkaku now." Hank adds, "But to gain access, you may need to give the Japanese defence minister a call."

"Inada-san?" He glances at his watch, doing a quick mental calculation of the current time in Tokyo. "That's fine. I'll give her a call in the morning. Keep me informed."

Hanging up the phone, Mark leans back in his chair, taking a deep breath. He closes his eyes, the fatigue of the day washing over him.

He knew if he dangled the bait before the professor, she would find the idea impossible to resist. Georgia is a smart woman, proud of her own intellect. But humans are fundamentally emotional beings, and everyone has a sensitive point. Mark learnt very early on in his career that it's all about getting that emotional leverage: once you find it, and apply pressure to the right spot, you'll just about get whatever you want out of anyone you meet.

He stands and walks over to the floor-to-ceiling window, absorbing the breathtaking view overlooking the Sydney Opera House and the Harbour Bridge. The glow of the full moon reflects upon the dark water, paving a silvery path to the horizon. Colourful lights have been projected onto the façade of the Opera House, making a psychedelic display of the Australian icon.

He smiles.

Smart girl, Georgia. You're progressing a lot quicker than I'd thought.

9

Three weeks later, Senkaku Islands

THE RYUKYU ARCHIPELAGO is a chain of volcanic islands that stretches over a thousand kilometres between Kyushu, Japan, and Taiwan. Together, the isles make up Japan's Okinawa Prefecture.

In Wang Jian's letter, Hsu Fu claimed there were fire-spewing sea monsters in this region, and it would have been true. It is likely the islands would have experienced sporadic eruptions back then, oozing out smoke, ash, and molten lava. Georgia can imagine how frightening a journey it would have been, sailing close to the islands and witnessing such events. It would not have been good for the crew's morale.

She wonders if Wang Jian did indeed traverse these waters himself. The stretch of archipelago would have made easier sailing than being in open waters, as he could have travelled from one island to another whilst searching for Penglai Mountain. But she highly doubts he made it as far as the

Senkaku Islands, which lay over 1,500 kilometres from Shingu.

She settles into a fold-out chair before her tent, studying a detailed map of the area. This uninhabited group of small rocks and isles has been the heart of an ongoing political dispute between China and Japan for many years. Despite their apparent insignificance, they in fact offer rich fishing grounds, and are also close to important shipping lanes and potential oil and gas reserves.

Georgia has been on the Senkaku Islands for almost two weeks now, spending most of her time on the larger isle, Uotsuri Island, which the letter claimed to be Penglai Mountain. The island is only 4.3 square kilometres in size, and completely deserted, save for a few Japanese coast guards who have set up camp in the area in an attempt to ward off any potential Chinese soldiers staking their claim.

It is evident Lambert's influence stretches further than she previously thought possible. Within a few days of her phone conversation with Hank, he somehow managed to organise her flight to Ishigaki Airport in Okinawa, where she boarded a Japanese coast guard ship bound for the Senkaku Islands. Hank even sent an assistant to help her set up camp on the island, a stocky, solidly built Japanese man named Tanaka, who has limited English skills but excellent navigational and camping experience.

Tanaka-san came well-equipped with trekking and camping equipment, satellite phones, archaeological tools that Georgia required, and food to last them for two weeks—which was the length of time Hank could negotiate for Georgia's visit. Tanaka-san has even brought a remote-controlled drone for aerial surveys, as well as a GPR, Ground Penetrating Radar, to image the subsurface of the terrain. One thing's for certain: Lambert has ensured that Georgia has every resource at her fingertips. Without even requesting it, she has been sent every available NASA satellite and laser survey image of the islands, taken with every possible filter for her analysis.

She could certainly get used to this.

With Tanaka-san's help, Georgia explored the whole of Uotsuri Island in detail, no small feat given its mountainous terrain, its highest elevation being 383 metres. Mostly they searched for caves, as these would have been the easiest places to live in this hostile landscape. They even visited the two smaller islets to the east, Kita and Minami, looking for the giant caverns Wang Jian wrote about in his letter.

And yet, they have come up with nothing that suggests previous habitation, or anything worthy of further investigation.

She's not sure these islands are what Hsu Fu claimed them to be. In truth, her instincts nagged at her even before she got on the coast guard ship. The islands are small, isolated, and too exposed. They are far away from any mainland, and the rocky terrain also makes it difficult for growing or sourcing food. These are amongst some of the very good reasons why they have not hosted any inhabitants in the last few hundred years.

The chance of finding any evidence of Hsu Fu's visit were minute in the first place. What's more, there is no chance of her performing any proper excavations due to the political standoff over the islands. Still, she cannot help but feel extremely disappointed.

And, a little foolish for being swept up by her excitement in the first place.

Why has she let herself believe things would be otherwise? All of the information she's been presented with is not backed up by any other historical evidence. Instead, it reeks of superstition and mythology, two things that are always dangerous and misleading in her line of work. She feels irritated with herself. Her inner sceptic seemed to have gone into hibernation for the past few weeks.

The man with the green eyes? She scoffs, lambasting herself for having fallen for it.

Her time on Uotsuri Island is now coming to an end, and she is due to return to Okinawa tomorrow. Lambert won't be happy that she came back empty-handed, but Georgia has certainly fulfilled her end of the bargain. Nevertheless, she's promised Hank she will resume her research in Sydney with the data collected over the past two weeks.

She highly doubts that she will uncover anything new.

As Georgia moves to fold up her maps for the last time, she catches a glimpse of a much larger island at the lower corner of the map.

Taiwan.

She cannot help but notice how close she is to her grandmother's home country right now. The thought of her amah tugs gently at her heart.

After living in Australia with her family for over thirty years, Amah decided to move back to Taiwan. She has always felt more at home there, and what's more, her English skills have deteriorated in her old age. Understandably, Amah is much more comfortable where she can communicate effectively with the people around her. Despite being ninety-two, the woman oozes vitality, and still maintains a sense of passionate curiosity about life. Georgia smiles as she thinks of her grandmother's busy social schedule, filled with dance classes, book clubs, and walking expeditions in the mountains of Taiwan. She also volunteers as a museum guide at the National Palace Museum twice a week.

Georgia hopes to be even half as energetic when she reaches Amah's age.

She sighs as she puts her papers away, admitting defeat. The sun is due to set soon and Tanaka-san will be back with their firewood shortly. Georgia stares at the last of the ready-meals on the fold-up table, feeling no appetite for the tasteless mush in the vacuum-packed bags. After two weeks of camping, she is sure looking forward to a shower and some fresh food.

She leans back into her canvas chair, staring out at the glistening waters of the East China Sea. This is her favourite time of the day on the island, with the dusk breeze soothing the blistering heat from the day. At this angle, the light reflects off the surface of the water in such a way that makes it a vast ocean of shimmering liquid metal. A scarlet sun hovers above the distant horizon, tinting thin strips of clouds every shade of orange and red. Georgia wonders if this means that it is going to be sunny tomorrow, or if it is an omen of rain ahead.

She decides that upon landing in Okinawa tomorrow she will organise a quick trip to visit her grandmother before flying back to Australia. It is Amah's birthday in a few days, and Georgia's also not been to Taipei for over three years. Who knows, maybe Amah's colleagues at the National Palace Museum can shed some light on some of Georgia's findings so far.

And, truth be told, she loathes the thought of returning to Sydney so soon, where her divorce papers will be awaiting her signature.

10

MARK LAMBERT EXITS his Sydney office building, strolling over to the curb where his driver is waiting patiently by the silver Rolls Royce. He slides through the door that Paul holds open for him, settling into the soft leather seat.

"Where to, sir?" Paul asks, buckling himself in the driver's seat.

"Let's go home." Mark exhales, leaning back on his headrest and closing his eyes.

"Yes, sir." Paul pulls the vehicle onto the road.

It's been a long week of merger negotiations, and even though it is still early in the afternoon, Mark is exhausted. His energy level is not what it used to be. Even though he has always been a fit and active person keen on regular outdoor adventures, lately he is finding that all of his exploits have been wearing on him. And now, he feels on the verge of collapse after a round of vigorous business negotiations, a task he once found easy to tackle.

This simply will not do.

He looks out the window and sees they are now crossing the Sydney Harbour Bridge, an iconic image of the city and one of the most photographed landmarks in Australia. At 134 metres, it is the tallest steel arch bridge in the world, and it was also the widest long-span bridge until 2012. He remembers being the first to climb it back in 1996. Getting permission from the government was a long and tedious process. The authorities were particularly twitchy about safety and weary of thrill-seekers who had illegally attempted the climb and invariably plunged to their deaths. He had to pull a lot of strings, pay an exorbitant amount of money, and take out a ridiculous insurance policy in order to gain access.

Mark remembers with clarity the morning he finally made his ascent: it was a sunny day, and he made it to the top of the bridge in under two hours. It was nowhere near the tallest thing he'd ever climbed, but standing at the top, with the breathtaking view of the Sydney Harbour sprawled out beneath him and the endless blue sky stretched above, he felt a familiar sense of exhilaration unfurl in his chest. It is the same feeling he experiences every time he has conquered something, a sensation he has actively sought out all his life.

The recollection of its first occurrence is never far from his thoughts: this sense of warmth that starts at his sternum and spreads across his chest, sending sparks of electricity through his arms to his fingertips, and tingles down his spine until his entire body is buzzing with energy. At moments like this, he is hyper-aware of everything around him: the flutter of butterfly wings metres away from him, the smell of an apple from across the room, the thunder of his heart beating rhythmically in his chest. All of his senses become acutely amplified, and a complete and all-consuming sense of contentment envelops him. It is only in these infrequent moments that he can quell the tenacious and fretful hunger in his heart.

Unfortunately, the experience never lasts, and then he is left with the ever-increasing desire to recapture it again.

A childhood memory resurfaces in his mind, the threads of its web curling around him to transport him back in time. He was thirteen, lying in his bed in the darkened room he shared with his younger sister. Nola was already asleep, her soft breathing soothing in the background. Mark was about to drift into slumber himself when he heard the loud slamming of the front door, followed by belligerent bellowing resonating through the house.

Father was back.

The walls of this small, dilapidated home were thin, and Mark could hear every single drunken word of abuse his father was hurling at his mum. Then, after her lack of response, came the predictable sound of loud crashing as things were being thrown around, followed by his mother's muffled screams as the bastard began to beat her.

Mark's entire body tensed, and despite his mother's previous warnings, he felt the urge to go out there and do something. He'd listened to this gruesome routine day after day for as long as he could remember, and sometimes these episodes were followed by his father coming into his room to give him a good beating too. He could still feel the bruises in his ribs from last week's encounter.

Mark hated his father, and he hated himself more for not being able to do anything about the situation. His mother had asked him, countless times, to forgive his father for his negligent ways. He was a sick man, she'd explained, and only God and his loving family could help him heal from the evil that had possessed his mind. She told Mark his father was not always this way, that once he had been a kind and loving soul. She asked Mark to pray for his father, promising that God would one day deliver the man she knew back to their family again.

Mark was already old enough to know his father's behaviour wasn't a matter of demonic possession. The man was just a sadistic animal who enjoyed beating up those who were weaker than him. But his mother had tearfully made him agree to never dodge his father's fists or fight back, for she feared it would only aggravate the situation and Mark, being thirteen and half the size of his father, would only get hurt even more.

Reluctantly, he had to comply. He could not stand it when his mother cried.

The sound of his bedroom door being opened made him freeze, and he closed his eyes to pretend he was asleep, hoping that the arsehole would just leave him alone. His father walked over to his bed, and Mark could smell the foul, sour scent of alcohol on his breath as he brought his face near. Mark braced himself for the beating that was to come.

But it never came.

Instead, his father turned and walked over to Nola's bed. Mark heard the creaking of the bed as the scumbag climbed in.

What the fuck.

He heard Nola's confused voice as she woke up, and her muffled question as their father hushed her. When Mark heard her squeal in protest, he got out of his bed.

He couldn't see what his father was doing. The man had his back turned to Mark, and his large frame blocked Nola. But Mark knew exactly what was going on, and it sickened him to the stomach. He slipped his hand under his bed and found the wooden cricket bat he kept there, and quietly walked to Nola's bed.

Without a sound, he brought the bat up high, and swung it down on his father's head with all his might.

The man fell out of the bed with a yelp, falling to the floor on his back. Mark kept bringing the bat down, attacking with everything he had. His father was a huge man, and on his better days would tower over Mark with impressive strength, but the blow he'd already received to his head left him dazed. He screamed like a wounded dog when Mark brought the bat down on his crotch.

"Mark, stop!" His mother was yelling at him. At some point during this assault she had come into the room, and she was trying to hold on to his arm, sobbing. "*Stop!* You'll kill him!"

He halted, looking at the man beneath him. Curled up on his side, whimpering and whining with hands protectively over the groin, his nose was bleeding, and he was blubbering like a child. Mark had never seen his father like this before. At that moment, the man was no longer the formidable bulky giant that was full of loud abuse and raining fists. He was reduced to a pitiful creature, crying at Mark's feet.

"*Leave,*" Mark spat at the older man.

Mark's father got up with some difficulty, and limped out the door.

Mark felt a growing warmth build within his chest. It turned into electric tingles and sent sparks throughout his entire body. He smiled triumphantly, almost laughed out loud with exultation.

That day, he learnt if he could defeat his hulking brute of a father, then there was nothing in this world he could not conquer.

11

THE CAPTAIN ANNOUNCES over the intercom that they are now descending towards Taiwan Taoyuan International Airport, advising passengers to follow the usual landing procedures. Georgia looks out the window and sees the familiar lush, mountainous terrain of her favourite island.

Also widely known as *Formosa*, meaning "beautiful island," Taiwan has a complex history of colonisation by the Dutch, the Spaniards, the Han Chinese, and the Japanese. It was finally taken over by the Chinese Nationalists led by Chiang Kai-Shek in 1949, when the generalissimo lost the Chinese Civil War against Mao's Communist Party. Since then, Taiwan's national identity has been an ambiguous one, with tense cross-strait relations and each side claiming itself to be the 'true China.'

These days, with mainland China becoming a formidable economic power, the international political status of Taiwan has become greatly weakened, with many regarding its sovereignty as undetermined. China, of course, considers Taiwan as part of Chinese territory despite its independent government, and is quick to quash any statements that may suggest otherwise. Many believe it's only a matter of time before the island is reabsorbed into Chinese rule, with or without the consent of the islanders.

As the plane touches down, Georgia's thoughts trail to her grandmother, and a strong sense of homecoming overcomes her. Within an hour, she exits the airport with her bags and climbs into a yellow taxi, directing the driver to head towards Tamsui, a seaside suburb on the outskirts of Taipei.

Growing up, Amah was the centre of her world. It was Amah who packed her school lunch and walked her to and from school every day, and it was also Amah who made sure she did her homework before bedtime. Her grandmother played a vital role in shaping the person she is today.

Though Georgia is a second-generation Taiwanese immigrant in Australia, her grandmother ensured their rich cultural heritage was passed down to her only grandchild. Amah's pride for her ethnicity is truly infectious. Whilst Georgia's other Australian-born Asian friends were brought up with English nursery rhymes and fairy tales, her bedtime routines were instead filled with stories of old China. Some of the tales were of Amah's family and life in China before she moved to Taiwan. Others told of great emperors and conquerors, philosophers, scholars, and poets. There were also, of course, legends of dragons, powerful sorcerers, zombies, and vengeful ghosts. As a child, the latter were her favourites. She loved a good scare and Amah loved to oblige, much to the chagrin of Georgia's mother.

Once, after story time had finished and still yearning to hear more, Georgia asked Amah if the people she spoke of existed in real life.

"What do you think, my darling girl?" her grandmother said in Chinese. Amah always insisted, and still does now, that Georgia speak to her in her native tongue.

"I think some are real and some aren't... But which ones are true, Amah?"

"Ah, I guess that's for me to know and for you to find

out." Amah winked, kissing Georgia on the forehead and leaving her to ponder that question.

Perhaps it was this prompting that led Georgia to a lifetime of pursuit, searching for relics from an ancient past that gives her a momentary glimpse into that magical world her grandmother once conjured. Somewhere in her subconscious, Georgia must have decided it a worthy challenge to take on, solving the puzzle that has plagued her since childhood. Amah was not raised as an educated woman, but Georgia discovered later that her grandmother indeed knows her history well.

Now, as the taxi slows to a stop before Tamsui train station, Georgia's heart swells with excitement at the thought of surprising her grandmother with her unannounced visit. Getting out of the car, she walks towards the apartment building her grandmother lives in, her mouth watering as a delicious scent envelops her from a street vendor selling grilled sausages.

It's good to be back.

She finds herself wandering over to the stall, having decided to pick up some snacks to share with her grandmother. The grey-haired woman standing behind the food cart smiles warmly at her, greeting her in the local Taiwanese dialect. Turning the sausages on the grill with great patience, the elderly vendor chats to Georgia affectionately as if she has known the younger woman all her life. By the time Georgia enters the elevator of her grandmother's apartment building ten minutes later, she has caught up on the latest neighbourhood gossip.

As the lift crawls slowly up the building floor by floor, Georgia begins to worry that Amah may not be home. She is a busy woman, after all, far more sociable than her bookish granddaughter. But the door is answered a few seconds after Georgia rings the bell. Opening it by a crack, a tiny old woman peers out, hesitantly squinting her cloudy eyes at Georgia.

"Amah," Georgia exclaims in Chinese, "it's me, Georgia! I've come to see you!"

"Georgia!" Amah flings the door wide open, throwing her arms out for a tight hug. "What a nice surprise! What are you doing here? Have you had lunch? *Aiya,* why didn't you tell me you were coming? How come you only packed such a small bag?"

"Oh, it was a last minute decision. I was in Okinawa for work," Georgia explains as Amah ushers her through the door and to the small settee. She looks around the tiny apartment, noticing that nothing has changed over the last three years. There is something nice about having some kind of consistency in your life. Amah has always been that for her, a reliable refuge no matter what was going on at the time.

"Okinawa! Tell me all about it." Amah busies herself in the small kitchen adjacent to the living room, making tea for both of them.

Georgia watches the older woman frown at the label of the tea canister, and asks, "How're your eyes?"

"Oh, you know, not great. But I can still see fine." Amah shrugs. "I'm just putting off the surgery for as long as I can."

Amah has cataracts, worsening her already poor vision from a head injury she'd sustained as a girl. Judging from the cloudiness of her eyes, Georgia worries her grandmother will struggle to get around on her own very soon.

"Anyway, I don't want to talk about my eyes," Amah says at Georgia's frown, giving a dismissive wave of her hand and insisting instead: "Tell me about Okinawa."

"Oh, I'd rather not, it was just work. *Boring* work." Georgia pouts, resting her chin in her palms and feeling like a child again. She watches Amah lay out the tea and snacks on the coffee table, shuffling around her apartment with efficiency.

"Boring? Work is never boring for you." She settles on the settee next to Georgia, pouring some oolong tea into their cups. Then she looks up and down at Georgia, assessing her closely and clucking her tongue. "You look skinny. Are you not eating well?"

Georgia rolls her eyes. Her grandmother is forever trying to fatten her up. "I'm eating fine, Amah, don't worry."

Amah furrows her brows, shaking her head. Then she pats Georgia on the knee. "Tell me then, how is everything at home? Everything settled?"

The corners of Georgia's lips slant down as she tastes the scalding tea to stall for time. Sighing, she says, "We're finalising the divorce next week."

"Hm." Amah puts down her cup, looking at Georgia intently. "Are you feeling okay?"

"No." Georgia's throat constricts as the fissure of her carefully patched heart threatens to crack open.

Her marriage didn't exactly fail out of spite or acrimony. If she is honest, a part of her still loves Lucas. But after Jacqui's death, everything about him reminded her of their daughter: his soft brown eyes, the subtle cleft of his chin, the slight cock of his head when he was trying to figure out something that puzzled him. Over time, she found his presence unbearable because it was a constant reminder of what they had lost.

She suspects Lucas would have seen ghosts of Jacqui in her too. Jacqui was in the silences that had become the norm in their home, a void pregnant with words that went unsaid. In the early days after Jacqui's death, her little figure hovered at the edge of Georgia's vision everywhere she went, the ghostly sounds of gurgling laughter ringing through the house as it used to. Georgia would find herself at the door to Jacqui's room, the air heavy with the little girl's absence, and her heart would collapse in on itself with grief.

As the months passed, the chasm between her and Lucas grew wider, each of them nursing their own wounds, and being in the other's presence brought a pain neither could face. Eventually Georgia felt the need to get away from the insistent reminder of the guilt that has plagued her since the day Jacqui was diagnosed: the guilt of not being able to save her, of giving her baby an incomplete heart, of remaining alive long past the death of her own daughter.

Georgia shakes her head, trying to dispel the gravity of her thoughts. "Anyway, let's not talk about Lucas." She reaches for some of the snacks on the coffee table, eating her bad mood away. "Enough about me, what have you been up to these last few weeks since I talked to you? Why aren't you out with your friends today?"

Smiling, Amah launches into a lengthy update of her social life, which makes Georgia's seem pathetic in comparison. Georgia is happy and relieved that her grandmother has such an extensive support network here. Her family were initially worried when Amah insisted on moving back to Taiwan after Georgia's grandfather died, but Amah wasted no time in reconnecting with old friends and making new ones. Despite their physical distance, Georgia and Amah have remained close, making regular video calls to check in on each other.

"So that's everything I've been up to, and I'm too tired to go out today after all that!" Amah laughs, finishing her report cheerfully. She pauses, redirecting her attention on Georgia. "How's everything going at the university right now?"

Georgia shrugs, knowing Amah is going to keep asking about work no matter how many times she dodges the question. "Work's been tough. Sarah and I spent two months on a scavenger hunt for money to keep this China dig afloat."

Amah frowns. "Is your job safe?"

"Yes," Georgia says reassuringly. "Yes, it's fine. I've picked up some freelance work on the side. That's why I was in Okinawa. But—well, it was just all dead ends really."

"Really?" Amah raises her eyebrows, curious.

Georgia sighs. "Yeah. I really shouldn't have taken the job in the first place, but the offer was one I couldn't turn down."

Amah pats her hand. "I'm sure you'll figure it out, Georgia. You always do."

They drink their tea and chat idly about the hot weather. Georgia considers for a moment how much to tell her grandmother about her search. After some time she ventures tentatively: "Amah, do you remember the bedtime story you used to tell me about Emperor Qin and the elixir of life?"

"Yes." Amah smiles from the memory. "That was one of your favourites."

"And about Hsu Fu who was sent to find the elixir, but ended up in Japan?"

"Ah yes." Amah nods, her filmy eyes focusing on something imagined in the distance. She whispers, "The man with the green eyes."

Georgia gapes at her grandmother. "*Green* eyes?"

"Yes, green eyes."

"You never told me that Hsu Fu had green eyes." Georgia frowns.

"I didn't?" Amah returns the frown, oblivious to the importance of this tiny detail.

"How do you know he had green eyes?" Georgia presses.

"Well." Amah clasps her hands together, staring at Georgia as her voice takes on a mysterious tone. "The legend is that Hsu Fu was the bastard son of a powerful witch. No one knew who the father was, or why Hsu Fu had such eerie jade-coloured eyes. Villagers suspected he didn't have a father, that the witch had conjured her baby from another realm. That was why he was both feared and shunned for most of his life. But his unique gifts in healing and sorcery won him a place in the community and in Emperor Qin's court."

Georgia shakes her head. For a moment she feels as if she is a little girl, listening to ghost stories again. "No, Amah, these are just tales of superstition. There's no reference anywhere in history that says he had those features."

Amah shrugs, looking a little disappointed that she cannot enchant her granddaughter with another story-telling session. "Well, there's a painting of Hsu Fu in the Gugong Museum. You can go see for yourself."

12

GUGONG MUSEUM, also known as the National Palace Museum of Taipei, is home to the largest and finest permanent collection of ancient Chinese artefacts in the world. Located at the foot of a mountain in northwest Taipei, its expansive compound includes two exhibition buildings, a library, and just under two hectares of Chinese garden reflecting the classical styles of the Song and Ming dynasties. The exhibition areas are housed within the traditional Chinese architecture of Naples yellow walls and turquoise blue roof tiles, with large archways and a wide avenue leading up to the main building.

Boasting a treasury of almost seven hundred thousand artefacts, it encompasses over eight millennia of Chinese history from the Neolithic age to the Republican period. Only around three thousand pieces of the collection can be shown at a given time, and it is speculated that there are still large reserves of treasure hidden in vaults under the mountain, precious antiquities that have never been shown to the public.

It is also one of Georgia's favourite places in the world.

Every time she sets foot in this building, she gives her silent thanks to Chiang Kai-Shek. Despite the controversy around the generalissimo's martial ruling in Taiwan, and the widespread corruption of his army and government, he also gave the world an enduring gift by preserving the heritage and legacy of the Chinese culture.

Taiwan's National Palace Museum shares its roots with the Palace Museum of the Beijing Forbidden City in China. The original collection of the Beijing museum was split in two after Chiang Kai-Shek lost the civil war to Chairman Mao. The Chinese Nationalist army retreated to Taiwan, taking with them some of the best pieces of Chinese heritage. Almost three thousand crates of artefacts were transported covertly with military escort during this time, though they only accounted for twenty percent of the crates originally transported out of Beijing. The rest were seized by the Communist army in 1949.

China has long claimed that the collection was stolen, but Taiwan insists it was a necessary act to protect the valuable treasure from destruction; especially during the Cultural Revolution, in which Mao encouraged his people to purge all remnants of 'capitalist and traditional elements' from society. Between 1966 to 1976, Mao's Red Guards destroyed countless ancient buildings, temples, relics and antiques. Mao persecuted thousands of intellectuals and scholars, and conducted frequent book burnings. He abolished the use of traditional text, introducing the use of simplified Chinese characters instead and effectively negated thousands of years of literature and culture that had evolved out of the art of Chinese calligraphy. The practice of many traditional customs and culture were also greatly weakened as a result. Indeed, some would argue that Taiwan became heir to the true Chinese legacy after the decade of ruination.

As Georgia walks into the main building of Gugong Museum, she is affronted by its transformation in the three years since her last visit. Gone is the serene place of reflective thought as one gazes upon the legacy of a great civilisation.

Instead, she feels as if she has just walked into the local wet market, with the throng of Chinese tourists making so much din and commotion it is difficult to navigate her way through the expansive foyer without having to push her way through the crowd.

Horrified, she walks up the wide staircase, having a near-miss with a group of screaming children playing tag. She sighs in exasperation. In the past decade the hostility between Taiwan and China has gradually thawed, and the two countries have opened their borders to cross-strait tourism. Understandably, over half a century of segregation from each other breeds a certain level of curiosity on both sides. It is estimated that every day, over ten thousand Chinese tourists land in Taiwan, most of them fascinated by the island and its history, and especially by its former head of state, the infamous Chiang Kai-Shek. As a result, anything associated with the previous martial ruler is extremely popular with the Chinese tourists, especially the museum housing the collection he supposedly stole from China.

She heads directly to the west wing of the second floor, where the painting and calligraphy section resides. There are fewer people here, as the section is less popular with the tourists. The permanent collection is usually rotated every three months, and Amah has assured her that the painting of Hsu Fu is currently on display. Amah has been a volunteer guide at the museum for only a few years, but her knowledge of the museum still never ceases to impress Georgia.

She walks through the west wing methodically, examining every painting before moving on. There are six areas of exhibits in total, and it is not until she reaches the fifth room that she comes across what she is looking for.

Standing in front of it, she draws in a breath. An ink and colour painting on a silk scroll, the work has yellowed with age and is frayed at the edges, but is otherwise in fair condition. It depicts two men, one of them obviously Emperor Qin, tall and stately. Qin is adorned in a black robe with strips of gold embroidery beneath the waist. As a crown, he wears a black coronet decorated with strings of beaded jade hanging in front and at the back of his head. One arm is extended towards the other man, as if to provide instructions. The other man, tall and thin, is leaning forward towards the emperor, his hands clasped within the wide sleeves of his pale robe. He has an unusually long, narrow face with square jaws. A goatee extends from his chin, and above his lips rests a thin moustache and an aquiline nose.

But the most striking feature of all is his strange green eyes.

Georgia looks down at the label next to the silk scroll:

Qin Shi Huang and Hsu Fu, 100-200 CE.

HE WATCHES her profile from the shadows of the dimly lit exhibition hall, furrowing his brow at this new development. Exhaling a sigh, the man runs his long, slender fingers through his matted hair.

It appears that Georgia has found the painting of Hsu Fu and Emperor Qin.

He knew she would find nothing at the Senkaku Islands. Those desolate islands are incapable of hosting anything but a few species of birds and rodents. It is a cleverly constructed detour designed to deflect and discourage any curious mind.

A detour that has always worked. Until now.

Knowing the kind of person she is, the man assumed she would have instantly dismissed the entire idea as a fantasy not worthy of investigation. But something, or someone, has managed to pique her interest.

And at her current trajectory, he fears it is only a matter of time before she achieves her goal.

13

"THIS IS ALL *VERY* FASCINATING, GEORGIA!" Amah exclaims, visibly excited as Georgia finishes her story.

Georgia cringes at Amah's enthusiasm, knowing Hank has warned her to keep quiet about the project. But after her discovery today, she felt as if she was bursting at the seams trying to keep this secret from Amah. Of course, her grandmother sensed this immediately, promptly interrogating her from every different angle until she finally relented and told her tale.

Earlier today, Georgia walked out of the Gugong Museum, completely stupefied after she found the painting of Hsu Fu and Emperor Qin. Here was a third reference to Hsu Fu's green eyes, confirming the information on Lambert's oracle bone and in the Hata scroll.

Could it really be possible that these pieces of information together prove that Hsu Fu's expedition actually ended up in Japan? And what of Hsu Fu's incredible healing abilities?

Does the elixir really exist?

The scientist in Georgia is in mutiny, violently rejecting the mere suggestion. But the part of her who grew up with

Amah's tantalising bedtime stories somehow finds the idea irresistible.

"Yeah," Georgia now replies to her grandmother, pushing the last bits of spaghetti around on her plate. "Yes it is. And very confusing and frustrating too."

They are sitting in a bustling, stylish vegetarian restaurant with an Italian twist. It is Amah's ninety-third birthday, and Georgia has decided to take her out for celebration. Amah is not accustomed to Italian food, but being who she is she has exclaimed in delight over every dish.

"What do you mean?" Amah frowns at Georgia from across the table. "What's so confusing and frustrating about it?"

She shrugs, making a face. "Well, all the evidence I've found so far is weak at best and probably won't stand up to scrutiny. Akiko Hata won't let anyone examine the scroll properly for authentication; and really, the painting at Gugong doesn't prove anything. The green eyes could just have easily been caused by a discolouration of the pigments." She blows out a frustrated breath. "I mean, all this talk of the elixir, of immortality—I feel like I'm wasting my time. It's just too far-fetched for me. I can't believe in the possibility that Hsu Fu could still be alive after two thousand years. It's just so—"

"So… what?" Amah interjects, "So airy fairy, so fantastical, so *unscientific?*"

"Yeah," Georgia admits as Amah takes the words right out of her mouth.

"*Aiya,* Georgia." Amah shakes her head, clucking her tongue. "The concept of being able to fill a room with light with the flip of a switch was fantastical to someone two thousand years ago. The idea of flying in a metal bird from here to America within sixteen hours was unscientific to people just over a hundred years ago. There are so many unknowns, so many possibilities that are not within our grasp right now.

What makes science so omnipotent, that anything it can't prove is immediately impossible and untrue?"

Amah reaches over to squeeze Georgia's hand. "I know you've been raised and educated in the West. I know being a scientist is important to you. But you are also my grand-daughter. You are the descendant of a culture which knows that the universe is far larger and more mysterious than a small human mind can fathom. Don't ever forget that."

Georgia's eyes well up as an unexpected ache spreads through her chest. Something about Amah's words, the feel of her paper-thin skin against Georgia's hand, and the way the older woman holds her gaze firmly but with kindness fills Georgia with a deep sense of longing. It is almost as if a part of her yearns to believe in the magic of her grandmother's words again.

Amah leans back into her chair, continuing, "So let's suppose for a minute that it *is* possible that Hsu Fu had found the elixir, and that everything in the Hata scroll is true. Think of what this could mean, Georgia! To be able to cure sickness, to end suffering once and for all. Isn't that something worth searching for? Isn't it something that would actually help the advancement of science?"

"Yeah," Georgia replies, "Mark Lambert said the same thing. He promised that he'd use the elixir to end child mortality, amongst other things."

Amah flinches at Georgia's tone. She frowns, placing a hand on Georgia's cheek. "Georgia. Are you still having the same dreams?"

"Like a broken record." Georgia grimaces. "Sometimes it feels like this pain I feel is all I have left of her."

Amah nods, letting out a heavy sigh. "Sweetheart, it hurts, I know. But you can't go on blaming yourself over it. Life is cruel sometimes, and there isn't anything anyone can do about that. You did everything you could. With Lucas too."

"Yeah, but that wasn't enough, was it?" Georgia lets out a

bitter laugh. "Jacqui is gone. And now so is Lucas. Nothing I did was good enough."

Amah falls silent, looking as if Georgia has slapped her in the face. Georgia bites down on her tongue, feeling self-indulgent with what she has said. This is Amah she is talking to, after all; and she has never heard her grandmother complain about anything in her life, even though Georgia knows she has been through some extremely challenging times. Amah's generation has always remained indomitable in the face of the brutality of life, and they never utter their grievances, much less wallow in their own misery. Instead, they are forever grateful to be alive.

After a long period of silence, Georgia almost feels the ridiculous need to apologise for what she has said. Before she does, though, a look of determination crosses Amah's face, and she pushes her chair back to stand.

"Come, Georgia." Amah holds her hand out to her. "I want to show you something."

———————

HER GRANDDAUGHTER FOLLOWS her into the elevator of her apartment building like a dutiful child, silent and brooding. All the way home, they have not said a word to each other, each engrossed in their own thoughts.

Amah wrings her liver-spotted hands, anxious about the tale she is about to share with Georgia: a story she has not told for decades. Not even her own daughter—Georgia's mother—knows of this part of her life. It was a past Amah had buried in the deepest corner of her heart, and were it not for the look on her granddaughter's face tonight, she would have happily left it there.

But sometimes, the past must be revisited.

The truth of this became clear to her at the restaurant tonight. Amah has not seen her precious granddaughter in person for years, and she was astonished to notice the change in her when the young woman showed up at the door: the gaunt, pallid face, the weight of pensive sorrow that seems to hover over her soul. Amah worries that if she doesn't intervene soon, the grief that Georgia is holding down like a balloon under water will soon snuff out the light in her eyes.

They finally enter her apartment, and gesturing to the settee in the lounge, she instructs Georgia as she heads for the bedroom: "Sit."

Inside the room, she reaches under the single bed, her hand encountering the familiar shoe box. She re-emerges into the lounge room with the package in hand, sitting down next to Georgia, who is looking at her with wide eyes. Without a word, Amah lifts the lid of the container, rummaging through its contents.

"Ah," she says when she finds what she's looking for.

She places it in Georgia's hands, watching as her granddaughter stares at the black and white photograph, its corners yellowing and the edges worn with age. Amah cannot see so well anymore, but she can picture the photograph vividly in her mind: an attractive young woman clutching a baby boy in her lap. She is wearing a *qipao*—a traditional Chinese dress commonly worn by women in the early 1900s. The one-piece dress is simple, with a mandarin collar and an opening from the neck to the underarm buttoned with a Chinese knot. There are dark trimmings around the collar and sleeves, but it is otherwise without any embellishments. The young mother's hair is pulled back, and she stares at the camera with a hint of mirth, as if she is holding back a smile. The baby boy in her lap has plump limbs and chubby cheeks, and grins unabashedly at the camera.

They look happy.

Georgia turns to her, eyes questioning.

"That's me, when I was very young," Amah explains

slowly. Then, tracing her index finger over the boy's flushed cheeks, she murmurs, "And this... was my son."

"Your son?" Georgia asks with surprise.

"Yes." Amah nods, continuing to caress her finger softly over the boy's face. "Yes, my son."

"Mum never told me." Georgia frowns. "I thought she was your only child."

"She doesn't know." She finally peels her eyes away from the photograph to look at Georgia. "I had him when I was fifteen, with my first husband in China."

Georgia arches her eyebrows, clearly unsure of what to make of another sudden revelation. She didn't know her grandmother had been married to another man, either.

Amah closes her eyes, the decades of her youth come rushing back. She searches through her mind, trying to order her thoughts and calm the rising emotions in her throat. After a few moments, she finally draws in a long breath, then starts to speak. She can scarcely recognise her own voice as she begins her story.

"My parents arranged our marriage," she says, "I didn't even meet him until our wedding night. That was the tradition at the time. My husband was much older, but he was very kind to me. A year after we married, I gave birth to our baby boy. We named him Yu-Lin.

"My husband owned a photography business in Nanjing at the time. He was the one who took this photo, you see, and life was good for us for a while. When the war started with the Japanese, we heard about the bloody battle in Shanghai. Everyone was nervous. I told my husband we should leave Nanjing, since it was the capital of China back then and everyone thought it was only logical that the Japanese would attack Nanjing next. He was hesitant at first about leaving his business behind, but eventually we decided to head for Hangzhou, where my family is from.

"But by the time we finally made the decision, the

Japanese army was marching towards Nanjing, and our own army began burning buildings and houses, destroying anything that might be useful to the enemy. They also destroyed boats, blocked the roads and the port to prevent civilians from leaving. We became trapped in our own city."

Amah pauses as she detects the tremor in her own voice. She takes a drink of water, her hand unsteady.

She can tell from the look of dread on Georgia's face that she knows exactly where this story is heading. Her granddaughter knows the history of China as if it is her own, and she knows that Amah is about to describe her own experience of the Nanjing Massacre: arguably the most horrific incident during the war between Japan and China. It is estimated that across a six-week period, the Japanese soldiers murdered over three hundred thousand unarmed combatants and civilians. And yet, to this day, Japan denies that the incident ever took place.

"There was a Safety Zone established by the last of the Westerners living in the city, and some refugee camps were set up," she continues, her voice soft. "We moved into one of them, the University Middle School, along with thousands of other people. Even though no shells were meant to be dropped on this part of the city, the Japanese soldiers would enter the Safety Zone every day—looting, raping, murdering.

"I can't begin to describe to you, Georgia, the horrors I saw during this time. It was like the whole world had descended into hell. The sounds of screaming and crying became a background noise in this city. We lived in constant fear. The kind of cruelty the soldiers inflicted on the people was something I hadn't imagined possible. They didn't just rape and kill their victims; they mutilated them, did unspeakable things to their bodies. I still have nightmares now, sometimes."

Amah's eyes widen as images of rape victims resurface in her memory. As if reading her mind, Georgia reaches for her hand, squeezing it firmly. Amah looks over to her with a small smile that twists into a grimace. Her lower lip begins to tremble as she tells the next part of her story.

"The night the soldiers came to the University, we heard them make a lot of noise in the building. They were yelling and banging around and there were people screaming. Gunshots were fired. My husband picked up the baby and yanked me by the hand. We ran down the hall searching for somewhere to hide, but one of the soldiers spotted us. Two of them came after us, and my husband pushed me into a class-room, shoved the baby into my arms, and shut the door, telling me to lock it. My son was crying, shrieking. I could see through the frosted glass of the door: my husband standing there, facing the soldiers, trying to hold them back. It was useless, of course. They stabbed him with their bayonets, and his blood sprayed all over the glass. He didn't even have time to scream."

Amah sighs, tears now welling in her eyes. She feels the familiar ache in her chest, something she has done her best to accept over the years. Beside her, Georgia gasps with emotion. This is the first time she has ever seen her grand-mother cry.

"They broke down the door, r-ripped—" Amah stutters, her words breaking off with a sob.

Georgia grips her hand with alarm. "Amah, it's okay. You don't have to—"

"No." Amah wrenches her hand away to wipe at her face. She takes a deep inhale. "No, Georgia. Some truths need to be told. And you need to hear this."

Her granddaughter falls silent. Recomposing herself, Amah continues her story with as much stoicism as she can muster.

"They broke down the door... ripped my son out of my arms... and, just for fun, one of them—" She draws another breath. "One of them threw him in the air while the other pierced him with a bayonet. They were laughing, but all I could hear was his little body hitting the floor with a thud, and then there was no more crying." She swallows the lump in her throat, tears streaming down her cheeks. "The rest of it was inevitable… I woke up in the hospital a week later with severe rape injuries and a stab wound in my neck. The doctor told me I had lost thirty percent of my eyesight from multiple head traumas."

"Oh my God," Georgia whispers as she chokes off her own tears.

"I was one of the lucky ones." Amah smiles grimly. "The nurses told me that. A kind-hearted man had picked me up after I passed out and brought me to the hospital. Most victims would have been left to die—there were just too many of them every single night.

"Of course, I didn't see it that way for many, many years. I hated that I was alive, Georgia. How was this luck, when I was left behind to mourn for my dead husband and son? I wished I had died the night my little boy was killed. I felt guilty for surviving when they didn't. I woke up every morning with a pain in my heart that made me cry. Like you, I tormented myself for a long time. I couldn't bear the thought of being happy when I shouldn't even be alive.

"After the Japanese left Nanjing, and once my wounds had healed enough, I eventually made my way to Hangzhou. Through some family connections, I managed to leave China and moved to Taiwan. Looking back, fate saved me once again because none of my family survived the things that happened after Mao took over.

"A few years later, I met your grandfather." She smiles, wiping her tears away. "And slowly, through his love, I began to see the errors of my thinking. When your mother was born, I realised life had given me a second chance when it'd been stolen from so many others who died during the war. I realised that life can be cruel, yes; but it has also been generous to me. People can be savages, but they are also capable of great kindness. Just like the man that brought me to the hospital in the nick of time.

"It was only because I let go of my suffering that I was able to live the life I had with your grandfather, your mother, and you. I finally saw that letting go of my pain didn't mean I was abandoning my son and husband. It didn't mean I'd forgotten them, because they are still in my heart and I still think about them every day. But now, I only think about all the happiness we shared. I am determined to live my life fully and gratefully, because I want to honour their deaths."

Amah now turns to look at Georgia, grasping her hands tightly. Her granddaughter, for all of her astonishing intellect, sometimes fails to see life for what it is. She knows her Georgia all too well: she clutched the dear girl to her breast when she was just a baby, whispering stories to her every night. She saw Georgia through her schooling years and teenage struggles, watched her grow into a capable and independent young woman. But all her brains and logic will not save her. Not this time.

"You listen to me, child," she says firmly. "I know it's hard for you to see this, but I am telling you this story to let you know that what you are feeling at the moment will eventually pass. Life doesn't end here. Life is generous. It will bring you other loves, and you never know—maybe even other children. This, I know for sure: life will bring you much more than what you can see right now. Don't ever forget that."

Her granddaughter breaks into sobs. This time it's impossible to hold her tears back.

14

GEORGIA OPENS HER EYES SLOWLY, blinking a few times against the bright morning light filtering through the curtains of her grandmother's apartment. Yawning, she stretches, massaging out the kinks in her muscles from falling asleep on Amah's small settee last night.

The sounds of clinking crockery ring out from the kitchen, and the delicious smell of her grandmother's cooking drifts over to her. Her stomach rumbles in response. She smiles as she listens to Amah hum a melody as she works in the kitchen. Rising from the couch, Georgia slips into the small bathroom to freshen up, catching sight of her face in the mirror and grimacing at her puffy eyes: the aftermath of last night's tears.

Sobbing into Amah's shoulder for over an hour, it was probably the first time she'd had a good cry since Jacqui's death. Georgia was exhausted afterwards, and only barely registered her grandmother placing a light blanket over her as she fell into a deep, dreamless sleep.

Rubbing her eyes now, she realises that despite the aches in her body from sleeping on the cramped couch, she feels surprisingly refreshed, as if a weight has been lifted from her spirit. She smiles at her reflection in the mirror.

As she emerges from the bathroom, a renewed sense of inspiration comes over her. She decides to send a quick text to Hank:

— *Doing some research in Taipei. I'll call in when I return to Sydney. G.*

"Georgia," Amah calls from the kitchen. "Breakfast is ready."

"Morning." Georgia gives her grandmother a quick peck on the cheek as she walks over to help her with the tray of dishes. They sit down on the settee with the food, Amah filling large bowls with steaming rice porridge.

"Yum," Georgia says, accepting one of the bowls. "Thank you, Amah."

Amah pats her on the knee. "You feeling better?"

"Yeah. I do, actually."

"Good. Good to cry it all out." Amah nods. "So, what are you up to today?"

She considers this as she chews on a mouthful of food. "I think I might head to the Gugong Museum again to see if I can find out anything more about that painting."

"Ah. Good." Amah smiles. "I'm glad you're going to have a proper look into it. Don't forget, Georgia, the best legends are often inspired by truths."

LING LING HSIA walks through the corridors of Gugong Museum, heading for the stairs that lead to the exit. She desperately needs a break. She's been cooped up in that windowless box that her boss calls an 'office' since six this morning, trying to get a report finished for tomorrow. But when her computer crashed for the third time, she decided she should get out and take a walk. The exercise will be good for her anyway, especially since her husband has been hinting she is getting a little soft and round on the edges.

It is early morning and they have just opened to the public, so there are only a few people around. This is the time Ling Ling loves the most in the museum, where there are only a handful of visitors dedicated enough to make the early morning visit before the arrival of the tourist crowd. These early visitors are usually researchers, scientists, and scholars who are sometimes more knowledgeable than many of the staff working on the premises.

Although the museum rotates the exhibition pieces, it is hardly possible to see everything in its immense treasury within one's lifetime. Even Ling Ling, who's been working at the museum for almost ten years, has not seen the entire collection herself. She's been inside the Gugong vaults only a handful of times—large, cavernous rooms hidden under the mountain that are accessed through long tunnels—but everything is encased in temperature and humidity controlled crates, and it is difficult to imagine all the objects they contain.

As Ling Ling walks through the west wing of the second floor, she spots a figure she instantly recognises. Her breath catches in her throat.

"Georgia?"

The woman spins around from the painting she was looking at, and Ling Ling sees that it is indeed her friend, Professor Georgia Lee.

"Ling Ling!" Georgia breaks into a dazzling smile.

Ling Ling booms with delighted laughter and closes the distance between them, embracing Georgia tightly. She looks at her friend, seeing that nothing has changed in the few years since her last visit.

Smart, accomplished and beautiful, Georgia is proof that

life is not fair. It is almost easy to hate her for it, but she is also endowed with a humble and kind character, which is why Ling Ling idolises her with no small amount of ardour.

"What a wonderful surprise," Ling Ling says, "I thought it was you! It's been a long time. You should've told me you were dropping by."

"I know." Georgia looks at her sheepishly. "It was a last minute decision to visit, I didn't even tell Amah I was coming before I showed up at her door." She laughs.

Ling Ling places a hand on her chest. "Bless your amah. She is such a beautiful soul, I just adore her. I look forward to the days that she volunteers at Gugong. Thank you so much for introducing her to the museum."

Three years ago, Georgia was invited to Taipei as a consultant. The Thirteenth Site Museum of Archaeology in the Bali District of Northern Taipei had a special excavation project, and had called upon Georgia's expertise. Her reputation as an archaeologist preceded her, and everyone on the project anticipated her arrival with both excitement and nervousness. But Georgia's easy-going nature soon put them at ease. She and Ling Ling worked side-by-side intensively over three months, and the whole experience dramatically expanded Ling Ling's mind and knowledge, leaving her thirsty for more. She sees Georgia as a mentor for her work, but also feels somewhat maternal towards the younger woman who is ten years her junior.

After completing the project, Georgia brought her grandmother to Ling Ling's regular workplace, and the two struck up an instant friendship over the museum's collection of bronzes from the Shang Dynasty. Georgia's grandmother has been passionately learning about the ins and outs of Gugong ever since.

"You know, I was just about to come and find you," Georgia says, then gestures towards the painting before them.

"Have you noticed that Hsu Fu has green eyes in this painting?"

"Huh." Ling Ling squints, looking at the work closely. "You're right, he does. That's really odd, I've never noticed it before." Then she shrugs nonchalantly and smiles at Georgia. "Must be a discolouration of the pigments."

Georgia frowns. "Yeah… must be."

"C'mon, I'm just taking a break. Come for a walk with me. Tell me how things are going with your dig in China." Ling Ling loops her arm through the crook of Georgia's elbow, redirecting her out of the exhibition room and down the stairs. They wander outside into the grounds of Gugong, catching up on each other's work and lives. The pair enthusiastically bounce ideas off each other about the possible owner of the tomb that Georgia uncovered in China.

Their aimless meandering ends up at Exhibition Area II, a separate building within the compound that hosts special exhibits; and looking towards the closed doors, an idea suddenly springs into Ling Ling's mind.

She whispers to Georgia with excitement: "Hey, you know, I'm not really meant to do this. But my good friend Ang is curating this *amazing* exhibition of Qin Dynasty manuscripts right now. It's opening in two weeks, but it's right up your alley and it'll be a shame for you to miss it."

Georgia raises an eyebrow, surprised. "Manuscripts? From the Qin Dynasty?"

Ling Ling nods, smiling widely. "The collection was donated back in 1965, and it's been in the vaults ever since. It's only now that the museum has decided to exhibit it for the very first time." They pause at the entrance to the building, and Ling Ling tentatively pushes open the side door, glancing around the foyer. "Everyone is out at a team meeting now, and they probably won't be back for a few hours, so I'll give you a quick sneak peek."

They walk into the exhibition room, pausing briefly by the

wall next to the entrance. There is a short blurb written by the director of the Museum and a small black and white picture underneath the text. The special exhibit, titled *The Qin Manuscripts*, consists of a collection of exceptionally rare bamboo scrolls and a few artefacts from the dynasty. The collection is the largest and most intact in the world, consisting of almost thirty pieces.

Very few manuscripts actually remain from the Qin Dynasty. The ruthless Emperor Qin was paranoid of any thoughts contradictory to his own, so during his reign he performed countless book burnings and buried scholars alive for voicing any radical ideas. As a result, almost all of the only written records left were those in the palace archives. What was even more disastrous for later historians is that when the Qin Dynasty was overthrown, the imperial palace and the state archives were also burned.

At the end of the brief written introduction, the Museum Director goes on to attribute thanks to the donation of the collection from a single collector who had made it his lifelong passion to acquire these rare relics. After extensive restoration by the conservators at the Gugong, this is the first time the museum has decided to exhibit the delicate pieces to the public, as part of its fiftieth birthday celebration.

Ling Ling watches as Georgia looks around the dimly-lit exhibition room, awestruck as she takes it all in.

Ling Ling chuckles under her breath. "I know, right? Not every day you see something like this." She pats Georgia on the back. "I really gotta get back to work, but take your time in here and call me later. Let's try to meet up for dinner while you're in town."

"Sure." Georgia gives her a hug. "Thank you."

GEORGIA SMILES as she watches her friend exit the exhibition room, feeling the lingering warmth of her presence slowly seeping away. It is truly wonderful to see Ling Ling again, her pleasant nature is always a delight, and she has the most infectious laughter Georgia has ever come across.

She walks slowly around the exhibition room. Though it is small compared to the other exhibition spaces in the main building, it still takes Georgia almost an hour to examine all of the pieces. She has never actually seen a fully intact scroll from the Qin Dynasty until now, as most of the remaining bamboo or wooden slips from the period have generally disintegrated due to age and lack of care. Without proper ongoing conservation, these works don't stand a chance against the test of time.

In fact, looking at the rare bamboo scrolls before her, she is reminded of the one that Akiko Hata showed her.

Glancing down at her watch, she decides she should prob-ably leave before the curatorial team comes back. She makes her way towards the entrance, and that is when she catches sight of the small, black and white photograph below the introductory text she only half-heartedly glanced at before.

Something about the image captures her attention, and she moves closer to examine it.

Judging by the hair and clothing of the people in it, the monochromatic image obviously dates back to the sixties. It is a picture of two men shaking hands: on the left, a portly pres-ence in a suit, smiling widely at the camera. The other man is in his early forties and has a thin, unusually tall stature. He is half-turned towards the front, and the wide-eyed expression on his face suggests he has been caught by surprise by the camera.

Georgia narrows her eyes and leans in. The thin man on the right appears to be of Chinese descent, no doubt, but there is something unique about his features. It takes her a few seconds to realise that he has light-coloured eyes.

Her eyes dart towards the small text under the image:

Hang Li-wu, Director of National Palace Museum, and Mr. Meng Jie, donor of the Qin Manuscript Collection. 1965.

She examines the man's face again. As was fashionable at the time, his dark hair is parted on the side, and sideburns frame his long angular face.

His striking, soulful eyes gaze back at Georgia. She stares at his unusual narrow face, square jaws, and the aquiline nose, and cannot help noticing the similarity of these features to the painting she was staring at only an hour before.

15

"SHE'S IN TAIPEI, sir. A detour before coming back to Sydney. She said she'll call in when she gets back." Hank's soft voice crackles over the phone line. "Mr. Tanaka said they found nothing at the Senkaku Islands. Would you like me to bring her in for an update?"

"No." Mark frowns, placing the pen down with his unsteady hand. "Just keep an eye on her movements."

He hangs up the phone, displeased with the news. Bringing his hands together, he rubs his fingers, trying to massage away the pain radiating up his arms.

What are you up to, Georgia?

The urge to know is almost choking him, but he knows better than to interfere with her investigations. Georgia requires a large degree of freedom and independence in her methods—he understood that the moment he met her. He also knows that once the project captures her curiosity, the obsession that takes over will be all-consuming. Mark has worked with plenty others who are the same: geniuses in their own right who also possess eccentric characters and peculiar work processes. Processes that must, above all else, not be interrupted.

Patience, he tells himself. He will not micro-manage her in her work.

Glancing at his watch, he reaches for the glass of water on his desk and swallows the three round pills Joseph left for him in a small bowl.

And yet—time is something he is now running short of.

16

GEORGIA LETS OUT A FRUSTRATED SIGH, slumping before the computer screen. Her cheek in one hand and the mouse in the other, she scrolls down the screen with growing agitation.

Nothing.

She has spent the past week in the National Archives of Taiwan, rummaging through its wealth of information. The mysterious donor of the collection of Qin manuscripts, Meng Jie, had a strong resemblance to the Hsu Fu depicted in the silk painting at the Gugong Museum. Excited with the discovery, her first thought was to come to the archives to find out more about the man. But aside from his generous donation to the museum upon its opening, there has been no other mention of him before or after the event.

This she finds rather odd. Collectors and donors usually hold high profiles in the community, and it was unlikely Meng Jie would have appeared so suddenly on the scene, only to disappear again without a trace.

Ling Ling called only a few moments before, with even less helpful news. As is to be expected, the museum holds a strict privacy policy in favour of its benefactors, and will not reveal their identities to the general public. Furthermore, no one at the museum has been in contact with Mr. Meng since almost fifty years ago, so the chances of reaching him at his last known address are slim.

"And besides," Ling Ling reasoned over the phone, "the photograph was taken half a century ago. It's hard to know if he's still alive. I will pass on your letter to the address we have on file, but whatever questions you have regarding the collection may have to go unanswered, I'm afraid."

Leaning back in her chair now, Georgia considers calling it quits, when she suddenly feels a prickling sensation at the back of her neck. Straightening in her chair, she turns to survey the room around her. It's a busy time at the large research room, with most of the desks occupied by people working on computers or flicking through the archive files. All of them have their heads down, silently concentrating on their own tasks and oblivious to her presence.

She shakes her head, trying to rid herself of the inexplicable feeling that she's being watched. She must be getting paranoid. Just a week ago, she had the same strange sensation at the Gugong museum, when she was searching for the painting of Emperor Qin and Hsu Fu.

Reaching for her phone, Georgia brings up the picture of Meng Jie again. She took a photograph of the one at the exhibition, and she's not been able to stop obsessing over it since. Zooming in on his face, she finds herself strangely drawn to his features. As a Chinese person, his long pale face and light-coloured eyes certainly make him stand out.

An idea flashes across her mind, and she puts down the phone to return to the computer before her.

Meng Jie had obviously collected historical artefacts before, and knew plenty about conservation: this much is clear from seeing the excellent condition of the Qin Manuscripts collection. Given his passion and knowledge, it is unlikely that a true connoisseur would have made only one museum donation. Typing quickly on the keyboard, she makes several searches, looking for similar donations to museums and galleries over the years.

It takes her hours to sift through the search results. She is almost about to give up when she finally stumbles across the website on the Asian Art Collection at the Denver Art Museum in the United States:

Our Asian Art Collection originated in 1915 with a donation from a single passionate collector who dedicated his life to acquiring Chinese and Japanese art objects which span from the first millennium BCE to the present…

Georgia feels her pulse quickening as she scrolls down the screen, searching for a picture. She finds it at the bottom of the page: a dated, black and white photograph of a thin man in a dark suit, looking rather regal in the vest, high-collared shirt, and tie. The chain of his pocket watch is visible in the open gap of his dinner jacket. He is sitting side-on with his face tilted towards the camera, his hair cropped short and parted down the middle.

The caption under the picture reads: *Mr. Q. Sun.*

Georgia zooms in on the small photograph, and finds the exact same eerie, light-coloured eyes peering back at her.

17

"JESUS, Georgia, I don't know what to say! This is just—" Sarah's voice rings in Georgia's ear, her volume much too loud. Georgia dials down her phone. Only minutes earlier, she emailed Sarah the photos of the two donors, and now her assistant is bellowing at her with excitement.

"I just can't believe this is happening. This can't just be a coincidence. I mean, they have different hair and dress styles, *obviously*, but their faces are practically the same. And those eyes—I don't think you'd mistake those eyes anywhere. What did you say this Denver guy's name was?"

"Q. Sun. I couldn't find any references to what the *Q* stands for." As with her discovery of Meng Jie, Mr. Q. Sun is another complete mystery: a man who has no other historical records besides his generous donation to the Denver Art Museum.

Georgia sighs, leaning back on the chair as she feels a headache looming between her temples. She's been staring at the computer screen all day, and she feels exhausted. Glancing at her watch, she looks at the research room around her. It is almost five, nearing closing time, and there are only a couple of others left in the room, working on last bits of research before they are asked to exit the building.

"They look like they're the same age too, did you notice that?" Sarah points out. "Have you shown these photos to Mark Lambert?"

"No, I don't want to call him unless I have something more concrete. I'm not quite sure what to make of it yet," Georgia says. "I mean, there must be some kind of logical explanation for this."

"Like what?" Sarah sounds sceptical.

"I don't know, maybe they are just historical doppelgangers, or maybe the two men are from the same family…" she trails off, unable to think of anything else. "I couldn't find any other information on either of them, though."

"Did you find any other donations that are similar?" Sarah asks.

"None that came with a picture," she rubs her forehead. "I did a search concentrating on donations of Asian relics."

"*And?*" Sarah's volume is now deafening, and Georgia winces, holding the phone a few inches away from her ear.

"There was one other that stood out. All the way back in 1865. A small selection of Song Dynasty statues and ceramics given to the British Museum. Again by a single collector. This one was named Yi Lee. And again, there is no trace of him before or after the donation," she whispers into the phone, trying not to disturb the other researchers. "That's all I could come up with for now with what I've got on hand here. I was hoping you could dig deeper with the resources back at the university."

"Okay, sure. Send me the details of everything you've got," Sarah says. "I just can't get over it, Georgia. I can't believe the legends might actually be true."

Georgia nods, feeling the same way. As she hangs up the phone, she leans her head on the back of the chair, closing her eyes as exhaustion overcomes her. The three names circle in her head, an enigma that plagues her mind. She knows she is not going to get any sleep tonight.

Meng Jie.

Q. Sun.

Yi Lee.

There is something about these names…

She suddenly bolts upright. Hastily grabbing her belongings and shoving them into her bag, she runs for the door.

18

GEORGIA STEPS through the doors of the National Taiwan Library, relieved it is still open until nine o'clock tonight. Quickly scanning the floor plans, she heads towards the section she's looking for: Classical Chinese Literature.

The library is almost empty as she walks with a singular purpose, the click-clacking of her shoes echoing in the near-vacant space. At a search station, she quickly types in the title she is after, memorising its location on the floor.

She finds the area she is looking for and walks down the aisle between tall shelves, scanning the titles as she goes. The book she seeks is one she hasn't read in a long time, but still owns a copy of at home.

As she nears the end of the aisle, she stops, looking up at the top shelf. Standing on the tips of her toes, she reaches for a large volume and brings it down. She holds the hardcover novel in her hands, feeling the weight of its some thousand odd pages, her fingers tracing the blue embossed Chinese title on the cloth-bound spine: *Romance of the Three Kingdoms* by Luo Guanzhong.

First published in fourteenth-century China, and hailed as one of the Four Great Classical Novels of Chinese Literature, its literary influence in East Asia has been compared to that of the works of Shakespeare on English Literature. An epic work of over eight hundred thousand words with almost a thousand dramatic characters, it is a historical novel set during the tumultuous years between the end of the Han Dynasty and the Three Kingdoms period. This work is probably the most well-known historical novel in the late imperial and modern China, influencing the creation of many plays, movies, games and other cultural mediums throughout other East Asian countries including Vietnam, Japan, and Korea.

The story is part historical, part mythical, and part legend, and many of its characters are based on actual historical figures. It depicts the conflicts, trials, and tribulations of feudal lords as they scrambled for power during the imminent collapse of the Han Dynasty. When Georgia was little, Amah told her different parts of the epic tale, and although she loved the stories of heroic warriors and dramatic sword fights as a child, she later baulked at the chauvinistic treatment of women in the book. She remembers one story in the novel that particularly nauseated her when she was old enough to read the entire text herself: it told of a hunter who couldn't find game to slaughter for his lord's meal, so he killed his wife to serve up her flesh instead. He was later handsomely rewarded for his 'sacrifice.'

Georgia walks to a nearby desk with the book and sits down, leafing through the pages. Tales of great battles and treacherous murders come flooding back to her, and she becomes more and more certain of her hypothesis as she scans through the book.

She stops when she comes to the title of Chapter 29:

Chapter 29

The Formidable Sun Ce Kills Yu Ji in Fury

His Green-eyed Son Succeeds Control of Yangtze's East

She scans through the chapter, and it's not long before she finds the name of the green-eyed boy: Sun Quan. This is the chapter where the warlord Sun Ce dies after being wounded in an assassination attempt against him. His brother and successor, Sun Quan, later becomes a successful and charismatic ruler. Sun Quan is described as having green eyes and a purple beard.

As with all Chinese names, the surname is always placed before the first name.

Q. Sun.

She flips further through the book, patiently continuing her search. She finds what she is looking for in Chapter 81, where the emperor asks a mysterious old man to predict the future of his state:

…Upon seeing the man, Liu Bei knew at once that he was in the presence of a venerable sage. The elderly man's soft white hair contrasted with his youthful complexion; his emerald eyes glistened with an arresting gaze…

The old man's name is Li Yi. Li is a spelling variation of Lee, but they mean exactly the same family name in Chinese.

Y. Lee.

Georgia's pulse quickens as she searches for the last name on her list, locating it a few chapters later in Chapter 89:

Kongming was about to announce himself, when a green-eyed and yellow-haired man emerged at the doorway, dressed in a girded white robe, with grass sandals on his feet and a bamboo hat on his head.

This green-eyed man, a recluse, is Meng Jie.

19

"Sir?"

Mark Lambert raises his eyes from the newspaper, seeing Joseph standing by the drawing room door.

"I have your breakfast ready, sir," he says, balancing the tray in his arms. "Would you like to have it in here, or in the dining room?"

"Here's fine, Joseph."

"Very well, sir."

The butler walks over to the coffee table next to Mark, laying out the various items of food and drinks for him: a bowl of berries, a couple of hard boiled eggs, coffee, water, and a small plate with three round pills.

"Thank you."

"A pleasure, sir." Joseph exits the room quietly.

Mark rises from the arm chair, taking the coffee with him as he walks to the French windows. He gazes out to the frosty grass plains outside, watching the pink sky slowly turn white then pale blue as the sun rises in the horizon. The grazing kangaroos retreat one by one as the morning light brightens.

His hand trembles. Fearing he'll spill his drink again, he places the cup down on the table next to the window. His eyes move over the picture frames on the table top, settling on the photo of his late sister. Nola is dressed in one of her ballet costumes—from *Swan Lake*, if he remembers correctly. She gazes at him with the same grey eyes that he possesses, her warm smile lighting up her beautiful face.

They were always close, siblings bonded by the struggles of their early childhood. Mark felt a strong sense of protectiveness over his sister ever since they were kids, and to others it always appeared he was the one who took care of his family after his father had finally left. What they didn't know was that Mark depended on Nola just as much as she relied on him. His sister was the calming influence in his life, the most kind and gentle person he has ever known. Without her, he is sure he would have derailed long ago, the energy and drive of his youthful years misguided towards criminal ventures.

Nola was an exquisite dancer. He remembers one of the times he watched her dance on stage: her debut performance as the hottest new talent in London. It was the ballet version of *Romeo and Juliet*, and anyone who was someone in the arts business was there. There was a lot of anticipation and gossip around this young ballerina nobody had ever heard of, yet who had somehow managed to score the lead role in the show. All of the critics were there, sharpening their pencils to write a damning review on the latest mistake the chief choreographer had made.

But when Nola finally took the stage, a hush descended on the entire audience. She emanated such a radiant beauty that over the next few hours of the show, she did not just prove the critics wrong, she bewitched them with her enchanting performance. Nola danced with such transcendental grace that it brought tears to Mark's eyes.

The performance was a resounding success, and when it was over the crowd rose to a standing ovation and clapped until their palms were raw. The next day, the newspapers were covered with stories of this spellbinding dancer who had astonished London. Contracts, tours, and acclaim quickly followed, taking Nola's ever-rising career all over the globe.

But it did not last long. Three and a half years later, when Nola was performing *The Nutcracker* in New York City, the audience noticed a strange jerkiness in her movements. She stumbled through a series of *Fouetté* turns, a ballet move she was most renowned for. And when the time came for her to descend the grand stairs on the stage set, she somehow missed a step and fell face first on the stage.

Even though she didn't fall far, Nola still came away from the accident with a broken nose and a sprained wrist. However, these injuries were insignificant compared to the tremendous shame she suffered. Mark insisted that the doctors run a full set of tests on her, given this was an unusual occurrence. When they finally announced the diagnosis, he knew his sister's dance career was over.

Over the course of the five years that followed, Nola Lambert, the most mesmerising ballerina the Royal Ballet Company had ever seen, was reduced to a writhing, twisted creature who couldn't control her own movements, her speech, or even her mind. Her usual demure and pleasant manner was replaced with aggressive outbursts and mood swings.

Mark couldn't even recognise his own sister anymore. In her more lucid moments, she would sometimes plead with him to end her life. She begged him, in her broken speech, to save her from the humiliating illness that would not kill her fast enough.

"Can't you see that I'm already dead?" she said, her eyes pleading.

Mark shakes his head, letting out a long sigh at the memory of Nola's distorted face, the strange and slow movements of her eyes, and the drool that never ceased to dribble from the corner of her mouth. How was it possible for such an angelic being to descend so far from grace?

His mind trails to Georgia. If the professor is as good as he thinks she is, she's the key to putting an end to all of this. Mark made a promise to his sister before she died, and he believes Georgia is the only one who can help him deliver that promise.

"Sir?" Joseph's voice brings him out of his brooding rumination. Mark turns, surprised to see his butler beside him. He didn't even hear him come in.

"Yes?"

"The car is ready for you sir." When Mark looks at him with momentary confusion, Joseph explains, "You have a flight to catch today."

"Right." Mark straightens, quickly recovering his composure. "I'll be out in a few minutes."

"Of course sir, I'll have Paul load your bags now." Joseph pauses before he leaves. "Remember to take your medication, sir."

"Yes. Thank you, Joseph."

The butler exits the room, and Mark walks over to the coffee table, taking the three round pills in the small saucer and washing them down with some water.

He rubs at the dull ache in his hands.

He would never want to end up the same way as Nola. So help him God, he'll end his own life before it happens.

20

"THIS IS REMARKABLE, GEORGIA!" Hank's usually soft voice is now animated with excitement. "Mr. Lambert will be thrilled. He was disappointed when your search at the Senkaku Islands turned up nothing, but this will definitely please him."

Back on the small settee in Amah's small living room, Georgia is doodling idly on her notepad as she talks to Hank on her phone, rehashing her findings over and over again to make sense of it all. She eyes her grandmother in the kitchen, busy preparing dinner for them both. Her mouth salivates at the wonderful smell.

"How did you even make the connection in the first place?" Hank asks.

She shrugs. "I've read that book half a dozen times ever since I was a kid. It's an important text, both in Chinese literature and history. And things just… stick with me, I guess."

Earlier today, she sent the black and white photos of Meng Jie and Q. Sun to Hank updating him with her discovery at the library. After the initial elation of the breakthrough, however, she is now left with more questions than answers. This man she is searching for has taken on names from characters of a novel, all of whom share his same unusual feature. But what does that even mean? And why *Romance of the Three Kingdoms?*

"I tried to search for more characters in the book who had green eyes," she says. "I was thinking that maybe this would be a way to locate him. But there are only three in the novel. I will keep digging around to see what I can find out about the donors."

"Okay, great," Hank says. "Keep me in the loop, and let me know if you need anything."

Georgia utters her thanks as she hangs up the phone. She turns her attention back to her notes, revisiting the facts before her.

Donation of Qin Dynasty manuscripts to Gugong Museum by Meng Jie, 1965.

Donation of various Chinese and Japanese artefacts to Denver Art Museum by Mr. Q. Sun, 1915.

Donation of Song Dynasty statues and ceramics to British Museum by Yi Lee, 1865.

She scratches her head. Maybe she is looking at this too closely. Maybe she needs to revisit the novel and look for clues in there. Leaning back in the settee, she looks up as Amah walks into the living room with a tray of food, placing it down on the coffee table.

"Look, Georgia," her grandmother says, beaming. "All your favourite dishes today."

Georgia lights up, grinning at Amah. She hastily puts down her notebook on the coffee table and accepts a bowl of rice, loading it up with small portions from each dish: three-cup chicken, braised eggplants, and preserved radish omelet. It's been a while since someone made a home-cooked meal for her. Lucas used to be the designated chef in the house, and Georgia has always been so terrible in the kitchen that she would rather skip meals than attempt making something for herself.

She eats gluttonously as her grandmother watches her. Amah nods with approval, a smile of satisfaction on her face. After a few moments Amah picks up her own bowl and chopsticks, sneaking a peek at Georgia's notebook on the table, a subtle gesture that is not missed by Georgia. She is reminded of the many times her grandmother would check her homework over dinner.

Amah chews on her food, thoughtful. After a while, she asks, "So what happens this year?"

"Huh?" Georgia says between mouthfuls of food, "What do you mean?"

Amah gestures at Georgia's notes. "You've got eighteen sixty-five, nineteen fifteen, and nineteen sixty-five scribbled there beside those three names. What's happening in twenty fifteen?"

"SARAH. The donations are happening every fifty years," Georgia says, gripping the phone tighter. "1865, 1915, 1965. The next in the sequence is 2015."

Silence ensues on the other end of the line, and Georgia marvels at the fact that Sarah has actually been rendered speechless.

At Amah's discovery last night, Georgia sent Sarah a message: *Do a worldwide search for museum donations happening THIS YEAR.* After a restless night in her hotel bed, Georgia woke early this morning and reached straight for her phone to see if her assistant has any news.

"And listen," Georgia continues, speaking faster now. "I

found out the three names all came from *Romance of the Three Kingdoms*. They're all characters with green eyes."

"Fucking hell," Sarah murmurs. "Just like Hsu Fu."

"Yes." Georgia hammers her fist softly on the table, as if to emphasise her point.

"They've all got to be the same person, Georgia. This can't just be a random coincidence."

"I think so too." Georgia nods. "Now, did you manage to find any similar donations this year?"

There is an audible pause on the other end of line. "Yeah," Sarah finally says, letting out a deep breath. "I did an extensive search, and also called around to see if anyone has heard anything through the grapevine."

"*And?*"

Sarah clears her throat. "And… uh… there's obviously quite a few that's happening around the world. I'm sending you the list I've compiled right now. I think you'd find number ten quite uh… *interesting*."

Georgia frowns at Sarah's now amused tone, unsure what the joke is. She logs into her email account and opens the attachment Sarah has sent her. Scanning down the page, her eyes stops at one particular donation:

10. *National Gallery of Victoria (NGV), Australia. Tang Dynasty paintings on silk and paper. Over 100 items. Anonymous donor.*

Georgia feels a little jolt somewhere deep in her belly. Her pulse quickens.

"Say Georgia," Sarah now sings, and Georgia can visualise her assistant twirling a pen playfully in her hand. Sarah always does that when she is in a teasing mood. "Correct me if I'm wrong, but doesn't that old flame of yours work at the NGV?"

"I've told you before, he's not an old flame." Georgia narrows her eyes. "He's a school friend and we had one drunken night a long, long time ago. *Way* before Lucas. I haven't seen him in years."

"Uh-huh," Sarah murmurs dismissively, and Georgia rolls her eyes as she hears Sarah type rapidly on the keyboard in the background.

"Well, well. Look at this." Sarah lets out a whistles. "Looks like he's recently been appointed the head curator of the Asian art collection. I think you should give him a call."

"Hm." Georgia chews on her lower lip.

"Yes, *hmm*," Georgia can hear Sarah biting back her laughter. "Oh lookie here, I just found a photo of him. Hmm. Maybe *I'll* give him a call. He's quite a looker—"

Georgia huffs in agitation. She grumbles her goodbyes, hearing Sarah chuckling away as she hangs up the phone.

21

MELBOURNE: home to the National Gallery of Victoria and widely considered the cultural capital of 'Down Under.' It is known for its Gold Rush era architecture, international festivals, galleries and theatres, culinary delights, and trendy bars. Ranking as one of the top hipster cities, it is a place where men with immaculately trimmed beards are seen sipping coffee in chic laneway cafes, and where edgy street art decorates the town. The birthplace of Australian football, its residents are both cosmopolitan and sports-mad.

It would have been the city Georgia calls home, if its winters were not so bitterly cold and plagued with bouts of vicious polar wind that chills you right to the bone. She is reminded of this as she exits the doors of Melbourne Airport, gripping the lapel of her coat to brace herself against the frigid air. Climbing into a taxi, she advises the driver of their destination. Then, leaning back on the headrest, she finally allows her mind to drift to Ethan.

Ethan is one of her oldest friends; Georgia has vague memories of them playing in the sandpit together in kindergarten. Their families lived one street away from each other in suburban Sydney, and they walked to and from school together every single day. The two were inseparable right from the beginning, a bond created not only from the closeness of their families and their shared common interests, but also from Ethan's protectiveness over her since they were little kids. Being the classroom nerd, Georgia received her fair share of bullying at school. She imagines the bullying would have been a lot worse if she didn't have Ethan hovering around all the time. He was always coming to her aid when she was cornered at the playground, breaking up the fights and picking her up when kids tripped her over.

When Georgia left high school with an early entry scholarship at Sydney University to follow her passion in archaeology, Ethan continued to be her closest friend because she was the only underage student in the entire class. She was left out of the extra-curricular activities that involved drinking—which, really, was pretty much all of them—and couldn't even join her classmates at the campus tavern for lunch. Nothing spelt outcast more than a kid in university who couldn't drive or drink or party. Her peers in undergraduate studies were not cruel like the kids she encountered throughout her schooling years, but Georgia still focused all of her efforts on her studies, not only because she loved it, but also for the lack of anything else to do with her time.

Eventually, Ethan moved to Melbourne to study visual arts when he graduated from high school. Despite the distance, they always remained close. That is, until the last few years.

As the taxi drives along the freeway over the Bolte Bridge, she stares out the window and looks towards the South Wharf, noting the changes to the city since her last visit. There are several buildings she hasn't seen before, and a brand-new Ferris wheel that reminds her of the London Eye. The sky is overcast with thick clouds, and a light mist hovers in the air, making everything a little fuzzy around the edges. A drizzle of rain begins to wash over the city.

She swallows, trying to calm the flutter of nerves in her stomach.

She chides herself for not calling first. After all, Ethan could be busy with work, and this may be a really bad time for him to see her. Or perhaps he's not even in town. But what was she going to say over the phone, calling him after all these years?

Hi, it's been a while. Congratulations on your promotion. By the way, do you mind doing me a favour…?

No. Ethan deserves more than that. After being such a lousy friend, she really needs to make a personal visit.

The taxi pulls up at the road side, and Georgia pays the driver as she gets out. Waiting impatiently for the electric trams to trundle past her, she tugs at her bag as she crosses the street towards the large grey building ahead.

Founded in 1861, the National Gallery of Victoria is the oldest and largest public art museum in Australia. The museum has an encyclopaedic collection of art, its diverse repertoire spanning everything from Australian art and historic artefacts, to international collections including European painting, prints, drawings, fashion and textiles, furniture, Pacific art, and photography. The Asian art collection grew big enough to warrant its own permanent gallery only a couple of years ago, and with its opening Ethan was appointed the head curator of the collection.

She enters the building, depositing her bags at the cloak room to the right. Then, taking a fortifying breath, she heads to the information desk.

The young woman sitting behind the counter looks like a graduate fresh out of art school. She has a retro-style, black and white polka dot dress on, and the straight bangs of her obviously dyed black hair don't quite reach her brows. She puckers her bright red lips as Georgia asks to see Ethan. Her thick-framed spectacles have no lenses, and she pushes them up on the bridge of her nose as she regards Georgia more closely, scanning her from head to toe.

"And your name is?" she asks Georgia with a slightly cocked brow.

"Professor Georgia Lee," Georgia blurts out, feeling strangely defensive under the young woman's stare. She frowns, realising she doesn't usually use her title—or even her full name—when she introduces herself.

"Ethan is out of town," the woman says, uttering his name as if staking a claim. Her perfect brow arches even higher. "I'm sorry, did you have an appointment?"

Georgia narrows her eyes, ready to fire back her reply, but is interrupted by a sudden tug on her arm. She looks down to see a perfectly manicured hand slip into the crook of her elbow, and looking up, she gapes at the young man standing beside her. He is a head taller than her, and everything about him is crisp and exact: his fashionable shirt and slacks are starched and neatly pressed, his hipster beard is impeccably groomed, and his dark hair is styled to reflect a wind-blown effect that makes her think of sandy beaches and sunshine.

"She doesn't need one," the man says to the woman behind the counter, his tone mirroring her malevolence. "Professor Lee is always welcome at the NGV."

Then he spins Georgia around, walking away with a purposeful stride as he pulls Georgia along. She peers over her shoulder to see the art school graduate watching after them with her mouth hanging open.

"Sorry about that, Georgia," the man now says, whispering in a conspiratorial manner. "Belinda has been lusting over Ethan ever since she got here. Not that I can blame her." He winks at her. "'Cause *damn*, that man has a fine arse on him, you know what I'm sayin'?"

He guffaws when her face is engulfed by a searing heat. Leading her into the elevator, he presses for the third floor.

"Come to my office. I'll make you a cup of tea. Your darling assistant called me this morning, said you'd be paying us a visit."

"Max." Finding her words at last, Georgia coughs out an incredulous laugh. "What on earth are you doing here?"

"I work here now, sweetheart," he drawls, "thanks to your glowing letter of recommendation. Ethan took one look at that and hired me straight away."

Max is an art conservation PhD graduate who did a three-month internship with Georgia early last year, restoring some fragmented ceramics she had uncovered. Their work together had formed the final pieces of the puzzle that ultimately led her to the site of the ancient tomb in China.

"I had no idea," she says.

"Yeah, I had no idea that you and Ethan were childhood sweethearts until after I got the job." Max wiggles his eyebrows dramatically. "I would have asked for higher pay if I'd known."

Unable to stop blushing, Georgia wants to deny what he's implying but cannot conjure a comeback. So she asks instead, "Is Ethan really out of town?"

"Yeah. Sorry, hun, you just missed him. He left on a last-minute trip to Taipei yesterday," Max explains. The elevator pings and they head towards his office. The term 'office' is an overstatement, because what she finds herself in is more of a closet with a work desk and a bookshelf crammed into the small space. At Max's prompting, she sits down in the only chair in the room. He lightly taps a finger on his lips as he considers a row of jars across the top of his bookshelf. "Now. I got *pu-erh* tea, you like that, right?"

"What…? Oh, yeah," she says, frowning as she watches him prepare the tea. "Um—what's Ethan doing in Taipei?"

Max sucks in a breath, spinning around abruptly on his heels to face her. The wide grin and the brightness of his eyes remind her of the time when he showed her a pair of vintage

Prada shoes he'd found on eBay. "Oh. My. God. Georgia, you are just going to die when you see this fabulous collection of Tang Dynasty paintings that was donated to us," he gushes, forgetting all about the tea and putting a hand on her shoulder as he brings out his smartphone, scrolling through the photographs. "I was in gay heaven when Ethan put me on the team. You know how I just *love* that period of Chinese history."

"Yeah, it's one of my favourites too," she says, confused about the sudden change of subject, "but—"

"*This*." He places the phone in her hand. "This is my favourite of them all."

She looks down at the image on the screen. It is a painting mounted in a traditional Chinese scroll format, depicting Tang court women in a garden. On a normal day, she would have appreciated the delicate beauty of the work, noting the details depicted in the dresses and the faces of the women. But right now, she can't seem to focus her mind on the image before her.

Max is talking quickly now. "The whole thing has been a logistical nightmare for us right from the beginning. I won't bore you with the details, but you know, this is going to be the most important Asian collection exhibition at the NGV *ever*. Ethan's really fallen in love with the works and wants to make sure he does everything right. We've all been working like dogs just to meet the deadline." He gives a wave of his hand and shakes his head. "Anyway, to cut a long story short, we decided to show the collection in two parts. The first part of the show opens tonight. The second part is about to be shipped from Taipei but there's been some last minute *booboo* made by our Cathy, who's over there documenting the works. So, going back to your question before, Ethan is in Taipei putting out last-minute fires before the paintings are crated and sent over here."

Taipei. This can't just be happenstance.

"See how well preserved these pieces are?" Max is craning over her shoulder, scrolling through other images to show her. "I just can't believe our luck in acquiring this collection."

"Yeah, about that," she says, turning to look at him. "Can you tell me about the person who donated it?"

"Never really met him. The guy would only deal with Ethan and Rob—the director—and no one else. You know how private some of these donors can be." He shrugs. "I did see him in passing once though, when Rob was giving him a private tour of the gallery. Only found out 'cause Rob's secretary whispered to me quickly that he was the mysterious donor." Max turns back to the tea as the kettle boils, pouring hot water into the small tea pot.

"Can you tell me what he looked like? Did he have any distinctive features?"

"Distinctive features?" He cocks his head, thinking. "Tall, thin. Maybe in his forties? Some kind of Eurasian, I think. And uh—" Max frowns as he gazes into the distance. "He had these really eerie green eyes. Gave me the shivers when he looked at me, like, for two seconds when we passed each other."

She sucks in an audible breath, her mind reeling.

"Georgia? You okay?"

"Yeah," she says, her voice hoarse. She clears her throat, accepting the cup of tea offered by Max. She sips it slowly, feeling the hot liquid warm the chill in her body.

Max's mouth forms a large 'O' as his mind visibly works on an idea. "Listen Georgia, you've *got* to come to the opening tonight. My date bailed on me, so you can be my plus one. You can't leave town without seeing these pieces. You can give me feedback on the first show I helped to put together."

She smiles at his infectious excitement. "Okay. Sure."

He sits at the edge of the desk before her, leaning back as

he looks her up and down, arching one flawless brow. She feels her cheeks warm under his scrutiny.

"What?" she asks.

A mischievous grin spreads slowly across Max's boyish face. "You better dress to seduce, Georgia girl. This opening is ultra VIP."

22

FOR THE SECOND time that day, Georgia steps into the NGV building, this time dressed in a form-fitting, silky red cocktail dress that shows the full length of her back. Her hair is artfully arranged into a springy mass of curls that cascades over her right shoulder and down her chest. Her face is expertly made up by Max, and she had to fight tooth and nail to stop him from sticking fake lashes on her eyelids. She feels as if she is dressed like a queen—and not in the good sense.

"Are you sure I'm not overdressed for this?" she asks Max again.

He rolls his eyes at her in reply, shaking his head as he chuckles softly.

To say that Georgia feels self-conscious is an understatement. To make matters worse, she is trying her hardest to not trip in her killer heels. She knows her back is going to hate her for it tomorrow.

"Stop fidgeting, Georgia," Max chides, "you're totally cramping my style, and I'm intending to pick up tonight."

She regrets letting Max take her shopping that afternoon, but she really had nothing to wear for the occasion. He spent hours dressing her up like his personal doll, taking obvious delight in the whole process even though Georgia groaned with protests the entire time. Evidently proud of his handiwork in her makeover, he has been unabashedly eyeing her up and down on their way here, grinning from ear to ear.

"If only Ethan could see you tonight," he now says, slapping his thigh theatrically. "Jesus, I'd probably have to pry him off you. That would definitely give Belinda something to bitch about!"

Georgia glows red in the face, uttering no reply.

As they drop off their coats at the cloak room and take the escalator to the Asian collection gallery upstairs, she can sense heads turning towards them. She cringes inwardly at the attention. Max, on the other hand, is vivaciously greeting everyone they are passing, oozing with infectious charm from every pore of his being.

As Max explained, the opening is reserved for only a select group of benefactors of the museum. She counts no more than fifty in the gallery at the moment, all of them dressed formally with expensive-looking diamonds and gems draped over the women's necks and wrists. There are waiters scattered about the room, each carrying trays of drinks and hors d'oeuvres, and Max waves one of them down.

"Here." He hands Georgia a glass of champagne, smirking. "Drink up. You look like you need it."

She complies mutely, trying to take her mind off the ache in her feet by focusing on the exhibition. The large gallery space is dimly lit, with subdued accent lights shining on the individual works. All of the silk and paper paintings are encased in glass cabinets, and as she moves about the room, she takes a deep breath, absorbing the beauty around her.

The Tang Dynasty, spanning 289 years from 618 to 907 CE, is generally regarded as a high point in Chinese civilisation. During this time, the state became the most powerful and prosperous country in the world, its economic, political, cultural, and military strengths reaching unparalleled levels.

Trade prospered along lucrative routes on the Silk Road. Arts and culture blossomed under this period of progress and stability, and many still consider it the Golden Age of Chinese literature and art. It was also during this time that woodblock printing was invented in China, making books more readily available. The cultural environment of this age was so vibrant that it extended its influence to neighbouring countries such as Korea, Japan, and Vietnam.

"Wow," Georgia utters as she looks at the paintings on display.

"I *told* you." Max grins. He grabs her by the elbow and leads her to a long, horizontal display case in the middle of the room. Inside, there is a long scroll stretched flat across the table. "This is it. This one is my favourite."

She studies the work before her, capturing all the details she skipped past on Max's phone earlier. A silk painting mounted on a traditional Chinese scroll, it is of Tang court women in various elegant gestures, adorned in colourful, low-cut dresses with long-sleeve chiffon coats. The ladies have pale, white faces, and some have hair piled elaborately above their heads while others wear extravagant head orna-ments and pearl necklaces. They have long silk scarves draped over their arms, and a few of them are leisurely enjoying the fragrance of flowers on a nearby tree.

Georgia smiles. The scene is typical of the lavish lifestyle during the most glorious days of the Tang Dynasty, and women of this time enjoyed a freedom of social rights and status that were unprecedented in China. They neither bound their feet nor led submissive lives. They could own property, participate in traditionally male activities like hunting, play sports such as polo, conduct business dealings, and even hold political positions at court. Many women gained religious authority by becoming Daoist priestesses, and high-class courtesans, who likely influenced the Japanese geishas, were well-respected and known as great singers and poets. It was within this liberal atmosphere that the only female emperor of China, Empress Wu, reigned for fifteen years.

Indeed, one of the reasons why this period of Chinese history is so attractive to Georgia—apart from being the pinnacle of ancient Chinese cultural development—is that it appeals to her inner feminist. Max, too, once confessed to her that this is exactly why he loves studying the Tang Dynasty. "Girl power," he said with a cheeky wink, gesturing to the Wonder Woman figurine he kept on his desk.

"Hey Georgia," Max now whispers as he looks distractedly around the room. "You're gonna have to excuse me for a few minutes, I've just spotted the guy I was telling you about."

She looks up, following Max's gaze to a lanky blond in a grey suit. He is talking to someone, animating his point with effervescent movements of his slender hands, a dimpled smile wide across his face.

"What are you waiting for? Go talk to him," she gives Max a nudge. "Take all the time you need."

"You'll be okay?"

She snorts a laugh. "I'll be more than okay. I want to have a decent look at these works without you yakking in my ear."

He glares at her with faux venom, poking out his tongue at her playfully, and walks away towards the blond across the room.

THE MAN SPOTS her immediately as he enters the gallery. Her dress is not entirely inconspicuous; in fact, she looks absolutely stunning and is turning heads everywhere she goes, especially with the exuberant young man accompanying her.

He frowns. *What is she doing here?*

He watches as her companion whispers in her ear, then walks away with a flamboyant spring in his step. Georgia shakes her head with amusement as she watches after him, and proceeds to study the exhibition pieces around the room.

The gallery begins to feel crowded as more people enter the room, the conversations growing loud. Yet she makes no attempt to talk to the people around her. It is obvious her mind is solely focused on the paintings on display.

He runs his long fingers through his matted hair. He does not know how, but she is getting close.

Too close.

"Good evening, ladies and gentlemen." A man's voice resonates through the speakers, and a hush descends across the busy room. The patrons shuffle slowly towards the centre of the room, where the director of the museum, Robert Clark, addresses the audience with a microphone. Robert begins to make a lengthy speech about the exhibition, thanking various staff and of course the benefactors of the museum who have made the exhibition possible.

The man remains at the back of the room as he watches Georgia through the crowd, intrigued by her.

Then, to his horror, she suddenly turns her head and looks directly at him.

23

Georgia's breath catches in her throat, and she immediately walks towards the back of the room.

Just seconds before, she had that prickling sensation at the back of her neck again—the nagging feeling as if she was being watched—which has started to become a familiar experience these last few weeks. When she turned to look behind her, she caught a face through the crowd.

A face that made all of the hairs on her skin stand on their ends.

It was there, but then all of a sudden it wasn't again. She pushes through the crowd, ignoring the glares and protests thrown at her as she makes her way to the spot where she spotted the face. Yet when she finally gets through the throng of people, there is no one there.

She frantically looks about her, then heads towards the door to the left, exiting as a waiter walks in with a jug of water, crashing into her and spilling the icy-cold liquid down the front of her dress. He fumbles for the glass jug, saving it before the catastrophic smash on the floor.

"Oh my God, I am so sorry!" the waiter exclaims. "Let me help you—"

But she's already out the door, half running and half walking in her ridiculous heels onto the escalator leading down to the ground floor. From here, she has an elevated perspective of the level below. Her eyes scan wildly around the building, coming up with nothing. Once at the bottom of the escalator she quickly walks towards the exit of the museum. There is no one around except for the attendants at the cloak room by the entrance, watching her with curiosity as she searches for the man.

What the…?

"Georgia!" At the sound of her name, she turns to see Max running down the escalator to catch up with her. "Are you okay? Look at your dress!"

She shakes her head, trying to catch her breath.

"Let's get you cleaned up. I'm going to make sure that waiter gets his arse fired!" He fumes, steering her towards to the restrooms.

"No, I'm fine, it's just a little water," she stops him. "Max, I saw him."

"Who?"

"The donor… the donor of the collection."

Max frowns. "Georgia, he's not here. He was given an invitation but he declined it."

"But I saw—"

"Honey." Max grips the sides of Georgia's arm. "He's not here. He's in Taipei. Ethan told me himself: he's gonna go through all the last minute paperwork with the donor in a few days' time."

Georgia's eyes widen. She can't be imagining things, she is sure of what she saw. She saw *him*.

Did she, though?

Georgia feels as if she is losing her mind.

"Are you okay, hun?" Max asks, his brow knitted as he guides her to sit down at a bench.

Seeing the concern etched on his young features, Georgia takes a deep breath, rearranging her face to compose herself.

"Yeah. Yeah—I'm okay, I just thought I saw someone who looked like the man you described, that's all. I wanted to ask him… ask him some questions about the collection, the pieces are just so remarkable," she lies. She is such a terrible liar.

Seeing that Max is unconvinced, she adds, "And you did such an amazing job with the pieces, you really did, Max. It's a beautiful exhibition."

His face lights up at the compliment. "You think so?"

"Absolutely," she says. Looking up, she sees that the lanky young blond is now coming down the escalator, gazing at them inquisitively.

"Hey, I'm keeping you from Mr. Hottie," she whispers to Max. "He's coming over here."

Max turns to look towards the escalator, then turns back to her, a huge grin on his face. "Oh. My God. He *does* like me, I knew it!"

"Look," she says, knowing this is the perfect time to make an exit. She gestures to the big wet patch on her dress. "I'm a mess. I'm exhausted. And these heels are killing me. I think I'm gonna have an early night."

Max frowns, still looking concerned, then conflicted as he sees his new friend walk towards them. Georgia puts her hand on his arm. "I'm fine. I promise."

He gives her a long look, then a small nod of his head. "Okay Georgia. Text me when you get back to the hotel."

She gives him a quick peck on the cheek. "You're such a gentleman." Then she pats him on the back. "Have fun."

Leaving Max to his new date, Georgia collects her coat from the cloakroom and fishes the phone out of her purse as she exits the building. Shivering from the cold night air, she hails a cab and quickly climbs in. Then she begins to dial the number she has long-ago committed to memory, her heart—

the damn thing—beginning to race as she brings the phone to her ear.

It only rings twice before it connects, not even giving her a chance to prepare herself.

"George?" the familiar voice says on the other end of the line.

24

ETHAN SOMMERS STEPS through the doors of Hyatt Taipei, scanning around for Georgia's face. The large atrium has an elevated glass ceiling all the way up at the third level, and of course no five-star hotel is complete without its own ostentatious marble fountain and crystal chandeliers. Its spacious foyer is dotted with guests and staff milling about, but he decides within seconds that she's not here yet.

He's always been able spot her in a crowd.

He paces, feeling anticipation laced with anxiety mixed with excitement. He hasn't seen her in—what, like five years now?—and a lot has changed since then. He's sure both of them have transformed in that time.

Ethan tries to remember the last occasion when they said more than two sentences to each other, and decides it was over six years ago, when Georgia flew to Melbourne for work. Lucas encouraged her to stay the weekend for a well-deserved mini break from the crazy lifestyle of a new mother. Jacqui was about ten months old back then, and Georgia had just gone back to work after her maternity leave. Naturally, being the pair of art-geeks that they are, Ethan and Georgia spent two full days in museums and galleries. And Georgia being Georgia, there was also a whole lot of food in between. It never ceases to amaze Ethan just how much the tiny woman can eat.

It's hard to imagine that they haven't seen each other for so long, but Georgia became distant after Jacqui's sudden illness and death; and sensing her and Lucas' need for space, Ethan wanted to give them time to grieve. Apart from his quick trip to Sydney for Jacqui's funeral, Ethan and Georgia have hardly maintained contact over the years.

He was therefore more than surprised to receive her call two nights ago, and equally surprised to hear she was coming to Taipei. He arrived here himself at the beginning of the week for work—a happy coincidence.

Ethan stops in the midst of his pacing, realising he's drawing a bit of attention to himself with his angst. But then again, it's hard to go around Taipei as a six-foot-one, light-haired, blue-eyed foreigner without attracting lingering looks from the locals. The Taiwanese seem to have a sense of awe towards anything that looks vaguely American, ever since the Yanks helped them during the war. There are even roads here named after Franklin Roosevelt and Douglas MacArthur.

He opts to sit down on the grey sofa instead, and lets his mind drift to a childhood memory, an incident that had happened when he was in grade five, and one he has replayed in his mind over the years.

———

THE SCHOOL PLAYGROUND was flooded with kids within seconds of the recess bell, with boys and girls squealing and laughing in the midst of play. Ethan ran straight for the monkey bars—his latest favourite—and hopped his hands from rung to rung, feeling the exhilarating sense of flight and freedom.

Something stopped him halfway. Across the playground, he saw a bunch of kids gathered in a circle, looking down at something on the ground. They were yelling with excitement, and he squinted to see in between their skinny legs, spotting a face he recognised.

He flew off the monkey bars, running towards the group and shoving the kids out of the way. In the middle of the circle, Georgia was on her hands and knees, her brand-new blue and white dress muddy and soiled, her books scattered across the wet grass. Misty was standing over Georgia, laughing shrilly.

"Oops!" Misty's voice dripped with sarcasm as she saw Ethan emerge, her hand flying to her mouth in mock remorse. "Watch where you're going, Georgia. Don't want to wreck your precious books." Then, staring at him, she tossed her curly brown hair. "Hi, Ethan."

Misty shrugged a shoulder to her posse of girlfriends standing around the circle, and they sauntered off, the girls still dishing out insults like "bookworm" and "teacher's pet" towards their victim. Clenching his fists tightly, Ethan glared after them with growing hatred.

"You okay?" He helped Georgia up, gathering her books and brushing the grass and dirt off the covers. Georgia smoothed her long black hair with shaky hands and looked down at her dress, tears glistening in her big brown eyes.

"My mom's gonna kill me. She told me not to make it dirty," she said, her lower lip trembling as she tried to hold back her tears.

"Don't worry about the dress," he said. "And don't worry about Misty. They're just jealous of you 'cause you're the smartest girl in class."

"Nah," she replied, wiping a stray tear from her flushed cheek with the back of her hand. She sniffled softly. "Misty's jealous 'cause you're my friend. She likes you, der-brain."

He gaped at the revelation, defensively stammering an awkward, "No, she doesn't!" But Georgia's conviction made her completely unconcerned with his protest. He handed her the books, and put an arm across her shoulder as if she was one of the boys instead.

"Well, George," he declared whole heartedly, puffing out his chest. "Misty will just have to get used to it."

The radiant smile that spread across her face shocked him to the core, and his heart did something funny in his chest. He decided then that he'd do anything to see that smile again.

ETHAN SPOTS HER NOW, coming down the escalator with the phone to her ear. She seems to be in deep discussion with whoever is on the phone. She steps off the escalator as she reaches the ground floor, standing next to the marble water fountain and finishing her conversation. He watches as she hangs up, a frown marring her near-perfect face as she stares down at the phone. Her chest heaves with a long sigh. She's obviously not pleased with whoever she was speaking to.

Then, after what seems like forever, Georgia finally looks up, meeting his gaze from across the foyer. Ethan's chest blooms with warmth as her frown is instantly transformed into a luminous smile. He beams, waving at her, his breath leaving him as he watches her walk—no, *skip*—towards him.

"Hi." She stops just short of running into him, now almost shy as she looks up at his face.

"Hey, George." That is his name for her—always George, or G—never Georgia. He likes the fact nobody else ever calls her that.

Grinning from ear to ear, he pulls her up for a bear hug, lifting her a foot off the floor. She squeals in delight, laughing with surprise, both of them transported back in time to their childhood days.

"Oh, Ethan," she whispers, holding on to him as he puts her back on the ground. "It's so good to see you. It's been too long."

Ethan breathes in the familiar intoxicating scent of honey in her hair, and he's suddenly aware of the soft crush of her breasts against his chest. He clenches his jaws to stop himself from the urge to pull her even closer.

Get a grip, mate.

Clearing his throat, he pulls back, holding her at arm's length. "Yes, it has," he says, "let me have a good look at you, G."

He scans her face, hands still gripping the sides of her arms. Her hair is longer. Her high cheekbones are slightly more defined than before. The years have made their mark with fine lines around her mouth and her eyes, and a few extra tiny freckles are now sprinkled across the bridge of her nose. But the unmistakable, intelligent, fierce passion still blazes in her eyes.

She is still the same Georgia, *his* Georgia. The next-door girl he has always known. And she is still devastatingly beautiful after all these years.

"You look good, George," he announces decidedly, finally letting go.

She laughs, the light-hearted sound tickling his chest. A blush colours her high cheek bones. "So do you." She takes a self-conscious step back, giving him a playful punch on the arm.

"So, moving up in the world, eh, G?" He gestures around them. "This is pretty fancy where you're staying. Either you found yourself a new career, or your department got some secret funding that no one else managed to get their hands on."

She wrinkles her nose. "No, I'm on a private job actually. The client has a taste for luxury."

He raises an inquisitive eyebrow, waiting for her to elaborate. When she doesn't, he ruffles the top of her hair, putting his arm across her shoulder as he has always done since they were kids. Guiding her towards the exit, he says, "Well, what do you say we get outta here and find some *real* Taiwanese food, and you can tell me all about it."

25

THEY END up at Shilin night market, Georgia wanting to show Ethan a selection of the quintessential Taiwanese street food: little sausage in big sausage, giant deep fried chicken schnitzels, pork belly buns, scallion pancakes, and of course, the famous bubble tea in all possible flavours.

Considered the largest and most famous night market in Taipei, Shilin contains mostly food vendors and small restaurants, with surrounding shops selling clothes, shoes, accessories, and various knick-knacks and souvenirs. It's a steaming hot night, and the place is bursting with people, but neither Georgia nor Ethan would have it any other way. Both having spent much time around the developing countries of Asia, they consider street food to be the most authentic and delicious cuisine a country can offer. More than that, it provides an in-depth insight into the culture of its people.

Georgia and Ethan move from stall to stall, grazing through their progressive dinner, putting away copious amounts of food as if it is an eating competition. After placing their order at what must be the fifteenth stall they've been to, they sit down at a crowded table side-by-side, and crack open a couple of beers.

Ethan leans back in the plastic chair and takes long swigs, obviously in high spirits. He's wearing a T-shirt that matches the soft blue of his eyes, the fabric pulled taut against his defined chest and muscular biceps. Georgia swallows her drink as she gazes at her friend, noting the changes since their last meeting: the few specks of silver in his sandy blond hair, the cleanly shaved, perfectly chiselled face where there was once a bushy beard, and the lines around his eyes whenever he flashes his trademark dimpled grin at her. She feels her heart flutter and briefly wonders how their friendship could have remained platonic all these years. Then she shakes her head, pushing the idea away. She reminds herself that ever since they were little Ethan has treated her more as a brother than a member of the opposite sex, always roughing around and hell bent on getting a rise out of her. She is, and has always been, his best friend—nothing more.

Except for that one night, so many years ago. But really, it doesn't count when there was so much alcohol involved.

"So." Ethan flicks the beer bottle cap in her direction to break her out of her musings. "What are the odds that we both end up in Taipei at the same time?"

She shrugs, trying to make light of the apparent coincidence. "I was in Melbourne on the way to Taipei, so I came by to the NGV to say hi, but Max said that you were already here." She loathes having to lie to him. "I'm just chasing up some leads on this private job for a client. The Gugong Museum has been very helpful."

Ethan's face brightens with interest. "Tell me about this job. Was it the client you were on the phone with at the hotel?"

"No." Her heart drops, the smile on her face fading. "No, that was Lucas."

His brows furrow. "Everything okay?"

She sighs, not wanting to go into it again. Shaking her head, she admits, "We're getting divorced."

"Shit." Ethan's face scrunches up with worry. "I'm sorry to hear that, George."

"Yeah, we've been separated for a long time now," she replies, taking another gulp of her beer. "But I really don't want to talk about it."

He studies her for a long moment. "Look, George, I've been meaning to say that I'm sorry. I know things have been tough for you. I really wish I could have been around more." He rakes a hand through his sandy blond hair, looking uncomfortable. "I should have... done more."

She shakes her head, giving him a wry smile. "There's nothing anyone could have done. I'm sorry that I haven't been in touch all these years. I just... I needed time."

"Of course." He nods, reaching over to draw her close. She feels the brush of his lips on the top of her head, and her heart goes into overdrive.

With perfect timing, the middle-aged stall owner serves up their food. Ethan straightens and lets go of Georgia. He gives the older woman his most charming smile, who enthusiastically explains each dish to him in broken English.

"Stinky tofu, good, very good." She sticks up her thumb with pride. "Oyster omelette. You try. Good."

"*Xie xie*," he thanks the older woman in Chinese.

"You speak Chinese! Good!" The stall owner walks away giggling, looking a little flustered.

Georgia rolls her eyes at Ethan, knowing that 'thank you' is the only word he knows in the language. "Oh, I bet you just *love* being a foreigner in Taiwan."

"Hey, it's not every day I get treated like a celebrity. Give the man a break. Let me live a little." He winks at her.

"Yeah, just don't charm the pants off every stall owner we walk past," she retorts.

"Jealous much? G, you're still my favourite Taiwanese here, I wouldn't worry."

She narrows her eyes at him and ignores his chortle, grabbing some chopsticks and digging into the food. Then she pauses to watch Ethan's face as he picks up a piece of the stinky tofu and puts it in his mouth, chewing on it hesitantly. Stinky tofu is one of the local delicacies here, and as the name suggests, the fermentation process makes it smell of something akin to dirty socks. Most tourists steer away as soon as they encounter the pungent odour, but she wanted Ethan to try the dish because no culinary experience in Taiwan is complete without it.

And also, perhaps, for the joy of seeing him gag at the stench.

"Well?" she asks, waiting for his verdict, puzzled at his mild reaction.

"Well." He swallows and blinks as if surprised. A myriad of expressions crosses his features before he answers. "I don't hate it. It's actually pretty good—*definitely* tastes a lot better than it smells."

She laughs, an unexpected pleasure swelling in her chest. They fall into an easy and casual conversation, catching up on all that has happened in each other's lives since they last met. She smiles widely as Ethan chats at length about his new role at the NGV, already feeling giddy from the beer in her hand. She realises—for the first time in a long, long while—that she is actually enjoying herself.

"So," Georgia says after they finish their food and move on to a shaved ice dessert stall. "How are things on the love front? Seeing anyone at the moment?"

Ethan gives a non-committal shrug. "Here and there, nothing serious."

"Belinda at the NGV seems to really like you," she presses, digging into her mango shaved ice lathered with a generous topping of condensed milk. When Ethan doesn't respond, she looks over at him, and is met with a lopsided grin.

"What?" She frowns.

"You *are* jealous, aren't you?" He cocks a brow, his grin getting impossibly wider.

"No," she scoffs. "I'm just saying that the girl almost bit my head off for asking to see you. Really, you can't have her respond that way to every visitor coming to the gallery. It's a good thing Max came to my rescue in time."

"Max told me you saw our latest collection at the gallery," he says in response, and she's not unaware of his less-than-tactful change of subject. She shrugs, deciding to drop it.

"I did." She smiles. "Oh, Ethan, it's so beautiful. You did an amazing job curating it."

"You think so?" He beams. "I can't believe in our luck, getting this donation. These works really belong to something like the National Palace Museum in Taiwan."

She nods in agreement. "Hey listen, I know it's a big ask, but do you think you can put me in touch with the donor?"

He raises his eyebrows. "Actually, I can't. The donor wants to remain anonymous. You know how these things work, G."

"Yeah, I know," she persists, "but can't you maybe just ask him to call me?"

He frowns, looking suspicious. "What's all this about, George?"

She gives him a nonchalant shrug. "Those paintings might give me some clues to the private job I'm on right now. I just wanted to ask him some questions about the collection, that's all. It could be the break I'm hoping for."

"What *is* this job that you are on? What exactly are you looking for?"

"I can't tell you, Ethan, I'm sorry," she says, yet she cannot help the excitement from seeping into her voice as she tells him, "But it could possibly be the greatest discovery of mankind."

"That's a big call." He looks at her for a long while, then shakes his head as if in defeat when she doesn't say anymore.

"But I know you, and you're not one to exaggerate things. What are you getting yourself involved in, George?"

He takes a long drink of his beer, and Georgia wonders if this is the fifth or the sixth drink they are on. She has already lost count.

"The best I can do," he finally says, "is to let him know my best friend is a big fan of the Tang Dynasty. I'll tell him you're an archaeologist and that you'd like to ask him about the collection. But all I can do is suggest this to him, and ultimately it's up to him if he meets with you or not. And knowing how private he is, I wouldn't get my hopes up."

She claps her hands together. "That'll be amazing. Thanks so much." She reaches over to give him a hug. "When will you be speaking to him again?"

"Tomorrow," Ethan replies. "That's part of the reason I'm here. We're meeting for lunch tomorrow to go over some final paperwork for the donation."

THE BALD, stocky man watches them closely as he pretends to queue for food at the next stall down the street. Ire simmers steadily in his veins as he feels sweat drip down his bare scalp, trickling over his neck and down the length of his back. He hates being anywhere near the subtropics in summer. This sweltering heat—sticky, relentless, and suffocating—can turn any civil man into an animal.

He strains to hear the couple's conversation, but the crowded night market makes it impossible to catch anything beyond a few fragmented words. Their body language tells him enough, though. He blinks with surprise as the professor throws her head back in hearty laughter at some joke her friend has told. She touches her companion's arm, and there her hand lingers as she accepts what must be her fifth beer.

This is a side of her that the man has never witnessed

before: this unrestrained, carefree version of a woman who is even more tantalising than her usual solemn self. And judging from the look on her companion's face, he is not entirely immune to her charm.

The man scratches the long scar beneath his goatee with irritation, studying this friend of Georgia's—the one she refers to as Ethan. Late thirties, tall, and athletically built, the blue-eyed Adonis has a mischievous, boyish grin that will entice the panties off any of the local girls that he comes across. He certainly is drawing a lot of looks around the stall, from both the women and the men. But Ethan's attention seems to be solely focused on Georgia. Whatever their conversation is about, he is fully engrossed in everything the professor has to say.

He observes quietly as Ethan stands to pay for their food and drinks, gathering themselves to leave the stall. Ethan drapes his arm protectively over Georgia's slender shoulders, and they walk straight past the bald man, oblivious to his existence.

As they walk on into the crowded market, the watcher catches Georgia's excited squeal, her words loud and laced with an intoxicated slur: "I know! How's *this* for the essential Taipei experience—let's go karaoke!"

The watcher frowns. This is the kind of distraction that Georgia does not need right now.

26

LIGHT FILTERS through the sheer curtains of the room and shines directly on her closed eyelids, rousing her from elusive dreams. Georgia stirs, groaning as she turns away from the day, her head protesting the movement with a sharp, jarring pain.

Exhaustion pervades her entire body, and yet, her mind is now refusing to drift back to sleep. Her eyes still closed, she sorts through the confused haze of her brain to remember who she is, where she is, and why there is an insistent, relentless pounding inside her skull.

Flashes of last night's memories come trickling back: a long-overdue mates-night-out that got very messy very quickly as empty beer bottles accumulated and gave way to drained shot glasses at the karaoke bar. She vaguely remembers very bad, very loud singing from Ethan. Georgia chuckles now at the image, and groans again when her head rewards her with another bout of searing pain.

"Mornin'," a deep voice says next to her.

Her eyes fly open. She finds herself in an unfamiliar room, on an unknown bed. She blinks when she realises that she is looking at Ethan, lying next to her.

Naked.

She blinks again. Her jaw drops open. Her eyes travel across the bare expanse of his broad chest, his defined abs, and the thin sheet covering him below the waist. Then, more memories of last night come flooding back.

Drunk and acting like a couple of school kids, they made a spectacle of themselves at the karaoke bar. She guffawed over Ethan's dramatic and hilarious performance of 'Kiss' by the artist formerly known as Prince. She sang her heart out and her throat raw with Alicia Keys' 'If I Ain't Got You.' And they even received a standing ovation to their duo rendition of Aqua's 'Barbie Girl.' Then, when they ran out of English songs to torture their audience with, Georgia wailed about having the sudden and irrepressible urge to dance.

She remembers dragging him to a nightclub, going straight onto the dance floor after a few more shots of vodka. Georgia moved to the loud, all-encompassing music like a possessed woman. It had been aeons since she last danced, since she let go of herself like that. Bathed in the flashing lights of the dance floor, amidst the mass of bodies writhing and twisting to the beats, she felt like she could forget every-thing, abandon who she was and pretend to be somebody else.

She's not entirely sure who started the kiss—maybe it was him, or maybe it was both of them—but when it happened it felt like the most natural thing to do in the world. She looped her arms around Ethan's neck, their bodies pressed together and swaying in sync to the music. Her body was on fire as his hand travelled down from her waist to the swell of her arse, and she felt the evidence of his arousal as she moved against him.

Georgia doesn't recall how they ended up back at Ethan's hotel room, but she remembers enough. She remembers the way they crashed onto the bed, ravenous for each other as they undressed with haste. She remembers the heat of his lips as he trailed kisses down her body, his hands touching her as if he was trying to memorise every inch of her skin. She remembers begging him to end the torment, and his soft chuckle as he shifted to look at her, his eyes ablaze with lust. She remembers the weight of him above her, and how they moaned in unison as he sank slowly into her heat.

The strain and flex of Ethan's arms as he rocked against her is forever etched into her mind, as is the look of unbridled, joyful ecstasy on his face as they both found their release. At the last moment he cried out her name, his voice hoarse: not George, not G, just a simple *Georgia*.

A shiver travels up her spine.

"G?" Ethan says now, his voice laced with concern. With some difficulty, Georgia's eyes refocus back on his face. Strain is etched in his face as he studies her. "You okay? You're not saying anything."

Georgia blinks, feeling a rush of panic. She closes her still gaping mouth. Then she opens it again. "I'm sorry, I—" she stammers unsuccessfully. "Last night—last night was—"

"Last night was amazing." Ethan says firmly, finishing her sentence for her. His hand reaches over to cradle her face, his eyes soft and almost imploring. "*You're* amazing, Georgia."

For a moment she closes her eyes to his soft caress, her mind searching for words to say. When she comes up with nothing, she hears Ethan sigh.

"You know," he says, "for someone so smart, you seem to have totally missed the fact that I've been in love with you for pretty much all of my life."

Her eyes flutter open and she stares into his eyes. In this light, they are a deep blue that makes her think of sailing on the open ocean. She feels her chest swell with a multitude of emotions she cannot define or name at that moment. This is a side of Ethan she has only seen a handful of times over the years: the vulnerable, sensitive, squishy-on-the-inside Ethan beneath all of his jokes and easy charm.

Hot tears—unexplained, unexpected, and unwelcome—sting her eyes. She smiles, nodding, unable to speak.

Seeing her eyes well up, he reaches for her, pulling her into an embrace. She hears him exhale heavily as he buries his face in her neck, setting off a slow burn of heated desire through her.

"God. You smell unbelievable, you know that? The things you have done to me over the years… Just being near you like this, just catching your scent… it drives me insane," Ethan says, the sound of his voice a rumble of vibration through his chest.

He shakes his head, his jaws clenched with effort as he pulls away. "I know it's awful timing, G—with your divorce, Jacqui, and everything with work. I know it's probably all a bit confusing right now. I can understand if you need to take some time to think things through."

She nods again, giving him an appreciative smile.

A long moment of silence passes as Ethan waits for her to say something, and yet as always she finds herself ill-equipped to deal with these emotionally charged occasions. Her mind blanks, and she feels something within her begin to fidget with discomfort.

Ethan cocks his head to the side, a look of understanding on his face. Then, something flickers across his azure eyes—and Georgia instantly knows that the rascal version of him is back.

He grins.

"Jesus, George. I've never known you to be so quiet. You really should try to get laid more often. It'll help to ease the shock over time."

She gapes at him, choking out an exasperated huff as she punches him hard on the arm. "Shut up!"

Ethan jumps out of the bed to dodge more of Georgia's punches, grinning from ear to ear, completely careless to the fact that he is now standing stark naked before her. She glows red in the face and tries—without success—to stop staring at his glorious body.

"Ow." He rubs where she punched him, a mock expression of hurt on his face. "Looks like we're gonna need a bit of a chat about post-coital manners, too."

"Oh my god! You are *such* a little—" She starts after him, only to realise that she is also naked when the sheets fall away.

She pulls the covers up quickly, shooting venomous darts at him with her eyes. Triumphant, Ethan lets out a loud cackle and strides cockily into the bathroom.

Georgia hears the shower start in the adjacent room and settles back in the bed. In spite of herself, a little smile creeps across her face. She shakes her head and lets out a happy sigh. He is still the same Ethan she has always known.

In the recent turmoil of her own life, this is somehow reassuring. From the first of their sandpit days when they were toddlers, she was always the quiet, contemplative kid happy to play on her own. And Ethan was always the boy who'd constantly hovered around her, ruffling up her hair, teasing and prodding her until he received some kind of animated response. Then, satisfied, he'd laugh and walk away, only to return not too long after to repeat the same annoying process all over again.

It was not until after they were living in different cities and she missed their constant contact, that she realised this dear childhood friend was the one who had always kept her from taking life too seriously. Whenever she found herself focusing on a problem and thinking herself into a rut, Ethan would always be there, prompting a laugh or an exasperated growl from her: anything to shake her free into a different mode of being.

Georgia hugs her pillow. She has really missed her friend.

"Are you gonna get out of bed sometime today, or am I gonna have to tickle you out of there?"

She turns to see him walk out of the bathroom with a towel hanging low around his waist. *God, he is something to look at.* Her eyes linger a few seconds too long, and Ethan raises an eyebrow, the corners of his lips hitching up into an irritatingly sexy smirk.

"Not expecting another round, are ya?"

She hurls her pillow at him, satisfaction surging through her when it lands squarely on his face. Suppressing her laughter, she asks, "What time is this lunch of yours?"

"Twelve-thirty." He glances at his watch. "Shit. I better hurry or I'll be late."

She watches as he moves about the room, hastily getting dressed and throwing some paperwork into his laptop bag. She notes the tangled mess of their discarded clothes and shoes, the extra cushions and pillows scattered around the room. There is a bedside lamp toppled over, and bits and pieces of Ethan's belongings strewn all over the floor, obviously pushed from the bedside tables.

She bites her lower lip. They really went at it last night.

Within minutes, Ethan is ready. He crosses the room to sit beside her on the bed, looking very torn about leaving. "Sorry G—but I really gotta dash. You'll be okay here? Hang for as long as you want. I'll give you a call when I'm done."

She nods, suddenly feeling awkward. "I'll let myself out."

Before she can react, he reaches for her and gives her a tender, lingering kiss. She melts into him, savouring the freshness of the minty toothpaste on his breath. When Ethan finally pulls away, he smiles, and for the first time she cannot decipher the expression on his face.

"See you after?" he whispers.

"Yeah," she says with a smile.

GEORGIA STARES at the hotel room door, long after Ethan has gone. The warmth of his presence has dissipated, and she suddenly feels cold. Shivering, she pulls on one of his T-shirts lying on the chair—pausing to breathe in the familiar Ethan scent—and half contemplates going back to bed to sleep off her pounding head.

Her phone vibrates somewhere in the room, and after some searching she finds it buried under her pile of clothes on the floor. She smiles when she sees the caller ID.

"Miss me already?" she teases.

"Yes," Ethan says with all seriousness, and her throat goes dry. "But that's not why I'm calling."

"Why are you calling then?"

"Can you check if I forgot my organiser? I might have left it on the desk."

Georgia shakes her head. Ethan has always been forgetful like that. When they were kids, his mother was always making multiple trips to the school because he'd forgotten to bring his lunch, or his sports gear, or an assignment that was due.

She hops out of the bed and walks over to the desk. Removing a cushion that must have been thrown across the room last night, she discovers his black organiser underneath.

"Yes you did, doofus. Do you want me to meet you somewhere with it?"

"Shit." He huffs a sigh. "Nah, it's fine. I'll live without it today."

"Okay."

"Miss me," he suggests.

She laughs. "Sure."

Hanging up the phone, she starts to rummage through her handbag for some painkillers. Her phone vibrates again—a message this time. She frowns when she sees the sender: Hank.

— How is everything going?

Georgia realises that she has not updated him since her discovery at the Taiwan National Library. She didn't want to let him know she was going to Melbourne, not with Ethan involved. Sitting down on the chair, she types a quick reply.

— Okay. May have a lead. Let me call you in a few days when I have something more concrete.

Hank responds with an image of Muffin, his Rottweiler grinning happily at the camera, slobber swinging in white strings from her jaw. Under the picture the caption reads:

— Sure. Muffin says hi. We are off to the beach today.

Georgia smiles at the photo, remembering now that it's Sunday. It appears Hank never stops working even on his days off. But that is not exactly a surprise considering who he works for.

She places her phone on the desk, strumming her fingers on the polished wood surface as her mind is brought back to her search for the mysterious green-eyed man. It seems she is now so close to getting all of her questions answered—and yet, she still has no way of contacting Ethan's anonymous donor unless the man agrees to meet with her.

Somehow, she's not too sure he'll be inclined to.

If he doesn't, then she'll lose her one chance at meeting him. Who knows which country or city he will be in tomorrow, or if she'll be able to track him down again. Hell, it may be another fifty years before he reappears.

She eyes Ethan's black organiser on the desk.

Ethan told her his lunch is at twelve-thirty, but he never mentioned where it was, and she had the good sense not to ask. But if she could just find out where Ethan is meeting this man, and wait outside the restaurant for a peek at the guy, then she could at least make sure it's not the same person she saw in the photographs. She can then tell Lambert she has tried her best, that she had uncovered some coincidental clues but ultimately ended up with nothing.

Because it really can't be the same guy.

Can it?

Suddenly Georgia feels she has to know, that she can't possibly walk away without finding out.

She looks over at the organiser again, feeling guilty for what she's about to do.

"Ethan won't know," she tells herself, reaching for the black volume to search for today's entry. "I'll just get a good look at the guy and be on my way. He'll never even know I was there."

27

As Ethan steps out of the taxi, he gazes up at the Taipei Grand Hotel and lets out a soft whistle. A notable landmark in Taiwan, both for its architectural style and its historical significance, it appears frequently on postcards of the city. It is one of the world's tallest Chinese classical buildings, its striking exterior adorned with scarlet pillars, sweeping roofs and glazed golden tiles. To passers-by, the establishment looks more like a majestic fourteen-storey Chinese palace. Indeed, in its 1960s heyday, it was hailed as one of the top ten hotels in the world.

Established in 1952 by Chiang Kai-Shek, the Grand Hotel was originally constructed for the purpose of accommodating foreign dignitaries. Back in the days when the generalissimo was still rallying foreign support for his fight against the Chinese communists, promoting foreign relations and diplomatic goodwill was a matter of priority, and state-level guests would be housed in the finest rooms at the hotel. Up until recently, any visitors wishing to book the presidential suite still had to get approval from the Taiwanese government. In its glory days, the establishment hosted many notable guests, including heads of states and celebrities such as Elizabeth Taylor, Margaret Thatcher, and even Nelson Mandela.

Ethan walks into the main building, marvelling at the bright red interior. Chinese lanterns hang from the elaborately decorated ceiling, which is supported by rows of red cylindrical pillars similar to those on the outside. An expanse of scarlet plush carpet leads up the wide grand staircase to the second floor. The hotel is busy with groups of tourists checking into the hotel, wandering around with their selfie sticks as they capture photographs of the foyer. These days, the most dominant patrons are Chinese tourists—most of them, again, satisfying their curiosities towards the infamous Chiang Kai-Shek.

Ethan briefly read up on the history of this iconic building before his visit, discovering that Madam Chiang Kai-Shek, who believed deeply in the art of Feng Shui, chose its specific location because it is especially auspicious. Towering high on Jiantan Mountain, with Keelung River before it and the mountainous national park to its rear, its position is considered to be 'the entrance to the lair of the dragon.' Henceforth, the hotel has been dubbed as 'The Dragon Palace' for this reason, with twenty thousand dragon motifs intertwining throughout the various structures, decorations, paintings, and carvings in the building.

He climbs up the wide grand staircase, making his way towards the Golden Dragon Restaurant at the back of the main building, noting the many dragon designs in the ceiling and on the walls. Glancing at his watch, he realises he is actually fifteen minutes early for his appointment. He slows his pace, exhaling a sigh of relief. It appears there was not really a need to race out of the hotel after all, leaving Georgia still naked in bed.

At the image, he swallows thickly, and a sense of warmth floods his chest, moving lower towards his groin as his thoughts trail to last night. The scent of her skin fresh in his mind, he wonders whether she is still in his bed, wrapped in the tangled sheets in which they made love. Georgia has never been a morning person, and with the amount of drinks they put away last night, he is surprised she woke before noon.

This morning in his bed, Ethan saw with clarity the panic flicker in her eyes. And when he poured his heart out to her, she was so damn quiet the entire time. The only thing he can seek comfort in is the knowledge that she has never been very good with feelings or words. But really, did he have to launch into some dumb joke again, even to save himself from embarrassment or possible rejection?

Way to go, jackass.

He's already missed his chance of being with her once before: all those years ago when he was still in art school. He'd been home in Sydney for the summer break and decided to spend the entire holidays hanging out at Georgia's office doing an informal internship with her. Georgia was already a PhD graduate by then and was doing some pretty impressive work at her university, paving her path towards professorship. He loved all the ancient ceramics she was working on at the time and the project later informed his graduating art piece. One night, after a campus party with too many drinks, they stumbled back to his student accommodation and he finally mustered up the courage to kiss her. In his wildest dreams he'd never have known what a passionate person Georgia can be in bed. When she is sober and dressed, she is always such a solemn person—she has always been so since they were kids. But the side of her she revealed to him that night all those years ago made him fall in love with her even more.

It made him crave for more.

When he woke up the next morning, however, she was already gone. Georgia went out of her way to avoid him for days after, and when they finally did see each other, she pretended that nothing had happened, as if she did not remember a thing from that drunken night. He was confused and shattered, but to save himself from further embarrassment and the fear of losing her friendship, he went along with it.

After that summer, he went back to his studies in Melbourne. Not long after, Georgia met Lucas.

Ethan scrubs his face, exhaling a huff of air, almost desperate to go back and see her now. He doesn't want to push her, but they need to talk. He needs to reassure her he is willing to wait for her, that she doesn't need to get all weird again because of what happened between them last night. God knows he's waited all his life. But the one thing he can't do is not see her again for another six years.

He has missed her. More than he would care to admit.

He finally locates the restaurant after some wandering in the corridors, and climbs the five flights of short steps to its entrance. The maître d' smiles at him as he tells her the name of the reservation, leading him promptly to a table in a secluded corner. Golden chandeliers wind across the ceiling in the shape of a dragon, and the restaurant is lined with a wall of windows that overlooks Keelung River.

It was the donor who suggested the place and made the booking for them, and Ethan can see why. There aren't many customers here on a weekday, and their table is located in a separate nook that offers the privacy that the donor prefers.

He takes out the paper work in his briefcase, anxious to get this lunch over with so he can see Georgia again.

28

It is now 12:40, ten minutes after Ethan's scheduled lunch, and she is hoping that they are already seated. She does not want the awkwardness of running into them face-to-face outside the door.

Georgia finds a bench not far down the corridor from Golden Dragon Restaurant and sits down, pretending to be reading on her phone whilst keeping an eye on the trickling of people walking up the short flight of steps into the entrance. For the hundredth time since finding out about the location of Ethan's lunch, she starts having serious doubts about coming here.

She really has not planned this out at all: she is sitting outside, hoping to catch a glimpse of this anonymous donor, but she cannot see inside the restaurant unless she walks up the steps leading to its entrance. If she does that, she risks being seen by the patrons inside. What if Ethan sees her? She does not want that to happen. She has not even thought to disguise her appearance to avoid being recognised.

Stupid, stupid, stupid.

Guilt grips her, and she considers leaving. She is being ridiculous, staking out like this. She's a respected archaeologist, for God's sake, not a private detective. Besides, Ethan has already promised to make the request on her behalf. What would he say if he realises she had gone through his stuff, and that she is stalking him like this?

No. This is wrong. She shakes her head, gathering her bag to leave. Then, out of the corner of her eye, she sees a figure pass by.

She looks up, and instinctively she knows without a doubt that it is him.

A tall, wraith-like figure, he walks swiftly in wide strides, unhurried and yet efficient; there is a sense of weightlessness about him. Even from this distance she can sense there is something different about this man—an air of... she's not sure what. She feels pins and needles all over her scalp, and she looks down her arm to discover she has broken out in goosebumps.

She only catches a glimpse of the side of his face as he seems to float up the steps towards the restaurant entrance. Then he turns away, addressing the maître d' at the door.

Georgia stands abruptly, then hesitates, unsure of what to do. Deep down, she did not expect to see this man at all, not really. Up until now he has been a mere hypothesis, a ghost from Lambert's fantasies that she has chased from Japan to Taipei to Melbourne and then back again. But now that he is here, really here, Georgia realises she is at a loss as to how to approach this. She watches the maître d' talk to the tall man as if she is familiar with him. The older woman laughs candidly at something he has said, and they make some more idle chit-chat before the woman turns, gesturing for him to follow her. But before he enters and disappears from Georgia's sight, he pauses, tilting his head to the side as if listening to someone whispering in his ear.

Then, as if sensing her presence, the man turns his face to look at her.

Her breath catches in her throat, and her heartbeat

hastens. She notes his narrow face, square jaws, and the aquiline nose. She takes in the almond-shaped, brilliant green eyes. It is him, all right; no question about it. He looks different with his shoulder-length matted hair, and there is something scraggly about this version of him, but he is the man in the photograph at the Gugong Museum, the same one who made the donation in Denver a century ago, and the same face she saw amidst the crowd at the Melbourne NGV.

He holds her gaze with those strangely hypnotic eyes for what seems like minutes, and she gets the ridiculous notion that somehow he knows her, that he is looking straight into her soul. Her lips part as if to speak, and yet she utters no words. She forgets to even blink.

And then, just as quickly as he turned to look at her, he turns away again and walks with the maître d' into the restaurant.

The air suddenly seems to have been sucked out of the room.

The spell broken, Georgia stumbles to the nearby exit, bursting through the automatic sliding doors and into the humid heat outside, her hands on her knees as she takes in big gulps of air. Her whole body trembles despite the warmth. A couple walks past her, looking at her with curiosity. The valet attendant approaches with concern.

"Are you okay, miss?" he asks.

"Yes," she responds in Chinese, waving off his extended hand. "Just need some fresh air."

It takes her a long while to calm herself down, and she sits on a bench to try and think things through. Her mind is racing, and she cannot think of what to do next. The image of the man's eyes has been burned into her mind.

She cannot go into the restaurant. Ethan is there, having lunch with the man. But she cannot just walk away, either. Now that she knows he is real, she cannot simply leave and not ask all the thousands of questions that are threatening to burst out of her.

Should she wait outside until they finish, with the hope of approaching the man then? Or should she just call Lambert now and hope he will know what to do? Georgia feels totally out of her depth here.

Suddenly, a new thought occurs to her and anxiety ripples through her stomach: What if he recognised her from the NGV opening, and realises she is tracking him?

What if he has already left?

She stands quickly, spinning around to go back into the building. She is stopped short when she runs straight into someone coming out the door.

"Sorry—" she begins, looking up at the stranger. When she sees his face, her mouth goes dry.

"Hello, Georgia." He smiles.

29

GEORGIA STARES at the man before her: the person she has been searching for over the past two months. Her eyes roam over his long, matted hair, the facial features she has already committed to memory, and those piercing eyes that look like emeralds in this light. Everything about him appears to be elongated: his neck, his torso, his long slender limbs. His waifish appearance is accentuated by his white linen hippy attire: the wide slacks and top hanging loosely as if they would blow off his thin frame at the slightest hint of a breeze. And yet, he stands like a man in full command of his body, from his head to his feet. He seems to be towering over her at this close proximity.

He's got to be, what, over six feet tall?

She feels dizzy. Taking an unsteady step back, she tries to compose herself.

What is wrong with me?

She sees that he is looking at her, expecting her to speak.

"Hello," she finally manages to utter. Then, as realisation dawns, she frowns. "How do you know my name?"

The corners of his eyes crinkle as his smile broadens. "Have you not been trying to contact me since you got here?

Your friend, Ethan, was just saying you wanted to meet with me."

Her frown deepens at his cryptic answer, but she swallows the deluge of questions erupting from within. Straightening up to meet his steady gaze, she tries on the most charming smile she can muster.

"What's *your* name?" she asks the stranger.

He laughs, a deep rumble in his chest. "Oh, I have had many of those." He nods at her. "You know some of them, I am sure."

"Meng Jie?" Georgia asks.

He nods, cocking his head in amusement.

"Quan Sun."

He smiles his assent once more.

"Hsu Fu?" Her voice escalates in spite of herself. She suddenly feels faint.

The valet attendant by the door looks over at Georgia's outburst, curious of the drama unravelling.

The stranger catches her by the elbow as she begins to sway. "How about we talk about this somewhere more private?" he suggests gently.

She gives him a weak nod, following him as if in a trance while he leads her back through the sliding doors into the hotel. He guides her back to the bench where she was sitting before he showed up at the restaurant.

"Sit here," he says. "I will be back promptly."

Worried that he will abandon her here, she gives him a questioning look. He chuckles softly as if reading her mind. "I am sorry, Georgia, but you caught me by surprise today. Trust me, I did not want to meet you under these circumstances. I know you have a lot of questions and they will all be answered in time, I promise. But this is not where we should be having this conversation. I am good friends with the manager here and I am going to ask her for a space in the building so that we can have some privacy... unless you have other suggestions?" He cocks his head again, his eyes kind.

"No," she says. "That sounds… good."

He gives her a quick nod, turning to walk away.

"Wait."

He looks at her again.

"You still haven't answered my question," she says. At his raised brow, she explains, "You still haven't told me your name."

Amusement gleams his eyes. "I go by Charlie these days. You can call me that if you like."

Then he turns and disappears down the corridor silently.

———

"SUBJECT HAS MADE CONTACT, sir. We're ready to move in."

His grip tightens on the phone. A smile radiates across his face.

About fucking time.

"Awaiting your instructions, sir."

He barks his orders at the phone, "Hold off for now and observe. Let's wait until they're out of the public eye. I want this job clean and discreet. No loose ends."

"Yes, sir."

"And keep your weapons stowed. I need the professor unharmed."

"Yes, sir."

"Make sure you station your men at all exits of the building. We may never get an opportunity like this again."

"Copy that, sir."

He smiles again, leaning back in the seat of his car. He is so close, so close to getting everything he has ever wanted for as long as he can remember.

"Well done, Professor Lee," he murmurs. "You have proven yourself to be very useful."

30

WHEN HE RETURNS to the bench in the corridor, Georgia is sitting in the exact spot he left her, deep in thought, her crossed legs jiggling anxiously. At the sight of him, she stands quickly, relief evident in her eyes. He has never seen her so unsettled before.

"Charlie," she says when he reaches her, as if to practise articulating his name.

He gives her a warm smile, holding up the key to show her. "The manager gave us a room so we can talk properly. Is that okay with you?"

He watches Georgia hesitate briefly. Then, determination flickering across her dark eyes, she gives him a firm nod. Together, they head towards the elevator down the corridor, and he presses the button for the sixth floor.

"What about Ethan?" she asks. "I thought you were meeting with him to go through some paperwork?"

He laughs, understanding dawning within him. "Ah, I should not have been surprised. That is how you tracked me down. I suppose you *are* best friends after all."

"No." A line forms between her brows. "Ethan didn't tell me anything, I swear. He doesn't even know I'm here. I—I

169

went through his organiser to find out where you were meeting and came here myself. I was just hoping to catch a glimpse of you, just to make sure—"

"Just to make sure that the legends are not true?"

She purses her lips. "Yeah."

He chuckles again. "Well, they are. Some of them anyway. But we will get to that later. And do not worry about Ethan. We took care of everything within five minutes. I told him something last minute has come up and I needed to go. He seemed happy I was cutting this short anyway—something about a girl he needs to talk to?"

Her cheeks flush at this, and she looks down to avoid his gaze, so he does not press her on the matter. Up close, she is even more beautiful to behold. It is not difficult to see why Ethan is so obviously enamoured of her—Charlie could tell just by the way the younger man uttered her name. But the professor is endowed with more than just good looks. Charlie considers the way she has tracked him down, and decides that probably very little escapes her scrutiny.

He will have to handle this very, very carefully.

The elevator pings, and they walk down the carpeted corridor in silence, quickly locating the room. He slides the key into the door, hearing the soft click of the lock, and pushes it open. Lights and the air conditioning kick in as he places the key card in its designated slot on the wall. Charlie surveys the space. They are in a small suite; a king size bed dominates most of the room, which also contains a small round table and a couple of arm chairs. Sheer curtains veil the sliding doors that lead out to the balcony.

This will do.

"Please have a seat, Georgia."

Walking over to the mini bar fridge, he offers her a bottle of water as she settles down in one of the arm chairs. He does not miss the slight tremble in her hand as she takes it from him. Giving her some space, he walks over to the sliding door to look out over the balcony, ruminating over all of the things that need to be said.

After a long period of silence, with his back still turned to her, he speaks. "As I was explaining before, I know you have been trying to contact me since you got here. The people at Gugong Museum sent me your letter. So, of course, I looked you up too."

"You were the one at the NGV opening," says Georgia. "You were the one I saw through the crowd."

"Yes. You caught me by surprise there, too. I went to the exhibition to see what the paintings looked like in the gallery. They always seem so different when they are presented in that context. I did not expect you to be there." He pauses, turning to meet her gaze. "I guess we do not have to go through how you found me. You must have seen my photograph at the Gugong exhibition since you were asking about Meng Jie, and at the Denver Museum too if you know about Quan Sun. My question to you, though, is what prompted you to start digging? How did you know to search for my existence at all?"

Georgia takes a deep breath, holding his steady gaze as he walks over to sit down in the other chair. When she starts speaking, her words are remarkably candid as she tells him of Mark Lambert, the oracle bone, the ancient Hata scroll, and Wang Jian's descriptions of his search for Hsu Fu. She recounts each finding that led her to this room with him, and his heart fills with dread as he listens to her story. Everything he has been trying to avoid for so long seems to be inevitable now.

When she finishes her tale, it is his turn to take a deep breath. He exhales with a long sigh.

"This Lambert," he asks, "does he know that you are here? That you have found me?"

"No," she answers. "The closer I got to you, the less I wanted to tell him."

"Why?"

She blinks, considering this. "I don't know. I guess I didn't want to quite believe this whole thing myself. But when it started looking like it may be true…" She shrugs. "Would you tell a person you were close to finding what he wanted, if you suspected that he may not have good intentions for his prize?"

"No, I suppose I would not," he affirms. "You do not trust him."

"I don't know," she says. "I guess I need more time to process things before deciding what to do with… this."

He nods, considering his next words. "I assume Lambert has persuaded you to go on this search in the first place because he promised to find a cure for all diseases for mankind."

"Well, he did—" she starts.

"And he probably succeeded," Charlie continues, "when he mentioned that he would cure infant mortality, too."

A deep frown knits Georgia's brows.

He sighs, remorse filling him. He speaks with more gentleness as he reveals: "My boy had the same thing, Eisenmenger Syndrome. I know what it feels like to sit at your child's bedside, watching each breath he takes, praying that it will not be his last. To hold his hand, trying to memorise what it feels like… so you will never forget. That kind of experience can drive a parent to try anything, believe anything, if only they could save their child."

She flinches as if he has kicked her in the gut. "How—how did you—"

He shakes his head, looking away. "I will get to that later. But first, Georgia, you asked me a question earlier that I have not answered yet."

There is a moment of silence. Then, she says, "Are you Hsu Fu?"

Charlie opens his mouth to answer her, but a knock on the door interrupts him.

He frowns, his body stiffening. Lowering his voice, he asks Georgia, "No one knows you are here?"

"No," she says, looking equally surprised.

Rising from the chair, he walks silently to the door to look through the peep hole. The distorted view shows nothing but the empty corridor outside, and yet the back of his skull tingles with intensity. The realisation washes over him like a bucket of ice.

This is a trap.

31

"WHAT'S WRONG? WHO IS IT?" Alarmed at Charlie's stiff posture, Georgia stands, an inexplicable fear rising within her.

Charlie turns away from the door and crosses the distance between them in a few strides. Taking Georgia by the hand, he pulls her towards the window.

"You have been followed," he says in a hushed tone. "I should have foreseen this."

"Followed? By who?"

The knock sounds again, louder this time. Ignoring her question, he opens the sliding door and steps onto the balcony. She looks out to the large, tiled area that encircles the entire outside of the building, seeing it is shared with all the adjoining guest rooms. There are one-metre-high Chinese-style balustrades that partition off private spaces for each room.

"What are you doing?" she asks as Charlie begins to climb over the balustrade.

"We have to go, Georgia. We cannot risk being captured."

"No, wait—"

But Charlie is already over the partition and heading for

the next one. Behind her, the insistent banging at the door grows loud and aggressive, and she makes the split decision to follow him. She is just climbing over the balustrade a couple of rooms down when a loud crash issues from their room.

They burst into a run, jumping over each partition they come across. Georgia tries to keep up with Charlie, who moves with fast, graceful precision. He makes it to the last room on the corner and takes a left, disappearing from sight. She looks behind her to see two tall, Caucasian men pursuing them. A third is speaking into his two-way radio.

Stumbling over a chair that she didn't see, she crashes to the floor, yelling out in pain. Before she can recover, one of the men has already reached her. As he bends down to grab her she sees with horror there is a gun in the holster on his hip.

Charlie appears out of nowhere, and before she comprehends what is happening, he has smashed a ceramic vase over the man's head, knocking him unconscious. Picking up the balcony chair, Charlie hurls it at the second assailant, who stumbles back and crashes into the balustrade, his skull making a loud crack against the concrete.

Charlie pulls Georgia to her feet. "Come. Hurry!"

They round the corner to the next balcony. Charlie grabs another chair and throws it against the guest room window, shattering the glass. They run through the room, bursting through the front door and into the corridor.

Charlie leads her down a fire exit stairwell beside the lift. At the bottom level, panting from their run, he edges the door open slightly as he peeks outside. Satisfied it is safe, he grasps Georgia's hand as they enter into the lobby of the hotel.

"Walk calmly. Do not draw attention to yourself."

It is now late afternoon and there are a few new groups of tourists arriving in coaches, spilling into the already busy foyer and wandering about with their cameras. As Charlie and Georgia walk swiftly towards the main entrance, they spot two Caucasian men standing near the door. Even though they are dressed casually, their height, build, and the standard military crew cuts make them stand out in the Asian crowd. One of them is talking into his two-way radio.

Charlie motions for Georgia to turn around, and they walk back towards the rear of the building, only to see in the distance two more men bursting out of the stairwell.

"Shit," Georgia mutters. "What now?"

"I know a way," Charlie says, pulling at her hand. "Come with me."

They veer left in the opposite direction, just as the men from the stairwell spot them and start running over. The swarm of tourists hinders the men's progress as they try to dodge through the vacationing crowd.

Charlie leads them quickly down another set of stairs to the side, heading into the basement of the building. Down here, the ceiling is a lot lower, and Georgia can hear the clinking of crockery and smell the aroma of food in the air. They must be on the kitchen level. They round another corner and come to an abrupt dead end, faced with a feature wall painted with the view from the hotel balcony, overlooking Keelung River at night.

"Charlie?" She panics. She hears hurried footsteps on the stairs.

Charlie rushes over to the feature wall and pushes against it, and to Georgia's surprise, it gives way to reveal a dark passage beyond.

Sudden realisation comes over her. This must be the tunnel that has been long speculated over since the opening of the hotel. When Chiang Kai-Shek built the Grand Hotel for the purpose of entertaining state-level dignitaries, there was a rumour that he ordered secret passages to be constructed. Allegedly, one of these tunnels ran from the premises to the nearby presidential residence for his convenience, and also for safety in the event of an air strike from the communists.

In 1995, two air-raid tunnels were accidentally uncovered after the hotel suffered from a major fire. Each tunnel was a hundred and eighty metres in length, with the capacity to shelter ten thousand people. Both of these passages connect to nearby parks: one heading east and the other west. To this day, the one rumoured to lead to the former presidential residence has not been found.

As Georgia approaches the doorway to the tunnel she sees this must be the western passage, as it is equipped with what's said to be the world's longest concrete slide, polished smooth and painted white. It was supposedly designed for disabled access—or for the elderly generalissimo Chiang—as an alternative to the long flight of descending stairs. Though, judging by how steep the slide is, Georgia would rather take the steps. It looks like a giant water slide at an amusement park, plunging into darkness, and she's not sure there will be a soft landing at the other end.

But Charlie is already climbing on. "Hurry, Georgia," he says. "It will be quicker this way." With a push of his hands, he disappears into the dark abyss.

She climbs onto the smooth, cold surface, surprised at how slippery the varnished concrete is. With an involuntary yelp, she glides down the steep decline, picking up speed as she descends. She feels it veering left and right, spiralling into the darkness in an uncomfortably high-speed course.

It seems to go on forever, and then all of a sudden the solid surface disappears from underneath her, and she is flying into the black void. She lands in Charlie's arms as he catches her.

"Are you okay?" He steadies her, then pulls them through a set of metal doors into the light. She sees they are in a park, the entrance to the tunnel concealed behind a rock.

"Yeah," she gasps, still reeling from the roller coaster ride.

"Hand me that." Charlie shuts the metal doors behind them, pointing at the fallen branch on the ground next to

Georgia. He jams it through the handles as she passes it to him.

They walk briskly away from the exit and into the afternoon light. Moments later, a loud banging booms from behind them.

32

THEY RUN through the park to the main road and hail a yellow taxi. Charlie holds the door open for Georgia and climbs in after her.

"Towards Tamsui," he instructs the driver in Chinese. "Hurry, please."

The taxi speeds off as Georgia spots the two men running through the park in their direction.

"Who're those men?" Georgia turns to Charlie, her heart still racing. "They were armed!"

"I do not know," Charlie shakes his head. "But they are clearly after us because they believe you have achieved your goal. My guess is that Lambert sent them."

"Why would he do that? I work for him."

"Yes, but does anyone else know about this quest Lambert has commissioned?"

"Apart from my assistant and my grandmother, no."

"And when was the last time you updated Lambert on your progress?"

"When I found the names in the *Romance of the Three Kingdoms*... I told his assistant I would update them in a few days' time when I had something more concrete."

Charlie gazes ahead, considering this. "If I were a powerful man who had hired someone to search for something I wanted desperately, I would probably have her followed to keep an eye on her movements, in case she neglects to report all of her findings. The fact that you have been keeping your progress from him will most likely be read as an act of betrayal." Charlie looks at her in the eyes. "And besides, his prize is now in sight; all he has to do is grab it."

She chews on her lip, working over his theory in her mind.

The taxi slows, crawling to a stop. Up ahead, cars are at a standstill as far as she can see, waiting for the traffic to break.

"Damn," Charlie mutters, "Taipei traffic."

He pulls out his wallet and hands the taxi driver some cash, opening the door. "Come, Georgia, we have to keep moving."

She climbs out of the taxi and follows him, half-jogging to keep up. Charlie is heading directly towards the metro station entrance across the street.

"I think we have lost them," he says, looking behind them. "I do not see anyone following us."

They enter the gates of the station, taking the escalator up to the platform for Tamsui.

"Where are we going?" Georgia asks.

"We need to get to my place," he replies. "I have something to show you."

———

EX-LIEUTENANT MICHAEL KERR holds the phone away from his ear as the enraged voice of his client bellows over the line.

"What do you mean, *you lost them?!*"

"Sorry, sir," Michael replies, trying to quell his own rising frustration. "They escaped down an air-raid tunnel, that was not something we'd anticipated—"

"I don't care, just find them!" his employer yells.

"Yes, sir—" he says, but the client has already hung up the phone.

Michael stuffs the device into his back pocket to resist the urge to throw it against the wall of the surveillance van. Only a couple of years out of the military, and he is already beginning to miss being in the forces. Not that he has an option of going back, after being booted out for what he did to those women in Iraq. A god-damned, unwarranted mess, that was. He only gave them what they rightly deserved.

After wallowing in an inebriated state of self-pity for months, it was his best friend who convinced him to go private. Colin had started the firm a while ago and needed a right-hand man for his growing business, promising Michael freedom and lucrative returns as a hired gun. But instead of carrying out serious operations of importance, Michael is now reduced to babysitting rich, spoilt kids and running errands for arrogant clients such as the one who was just on the phone.

His jaw tightens.

When he took on this job, he didn't understand the need to deploy so many men. The brief was simple: all they had to do was locate the couple and bring them in. They looked harmless enough. The woman is a small and petite Asian, and the man looks like he hasn't eaten in weeks. But the client insisted on bringing in more cavalry. Money was not an issue, he said. And now Michael knows why—judging by the way the tall man handled two of his assets, the subjects are not to be underestimated.

This is precisely why he always asks for full disclosure when taking on a job. But Colin, his best-friend-turned-boss, insists that some clients like their privacy. It's what they pay for.

Just get in, get the job done, and don't ask any questions.

That motto has not served him well today.

"Sir?"

"What?!" he barks at the rookie on the computer.

"Er… we picked up this footage, sir. From the Taipei Metro CCTV. I think it's our subjects—"

Michael whirls around to fix his eyes on the monitor. A woman and a tall man stand in the train, huddled close. The image quality is not great, but there is no doubt they are the couple he's looking for.

"This is live?"

"Yes—"

"Which metro line is it?" he asks, already dialling on his phone.

"Tamsui, sir. They're headed towards the end station now."

33

THE MAN HANGS up the phone, rubbing his bare scalp with irritation. The old scar that runs from his chin to the right ear throbs with a dull ache.

Imbeciles.

It was meant to be easy. His prize was right there in sight. All they had to do was bag them both, and bring them in.

The mercs are not worth a cent of the money he paid them.

He hurls the phone across the room, feeling none of his rage lessen as he watches it shatter against the wall. Grabbing his briefcase, he checks that he has his passport and everything else he needs before slamming it shut. He stalks towards the door.

It looks like he's going to have to do this himself, if he wants the job done right.

CHARLIE PULLS open the door to his apartment building. It is a worn, humble construction that is typical of the old Tamsui area, located in a quiet alley not far from her grandmother's home. A row of cars is parked along one side of the road, leaving barely enough room for traffic. Several buildings down, two elderly women speak loudly as they catch up on the latest complaints about their children and grandkids.

Georgia follows Charlie up the steps to the third floor, and he unlocks one of the two doors, leading her inside. She walks into the cosy space, surprised to see that it's even smaller than her grandmother's place. A mere studio apartment, its furnishings are simple: a single bed against the far wall, a small desk to the side, a couple of bookshelves bursting with volumes, a pedestal fan, and a meditation cushion in the corner. There is a small wardrobe, a bathroom at one end, and a kitchenette at the other. She sees no TV, no computers, no dining table, or even a settee.

Hardly the mansion of a man who has just donated a collection worth millions of dollars.

"This… is your home?" Georgia asks. She's not sure what she was expecting, but it surprises her.

"My current one, yes." Charlie smiles at her expression. "I like to keep my life simple. I do not need much; this is all I ever use in my daily life. In fact, this is all anyone ever really needs, when it comes down to it."

She nods, watching as he walks to his desk and opens the drawer, retrieving a thick notebook. He slips it into a knapsack, along with some changes of clothing, and slings it over his shoulder.

"What's that?" she asks.

"I will tell you in the car," Charlie says as he grabs the car keys hanging on a hook by the door.

"Where're we going?" asks Georgia as he ushers her out of the door.

"We have to keep moving. They could still be following us."

His reply spikes her anxiety, and she follows him without another word, down three flights of stairs and out onto the street. Charlie stops next to a small, old Proton and unlocks the doors, starting the engine as Georgia climbs into the passenger seat.

Behind them, a black van swerves around the corner about a hundred metres away, gunning up the street.

"Damn." Charlie quickly puts the car into gear, pulling it out of the parking spot.

"Is that them?" she exclaims, turning around to see the van. The dark tinting on the windscreen makes it difficult to make out the driver.

With all of the vehicles parked along the road, the narrow alley can only accommodate one-way traffic. Charlie navigates the myriad of alleyways with familiarity, making a few quick random turns, losing sight of the black van each time. But moments later, Georgia sees the same vehicle pursuing them again.

They speed up, merging onto a main road. But this is Tamsui, on the outskirts of Taipei, and there is only one double-lane road that leads in and out of the seaside suburb. The traffic is intense as Charlie switches from lane to lane, trying to gain distance on their pursuers. Georgia keeps turning to gauge their progress, each time noticing the unmistakable van trailing not far behind.

She glances at Charlie, wondering how he can appear to be so calm, even now.

"As long as the traffic does not stop, and we can keep moving, we will be okay," he reassures her as if reading her mind, keeping his eyes on the road. "If they intended to shoot us, they would have done it already."

He switches lanes a few more times, earning them plenty of honks as he squeezes into each narrow space between the moving cars.

Georgia grips her seat, gasping at every near miss.

Their car reaches an amber light that turns red as they approach, and suddenly Charlie slams down the accelerator, speeding through the intersection as cross traffic comes at them. Georgia squeezes her eyes shut, hearing the screeching of tyres and the loud honks, expecting a collision that never comes. When she opens her eyes again, she whirls around on her seat to see they are the only vehicle that made it through the crossing.

"I think we've lost them," she says.

Charlie flashes her a reassuring smile, then looks back to the road, driving silently. They merge onto a freeway and begin to pick up speed, and after she has looked back several times to make sure they aren't being followed, she leans her head back and exhales a long sigh.

Her phone vibrates in her pocket, and she pulls it out, looking at it for the first time since that morning. She has missed quite a lot of calls: four from Ethan, a couple from Sarah, and even more from Hank. Clicking into her messages, she sees a long string of texts from Hank:

— *Georgia, haven't heard from you, everything okay?*

— *Georgia, Mr. Lambert would like you to update on what is going on. Can you please give me a call.*

— *I have left you a few voice mails. Please call me.*

Georgia switches off her phone, slipping it into her bag.

34

As THEY SPEED down the freeway, Charlie can sense Georgia's intense stare.

"Are you okay?" he asks, casting her a glance.

"No." She shakes her head, visibly agitated. "No I'm not. I want you to pull over."

"We are on the freeway right now," he protests.

"I don't care," Georgia says, still shaking her head and raising her voice as she becomes more upset. "I don't want another minute of this. I've had people come after me with loaded guns. I've been in a car chase. We could've been in an accident back there. I have no idea where we're going, and you still haven't answered my questions!"

"Okay, calm down, Georgia," he coaxes. "What questions?"

"Where are we going?" she demands.

Charlie shifts his eyes back to the road. "We need to get out of the city. Lambert probably has men staking out at all the familiar places you go to, and they will not stop until they track us down. I helped out a friend some time ago, and as a token of gratitude, he lets me use his holiday house on the north-east coast, near Yilan. It is secluded, and we will be safe there until we figure out what to do."

"Your friend will be there?" she asks, her tone softening slightly.

"I doubt it," replies Charlie. "He is hardly ever in the country. But he is happy for me to use the place whenever I like."

Georgia opens her mouth, only to close it again. Then, she whispers, "Are you Hsu Fu?"

Charlie takes a breath before answering; it feels so strange to hear that name spoken aloud.

"Yes," he finally replies. "A long, long time ago."

"Prove it."

He snaps his gaze to her, and seeing the resolve in her eyes, he smiles. Keeping an eye on the road ahead, he reaches for the car cigarette lighter, pushing it in to activate the burner.

"What're you doing?" she asks.

"I am going to prove it to you."

Georgia looks as if she is about to say something else, but frowns in silence instead. After a long minute, the lighter pops back up in its slot. Charlie grabs the knob with one hand, keeping the other on the wheel.

"Okay." He breathes. "I am only going to do this once, so watch carefully."

Gritting his teeth against the searing pain, he presses the burner against the back of his hand on the wheel. The hiss and smell of burnt flesh fills the air in the enclosed space. Beside him, Georgia is watching in silent horror, her mouth agape.

"This is going to be the neatest party trick you have ever seen," he jokes, and is rewarded with an apprehensive stare.

His attention back on the road, Charlie extends the injured hand towards Georgia to let her see the evidence she has requested. Already, the area of the burn has gone numb. Over the next minute, the tissues around the region will work to repair themselves until all trace of the wound has disappeared.

Even from the corner of his eye, Charlie notices Georgia's face blanch as she stares at his outstretched hand. She looks as if she is about to be sick. Charlie is half expecting her to actually throw up as she absorbs the implications of what he is unveiling, and he contemplates pulling into the emergency lane. But his level of respect for Georgia is raised another notch when he sees her swallow thickly, quickly regaining her composure to turn towards him.

"How the…" she whispers. "How?"

"Ah. Where shall I begin?"

"Start from the beginning," Georgia urges.

"Very well." Briefly closing his eyes, he exhales. "I was born in the ancient Chinese state of Qi," he confesses, feeling something unravelling within him.

As Charlie begins to recount his personal history for the very first time, his mind turns to the years he has not allowed himself to ponder on for so long. He thinks of the Hata scroll that Georgia described, and he can almost sense the ghosts of Emperor Qin, Wang Jian, and Naaya surround him. Charlie feels himself pulled by their familiar presence—these people whose very actions have shaped his destiny—and he finally gives in, drifting back to those fateful events that made him the person he is today.

35

211 BCE, Japan

HSU FU CAST *a backward glance as he hurried along, climbing uphill through the forest. Stumbling over some protruding tree roots, he frantically grabbed the trunk to regain his balance. The rough surface cut into the skin of his palm, but he did not even feel the pain. He was feeling very little at this point.*

Very little except for the terror consuming his entire being.

He paused to look behind him, feeling certain he had made a clean escape. The sun was directly overhead now, its harsh rays beaming down through the foliage of the trees, a reminder that he had been half running, half walking without pause since before dawn.

Hearing the trickle of water, Hsu Fu quickened his pace in spite of his protesting limbs. After a few more minutes following the sound, he was rewarded with the sight of a small stream through the trees. He scrambled to the edge of the water and fell to his knees, guzzling with frenzy.

His stomach full of the cool liquid, Hsu Fu fell on his back, gulping for air. Here in the silence of the forest, he felt both sated and exhausted as he tried to assess the situation and consider his options. For the first time since he was captured by Wang Jian, a swell of emotions rose within his chest. Despite efforts to swallow it back down, it erupted out of his throat in the form of a strangled sound. Hsu Fu began to sob uncontrollably, his body convulsing with tremors. His outburst echoed through the trees.

It took a long time to calm himself down. His diaphragm still spasming, Hsu Fu wiped at his nose with tattered sleeves as he fought hard to think of what to do next. Rising, he took off his clothes—or what was left of them—to soak the bloody fabric in the stream, wiping at the stains on his face and body. What a sight he must be right now, with three days of blood caked all over him. That murderous Lu Hsing, the general's interrogator, was relentless with each session of torture, carving at Hsu Fu's flesh day after day: slowly, mercilessly, taking care to avoid major arteries that would kill immediately. But even the bloodthirsty fiend began to tire when Hsu Fu continued to heal every day. The general, however, seemed to have stomach for more.

It had taken Hsu Fu most of last night to break free of the bonds that Wang Jian's men had put him in. He had to dislocate both of his shoulders, the rough lengths of rope digging into his flesh as he tried to struggle out of them. The bastards had fastened them tightly, and his wrists still burned at the memory of his restraints. He rubbed at the now-unblemished joints self-consciously, as images of his torture came flooding back.

Hsu Fu squeezed his eyes shut, shaking his head to expel the sounds of his own screams.

He could feel the same panic and terror gripping his heart again. Reasoning with himself, he tried to remain calm. He was miles away from the camp, having escaped hours before the men were due to awaken. No one had seen him, Hsu Fu was sure of it. Even if they tried to come after him, they would not be able to travel as quickly as he had. The general's deserters had taken all of their horses, and the men who remained were not travelling as lightly as Hsu Fu.

Besides, now that Wang Jian knew about the elixir, Hsu Fu

suspected the general would be setting his sights on the true prize instead of pursuing a worthless alchemist.

At least, that is what Hsu Fu hoped.

There were a few times, during the delirium of excruciating pain, he had feared unwittingly speaking about Naaya and her true location. When Wang Jian threatened the Nine Familial Exterminations on the Hsu clan, Hsu Fu knew he had to do something. The general was vowing to hunt down every one of his relations in China and submit them to the same torture and eventual death.

Hsu Fu could not let that happen. He had to protect his family.

So he gave the general what he wanted.

Hsu Fu had not lied when he spoke of that island and its location. It did exist, and Naaya had been there. This he knew, because of the drawings depicting its peculiar shape on Naaya's walls, and the stories she had told. But Hsu Fu had described the island to Wang Jian as if he himself had actually been there, and judging from the reaction, it seemed the general had bought the story. With any luck, all of Qin's accursed men would be on a boat right now sailing south.

And if they ever found the island, they would discover nothing but birds living there.

Hsu Fu had always been a gifted storyteller, narrating enough details to capture the listeners' attention, leaving out just the right amount for their imagination to take over. This was how he had convinced Emperor Qin of the existence of Penglai Mountain and the Immortals, and of the giant sea creatures blocking the path when he had failed to return with the elixir from the first expedition. The secret to a great lie, he knew, was to interweave as much truth as necessary to make fiction come to life.

Hsu Fu rinsed the makeshift rag in the brook again, wringing the last drops of water out and putting his clothes back on. The damp material against his skin was a welcome respite from the midday temperature. Looking down at his shins and palms, he saw that the deeper cuts from the lengthy stumble through the forest had already begun to heal.

Amazing.

He was yet to become fully accustomed to this new body: the way it repaired itself, the efficiency with which it moved, as if it were made of air. Often, Hsu Fu had to remember to slow his movements just to blend in with others so as to not attract attention. As a medicine man, he was fascinated by how it worked. How was it possible that after receiving the elixir, one's body operated and mended itself with such efficiency that one would remain youthful forever?

Despite Naaya's repeated warnings, Hsu Fu wanted to share this marvel with the rest of the world. He believed whole-heartedly that this was a gift from the gods.

A branch snapped behind him, bolting him upright. Hsu Fu swivelled, searching amongst the trees for movement. A deer grazed innocently only fifty metres away, seemingly unperturbed by his presence. Looking up at the steep mountain ahead, he stood quickly, realising that he had rested for too long. He had better keep moving if he was to reach Naaya before sundown.

36

"So the Senkaku Islands were a lie?" Georgia asks, her forehead crinkling.

"Yes and no," replies Charlie. "Naaya did stay there briefly as she sailed from her home to Japan. But unlike what you read in the Hata scroll, the islands are not the promised Penglai Mountain. There was never a shipwreck, and I never ended up there. My fleet landed safely at what is now known as Shingu in Japan—myself and five hundred other brothers and sisters of China who were victims of the oppressive Qin regime. Japan became our new home, our haven from the tyrant who had taken over our lands."

"Wait. You mean to say that all of this—the expedition that you convinced Qin to send you on, the stories about Penglai Mountain and the Immortals—all of it was just a ploy for safe passage out of China?" She is incredulous. "And you made the emperor *pay* for it too?"

A crooked smile spreads across Charlie's face. He was right; not much escapes her scrutiny at all. "You are an archaeologist, Georgia. You know how Qin treated his people. Qin was all about unification: one language, one measuring system, one ruler for all that vast land. There was never any room for diversity or differing opinions. And I have always been different, all of us were. We had all been shunned one way or another by our community, and we saw the dangers for us as Qin became emperor. That was why we needed to find a way to leave China and find a new home for ourselves.

"I was familiar with Qin's greed. His appetite for power drove him to madness, and when he became ill, he was desperate to try anything so that he could live forever. I saw my opportunity, and I took it."

Charlie pauses, then adds, "We were careful, of course. Sailing in uncharted waters was not something I would risk with so many innocent lives on board. That was why I planned a smaller first voyage to map out our path. When I returned empty-handed, I convinced Qin there was a giant sea creature blocking my path to Penglai Mountain. Years later, we sailed again with the complete fleet, with bigger ships to withstand the seas, and accompanied by five hundred men and women as sacrificial gifts for the Immortals."

Georgia is silent as she absorbs this.

"…And Naaya?" she finally asks.

Charlie smiles as he thinks of his mentor. "Naaya was my teacher, my dear friend. She taught me so much about herbs and healing. Can you believe that she was already several hundred years old when I met her in Japan?"

Georgia raises her brows, waiting for him to continue his story.

---

211 BCE, Japan

THE SUN HOVERED *above the distant horizon, setting the entire heavens ablaze. Hsu Fu paused in his tracks, taking in the spectacular scene unfolding before him. Up here, he felt closer to the clouds and the gods, and it was almost easy to forget the past week of hell he had endured.*

Almost.

A cool breeze swept through the trees, making him shiver and reminding him to keep moving. Hsu Fu resumed his climb, and soon came across a clearing in the woods. A small hut with a thatched roof stood at the far end, light emanating from within. At the sight, relief and exhaustion flooded him simultaneously. His stomach growled with fervour at the delicious aroma of simmering stew. He had not eaten for several days.

As if sensing his presence, Naaya emerged from the hut. She rushed forward as his knees gave way.

"What happened?" she cried with horror, helping him into the hut. Settling him on a straw mat, Naaya quickly soaked some clean cloth in a bucket of water to wipe at his face. Hsu Fu guessed there was still plenty of blood left despite his efforts to clean himself up at the creek earlier.

"The emperor's men found me," he explained.

"They tortured you," she observed, looking at his shredded, bloody clothing. At Hsu Fu's grim expression, she asked, "Do they know?"

He shook his head. "I told them the elixir is on an island two weeks' sail south of here. The general believes there was a shipwreck, that everyone else perished and I was washed ashore alone."

That was another lie he had spun. He had to protect the others so that the general's men would not go after them.

Naaya sighed. "I am sorry they did this to you." Washing the stained cloth in the water, she added, "You must stop coming to me covered in blood like this."

Hsu Fu gave her a wry chuckle. It had been almost a year since the day they met. He had been wandering in the woods not far from there, collecting the special herbs that grow so well at this altitude. The land of Wo offered an abundance of new plants he had never come across before, many of them with very interesting healing qualities.

Hsu Fu had been truthful when he told Qin of his desire to search for a cure. What Qin had not known, however, was that Hsu Fu was actually searching for a concoction that could heal his own son, not the emperor. Hsu Fu never had any intention of helping the ruthless despot prolong his tyrannical reign.

But when little Hsu An had died during their voyage to Wo, Hsu Fu had howled to the heavens with rage and despair, and almost turned the fleet back to China. The only thing that stopped him was the promise he had made to the five hundred men and women of a new home, and of course, the knowledge that Emperor Qin was likely to behead him for a second failed attempt.

It was Hsu Fu's greatest pain in life to be able to heal so many people, but not his own son. He believed his wife secretly blamed him for it too. The death of Hsu An had created a irreparable fissure in their marriage. Unable to console her or even deal with his own grief, Hsu Fu had plunged himself into work.

One day, as he was hiking in the forest, searching for a new tree fungus he had recently discovered, he encountered a black bear attacking a termite mound. A few metres away, there was a cub foraging on the ground, probably looking for mushrooms.

Hsu Fu froze. Only the week before he had treated a farmer who had been brutally attacked by a bear protective of its cub. The man had suffered horrific wounds to his face and head. Despite everything Hsu Fu tried, the poor farmer had died within a day. He wondered if it were the same bear that now stood only twenty metres away from him.

He backed away slowly, carefully, hoping to escape undiscovered, but the creature must have caught his scent. It looked up from the termite nest and straight into his eyes. In a split second, leaping and bounding, it closed the distance between them. With a thunderous roar, the beast reared up on its hind legs. Hsu Fu stumbled back a few steps in fear, tripping over a log and landing on his back. The last thing he remembered was a giant paw swinging at his face.

When he woke up, it was to a similar sight to the one he had described to Wang Jian. Hsu Fu found himself in a hut, a fire *burning bright, and a figure crouched beside it, preparing some kind of concoction in a bowl. He was delirious, his body burning up as if it were ablaze, his throat so dry he could not swallow or speak.*

He lost consciousness, awoke again, and drifted between sleep and wakefulness many times.

When he finally regained full consciousness, he opened his eyes to see a girl sitting beside him. She had long, silver hair that reached to her lower back, though she looked no more than fourteen. Her robust frame and facial features differed from the people of Wo. She had larger, deep-set eyes, full lips, a more prominent nose, and darker skin. Hsu Fu could tell straight away that she was not from around there.

As he studied her, Hsu Fu realised she was the silver-haired witch the villagers in the valley spoke of. They talked often of a frightful apparition they glimpsed in the woods, one who moved swiftly like a ghost and was likely to cast a curse on anyone she came across. Yet the girl before him did not seem to be the forest-dwelling monster everyone feared. Even before she spoke, Hsu Fu could feel the kindness that seemed to radiate from the core of her being.

Her name was Naaya, she told him.

"You were badly injured by a bear," she explained, and memories of the beastly assault resurfaced in his mind.

Hsu Fu sat up quickly with alarm, looking down his limbs and body, touching his face to feel for injuries. All that remained of the bear attack was his tattered clothing, but he could not detect any pain or wounds. Confounded, he looked to Naaya for answers.

Her expression was strangely apologetic, and Hsu Fu wondered at the sadness in her eyes.

"When I found you in the forest, you were delirious with pain. The bear had torn the scalp off your head and left gaping wounds on your face. I would not have recognised you but for the green eyes. You kept begging me to help you, to save you."

"Have we met?" Hsu Fu asked, confused.

"No," replied Naaya, straightening her back. "But I have

watched you collect herbs in the mountains, and I have seen you help the people in the valley with the medicine."

Still marvelling at the lack of injuries on his body, he asked, "But how? I do not understand."

"You begged me," said Naaya, guilt in her dark eyes. "You held on to my arm with your bloody hand and you asked me to save you. So I… I did."

Something in her voice alarmed Hsu Fu.

"What did you do?"

37

"I THOUGHT no one had followed me when I went to Naaya's hut. I was wrong, and that mistake cost my friend's life," Charlie admits.

Georgia frowns, waiting for him to go on. Mostly silent for the past hour, she is quietly digesting his story. The towering street lamps along the freeway flicker on in the waning afternoon light. More vehicles join them on the road as they approach rush hour, but the traffic remains smooth closer to the country town of Yilan.

Her face is tilted as she watches this stranger: the long, slender fingers curled around the steering wheel, his expressions calm and difficult to decipher. Georgia searches her mind to pinpoint exactly what she finds unnerving about the older man's presence. Ever since their meeting earlier today, she's been having trouble gauging his reactions. Even when she gave him the lengthy confession of how she found him, she wasn't sure if he was going to burst into laughter at the preposterous story, or confirm her tale. The uncertainties worry her.

Charlie has a peculiar way of speaking that becomes evident after listening to him for a length of time. Although he largely uses colloquial speech, at times he slips into bouts of long, eloquent prose, using obsolete words that make him sound almost like a character out of a historical documentary. There's also his accent, which she can't quite place. It sounds like a mixed bag of various origins: some American, all different kinds of British, and even a bit of South African.

"What happened?" she asks after Charlie has paused for some time, staring out the windscreen.

"Naaya was killed when Wang Jian found us a day later. One of his men had picked up my trail and brought the general straight to Naaya's hut. I went out to collect some food early morning, and when I came back I found a man holding Naaya down while Wang Jian cut off her head."

"Jesus," Georgia whispers.

"You see, Georgia," Charlie continues, "this is how the elixir works: it accelerates the healing processes of the body, making all of its functions much more efficient so that instead of deteriorating, the cells are renewed every day. Of course, any scar tissue from previous injuries are never erased; I have one on my knee from a childhood tumble that is still there. But for cuts received after one drinks the elixir, it is a different matter. Small wounds heal within seconds, as you have witnessed. Deeper ones take longer as there are more tissues to repair. But some wounds cannot be healed at all."

"So it's still possible to die."

"Yes," he confirms. "When Wang Jian saw me returning the hut, he threw Naaya's bloody, severed head at me. He was laughing. *Damn witch,* he said, *let us see her grow another, if she can.*" Charlie shakes his head. "That is when I lost it. All I remember was grabbing for the man closest to me. It was over within minutes, and I had the general's sword pressed against his own throat.

"Wang Jian did not even utter a word. He did not beg for his life. All he did was stare defiantly into my eyes. I had so much hatred for him at this point: he had hunted me, tortured me, and now he had killed my friend—the person who had given me a second chance at life, and taught me so much. Before I knew what I was doing and before I could stop myself, I sliced open his throat, and I walked out of that hut, leaving him to die."

Charlie stares at his hands, murmuring almost to himself. "That was the first time, the only time, I have ever killed. Sometimes I can still hear the gurgling sound he made as I walked away. For years I had nightmares about that night."

They fall into silence, Charlie's gaze distant as he drives on, Georgia chewing over all the information that has been revealed.

After a few moments, he sighs. "So ever since then my life has been a semi-nomadic existence. I move frequently to avoid suspicions concerning my unchanging appearance. I try to keep a low profile, most of the time."

"That must be a lonely way to live."

"Yes, I suppose it is. But over time, I learnt to deal with it. I learnt to appreciate the transient nature of my life. There are not many parts of the world that I have not yet visited," he turns, smiling at her now. "I kept learning. After so many years, I am still learning—about life, about medicine and healing, and about all of the wonderful new scientific discoveries we make year after year. I began to meditate, and I have studied with many, many teachers and sages in my lifetime."

"And you also collected ancient artefacts to donate them to museums."

He laughs, the sound a deep rumble in his chest. "Yes, well, when I collected a lot of those items, they were still contemporary. It is a practice I picked up when I saw Emperor Qin destroying all the writings he did not approve of. I believe it is important to protect our cultural heritage and to give it back to the public, so that the new generation can learn from the past, do you not agree?"

Georgia smiles, nodding. So much of the world's cultural

history has been destroyed by wars, and humanity only sees the value of artefacts hundreds of years later.

Then she frowns as a thought crosses her mind.

"There's one thing I don't understand," she begins. "Why are you telling me all of this? You barely know me, and I'm meant to be working for a man who wants to make the elixir available to the rest of the world. I gather that's not what you want, or you would have done it already. All this time, you've avoided being discovered, and I suspect you're very good at it. How is it possible that I still managed to find you, especially when you *knew* that I was looking for you? Unless— unless you *wanted* to be found…" She falters at this thought.

Charlie is quiet as he turns to her, a wry smile on his face that she does not comprehend. "Georgia. You did not find me, *I* found *you*."

38

HANK STANDS before Mark Lambert's desk, quietly watching as his boss processes the lengthy report he has just delivered regarding Professor Lee. A feeling of dread sits low in his stomach as he awaits a response.

He did not anticipate Georgia disappearing on him the way she did. It puzzles him immensely. The professor is a low-maintenance kind of girl; she seems meek enough, and they've developed a friendship—albeit over the phone—that made him believe managing her would be easy. Well, easier than the others he's had to babysit. God knows he has enough on his plate, working for the man sitting at the desk before him.

Women. He'll never understand them.

Lambert is silent, his face dark and unreadable. He slowly leans back in his chair, then raises his eyes to meet Hank's. Instantly, Hank recognises that look: he has only seen it a few times over the years, but each occurrence has been memorable.

"Tell me, Hank, how long have you been working for me?" Lambert's voice is frighteningly calm.

"Almost ten years now, sir."

"Those have been ten good years, and your exemplary service has been appreciated."

"Thank you, sir," Hank says, feeling unsettled by Lambert's tone.

"And in those ten years of working as my right-hand man, have you ever seen me tolerate any kind of mistakes or incompetence from my staff?"

"No, sir." Hank swallows past the lump in his throat.

Lambert fixes Hank's gaze with a steely stare. "Then consider this a courtesy: I suggest you find the professor before you lose your job, Hank. I will not warn you again."

"I DON'T UNDERSTAND," Georgia says, confused by the revelation.

Charlie sighs, shifting in his driver's seat, his gaze fixed on the road before them. When he finally speaks again, he does not address her question straight away.

"My wife, Hsu Yin, grieved for our son's death for a long time. The sadness became chronic, and her health suffered thereafter."

Georgia furrows her brows at the sudden change of topic. But she decides to go along with it. "She didn't take the elixir?"

"No, there was none left. Naaya had used the last dose on me." He shakes his head. "And in any case, Naaya did not think Hsu Yin would have handled the change well—especially with the depression. But I did not believe that. I thought if we could heal Hsu Yin's body, her mind too would heal over time.

"After Naaya was killed, I searched for the elixir. There were clues that Naaya had left—in her drawings and writings—but it took me a long time to decipher them all. By then, it was too late. Hsu Yin died a few years after Naaya was killed. Before she died, she gave birth to our baby girl, Hsu Jen."

"You had a daughter?" Georgia says, surprised.

"Yes." Charlie smiles, his face lighting up in the dimming light. "Oh she was beautiful, Georgia. She was kind, just like her mother had been. She was strong-willed, smart, so curious all the time." He pauses, turning to look at Georgia thoughtfully. Then, his voice soft, he continues, "For a long time, I kept searching for the elixir. Every day, my daughter grew and changed. Every day, I remained the same. I was constantly terrified of losing her. I had watched my son die, clutched his small, lifeless body against my chest and howled and sobbed until there were no more tears left in my body. I could not imagine doing the same with Hsu Jen. I could not go through the agony of watching my child die again.

"But the secret of the elixir was lost when Naaya died. And as Hsu Jen grew up, she began to see my desperation for the elixir. My daughter… in so many ways, she was a much wiser person than I was. Hsu Jen was a deeply spiritual person. It was she who encouraged me to ground myself in meaning, learning, and spirituality. She saw that this was the only way I could live with my condition."

"Your condition?" Georgia asks, puzzled.

His response is a sardonic smile. "On the surface, immortality may look like a desirable thing. But I assure you, Georgia, it comes with a price.

"Even as I was searching for the elixir, Hsu Jen saw this truth. She told me she did not want to live forever, that the most revered masters and teachers had taught about the impermanence in our world, and it is because of this that we suffer. It is also why we must learn to not cling on to what is never meant to be forever. Of course, at the time, I could not understand her, or even hear what she was saying to me.

"I began taking long journeys away from Japan for my search, looking for where Naaya had come from. I knew it was where I would find the elixir. I visited every island I could find south of Shingu. I was away on one of these voyages when Hsu Jen died at home, in Japan."

Charlie sighs. "All that time I was away, searching for something to make our relationship permanent, and I did not realise I had neglected to make the most out of the precious little time that we actually had together. It is the ultimate irony, is it not? But that is exactly what we all do. We spend our time trying to obtain what we do not have, and forget to cherish what is right before us." He shakes his head.

Georgia sees the sadness in Charlie's eyes, and she feels an ache rise within her chest. The sentiment feels all too familiar. They drive on in silence, taking the next exit off the freeway. From here, they will have to travel via meandering country roads up into the mountains.

A questions floats around in her mind, and she takes the opportunity to voice it. "What *is* the elixir?"

"Ah," Charlie says, his jade green eyes twinkling at her in the fading light. "See, this is why I came searching for you."

39

THE ANNOUNCEMENT for boarding flight EV203 for Melbourne issues from the airport intercom, and for the fifth time that minute, Ethan stares at the phone screen.

Nothing.

No messages, no missed calls. Ethan frowns, unsure if he should be worried or pissed. He racks his brain, going through every detail of all that happened before they said goodbye at the hotel this morning. He kissed her goodbye, held her in his arms. He asked to see her after his lunch meeting, and she said yes.

Georgia did say yes, right?

She did, he's positive she did. He thinks back to the smile she gave him as he left the hotel room. That radiant smile... it made his knees go weak. It held promises. Hell, it damn well nearly made Ethan cancel his lunch to spend the rest of the day in bed with her. In the light of that smile, it makes no sense at all that Georgia would not show up as agreed. It also makes no sense that her phone has been switched off ever since, and that she hasn't returned any of his messages.

Ethan watches the queue of passengers gradually disappear through the boarding gate, wondering what to do. He really needs to get on this plane. There are a million overdue things waiting for him to attend to back at the museum. The Tang Dynasty show is the biggest Asian collection NGV has ever exhibited, and it's either going to make or break his career. But how can he leave Taipei now, when he has no clue where Georgia is?

What if she's hurt? What if she needs him?

Something's not right. Ethan feels it in the seat of his gut, gnawing at him with no reprieve.

He tries her number again, growling with frustration at the voice mail greeting he has by now memorised.

"Hi, this is Georgia," her voice says brightly on the line. "Please leave me a message..."

Hanging up, Ethan taps his phone on his hand. A thought suddenly washes over him like a sheet of ice, making his chest constrict with pain. *Think about it, dumbarse. Georgia's most likely not missing. She's probably avoiding you, just like last time.*

"This is the final boarding call for flight EV203 bound for Melbourne," the ground staff announces. "All remaining passengers please go to gate D13 immediately."

He quickly types out one final message. *Call me. Please.*

As Ethan walks towards the gate and hands over the necessary documents for boarding, he can't shake the fear that he may have lost her again, perhaps for good this time.

40

"Before I explain the elixir," Charlie begins, "I have to tell you about Naaya."

He senses Georgia sitting up a little straighter, giving him her full attention.

"Naaya was of Austronesian descent," Charlie explains. "Her people lived on a land several weeks' journey south of Japan. Her father was the village shaman, and had mastered the use of herbs for healing. Naaya told me once that when she saw me collecting herbs in the forest, she was reminded of him. I suppose that may have been the reason that compelled her to save me.

"Naaya loved to help her father with his work, and she dreamed of one day becoming a healer too. He trained her to identify plants and would often send her out to collect the medicines he needed. One day, while she was searching in the forest, she came upon a pool of water in a cave. She drank from it, and when she eventually realised its healing powers, she went back to her father and told him of her discovery. They began to collect the water to cure all sorts of ailments for the villagers, until they realised those who drank from it neither aged nor died. The cave became hallowed ground, and her people went there regularly to worship its sacred waters. They believed the magical pool was a gift from the revered and powerful mountain god, Zai.

"After a while, though, Naaya began to notice a change in her people as they lived on through the decades. The initial euphoria of becoming immortal eventually wore off. Gradually and steadily, people became despondent."

"Despondent?" Georgia asks, bemused.

He nods. "Imagine, Georgia, if you knew you had eternity ahead of you, that over time you could achieve everything you've ever dreamed of. What would you do with your time?"

"I'd do everything," she responds without hesitation. "Travel to all the places I've always wanted to visit. Learn free diving. Study neuroscience. Take all the drugs I've been curious about trying."

He laughs softly. "Would you really? Or would you end up doing nothing, *because* you knew you had all the time in the world?" He glances at her to see her frowning at the idea. "The things you described are actually a bucket list; it is what people do if they find out that they are dying, not if they think they are to live forever."

As she ponders on the thought, Charlie continues, "In all my years, I have come to realise that what makes human life precious and magical is ironically its fleeting nature. When you think about it, it is surprising how much death drives all that we strive for in life. It is the knowledge of an imminent deadline that motivates us to actually do the things that we have hoped for in our lives. It is also what makes us search for meaning in our seemingly minuscule existence. Everything—technology, art, literature, music—civilisation as we know it has been a product of human beings' desire for significance and importance. Death being a certainty makes people *live*. It makes us want to create a legacy for ourselves. I would wager that without it, we would not have Beethoven's symphonies, nor Monet's lily ponds, and certainly no pyramids or missions to the moon."

Charlie pauses, looking out into the night with his hands resting on the steering wheel. The roads are deserted at this hour in this remote part of Taiwan, and he is relieved to know for certain that they have lost the men who were pursuing them. He has not seen any other cars on the road for almost half an hour now. Making a turn as they come to a crossing, he takes the road that heads up into the mountains. He turns on the fog lights as they leave the illuminated streets behind.

"That is essentially what happened to Naaya's people," he explains as Georgia listens quietly. "They became miserable, depressed, and bored. Being drowned in that overwhelming sense of futility is a most dreadful thing. To have nothing to want for can make a person lose all of their hope in life.

"What is more, the elixir cures only physical ailments, not emotional or spiritual ones. Without guidance, the fragile psyche of one simple human being cannot contain so many years of emotional baggage. For many, death becomes a welcome respite after a short lifetime with their own inner demons.

"The elixir eventually drove Naaya's people mad. They became a people who had lost their sense of purpose and their sense of God: for now that they were immortals, what could possibly be greater than themselves? Morality and decency became a thing of the past. People became unkind and cruel to each other. Their once thriving culture collapsed into chaos. Insanity and mayhem ensued. Within a matter of decades, her people all but disappeared, perishing at their own and each other's hands. And for those who had taken the elixir, death only comes with extremely violent and painful means.

"Naaya blamed herself, of course, for discovering the cave in the first place, and for introducing her people to the elixir. Her hair went from a beautiful jet black to grey with grief. So she sealed the entrance to the cave to make sure no one would ever stumble into it again. Then she left her homeland, banishing herself by living in exile. She travelled north, sailing from one island to another, never settling for too long at a time, and always living in isolation.

"This semi-nomadic lifestyle suited her for a while, but it was also a very isolating existence. I know she was quite conflicted when she finally gave me the elixir to save my life. On one hand, she would be gaining a friend. On the other, she felt she was actually placing upon me a terrible burden."

"So she brought some with her when she left her home?" asks Georgia.

"Yes. She wore a small vial of it around her neck, as a constant reminder of her sins."

"Wow," Georgia breathes.

"Yes, I know." Charlie sighs. "I spent a long time trying to persuade her our condition could actually be a gift, that with this gift, we could do a lot of good for humanity. But Naaya became convinced the elixir was a curse when she saw the destruction it brought to her people, and I am not sure that she ever managed to find peace in what had happened."

He pauses as the car jolts and bounces over a section of unsealed road. Squinting into the inky night, he spots the little red mailbox ahead and makes a sharp left turn, taking the car up a steep driveway lined by trees. Up ahead, a large two-storey log cabin comes into view, illuminated by the Proton's headlights. The windows remain dark as he pulls the vehicle up to the house. As he suspected, the place is unoccupied.

He turns off the engine, but makes no move to get out of the car. The moonlight beams in through the windows, bathing everything in silver. Georgia also remains in her seat, seemingly expectant of his next revelation.

"It took me a long time to figure out Naaya's path," he says. "After she left her home, she travelled from one land to the next over many years, finally landing in Wo, where she and I met.

"Through her drawings, her writings, and the stories she told me, I compiled and sorted out a list of places she had been. None of them were called what they are now, of course. Some of the islands Naaya went to didn't even have names. I noted each landmark of all the different locations she had travelled to on the way, trying to figure out exactly which islands she had been to, and which one she initially came from. I finally realised that Naaya had travelled up the Ryukyu Archipelago to eventually reach Japan. I believe that I have managed to track her path back to the origin." He pauses.

"And?" Georgia asks. "Where was she from?"

Charlie looks at her, seeing fervent anticipation in her dark eyes. "She was from here, Georgia. Her people were a native tribe of Taiwan. That is one of the reasons why I am here."

41

GEORGIA GASPS as realisation washes over her.

"You're still looking for the cave?" she asks. "Why?"

Charlie nods in confirmation. His gaze is distant as he looks out the windscreen. "Let us talk about this inside the house."

They exit the car and walk up the path towards the log cabin, Charlie's knapsack slung over his shoulder. It is a balmy and humid night, the deafening sound of cicadas permeating the air. The house is located in a clearing and surrounded by trees, with dark mountains looming at the back. Charlie was right; the place is secluded. She hasn't seen any artificial light on their way here for some time.

Charlie unlocks the front door and flicks on a switch. Warm light floods the minimalist interior, and Georgia sees it is sparsely but elegantly decorated with sixties-style designer furniture. The walls are lined with bookcases filled with volumes, the floors are constructed of polished grey stone, and there is a large fireplace in the living room. There is an overall masculine warmth to the décor.

"My friend calls this his man cave," Charlie smiles, accurately describing her general impression of the place. "Somewhere to escape the daily grind. Unfortunately, he does not get much time to use it at all."

He guides her into the country-style kitchen next to the lounge, where everything is constructed of either polished wood or stone. There is a dining table of mammoth scale in the attached dining room, with floor-to-ceiling windows looking out to the darkened forest beyond. Charlie pulls out a chair, motioning for her to sit while he walks to the sink to fill the kettle.

"Cup of tea?"

Georgia nods. "Yes, please."

Charlie rummages through the pantry, producing tea canisters and packets of crackers. "I will go and pick up some food from town in the morning. Until then, this is all we have if you are hungry. There may be some instant noodles some-where too, if you are desperate."

Georgia shakes her head. Her stomach is still trying to unwind after the stressful day she's had. "I think I'll just settle for tea. I really don't think I can eat anything right now."

She watches impatiently as Charlie prepares their drinks, then sits down at the table beside her.

"I told you before that Naaya had carried a last vial of the elixir around her neck," he begins. "But she did not just save it as a reminder of what had happened to her people. She also kept it for another reason."

"She'd meant to give it to someone else?"

"No. She believed it was her way out."

"Her way out?" Georgia raises her eyebrows. "Out of what?"

"Out of the immortal life," explains Charlie. "Naaya thought the spring water which gave her enduring youth was also the cure for its affliction. She believed taking the elixir again would reverse its effects. She had saved the vial for herself, to take it one day when she decided that she had lived out her sentence for causing the demise of her own people."

"That's really screwed up." The words are out of Georgia's mouth before she can stop herself.

"Yes. I know you may see it that way. But you have to understand Naaya's people. They were idealist. They valued honour and loyalty above anything else, and they also held very romantic ideas about life in general. To Naaya, this was the only way she could redeem herself."

Charlie pauses to take a drink of his tea. "Unfortunately that last vial of water was used on me when she saved my life. I suppose her self-inflicted punishment ended when Wang Jian murdered her. In any case, the elixir was lost."

He reaches into his knapsack and brings out the notebook they retrieved from his home. Leather bound, with a string that wraps around its bulky volume, it is bursting with paper inserted through its pages.

"When she was alive, Naaya liked to draw and write," says Charlie. "She did it almost obsessively. She often told me she needed to put those images outside of her, instead of leaving them to fester within. It was her own way of releasing the deep guilt and sorrow she felt. The day she was killed, I took her writings and drawings with me when I left her hut."

He rubs his palm over the brown leather cover. "This note-book contains the translations of all of her writings. It also has everything I have compiled in my research. It has taken me all this time to narrow it down to Taiwan. I have been searching all over this island for many, many years, but I still cannot pinpoint where the cave is. I do not have enough anthropo-logical or archaeological knowledge to do that."

Georgia nods, apprehension dawning. "This is why you came searching for me?"

Charlie nods. "I want you to help me find the cave, where it all began."

She takes the book from his outstretched hand, noting its

worn covers and its dog-eared pages, feeling the bulky weight of its contents in her hand.

Within these pages are the secrets to eternity.

She is almost breathless at the thought. Her next words come out as a whisper, "Mark Lambert said he has an army of scientists who can study the elixir. He said they could synthesise it for the whole world."

Charlie purses his lips, exhaling a long sigh. Shaking his head, he says, "Georgia, do you really believe that is what he will do?"

"I'm not really sure." She shrugs. "But honestly? I don't think I ever gave it much thought, because I didn't believe the elixir actually existed."

"In my experience, wealthy and powerful men like him are usually more interested in what they can gain out of a discovery like this. Judging by the mercenaries he sent, it looks like Lambert is willing to do anything to get what he wants. I am not convinced that he intends to share the findings with anyone else. Even if he does, it would most likely come at a price to all those who desire it. And putting the elixir in the hands of a powerful few would be a very dangerous thing, Georgia.

"I know it is enticing, the idea of being able to save people from incurable diseases. It is a noble intention to have. But let me ask you this: do you really think eternal life would give people happiness? What befell Naaya's people is only a small taste of what would happen to the entire human race if you were to give the elixir to the world. It has been two and a half thousand years since Naaya first discovered the gift of eternity, but human consciousness as a whole has not yet evolved or matured enough to carry the responsibilities of immortality. If anything, it has probably regressed since."

Charlie pauses, silently pensive. When he speaks again, his voice is so quiet that Georgia has to strain to hear him. "It has worried me for some time now that we are rapidly coming to the end of our times. In all of my life, I have never seen the kind of destruction our people are now bringing to the world. Over-population and over-consumption coupled with our wasteful culture means our natural world cannot provide for our habits much longer. People have become emotionally distant from each other, and more people now suffer from depression, anxiety, or some form of mental illness. If the elixir is given to humanity now, the results will be catastrophic. The problems would not be solved, they would only be amplified. We would destroy each other, and the world, too."

There is a long moment of silence, and for a while Georgia contemplates on the truth of Charlie's words. Logically, she knows he is right. But the survival instinct in Georgia, and the mother within her who has experienced the death of her only child, repudiates his arguments. There is also a part of her, naïve as it may be, that believes in humanity's capacity for change. Sure, there are a lot of things wrong with the world they have created, but in spite of all of that, she is still hopeful.

Studying his profile, she finally says, "Can I ask you something?"

Turning, he smiles at her. "Of course. Anything."

"How have you done it, living all these years? How is it that you've managed to do what Naaya's people couldn't?"

Charlie takes a deep breath. "Well. It has not been without challenges, I can assure you. But I believe I have been given a gift, a precious opportunity that must not be squandered. In my lifetime, I have done my best to contribute to the human cause. And like I said before, I have tried to better myself through continued learning. I feel that I have lived a very enriching life."

At that moment, Georgia suddenly understands why Charlie is asking her to help him locate the cave. She frowns, looking up to meet his eyes. They seem to glow a dark aquamarine in the warm light.

"You want me to help you find the cave," she says, "because you want to see if Naaya is right. You want to see if taking the elixir again will reverse its effects. You want to stop living."

Charlie nods slowly, giving her a small smile. Suddenly he looks exhausted and worn, decades beyond the apparent age of his body.

"I feel it is time, Georgia."

42

"I DON'T UNDERSTAND. What happened to contributing to the human cause? What about helping us in a time when we need it the most?" Georgia asks, now visibly upset.

Charlie gives her a wry smile. "If you lived for as long as I have, Georgia, you would discover that despite everything you do, the world has a way of doing its own thing. The only thing you really have the power to change is yourself. The conditions of our society have gained a certain momentum. It is hurtling along a path that will end in devastating consequences. Or—who knows—it is also possible a drastic event may happen in time to turn things around. That certainly has happened before. One way or another, a dramatic change is imminent. But all of this, Georgia, is just the ebb and flow of life. In the bigger scheme of things, life goes on. The planet will go on, and the universe will certainly survive—with or without humans."

She shakes her head, unwilling to accept this. "How can you be so nonchalant about it all? We're talking about millions of years of evolution, and over seven thousand years of civilisation—"

He reaches over, putting a hand on hers, and he can

almost feel the exasperation seeping out of her. "I know, Georgia," he says. "It is difficult for you to understand my wish. But I have lived for two thousand, two hundred and seventy years. That is more than anyone can ever ask for, and to be frank, my soul has grown weary. An average human consciousness can only cope with eighty, ninety, and—at a stretch—maybe a century of life on earth. It is time for my soul to rest."

"But you have so much to teach. You have seen so much, learnt so much… how can we just throw all that away?" She trails off, looking defeated when he does not respond.

He gives her some time to process this, the tea growing lukewarm in their cups. After a few moments, he decides to raise the issue that has been plaguing his mind since their conversation at the Grand Hotel.

"You know, now that Lambert knows I am still alive, neither of us is safe. I have a feeling he will not give up until his scientists have a chance to study and experiment on me. I cannot allow that to happen. It is imperative that I protect the elixir.

"I have anticipated something like this would happen soon. With the internet, surveillance, and technologies of the modern world, it has becoming more and more difficult for me to cover my tracks, to remain untraceable. It was only a matter of time, and I fear I will not be able to keep this secret for much longer.

"Even if Lambert never finds us, there will still be other men—maybe even more dangerous ones—who will eventually come after me. But if I am able to reverse the effects, if I become mortal again, Lambert will have nothing left to study, and nothing to synthesise. That also puts *you* out of danger."

Georgia thinks this over, then shakes her head, looking unconvinced. "It just doesn't make any scientific sense. I can accept the possibility that there was something in that water which caused a radical change in the physiology of your body, and that because of this, your cells heal the way they do now. But how would drinking the water again reverse its effects?"

"That, I do not know, Georgia," he says. "All I know is Naaya was convinced of it. I am a man of medicine, and I have spent many years studying my own body to understand the how the elixir works. I know from comparing my blood with others that there has been a fundamental DNA change in me because of the elixir. It works almost like a virus, infecting the host and taking over cells to insert its genetic material into the host's genes. But there is a missing link to understanding this transformation, and the way to reverse it. I am hoping, that even if drinking the water again does not reverse its effects, at least I can study it, to—"

"To find an *antidote?*" Georgia finishes his sentence for him.

He shrugs. "Yes, I guess you can call it that."

"Why not just kill yourself?"

Charlie snickers. "Oh, I have thought about it, believe me. But as much as I tried, I still could not go through with it in the end. It may seem a minute distinction to you, but fundamentally there is a colossal difference between wishing to die a natural death, and committing suicide. The intentions are a world apart. And, like I said before, for someone like me, death only comes via very painful and violent means."

Charlie watches as Georgia opens her mouth to further argue a point, but instead she closes it again as she reconsiders everything. After a long time, with resigned acceptance, she finally says, "How do you need me to help you?"

He smiles. "You are one of the most brilliant archaeologists in the world, Georgia, and you know this island well. I have been following your work for a while now, and it is no surprise Lambert also chose you for this expedition. I was studying you, trying to gauge if I could trust you with this secret. Imagine my surprise when *you* started searching for *me*."

He gestures to his notebook. "I know every page of this book by heart, but I cannot seem to come up with anything new. I really need a fresh pair of eyes. *Your* eyes. Will you look it over for me?"

43

GEORGIA LIES on the king-size bed, feeling the silkiness of its luxurious sheets. Charlie has given the master bedroom to her and is sleeping in the smaller room down the hallway. The moon outside the window hangs low in the sky, telling her it is late—or, rather, getting close to early morning—yet sleep evades her.

She tosses and turns, unable to rest despite her exhaustion. Then, giving up altogether, she turns on the bedside light, eying Charlie's notebook on the table. Curiosity taking over, she reaches for it, unwinding the leather string around the volume. Flipping through the pages, she sees it is filled with notes, drawings, maps, and photographs. Charlie has obviously spent years studying these; everything is meticulously ordered and translated into modern text.

Georgia finds it fitting that the elixir was found in a cave. She remembers seeing a documentary recently about these unexplored, underground worlds, where whole ecological systems have evolved in isolation over millions of years. The lifeforms in these segregated microcosms are completely alien to ours on the surface of Earth, and even though humanity knows almost every part of our planet's surface, we have little understanding of what is within the depths of the oceans or hidden inside the earth. According to the film, it is estimated that at least ten million kilometres of caves still remain uncharted around the globe. Who knows what chemistry could brew in one of these unexplored realms?

As Georgia reads on, she feels herself transported to a world that existed on this very land, millennia ago.

44

520 BCE, Taiwan

HER FATHER CAME to wake her before daybreak.

"Naaya, sweetheart," he cajoled, knowing his child was a glutton for sleep. "I am sorry to do this, but our neighbour Nin is still sick. He had high fevers all night. I fear the worst."

Naaya blinked at him with sleepy eyes. "What can I do, Father?"

"I need you to gather some herbs for me. One of them is not easy to find, but it may be his last chance for survival." He listed the plants and Naaya nodded, committing them to memory. "Please hurry," her father added.

It was the beginning of the hot season, but the mornings were still quite cool, especially in the mountains. Dew gathered on the foliage of trees, and she drank from the leaves, the cool liquid waking her. She gathered her collecting basket, a digging stick, some food and water, and set off across the river before the sun appeared over the peaks.

Her father had given her a list of four things to collect. The first three were easily found and readily available this time of the year, and Naaya located them quickly near the banks of the river. The last, however, was an extremely rare mushroom that grew only deep in the mountains and involved an arduous climb which would take most of the day. She would not be able to return home until after the sun had moved more than halfway through the sky. So Naaya set a steady pace, first crossing the small creek that ran from the northern peaks, then climbing high enough along the northern face of the gorge to follow the river due west, heading deep into the mountains.

Father had shown her this path on her last birthday, and they'd traversed it a handful of times since, but this would be her first time making the outing on her own. Father had to be with Nin, to look after the poor boy. But Naaya also knew that this was his way of telling her that she was now a grown woman and no longer a child. She was pleased that her father finally trusted her to complete the task by herself.

She was desperately eager to prove to him that he was right.

It was with this motivation that she climbed over giant boulders and edged herself across treacherous cliffs, noting every tree and rock that Father had previously pointed out to her as markers along the path. She had a single-minded focus, and did not take the time to explore the forest as she usually would have done on trips such as this.

For Naaya loved the forest. She loved to explore all of the treasures that it offered. She relished taking her time to daydream while she wandered amongst the big, beautiful trees. But today was not a day for adventures or musings. She was so focused on the task at hand that she even forgot to sing.

Warming up quickly from the exertion, her body dripped with sweat as the sun ascended the sky. Before long, Naaya realised her water was running low. Fortunately, she had reached the small flatland where the mushrooms grew. It took her a little while to collect the amount her father needed. Then, mission accomplished, Naaya sat down to nibble on some food whilst contemplating whether to return home straight away, or to continue her westward path towards the second creek to refill her water bladder.

In the years to come, Naaya would often revisit this day,

mulling over every tiny, minuscule decision she had made. There were so many things that could have been done differently to change the course of her fate. She could have drunk less water, paced herself so that she still had enough for the trip home. Or she could have refilled her water bladder on her return journey instead, at the first creek that ran from the northern peaks. There were so many other options that could have been taken to avoid travelling further west.

But Naaya did none of these things. Instead, she chose to continue onwards, a decision which would ultimately culminate in the destruction of her people. She would regret making this decision until the day she died.

Perched on that rock, Naaya told herself it would not take long to get to the second creek. Besides, this brook ran from where the mountain god Zai resided, and her mother had always told her its waters were more nourishing. She reasoned that it would be helpful to bring some back for Nin, to aid his healing.

This was the rationale she had in her head that day, but deep down she knew she was just feeling hot and thirsty, craving some time in the cool stream before making her way back home.

On her westward path, as she neared the creek enough to hear its trickling waters, Naaya spotted a Panna tree several paces to her right. She stopped dead in her tracks. This was the second Panna tree she had ever seen, for they are even rarer than the mushrooms that she had just picked. Mother always spoke of their special leaves, for when pounded into a pulp they made a concoction for washing one's hair that rendered it beautifully shiny and strong, and as black as a moonless sky.

What happened next was the second dreadful decision she made that day, for she walked quickly towards the tree, intending to collect some leaves both for herself and for her mother. This was the very last thing she remembered of that day.

The next thing she knew, she was awakening from a slumber of unknown duration, finding herself on her back, blinking at the total darkness that surrounded her. She panicked, wondering if she had

gone blind, reaching her hand out before her eyes. The sudden move-
ment was what brought on the searing pain.

Oh, the pain. It was a total, all-encompassing sensation that
engulfed her entire being. She cried out, tears streaming down her
face, and this triggered a coughing fit that had her choking on the
liquid which suddenly filled her throat. She convulsed, rolling to her
side to expel the warm fluid. It was violent and agonising, and she
thought it would never end. But slowly, the spasms subsided, and
she rolled her tongue in the coppery taste of blood in her mouth.

Echoes of her outburst reverberated around her. Naaya realised
then that she was in a cave. She searched the depths of her mind to
remember how she had gotten there. But at that moment, lying on
her side with blood trickling from her lips, the very last thing she
could recollect was her father coming to wake her, asking her to
gather herbs for him. Had she been mauled by a bear in the forest
and dragged into this cave? She did not think bears did such things.

It was stifling and humid, and her lips were parched, her throat
burning with thirst. She could smell the tinny, sharp odour of fresh
blood and she wondered where else she was bleeding from. Slowly,
gently, she pushed herself up into a seated position, gasping with
pain, and she tried to stand up.

She could not feel her legs. She could not command them to
move.

Tears streaming down her face, Naaya lay back down, quietly
weeping. She cried over her pain. She wept over her hopeless
predicament. She grieved for the legs that no longer had any sensa-
tions. But mostly, she sobbed over her loneliness. Naaya knew she
was to die here, alone.

Time passed. Slowly, a faint glimmer of light glowed above her,
growing steadily brighter. Naaya thought that she had died, that
this was the light all souls saw at the moment of death. But instead
of blissful freedom, all she felt was the same agony. It was some time
later that she realised the light was the silvery glow of the moon
through a hole high above her. She decided it must be the hole she
had fallen through.

As Naaya lay there, she began to register the slow dripping of water, and the thirst in her throat suddenly became overwhelming.

Drip. Drip. Drip.

A coughing fit seized her again, and the harsh taste of new blood made her gag. Her stomach contracted, but all she threw up was bile and more blood.

Drip. Drip. Drip.

The echo of the dripping sound haunted her. She was overcome with thirst, with the desire to wash out the vile mixture of vomit and gore that was swirling around her mouth. Finally, grunting with effort and wincing in agony, she turned and used her arms to crawl towards the sound of water.

Drip. Drip. Drip.

She did not have to go far. After a few paces, her hands felt the cool water before her, and she cupped the liquid with her hands. Naaya drank slowly, and for as long as her stomach would tolerate it.

Then she laid her head down by the water and let the deep darkness engulf her, knowing she would never wake again.

45

GEORGIA WAKES WITH A START, the sound of her rapid breath rasping in the silence. Remnants of her dreams linger, their tendrils curling around her mind, unwilling to let go. Sleep, when it finally came, took her to a dark place where she was trapped and scared, fearful of being captured by faceless men.

She blinks a few times, chasing away the slumber. It takes a couple of seconds to recognise her surroundings and remember how she got here. The house is quiet, and the only sounds she hears are the birdsongs outside.

Once dressed, she heads downstairs, discovering from the wall clock that it is now past noon, and that she is alone in the house. Charlie has left a note on the kitchen island, advising that he has gone into town for groceries. He has left the coffeemaker on, the aroma of the fresh brew making Georgia's mouth water.

Good man.

Strong coffee is exactly what Georgia needs. She's been up all night, going through the drawings and writings in Charlie's notebook. Sipping the hot drink, she eyes the vintage house phone on the kitchen counter, next to the fifties-style fridge.

The owner of the house has retro tastes. She smiles as she picks up the phone receiver, dialling a number she knows well, waiting patiently between every number as the rotary dial rotates back to its original position each time. After a brief pause, it begins to ring.

"Hello?"

"Sarah, it's me."

"Jesus, Georgia, you had me worried half to death! Where are you? Why haven't you picked up your phone?"

"It's a long story," she says. "Look, I can't talk long, I just wanted you to know I'm safe. Can you also call Amah and Ethan to let them know that? Tell them I'll call when I get a chance."

"O-kay…" Sarah's voice is full of suspicion, but she doesn't question Georgia the way she normally would. Instead, she says, "Georgia, you need to know something."

Georgia is quiet as she listens to Sarah speak with urgency, uneasiness curling in the seat of her belly. She hears a car pull up to the house and turns, seeing through the window that Charlie has returned.

"No, don't do that," she says quickly in response to Sarah's question. "Hey, I gotta go now. I'll call again later and explain everything, okay?"

"Okay. Be careful—"

Georgia hangs up before she has a chance to hear the rest of her assistant's sentence.

***

Sydney

SARAH WU IS NO FOOL, and she certainly doesn't appreciate being treated as one.

Fifty-eight years of age and a mother of three, she has long ago developed a strong nose for bullshit. It is, therefore, extremely rare for her to be hoodwinked.

And that's exactly what's happened, judging by what she found out today. It had her huffing with anger all day, throwing her weight around the university campus like a woman possessed. Even the other professors in the department have avoided her, sensing trouble whenever she neared.

That Lambert has some balls on him, fucking with Georgia like that.

And whoever messes with Georgia is messing with her. Sarah clenches her jaw. Oh yes, she takes it all very personally. She was about to pick up the phone and tell the bastard exactly that, when she received the phone call from Georgia. Sarah has no idea where the girl is, and she must admit that this turn of events has her worried.

She exits the building of the Department of Archaeology, carrying her bag over her shoulder as she walks briskly towards the car park. It's late, and there are no other souls around as she walks towards her car. Sarah has been working late all month, corresponding with China and managing the dig on Georgia's behalf to the best of her abilities. She's been anxious for Georgia's return for a while now—handling both of their jobs at the same time is hardly sustainable, and that Professor Chang from Peking University is getting mighty bossy. Plus, the paperwork is starting to pile up.

She reaches her car and fumbles in her bag, trawling through various documents and miscellaneous items for the key.

Where is the damn thing?

That's when Sarah hears the footsteps behind her.

The hairs stand up on the back of her neck, and she turns to see who is approaching. But the movement is interrupted as a hand closes over her face. She struggles, trying to break free, yet strong arms have wrapped around her, holding her still. She shrieks as she feels a sharp prick in the side of her neck, her scream muffled by the attacker's hand.

"Shhh…" a voice says.

That is the last thing Sarah hears before her mind slips into darkness.

46

GEORGIA SPENDS the rest of day sifting through the contents of the notebook with Charlie. They sit in the living room, poring over the old photographs of Naaya's drawings and writings on barks and scrolls. According to Charlie, most of the originals have crumbled to dust by now, despite the care he has taken with their conservation. The ones he could not save in time to be photographed, he replicated by hand.

Naaya was a talented artist, sketching out her story and journey in exquisite detail. It is clear from these records that her home was somewhere in the mountains. But that information means next to nothing in Taiwan, because almost two-thirds of the island is rugged, forest-covered, mountain terrain. What's even more discouraging is the fact that there are very few publicly known natural caves here. The instability of the region means many caves are inaccessible or dangerous, and the local authorities tend to discourage tourists from exploring them. Possessing more than two hundred peaks over three thousand metres, Taiwan lies along the convergent boundary between the Philippine Oceanic Plate and the Eurasian Continental Plate. As a result, there are frequent earthquakes, and a few dormant and possibly active volcanoes in the area. Furthermore, every year the island is visited by multiple typhoons of varying strengths, and the strong winds and rainfall usually cause widespread destruction as well as catastrophic landslides, especially down south and on the east coast.

Georgia can understand why Charlie hasn't been able to locate the cave on his own. This is not going to be an easy task at all.

To make matters worse, she hasn't been able to focus on the task at hand. Her phone call with Sarah earlier today has left her perturbed and distracted. Her mind keeps returning to Sarah's warning.

Be careful —

"Are you okay, Georgia?" Charlie asks now, as if reading her mind.

"Yeah." She forces a smile. "Why do you ask?"

"You keep looking out the window as if you are expecting someone to show up. And you look worried. Is everything alright?"

She shakes her head. "I spoke with my assistant at the university earlier today."

Charlie frowns, a rare expression on his usually tranquil features. "Trouble at home?"

She chews on her lower lip. "Remember when I told you about how I came to accept Lambert's assignment?"

Charlie nods, thinking. "You were having trouble securing funding for your excavation project in China. Then his assistant called and invited you to dinner at Lambert Manor."

"Sarah's brother, David, knows one of the funding board members for our dig in China," she tells him. "The board member told David that Lambert did everything he could to block our funding."

Charlie leans back on the sofa, his face impassive and calm.

When he doesn't say anything in response, Georgia asks, "Why would he do something like that?"

"I think you already know the answer to that question," Charlie replies quietly, meeting her gaze.

Indeed she does, but she has been unwilling to contemplate it all day. Now, she finally voices her suspicions. "Because he knew that, being the scientist that I am, I would have refused to take on the project. I would have dismissed it as the fantasy of a narcissist who's just afraid of the thought of his own mortality. I would've thought he was wasting my time. Lambert needed me desperate enough to go to him and accept the job."

Charlie nods in agreement. "It was just his luck that the government had also cut funding to your entire university at the same time, so you were not only trying to save just your project, but your job too."

He continues as Georgia remains silent. "I know men like Lambert. He would have done his research before meeting you, and someone of his resources could find out things you would not even know about yourself. He would have made sure he knew your favourite foods, your financial situation, what you ate for breakfast, even your favourite TV shows—everything to prepare himself so that when you met, he could create the most affable and agreeable atmosphere possible, one in which you would be likely to accept to his offer."

Georgia thinks back to the night at the Lambert Manor. It all seemed delightfully coincidental at the time: the sumptuous meal at which every dish was what she loved, the expensive Bordeaux superbly matched to her taste in wine, the engrossing subject matters they discussed over dinner, the art collection on display, and even Lambert's comments about her favourite artist, O'Keeffe. Everything that night was somehow perfectly aligned to her own interests and tastes. She wonders now if it was all a matter of careful planning, if

Lambert had indeed set the stage so she would regard him more favourably than she did initially.

Georgia puts her head in her hands, absorbing the implications of it all.

What if Charlie is right? What if she has been manipulated?

The thought fills her with a raging indignation, which makes her all the more determined to make sure Lambert doesn't get what he wants. She looks out the window, seeing the darkening sky. The sun has now set, and the roaring sound of cicadas in the forest has returned. Rising from the couch, she makes her way into the kitchen.

"Georgia?" Charlie asks, puzzled at her abrupt departure.

"I'm just getting some more coffee," she calls over her shoulder. "I'm going to need a clear head to figure out where Naaya was from."

IT TAKES her almost a week to make sense of all the information. She makes use of the huge dining table, piecing together every clue over its expansive surface.

Naaya's people lived close to the sea; they were confident seafarers who possessed impressive navigational skills. Although they were skilled at farming, hunting and fishing remained an important part of their food source. All of these details are consistent with the practices of the Neolithic peoples of Taiwan, who were trading with South East Asia as early as four thousand years ago, and who were also in frequent contact with other tribes in China.

According to Naaya's writings, strong storms hit the coast every year during the hot season, destroying their crops and homes. Eventually, they moved to a plain in the mountains, sheltered by the surrounding peaks. They stayed close to the ocean, though, the shore only a morning's hike away.

Naaya's writings are full of regret and longing. They describe an admirable people with a kind and honourable nature who had flourished on this plateau and were developing into a strong and powerful tribe before their abrupt end. Immersed in the power of Naaya's words, Georgia feels a growing sadness as she witnesses the catastrophic decimation of a culture.

47

450 BCE, Taiwan

THE SCREAMS WERE ECHOING through the gorge.

Naaya stumbled down the hill, trying to put as much distance between her and the village as she could.

They had all gone mad. All of them.

She had been worrying over the way things had been in her village for a long time now, but she hadn't expected it would come to this.

It had started out innocently enough: a simple contest between two brothers, Raha and Ren. They were two of the best hunters in the region, and also the most beloved young men in the village. Both of them possessed the height and build of formidable warriors, the good looks of their late father, and the charm of their endearing mother. Somehow, during one of their hunts a few months ago, they had decided it would be more fun to compete against each other over how much prey they could kill.

Naaya's people had never hunted this way. To them, daily tasks were a matter of team effort, where each member played a valuable role in achieving the end goal. To compete in hunting, or indeed, in anything, was a completely radical thought.

It was fun for Raha and Ren at the beginning. It brought an exhilaratingly novel experience to a chore that had become dull and repetitive ever since the end of death for their people. For now that the act of hunting itself posed no more danger to the hunters, where was the thrill in it all?

But the contest became more and more heated over time, with Ren claiming that Raha had cheated, and Raha asserting that Ren had an unfair advantage because of his height. A once amicable brotherhood descended into one of rivalry and jealousy. Worse still, the toxicity of this relationship emanated and spread its influence around the village.

The villagers took sides, each with their own reasons for which brother they loved best. They would enter long arguments about who was the best hunter, and who had not played the game fairly. It was subtle, but it created a divide amongst the people.

Then, a few days ago, the bickering between the brothers had spiralled into physical violence. To this day, Naaya was still not sure how the whole thing had started, but when she arrived at the scene, she saw Raha lunge at Ren, splitting his head open with a rock. Instantly, there was blood everywhere.

And that was how it began.

The villagers stepped in to break up the fight, but all the tugging and wrestling quickly escalated into a massive brawl. Once the violence started, it was like a wildfire that could not be contained. The insane rage coursed through everyone present, and they attacked each other as if they were possessed.

This sort of eruption of fury had happened from time to time over the past few years, each incident with its own obscurely mundane and stupid reasons. But the previous occurrences had never been on this scale, and they had always died down quickly, with the parties involved all retreating to their own huts, waiting for their wounds to repair themselves. At the end of the day, it had been mostly harmless, for everyone had healed from their injuries within a matter of minutes, or hours.

On this day, however, Raha took a large knife and plunged it into Ren's heart, stabbing him repeatedly. Raha was roaring like a wild, savage animal: it was as if he'd been taken over by a fearsome demon. He pierced Ren's chest over and over again until it was a pulpy mess. Then, reaching his hand into the open cavity, he ripped out the heart and tossed the organ away.

The villagers stopped their brawling. They watched as Ren's mutilated organ rolled away from his body, the flesh still warm and steaming in the cold mountain air. Ren's body lay limp and lifeless, a half-formed scream frozen on his open lips.

The reek of blood and terror and ripe faeces filled the air.

Ren's wife howled in a fit of passion that shook the earth, and ran to attack Raha, who struck her in the head with such force it sent her flying backwards. Then it was a mad blur of everyone either seeking retribution or defending their loved ones, all furiously battling against each other.

That was two days ago, and the fighting had not stopped. The mass brawl turned into open war between the divided groups; now, as numbers dwindled and the dead accumulated, it was survival of the strongest.

Naaya, sprinted through the woods, searching frantically for somewhere to hide. That had been the only way she had survived the last few days: hiding. She did not even know who was fighting on which side anymore. It seemed as if an acrid fog of pure evil had settled over the village and permeated the hearts of her people, turning them into barbaric savages that she did not recognise.

She spotted a crack between two large boulders to her right, and slipped into the small, dark space, hoping desperately that it would be wide enough to take her in, praying that it would conceal her. It was shallow and narrow, with not even space enough for her to sit. But she wedged herself in the deepest part of the crack, and there she waited.

Her head was spinning. She was panting from exertion.

Her heart almost jumped out of her chest when a shadow flashed past the opening. She clasped her hand over her mouth to stop a cry from giving her away. Then, moments later, another figure flew by in pursuit of the first, uttering a blood curdling scream.

Naaya kept her hand tight over her mouth. She squeezed her eyes shut as tears streamed down her face.

This was all her fault.

48

NAAYA'S graphic account of her people's descent into madness affects Georgia deeply, and she finds herself torn between the promise of alleviating the world's physical suffering, and the dangerous consequences that could arise from finding the elixir. Doubt seeps into her heart as she continues her search, and she does her best to push it aside; yet it lingers, lodged in the back of her mind.

Through the descriptions in the notebook, she decides that Naaya's people must have lived somewhere on the east coast of Taiwan: they fit the weather patterns, the landscape, and the proximity of the mountain range to the ocean. What's more, the tribe's customs and their ways of life have a strong resemblance to those of the Chi-lin Culture. Georgia studied the Chi-lins when she worked as a consultant in Taiwan a few years ago, as part of her extensive research into the prehistoric peoples of the island.

"The Chi-lins were a Neolithic race that lived along the east coast of Taiwan," she explains to Charlie. They are sitting in the kitchen, looking over the information that Georgia has carefully mapped across the dining table over the past week. "Recently, evidence of their existence has been found in one of the Bashian Caves, an important archaeological site in Hualien County. Even though these seaside caves are better known for the relics found concerning the earlier Paleolithic culture of Changping, with the discovery of Chi-lin remains, it's now clear that more than one group of people have inhabited the caves over the millennia."

"Bashian?" Charlie repeats the word in Chinese. "As in the Eight Immortals?"

"Yeah. The Eight Immortals Caves." She looks at Charlie pointedly.

"The Eight Immortals of Penglai Mountain, which Emperor Qin was so desperately looking for," Charlie muses.

She nods. "Here's another interesting fact for you. Taiwan lies along the boundary between two tectonic plates, and four million years ago, these two plates collided, causing what's called the *Penglai Orogeny*. The Penglai Orogeny was responsible for forming not only the mountain ranges of the east coast region, but also the whole of Taiwan itself. Northward, it also formed the Ryukyu chain of volcanic islands, and southward, the Luzon Volcanic Arc to the Philippines."

"Penglai Orogeny. Penglai Mountain," Charlie mutters.

"Exactly. Now, these may just be coincidental names, but in my experience, sites are rarely named at random. Their names are usually chosen for historical reasons, because of stories and legends that have been passed down over time." Georgia pauses, then continues, "I've been to Bashian Caves once, a few years ago. At the time, I'd thought the caves were named because of the constant, thick ocean mist drifting around the area. The scenery resembles the stories and legends of what the deities saw when they crossed the ocean to come to Penglai Mountain."

Charlie furrows his brow. "But they are not underground caves in a forest," he points out.

"No," she replies. "Look, I'm not saying Bashian Caves is the place we're looking for. All I'm saying is that the region seems to fit everything Naaya described: the people who existed in the area, the climate, and the landscape." Georgia stretches out her back; she has been leaning over the dining table for hours now.

"In Naaya's writings," she continues, "It's clear her people moved around many times, splitting into different groups as they went, until they settled on a mountain plateau that was sheltered from the vicious typhoons that hit the east coast every year."

She points to a particular drawing in the notebook. "This particular plateau was surrounded by mountain peaks. It was two-tiered, and perfectly suited to their needs: they grew different crops on each tier, creating unique microcosms for rudimentary agricultural experimentation." She flips to a page bookmarked with a piece of paper. "In this section, Naaya talks about how her father was starting to attempt growing his own herbs instead of gathering them in the forest all the time."

Charlie nods as he absorbs the information, quietly urging her to go on.

"And the other reason why I really like this Chi-lin theory," Georgia explains, "is that the Chi-lin people were an initially hunter-gatherer culture that eventually became knowledgeable in sedentism and farming. They reached a considerable degree of cultural complexity, and evidence suggests that they had a short-lived population explosion, before disappearing altogether around four hundred BCE. Scientists have been speculating that the cause was climate change or destruction by a competing tribe, but there is still no conclusive evidence for either of those theories. To this day, the disappearance of the Chi-lin people remains a mystery."

"Four hundred BCE…" murmurs Charlie. "That was around the time Naaya's people destroyed themselves."

"Yeah." She nods.

"And the population explosion just before their disappearance could have been caused by the elixir," he speculates.

"Precisely."

Charlie smiles, nodding as pieces of the puzzle fall into place. "I am impressed, Georgia."

She blushes at the compliment. Her stomach growls loudly in response.

Charlie laughs, pushing his chair back to stand up. "Let me fix you something to eat, it seems like you are making plenty of progress without my help anyway."

She smiles, watching him walk over to the fridge. Turning her attention back to the notebook, she flips to an entry where Naaya recounts the day she left her village. Naaya had made a detailed drawing of her home before she left. There were at least twenty huts dotted across the wide plains, with majestic mountains looming in the background. It would have been a beautiful place to live.

Georgia examines the drawing closely, furrowing her brow. As she said to Charlie, she is pretty sure that they lived on the east coast.

But *where*, exactly?

49

WHEN SARAH FINALLY REGAINS CONSCIOUSNESS, her body feels like a rubbery mess that doesn't belong to her. Her mind is foggy and confused, her vision blurred. She groans at the stabbing pain in her head.

As her mind slowly clears, Sarah realises she's sitting in a chair with both wrists and ankles bound to its frame. Suddenly, memories of her last waking moments resurface: the abandoned car park after a long day at work, someone grabbing her from behind, and the sharp jab in the neck before she lost consciousness.

She blinks a few times and looks around as her eyes regain focus, seeing that she's in a basement. It's dimly lit, windowless, and mostly empty, and every sound she makes echoes off the bare concrete floor and walls. Two bare bulbs scarcely illuminate the large space, and there's a set of stairs to her rear. Underneath the stairs, there's a sink and a toilet without a lid or a seat, its ceramic surface glistening white in the shadows.

Creepy.

There's a desk and chair in the far corner in front of her, and above the desk, photographs and words fill the entire concrete wall. Whoever stuck them on there seems to be mapping something out, neatly and meticulously. Sarah squints as she looks harder at the photos and words from this distance. She inhales sharply when she spots something familiar.

What the —

The sound of the door being unlocked startles her, and she turns to see a man walking down the stairs. Somewhere in his late twenties, he is short and stocky, his head cleanly shaven, his chin covered by a goatee. Pigeon-chested and built like a bull, the man is dressed in black, tactical gear that makes her think of the Special Forces.

He smiles at her on approach, but the expression does not reach his eyes.

"Who the fuck are you? What the *fuck* is this?" she demands, tugging at her restraints.

The man chuckles at her outburst. She glares at him with all the hate in her body.

"This," the stranger replies in a surprisingly soft voice, "is just a little chat we're going to have."

He saunters over to the desk, opens a drawer, takes out a few items, and fiddles with them for a while, his back turned to her. Then, he drags the chair across the room, the scrape of its metal legs wreaking havoc on her skull, before sitting down in front of her. Sarah eyes the syringe in his hand and the clear liquid inside it, and fear creeps over her.

"What the hell is that?" She jerks as he rolls up her sleeve.

He chuckles again like it's all a big joke. "This is sodium pentothal," he says, placing his big paw on her shoulder to hold her still.

She flinches at the sharp jab on her arm.

"Easy, Sarah, it's just something to relax you a little. Like I said, we're only going to have a chat. And don't worry: you probably won't remember a thing."

"Sodium pentothal," she repeats, feeling dread as she watches him push the liquid into her arm. "Truth serum?"

"Someone knows her chemistry." He looks impressed.

"I thought it doesn't work," she says, thinking of the many crime novels she has read.

"Ah, it works alright." He smiles with pride. "This version is a special little cocktail I came up with myself, perfected over the years. It takes a skilled interrogator, knowing the exact dosage to administer. You need to word the questions in the right way, of course, and in the correct sequence. I've had plenty of experience in that, trust me." He gives a casual shrug. "Sometimes it may take a few goes for the more resilient ones, but I always get my answers."

"I'm not telling you shit," Sarah spits out, despite the sudden dryness in her mouth. At this close distance, she can see a long scar running down the side of his face, partially concealed by his goatee. She wonders how he got such an ugly wound. She'd like to give him one herself.

The stranger just sits before her, smiling like he's enjoying himself. He scratches his goatee playfully, then gestures to the wall of photographs behind him. "You know, Sarah, I know everything about Georgia. I've been keeping an eye on her for a while. In fact, I probably know her better than you."

"What do you want with her?" She stares at him suspiciously, already starting to feel disoriented. Her brain feels like it's swimming in a pool of grog.

The man rubs his bare scalp. He leans towards her, fixing her with his dark eyes. What he says next comes in a whisper, and Sarah feels an involuntary chill run up her spine.

"There are people after her, Sarah. Don't you know she's in danger?"

50

Sitting at the dining table, Georgia rubs her temples with her fingers in an attempt to dispel the oncoming headache. A glance at the kitchen wall clock tells her that she's been studying Naaya's writings for at least three hours. It's now close to midnight, and she's getting nowhere.

Several days have passed, and she's no closer to pinpointing where Naaya's tribe lived. All of the entries are emotional accounts at best, and it's difficult to separate helpful facts from story to assist with the search. Perhaps she is far too engrossed in the details to see the bigger picture, and some distance is required.

Huffing a long breath, Georgia leans forward to rest her cheek against the smooth table surface as exhaustion overcomes her. She blinks slowly a few times, the drowsiness enveloping her like a warm blanket. The clock on the wall ticks on, strangely hypnotic.

Just as she's about to close her eyes, her vision focuses on the edge of the photograph next to her face. Frowning, she lifts her head, all the while keeping her gaze fixed on the object that has caught her attention. Her hand reaches straight for the magnifying glass, enlarging the peculiar design at the bottom corner of the image.

Georgia examines the rest of the photograph: it is of a bark drawing, depicting an annual hunting ritual of Naaya's tribe. Groups of men are returning to the village with game slung over their shoulders as women and children congregate around a big bonfire, singing and dancing.

She rummages through the other prints, studying them one by one. Several minutes later, she has compiled a collection of photographs depicting other symbols of similar nature, all doodled on the corners or edges of Naaya's drawings and writings. Georgia's eyes widen at the different shapes of circular, rectangular, and irregular designs, wondering how she missed them in the first place.

Her chair scrapes against the grey slate floor as she pushes it back to stand, and walking briskly into the living room, she finds Charlie on the sofa, his legs and hands crossed in a meditative pose.

"Charlie?"

He opens his eyes, his dark green gaze bright in the dim light.

"Do you know what this is?" Georgia approaches him with the first print she came across, pointing at the strange symbol on the bottom corner.

"Ah." He smiles as he looks at the drawing. "I asked Naaya about these once."

"And?" she urges. "What did she say?"

"She told me about a boy," Charlie says, smiling at the memory. "Someone from a neighbouring tribe that she was in love with. He was a jade craftsman's son, and these are some of the designs she helped him with, ritualistic and jewelery pieces that he then made with his father."

Her breath catches in her throat as her mind works over the facts.

"What is it?" Charlie cocks his head to the side.

"What happened to the boy?"

He shakes his head. "Naaya never told me. She did not want to talk about it. I have a suspicion that he was killed during the massacre, and it most likely compounded her sense of guilt." He pauses. "Why?"

Georgia sits on the sofa beside him, spreading out the other photographs over the coffee table, each with a strange symbol embedded in an obscure corner of the bark or scroll.

"These designs," she begins, "they remind me of the jade relics that were discovered at the Peinan archaeological site in Taitung on the east coast. The remains were stumbled upon when the government was building Taitung railway station in 1980."

Charlie lifts his brows, but says nothing as he waits for her to continue.

"The Peinan culture was actually quite similar to the neighbouring Chi-lin culture, coexisting in Taiwan at the same time around two, three thousand years ago. At the time, jade was used abundantly for accessories, daily utensils, and tools throughout Taiwan. Then, two thousand years ago,

Taiwan entered the Iron Age. This, combined with the growing scarcity of the raw material, meant that jade was no longer used."

"So these jade items could only have been made during that period," Charlie surmises.

"Yes!" Georgia nods enthusiastically. She points at the first drawing. "You see this particular design? It's a shape of two people standing side-by-side, with an animal above their heads. This shape has been made into one of the most iconic prehistoric jade objects in Taiwan—it has been found at different archaeological sites all over the island."

Charlie leans in, scrutinising the drawing with the magnifying glass Georgia offers to him. "What animal is it?"

"The popular belief is that it's the Formosan Clouded Leopard, which is now extinct," replies Georgia. "It's fitting, really. Naaya drew this design on the painting she made of her tribe's hunting festival."

"Okay," Charlie says, leaning back on the couch. "So what does this all mean?"

She sits up, excitement bubbling through her. "See, this is where it gets interesting. You mentioned the boy Naaya was in love with was from a neighbouring tribe, and that he was the son of a jade craftsman. Now, these jade pieces were mainly created around the Pinglin, Chungkuang, and Laoshan Archaeological sites, all within a ten-kilometre radius of each other in Hualien County. They're where jade was mined in abundance."

Charlie's brows shoot up. "You think that Naaya's tribe must be from near there."

"Exactly." She smiles. "Naaya and the boy's tribe must have lived within walking distance of each other. So based on the location of those three sites, I can narrow down our area of search through triangulation."

Charlie smiles broadens. "Brilliant."

Elated with the breakthrough, Georgia gathers the photographs to return to the dining table, all hints of her previous drowsiness now gone. She knows that with this finding in mind, she will be able to pick up something new as she reviews the information before her.

It's going to be a long night.

51

ALL WAS LOST.

Naaya sat down on a rock beside the river, her head in her hands as she wept.

It was difficult to contemplate that she was the last of her people, a thriving tribe that she had helped to destroy. She had spent the last of their days hidden until all was quiet. When hunger finally forced her to leave her refuge, she had crept out of the hole, fearful of what she would encounter.

But deep down, she had known exactly what she would find.

Dismembered bodies had been strewn through the woods, paving a macabre path back to the village. She had walked slowly, full of trepidation and grief, tears streaming down her face as she went. She could hear and smell the aftermath of her tribe's ruination before she reached the plateau: the sharp, sickly reek of rotting flesh and the dense black cloud of buzzing flies.

Everyone was dead.

It was certain that they had incurred the wrath of the mountain god Zai, for it must have been He who brought this monstrous curse upon them. Naaya had seen His grotesque features in the face of

Raha as he plunged the knife into his brother's chest. This, Naaya was convinced, was Zai's punishment for her stumbling into His secret cave.

Naaya walked through the village, sobbing with distress, finding no other survivors. The nauseating stench made her heave what little was left in her empty stomach. She halted in her tracks when she saw a sounder of wild boars in the distance, snorting and gnawing on some indistinguishable body parts. Her breath shallow, Naaya tried to backtrack before the pack became aware of her presence, but the largest amongst them looked up suddenly, its beady eyes zeroing in on her. She froze, staring at the animal's long, menacing tusks, her heart drumming hard in her chest. She was ready to bolt if it decided to run at her. But the beast only gazed at her briefly as it remained in the same spot, then it opened its jaws to give a languid yawn before returning to its feast.

Naaya spent the following days gathering what she could of the dead. Recalling her own mother's funeral, she tied the bodies to rafts. She placed bouquets of flowers all around the bodies and sent them downstream as she sang a special song. Father had told her before that this was the way they sent the dead to the afterlife, where they would travel down the meandering river and then out into the ocean as they are met by the gods.

Now, as she sat by the river, she looked at the boat beside her. This final boat was her own. She had loaded the last of her supplies a while ago, and yet, she was still reluctant to climb in. Instead, she stood and climbed up the bank of the river, heading back towards the village. Arriving at her family's hut, she sat down and made a final drawing of her home on a piece of bark. She detailed the mountains surrounding the plateau, the huts that populated it, and the forest beyond.

Then, she slowly walked back to the river and climbed into the boat. It was still early morning, and the bird songs accompanied her as she pushed the boat away from the bank, letting it drift downstream. Naaya knew she would reach the sea before the sun was overhead. Gazing at the glistening white rocks that lined the gorge, and the beautiful river that was eternally turquoise-blue, she committed all of these details to her memory, storing them away forever.

"Goodbye, forest, mountains, river," she whispered under her breath. "Goodbye, home."

GEORGIA GASPS, a rush of adrenaline washing over her. Her eyes traverse a particular line in the notebook again and again.

> *...the glistening white rocks that lined the gorge, and the beautiful river that was eternally turquoise-blue...*

She stands and walks into the lounge room, her eyes searching over the bookcases for a particular volume she spotted previously. When she finds it, she picks it from the shelf, tracing her finger over the gold embossed title on the cover.

Atlas.

Georgia quickly searches through the index at the back, finds what she's looking for, and flips to the corresponding page. Her eyes roam over the map, the breath catching in her throat when she locates her goal.

"Charlie!" she calls.

"What is it?" He pokes his head out of the kitchen, puzzled.

Georgia waves the atlas in the air, her words coming out fast. "I think I've got it! I know where Naaya's people lived."

52

When Sarah wakes again, she finds herself lying on a bare mattress, a new addition to the basement that has become her prison. Her wrists are bound behind her, the rough rope digging into soft skin with every movement. It's obvious she's been in this position for a long time, because her shoulders and arms are absolutely killing her.

Sitting up, Sarah moves around to get some blood back into her limbs. She blinks a few times to shake off the lingering grogginess from the drug the kidnapper has been using on her. Having been in and out of consciousness through it all, there's no telling how long she's been down here. It might have only been a day, it could have been much longer. The man has returned at least three times now, repeating the same interrogation process over and over again.

This is getting old.

Sarah can never remember anything afterwards. She's hoping, though, that the fact he keeps coming back means he's getting nothing useful.

She rises to her knees to stand, exercising muscles that have not been used for a while. Walking around the dimly lit basement, she searches for something—*anything*—to get her out of these ropes. Since the space is pretty much empty, the only thing to be examined is the desk at the far corner. Hoping her kidnapper has left something sharp behind, she bends at the knees and twists at an awkward angle to pull the drawers open with her bound hands, one by one. To her chagrin, she finds them all empty.

She heaves a sigh of frustration, looking at the wall above the desk and the photographs and writings plastered all over it. What's the man mapping here, and what's he trying to figure out? There are countless pictures and names, some clustered in groups, others just floating on their own.

Without a hint of context, Sarah has no idea how these people relate to each other. She doesn't recognise any of the faces, except for the one at the very top.

Georgia.

53

"You think that Naaya's people were from the Taroko area?" Charlie asks as she walks swiftly back to the dining table with the atlas.

She nods enthusiastically, grinning like a little girl. "It all fits perfectly!" she exclaims, pointing at the notebook. "All of Naaya's drawings, her descriptions... it all fits."

Taroko National Park is the famed region around Taroko Gorge, a popular tourist destination in Hualien County. The park spans more than ninety-two thousand hectares in the northern section of the Central Mountain Range, where the peaks rise above three thousand metres. Taroko Gorge, also known as 'The Marble Gorge', is an eighteen kilometre marble-walled canyon, a true natural wonder of the world. When Georgia was little, her family travelled there a few times on holidays. Georgia remembers walking along the beautiful gorge, hand-in-hand with Amah, listening to her explanations of how the glistening white marble cliffs were carved out by the river over hundreds of thousands of years. Amah also explained that the calcium deposits from this erosion made the water a startling turquoise blue.

The unique geography of Taroko was formed as a result of

the Penglai Orogeny, where the two tectonic plates collided, pushing thick layers of limestone rock from the marine depths to form lofty peaks, and the immense tectonic forces produced high pressures and temperatures to metamorphose these limestone rocks, turning them into marble. Before quarrying was banned, Hualien County was one of the biggest producers of marble in the world. For this reason, it was dubbed the 'City of Marble', a name it lives up to by the copious use of the material in many public buildings, and even its sidewalks and bridges.

"Here." Georgia points to a drawing in the notebook, showing an expansive, two-tiered plain surrounded by mountains. "This is the last drawing Naaya made of her village. The terrain is the kind of dramatic landscape that's typical of the Taroko area. She also described how her memories of home are always filled with the shimmering light glistening off the white rocks in the gorge, the sound of water flowing around the giant boulders, and the turquoise blue water of the river."

"Just like Taroko Gorge," Charlie murmurs, raising his brows. He hovers over the dining table, looking at the drawing.

"Yes!" She flips to another page. "Here, it talks about her last happy memory with her father, where they walked together from the village to the shore to collect shells for medicine. She described her journey as they headed east, following the river, all the way to the ocean."

She slides the atlas before them, tracing her finger over the map of Hualien County. "Look," she says. "The Liwu River is the main Taroko river that originates from the high mountains along the central Taiwan alpine ranges. It flows eastward through the marble ravine, directly into the Pacific Ocean. Now, Naaya wrote that it took them only half the morning to reach the shore on foot. Judging from the terrain of the area, they would have been able to walk about…" She does a quick mental calculation. "...ten kilometres within those hours."

She grabs a pencil and plots out the route, measuring the distance from the beach along the river.

"That would put their village roughly around... here." She circles the spot on the map.

"The Swallows Grotto?" Charlie says, bending over to read out the tiny inscription on the map.

Georgia stands back suddenly, goose bumps breaking out over her skin.

"Of course," she whispers. She can only think of one sprawling, two-tiered plain in the midst of this dramatic landscape.

"What?" Charlie turns to look at her, perplexed.

She exhales, meeting Charlie's eyes. "I think I know where the cave is."

54

THEY ARE DRIVING along highway nine on the east coast of Taiwan. As soon as the sun rose this morning, Georgia and Charlie left the cabin in his car, heading south along the coast.

They drive in silence, Georgia at the wheel as Charlie meditates in the passenger seat. She glances at his profile, seeing his peaceful composure, and a blanket of deep silence settles over her. She marvels at the sensation, having only ever felt this profound sense of quietness on one other occasion. It was many years ago, just after Ethan finished high school. He was going through an experimental phase and was passionate about all things hippie and New Age. Fascinated by Asian mysticism, Ethan took a gap year to spend months in India and Burma, studying under various yoga teachers and meditation masters. When he finally came back to Australia, he returned home to Sydney for a month before heading to Melbourne for his studies in the Visual Arts. One night, Ethan persuaded Georgia to join him at a meditation class. He wanted to spend time in Sydney specifically to meet with a revered meditation teacher he had heard about.

Georgia's impression of the guru was that he seemed to

exude an infectious, pervasive sense of calm. There were occasions when he walked into the room, and she would feel as if she was instantly transported into a soundproof room padded with acoustic foam, where all of her extraneous thoughts are silenced and absorbed. At times, she could almost hear her own heart beating when she sat next to him.

She continued to go to classes with Ethan for the month he was in town, but after he left, she soon lost interest. Georgia, a scientist and a fierce sceptic, could not reconcile who she was with attending a class on mastering something that she could not scientifically understand.

She guides the car down the meandering coastal road and sees that they are driving along the most famous section of the highway: Qing Shui, or Clearwater, Cliff. Georgia admires the rugged beauty of the coastline, where lush, untouched, forest-covered mountain meets the sea. The sheer cliff face descends almost vertically from the peak of the mountain right down to the Pacific Ocean, an impressive two-kilometre drop. This section of the road stretches for twelve kilometres alongside the turquoise seas, forming the most beautiful and the most dangerous drive on the island. The narrow and winding road is infamous for causing drivers to veer off path, and many superstitious travellers now throw joss paper money out the window as they drive along, a bribe for the spirits of the dead to ensure a safe journey for the living.

Georgia imagines how the coast would have appeared to sailors of Emperor Qin's time, traversing the seas through the ocean mist to suddenly come upon the steep, verdant mountains looming ahead of them. It's not difficult to imagine that the island would have been thought as Penglai Mountain.

"Beautiful, is it not?" Charlie says, stretching in the seat beside her. He seems to have finished his morning meditation.

"It is," she agrees. "I haven't been to Taroko Gorge in years. I forget how stunning this area is."

"Me too," answers Charlie. "My friend—the owner of the cabin—loves to come here to surf when he gets the time. He swears it is one of the top twenty surf spots in the world."

Georgia smiles in response, and they fall into a comfortable silence, both watching the sublime landscape unfolding before them as Georgia drives on. Not long after, they make a turn off the highway to head straight for their destination: Buluowan Terrace.

Flat land is scarce in the extreme landscape of Taroko National Park. Buluowan Terrace, however, is one location within the gorge blessed with sprawling plains. Formerly inhabited by the Truku Tribe, Buluowan means 'echoes of the canyon' in the native language. It's located downstream of Liwu River, a two-tiered fluvial terrace divided into the Upper and the Lower, with a height difference of thirty metres between the two. Today, catering to the bustling tourist trade, the Lower Terrace now houses the Tourist Centre of Taroko National Park, as well as an exhibition centre of the Trukuan history.

"So here is something that puzzles me," Charlie says as they arrive at the parking lot. "I always thought that the Truku tribe arrived in Taroko much later than Naaya's people."

"They did," Georgia says, exiting the air-conditioned interior of the car and feeling the August heat engulf her. "The Truku people actually migrated here from further inland about three hundred years ago. But the terrain at Buluowan lends itself to settlement and would have been home to a variety of people over the centuries. The flat land makes it easy to cultivate crops, it's sheltered by mountains in all directions, and it's also abundant in flora and fauna. So there would have been plenty of food all year round. It's also right next to the river, which would have been a reliable resource for transport and water."

It is still early in the morning and the parking lot is almost deserted, save for the few hikers keen to get a head start on the many walking trails that the park offers. Charlie and Georgia leave the parking lot and walk towards the lower terrace. Constructed of logs, the tourist and exhibition centre blends perfectly into its surroundings. Lush green lawns spread over the terraces, and the mountain ranges loom high above them, surrounding the entire plateau. Standing in front of the visitor centre, Georgia takes a deep breath as she absorbs the tranquil beauty surrounding her.

She sits down on the wooden step and pulls the notebook out of her bag, sifting through the contents. It takes a few moments to find what she is looking for.

"Here," she says to Charlie, "this is the drawing that Naaya made of her home before she left."

He nods, looking down at it. "That was one of her favourite drawings. I would catch her gazing at it at times, and the sadness in her eyes would just break my heart."

Georgia looks at the drawing more closely. "Here's where the two terraces meet," she says, pointing.

She stands again, trying to locate herself in relation to the perspective of the drawing. She moves about the plateau for a while, holding the drawing up before her. Surveying the mountains surrounding them, she compares the skyline with the lines on the drawing. Then she walks all the way up to the Upper Terrace as she continues her search.

"Look." She stops when she sees what she's looking for, the rise and fall of the peaks matching exactly the marks depicted on the drawing.

Charlie peers from behind her, seeing her discovery. He inhales sharply. "I cannot believe it. This is it. You found it, Georgia!"

She grins, feeling the familiar rush of excitement that comes with a significant discovery on an excavation site. She walks swiftly back to the tourist centre office. It's not due to open for another few hours, but there's a map of Taroko National Park pinned up outside. Her mind works rapidly as she studies it.

"Let's get a map and a pen. I have an idea where we need to go."

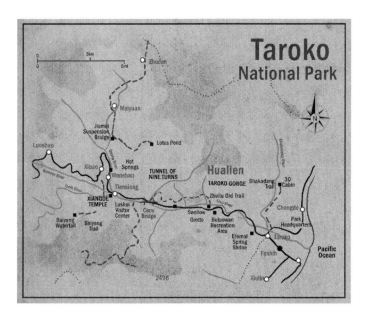

55

THEY MANAGE to find a souvenir shop and café on the premises that is open early to cater to hikers. On one of the stands, Georgia locates the same park map that's pinned up outside the office.

She sits down at a table, unfolding the map and spreading it out. Charlie walks over with their takeaway coffees, settling in the seat beside her. He hands her the pen he has borrowed from the cashier.

"Right now, we're here," she says, circling the Buluowan Terrace on the map. "In Naaya's writings, she describes the day she found the cave. She crossed the main river—that's the Liwu river next to us right now—and collected some of the herbs on the shore there."

She draws lines on the map, visualising Naaya's path in her mind. "Then she headed west, crossing a creek that ran from the northern peaks, climbing along the northern face of the gorge."

Georgia traces her pen to the west, encountering Badagang River, which originates from the north and meets the east-west Liwu River.

She feels her pulse quicken. "Then, she carried on along the Liwu River due west… and she fell into the cave before she got to this second creek from the north."

Her pen continues the line to the left, stopping just before the second, unnamed creek, and she marks the spot with an 'X.'

Charlie and Georgia both stare at the map, silent as they contemplate the location deep within the mountains.

"How are we going to get there?" Charlie finally asks, voicing Georgia's own concern.

This isn't going to be easy, Georgia realises as she chews on her lower lip. What's more, it's probably going to be dangerous. The Taroko region is well known for its unstable terrain. With all the water burrowing in and out of the rocks, corroding the structure over time, it would be more like standing on a sponge than solid ground. All visitors are advised to stick to the designated hiking paths, and tourists are encouraged to wear hard hats whenever they walk along the gorge. Every year, there are reported casualties due to rock falls.

Georgia shakes her head at the mounting obstacles in her mind. She looks into Charlie's eyes, feeling resolve strengthening instead.

"We'll trek," she replies.

IT TAKES several days to prepare for their journey, and they make frequent visits to the nearby Hualien and Taitung townships to source essential camping gear and food for the trip. Georgia gathers as many satellite images of the area as she can, hoping this will assist their search. She tries to call Sarah at the office for her help, but the woman never seems to be at her desk.

They plan out their route carefully, deciding to take the Zhuilu Old Trail for a large section of their journey. Justifiably famous within hiking circles, Zhuilu Old Trail is the most spectacular walking trail in Taroko Gorge. Once part of a garrisoned path built by the Japanese during the colonial period in the early twentieth century, it is a sinuous path snaking through tunnels, between steep mountainous peaks, and over azure rivers. The hike derives its name from the most hair-raising section of the trail, where the extremely narrow track hugs the sheer face of the 1,100-metre-high Zhuilu Cliff. Nothing but thin air separates the hiker and the vertiginous drop to the Liwu River below.

The trail begins at the Swallows Grotto near the Buluowan Terrace, starting with a three-kilometre vertical climb, then runs west along the northern wall of the gorge, and ends ten kilometres later at the Zimu Bridge. The path is long and narrow, its cliff terrain precipitous, and hiking it requires a good degree of fitness, as well as permits from the local police department and the national park office. There are frequent rock falls in the area, especially during the typhoon season. Every year, at least some part of the path will be closed due to damage from the treacherous weather.

Luckily for them, the trail has now reopened again after almost a year of closure.

As they wait for the mandatory few days for the trail permits to be processed, they decide to stay at the accommodation next to the tourist centre. The themed lodging is located on the upper terrace, and consists of wooden cabins designed to resemble a traditional Truku tribal village. Staffed by members of the Truku tribe, the hotel offers tourists an indigenous experience of Buluowan. It is well-known for hosting Truku-themed dinner parties every night.

Now, waiting for dinner to start, Georgia sits on the lawn in front of her room, ticking off the list of essential equipment they have composed for their trip. Finally, everything seems to be in order. Their trail permits arrived just a few hours ago, and they'll be able to set off early in the morning tomorrow.

Yet she gets the inexplicable feeling that she has left something off the list. It worries at the edges of her mind, something intangible that she cannot pinpoint, and it's making her feel anxious and unsettled.

Georgia knows that this is probably just her feeling apprehensive about the trip. The trek they are planning will be no small feat. If it were up to her, she'd have preferred to have more support, more time, more equipment, and more information for the journey. The need for secrecy is paramount, however, and with the limited resources at hand, they'll be attempting the journey on their own.

Nevertheless, she feels that she needs to at least tell *somebody* what they are about to do, before they go out of mobile phone reception range. Just in case they don't make it back at all.

Georgia searches through her bag and pulls out her phone. She has not turned it on since the day they escaped from the mercenaries at the Grand Hotel in Taipei. Somewhere in the back of her mind is the nagging fear that doing so would somehow make her locatable. But all of her address books, emails, and important data are on the little device, and not having access to it for the past two and a half weeks has made life very difficult.

She also wants to get Sarah on the phone, and though she's committed the office number to memory long ago, she somehow cannot conjure Sarah's mobile number in her mind. She blames it on her ever-increasing reliance on her smartphone.

Georgia looks at the device, arguing with herself that the chances of it being traced are pretty slim. She reasons that from the movies she has seen, it always takes several minutes to trace a call.

Then she chides herself for thinking like Sarah. *You've been watching too many spy movies.*

Pressing the 'on' button, she waits patiently for the phone to boot up. All at once, it starts beeping and vibrating as the backlog of messages comes flooding in. She ignores them and brings up Sarah's number instead, bringing the phone to her ear as she presses 'call'. There is a brief silence on the other end of the line, followed by the sound of Sarah's voice.

"You have reached Sarah Wu, I can't come to the phone right now…" the voice mail message begins.

"Damn it, Sarah." Georgia hangs up.

Where the hell are you?

AT THAT MOMENT, far away from the mountains of Taroko, a tiny red light blinks to life on the large flat screen.

Hank bolts upright, his eyes glued to the screen as he quickly taps a few keys on the keyboard. The satellite image zooms in on the transponder, showing its location.

A wide grin spreads across his face.

Gotcha.

Rising quickly from his workstation, Hank grabs his tablet and rushes out of the room. He hurries up the sprawling staircase to the second floor, taking two steps at a time. Stopping in front of a double mahogany door, he catches his breath as he taps on the door twice.

"Enter," Lambert's voice calls from within the room.

Turning the knob, Hank walks into the spacious office. His boss is seated in his usual spot, behind the stately desk and frowning at something on his screen. He has not even bothered to look up or acknowledge his assistant's presence. Hank can tell from his demeanour that he is not in the mood to be disturbed.

"Sir," Hank says, barely containing his excitement. "I have located Professor Lee."

Finally looking over, Lambert asks, "Where?"

"She's in the mountains on the east coast of Taiwan, sir." Hank taps at the screen of his tablet, bringing up the map to show Lambert. The little red light blinks rhythmically on the image.

Lambert takes the tablet and looks down on the map. "What on earth is she doing there?"

"I don't know, sir," Hank admits. "But I will go and find out."

He pauses, waiting for further instructions from his boss. When it doesn't come, he takes it as a silent assent.

"I will keep you updated, sir." He turns to leave the room.

"Hank."

Hank stops in his tracks, apprehension rising within him. "Yes, sir?"

"Get the jet prepared. Cancel all of my appointments for the next week," Lambert says, now looking back at his screen. "I'm coming with you."

56

"I'M CURIOUS," Georgia says as they are settling into their seats for dinner. "How many different countries have you lived in?"

Georgia and Charlie are in the main dining room of their hotel, a large space decorated with traditional Truku tribal carvings. A wall of windows gives them a sweeping view of the hotel compound: rustic wooden huts with a backdrop of lush green mountains, the warm glow of lanterns coming on one by one as the light wanes in the gorge. Guests enter the dining room in droves, each ushered to their assigned seats as everyone waits patiently for the festivities to start.

"I have not counted." Charlie smiles at her. "I have lived everywhere, really. I used to go for long voyages before air travel was invented. I would embark on whichever ship was leaving the dock that day, and get off months after at a completely new place. But recently, I have stuck around Asia —it just feels more like home."

"That must have been amazing," she observes, wondering at the complete freedom the lifestyle offers. Then she shakes her head incredulously. "I can't imagine what it's like, being able to experience all of humanity's history over the last two thousand years. There's just so much you can tell us, help us solve all the mysteries we've not been able to find an explanation for."

"Frankly, I think some things are best to remain as mysteries." Charlie shrugs. "In any case, humans have a habit of rewriting history as they see fit. At the end of the day, they will believe what they choose to believe in."

She frowns. "How do you mean?"

"I mean that history is a completely subjective topic," he explains. "Look at our history of conflict with each other, for instance. It all depends on who won the war—that determines who the 'bad guy' was in the end. Every culture and every country has its own version of events, and not all of them are based on facts."

"Like what?"

"Like the Mongol Empire, for one," Charlie points out. "According to most of the world, the Mongols were a savage, warmongering tribe that raped and pillaged their way through Asia and Europe. But this view is hardly complete nor correct, and people do not realise that developments which happened under the Mongol rule actually laid the foundation for the modern world."

"Do you mean how they fostered trade along the Silk Road?"

Charlie smiles. "I am referring to all of the ideals that the Mongols stood for: secular politics, religious coexistence, public schooling, international law, and free commerce. All of the paradigms that we take for granted today did not exist in the world at the time; especially in the West, where people still lived in feudal systems and the Church continued to persecute Jews and pagans. It was the Mongols' enlightened approach that paved our way to the civilisation that we live in today."

Georgia nods, considering his point. It is true that the Mongol Empire, and East Asian cultures in general, have been unjustly slandered through propaganda spread by the eighteenth-century Enlightenment writers, and by European colonisers a century later who were eager to persuade the public of the 'Yellow Peril.' Ironically, without the Mongols and their trade routes, vital inventions such as the printing press, the compass, and gunpowder would never have made their way from China to the West. Thanks to these critical technologies, Europe experienced a true rebirth. Or, if you will, the Renaissance.

Every year at the beginning of the semester, Georgia covers some of these ideas in her lectures for the first year students, and most of the time students are shocked when they learn the truth of Genghis Khan and his legacy. They are also equally astonished that the world still continues to subscribe to such a xenophobic view of a visionary race.

"Did you meet him?" Georgia asks. "The Great Khan?"

Charlie smiles. "No, I was living in Europe at the time. Back then, the world was a collection of kingdoms mostly separate from each other. The Asians knew nothing of Europe, the Europeans nothing of the Americas. No one even dreamed that Australia existed. But despite all of this, news of the Mongols and their formidable power *did* eventually arrive in Europe. That was the accomplishment of Genghis Khan. He forged links between the East and the West, and began the creation of this globalised culture we now live in."

At that moment, the waitress arrives with their meals, serving up platters of indigenous fare. Today it consists of roasted wild boar, wild vegetables picked freshly from the forest, rice steamed in bamboo tubes, and traditional millet wine. Charlie and Georgia give appreciative praise as the dishes are served.

Georgia sips her millet wine, watching as Charlie tucks into the meal with gusto. Strangely, this is one of the very rare moments that she finds herself unenthusiastic about the food laid out in front of her.

In her mind, she is frantically sorting through all the things she wants to say, trying to single out the most important one. There are so many questions she wants to ask this man: a man who has seen the rise and fall of civilisations, who has experienced the greatest wars of mankind, and who has been there for every significant leap that the human species has made. The invention of the printing press. The Industrial Revolution. Women's suffrage. Armstrong's landing on the moon.

The wisdom and knowledge accumulated over two millennia is contained within the person sitting directly across the table from her, and she finds herself at a loss for words.

"Something wrong?" Charlie frowns, noticing that she has not started on her dinner.

What do you ask such a man? What questions could possibly satisfy her desire to know more of this world, of life, of human existence?

Struggling to form her enquiry, she blurts out instead, "Why fifty years?"

Charlie raises an eyebrow, confused at her sudden question.

"You make significant donations to museums every fifty years. Why?"

"Ah," Charlie says, understanding dawning in his green eyes. He lays down his chopsticks to address her question. "For purely pragmatic reasons. It is long enough time for people to forget who you are. And it also seems to be the amount of time that it takes for me to run out of storage space. If I hold on to the pieces for longer than that, the collection just gets too big for me to manage and to conserve myself."

Georgia nods, satisfied with the answer. "And *Romance of the Three Kingdoms?* You took on names from the book over the years: Sun Quan, Lee Yi, and Meng Jie—benevolent characters that all have green eyes. Why?"

Charlie cocks his head to the side. "You know, I am surprised you even picked up the reference to that book. They were mostly minor characters that a person would not remember unless you knew the text by heart."

She shrugs. "I read the book a few times during school. And I've got a good memory, I guess."

He nods, his gaze lingering on her. "The opening of the novel, do you know it?"

"Sure. It's a famous line." She conjures up the text in her mind. Switching to Chinese, she recites: "*Thus it has been with the world: the lands under heaven, unify after lengthy division; then, after prolonged unity, shall divide.*"

"Thus it has always been, and thus it will always be," he echoes her words in English. "That is the transient nature of our existence, and it is also the enduring warring nature of human beings.

"The story of *Romance of the Three Kingdoms* has resonated with me. The book is metaphoric of our constant struggle as a species—for survival, for power, for a chance to rise above others. But more than that, in spite of all the destruction and treachery in our scramble for power, the story also speaks of the resilient sense of good and righteousness in people. Of loyalty, honor, and valour. I suppose it was a reminder to myself, to hold on to a sense of beauty for the world, to never forget the bigger picture.

"As for the names…" Charlie pauses, laughing light-heartedly. "Perhaps I fancied myself a tad poetic, taking on the names of the characters with green eyes."

Georgia nods slowly, understanding that within Charlie's lifetime, he must have seen so much of the ugliness and cruelty that is fundamental to humanity. Living for two thousand years without losing faith in mankind could not be easy, she realises. It is unsurprising, then, that Charlie holds such a gloomy view of the future for the human species.

"There's a lot of beauty in the world, and in people," she

agrees, "and that's why I think you should give us the benefit of the doubt. I know that it didn't end well for Naaya's people after they found the elixir, but should the mistakes of others dictate our future? What about the human capacity to change, and evolve into something much more than we have ever been?"

"Georgia," Charlie's smile fades into a forlorn expression. He shakes his head. "I understand what you are trying to say. Trust me, I once argued the same points myself with Naaya. But in the current condition that we are today, people are just not ready for the elixir right now. We may have evolved in technology over the years, but deep down we are still self-serving animals."

"But—"

Charlie reaches into the pocket of his pants and brings out a piece of paper. Unfolding it, he places it in front of her. She looks down at a printed news article, dated almost ten years ago. The headline reads:

Beloved Ballerina Dead at Thirty-Five

Beneath the headline is a picture of a beautiful woman in a ballerina costume, gazing up at the camera with a soft smile. Georgia scans the first few lines of the article:

Nola Lambert, former star of the London Royal Ballet Company, passed away last night after suffering long-term illness…

Puzzled, Georgia looks up at Charlie. "What's this?"

"I was searching on the internet about Mark Lambert today and came across this. Nola was his sister. She died of Huntington's Disease."

Georgia frowns, unfamiliar with the illness.

"Huntington's Disease is a hereditary disorder that causes the breakdown of the brain's nerve cells," Charlie explains.

"Over a number of years the patient experiences progressive muscular problems, difficulty in controlling movements, and a growing inability to perform daily tasks. The condition is fatal and once the initial symptoms emerge, patients only live for up to ten years. The probability of Nola's sibling also having it is at least fifty percent."

She stares at him, realising his point. "You think this is why Mark Lambert has commissioned me for this search. Because he's sick?"

"I believe it is safe to assume that. And it is also safe to assume that he is intending to keep the elixir for himself rather than share it with anyone else."

Georgia falls silent, mulling over this new information and battling with an unexpected sense of dejection. After a long moment, a thought presses at the back of her mind, and she asks quietly, "What was he like?"

"Who?"

Looking up, she meets Charlie's emerald eyes. "Emperor Qin. What was he really like, as a person?"

She catches a glimpse of emotion flittering across Charlie's elongated face, a brief contortion of his features that settles into solemnity.

"He was…" Charlie begins. "He was one of the loneliest people I have ever met."

Georgia raises her brows. She opens her mouth to ask more, but is interrupted by the hotel director speaking loudly on the microphone, making a lengthy welcoming speech to the guests. He announces proudly that an Aboriginal cultural show is about to begin, performed by the staff of the hotel. Young men and women dressed in traditional Buluowan clothing amble onto the stage, breaking into tribal song. Soon, some of the women begin to dance, inviting guests from the audience to join them. A young teenage girl beckons them with outstretched hands.

"Shall we?" Charlie smiles at her, all hints of the weight of their previous conversation gone.

Georgia pauses, then shakes her head, laughing. "Nah, you go ahead."

She watches as Charlie joins the group on stage, dancing, laughing, and learning the song with the others. For all of his wisdom and seriousness, he seems to be able to really let go and have fun. Georgia looks down at her now cooling food, and abandons it to wander around the dining hall, admiring the traditional carvings and decorations on the walls. She notices a small store selling souvenirs in the corner and saunters over, curious about the local handicrafts on sale.

The elderly indigenous woman behind the table greets her with a toothless smile. Her face is creased with age and covered with the tribal tattoos of the Truku people. Wide bands of geometric designs inked in dark green spread across her cheeks and join around her lips, a tradition that was performed on young girls to symbolise their rite of passage.

Georgia browses the colourful bracelets, key rings, wallets, and other trinkets. A necklace catches her eye and she picks it up to study it. A thin, hand-woven band of red, purple, and white, it holds a small circular pendant made of clay, a symbol carved in its centre:

"Hello," the elderly woman greets her, moving closer to make a sale. Like many indigenous people, her Mandarin is accented. "Looking for a gift, or something for yourself?"

"I'm not sure," Georgia smiles at her. "This is beautiful."

"My daughter made it," she says proudly, reaching over to trace the design with her finger. "This is an especially important sign for my people. It symbolises the mountain god, Zai."

"Oh?" Georgia raises her eyebrows at the woman, expressing interest.

"You should buy one," the old woman goes on. "It will bring you good health and everlasting youthfulness. Look at your beautiful skin. If you buy one you'll never end up looking all wrinkled like me."

"Is that right?" Georgia smiles with mirth. "I guess I will have to get one then." She reaches into her pocket to pay for her purchase.

The old woman beams, obviously delighted with her first sale of the night. Georgia leaves her smiling widely and returns to the table, finding Charlie back at his meal. She sits down, still looking at her newly acquired souvenir, feeling a strange familiarity as she studies its simple design.

"Hey Charlie," she says, eyes not leaving the pendant. "Remind me again, where did Naaya's people believe the elixir had come from?"

Charlie looks up. "From the mountain God of the north: Zai. Why?"

57

SARAH PACES the room with growing agitation.

She is getting hangry. *Very* hangry.

The kidnapper must have been satisfied with their most recent session, because he hasn't returned for a while. Sarah estimates that it's been almost twenty-four hours, but she can't be sure without a watch or any other means to tell the time. She has been sitting on the bare mattress butted against the wall, dozing in and out of the haze of the drugs, covered in a sheen of cold sweat.

It's a blessing that she hasn't had to see his ugly face again, but unfortunately it also means no one's brought any food or drink since. Will the man ever return at all, now he has what he needs? Or will he just let her die here, undiscovered until her flesh has rotted to the bone?

Chilling fear courses through her at the dreadful thought.

She rises, shuffling towards the sink beneath the staircase with her hands bound behind her. Reaching at an awkward angle, she grasps to turn the tap.

Nothing. Of course.

"Fuck," she mutters. "Mind-fucking arsehole."

Her mouth dry, she swallows against the grating in her

throat as she eyes the toilet bowl beside her, hoping that it'll never come to that. Then, feeling indignant about the whole situation, she stomps up the concrete staircase again.

"Hey!" Sarah yells, kicking at the door. "Hey! I'm starving here! Let me out, you freak!"

Unsurprisingly, there's no response. She presses an ear against the smooth, unpainted surface of the door, holding her breath to try and detect any minute sounds from the other side. Other than the hollow whistle of the wind, there is nothing.

There hasn't been much noise from the outside world throughout her time here. Nothing from a nearby street, or even minor vibrations from distant traffic. This tells her she's probably in the middle of nowhere and not likely to be rescued anytime soon.

Screw waiting. It's time to take matters into her own hands.

First, she needs to lose the ropes tied around her wrists.

Sarah looks around the windowless basement and begins tracing its walls, searching for anything that can break her out of the bonds. Her eyes roam over the bare concrete walls and floor as she walks along, looking for a nail or something sharp to grind her rope against. When she comes up with nothing, she repeats her path again.

Again, she finds nothing. She tries to quell the rising panic in her gut.

C'mon, Sarah, think.

Her eyes fall on the stairs leading up to the door, and the toilet bowl and sink underneath the staircase. Whoever had built the basement wasn't a stickler for surface finish. The concrete is rough and unpolished, and every corner is a jagged edge.

She walks to the space under the stairs, turning to bring her restrained wrists up to a corner, and begins to awkwardly rub the rope against the rough concrete.

This will take a while, but it'll do.

58

GEORGIA PAUSES as she stands at the beginning of the Zhuilu Old Trail: a suspension bridge barely a metre in width, spanning the gaping chasm a hundred metres above the Liwu River. Beneath her, white churning water rushes past giant, marble boulders. Natural hot springs spill out of the rocky cliff face, tiny steaming waterfalls that are prevalent in the area. She eyes the foot bridge before her suspiciously, noting several broken vertical cables. It looks in desperate need of repair.

Charlie is ahead of her, already walking down the narrow passage with the ease and speed he always moves with.

"Georgia? Everything okay?" He turns, sensing that she has stopped behind him.

"Yeah," she replies, making no move to walk towards him.

"Are you scared of heights?" he asks, knitting his brows.

"No," she says defensively. Then she mutters, almost to herself, "Just have a healthy respect for them, that's all."

She readjusts the weight of her pack, making sure that it's strapped securely over her chest and hips. They have prepared enough supplies to last for a whole week. She steps gingerly onto the bridge, the wooden boards creaking beneath her feet. Her grip on the guiding cables tightens involuntarily.

Charlie watches her walk slowly towards him with amusement. Then, apparently knowing better than to say anything, he turns to continue his path towards the end of the bridge.

When she joins him on the other side, she lets out a breath that she doesn't realise she's been holding on to. From here, there is a long, steady climb of almost a kilometre.

"All good?" Charlie smiles at her with encouragement.

"Sure," she nods.

They set a steady pace as they climb upwards. Georgia has maintained a good level of fitness over the years with her love of running, but it's the middle of August in Taiwan, and even though it's still early in the morning, the stifling, humid heat has her struggling to keep up. Charlie, on the other hand, ascends without apparent effort, pausing every now and then to let her catch up.

The climb seems to go on for aeons, and Georgia imagines what it must have been like for Naaya to make this journey alone as a young girl. The clear-cut path would not have existed then, and the climb would've been much more difficult to tackle in the untamed terrain.

They finally come to a small plateau overgrown with grass, and she pauses to catch her breath, wiping the sweat off her brow. Charlie offers her some water from his canister, then walks over to a couple of old, crumbling concrete pillars jutting out of the shrubbery. Eying them with curiosity, he places his hands on one of the pillars.

"This is the old settlement of Badagang," Georgia explains. "It's one of the villages that accommodated the Japanese soldiers stationed here. The clearing should be just up the hill somewhere. It used to have a clinic, a school, and even a hostel for travellers."

"The Japanese? Out here?"

"Yeah." She sits down on a nearby rock. "Before the Japanese took over, the whole island was largely undeveloped. The Japanese treated Taiwan as a resource-rich colony that they could pillage. The ripe soils, sub-tropical climate, and abundant seas meant there were plenty of fish and valuable crops to be harvested.

"The Truku people around here put up a fight, but after a long conflict with the tribe, the Japanese finally won a major battle. Then the military built the Zhuilu Old Trail to improve their control over the area. It allowed their soldiers to patrol the villages quickly on foot. There are ruins of fortified police stations all along this trail."

Charlie nods, still gazing at the pillars in silent contemplation.

"I've been thinking…" Georgia clears her throat, deciding to broach the subject that's been floating around her mind. "What's going to happen if we find the cave? I mean… what will happen if you drink from the pool of water?"

Charlie turns to look at her, an amused smile on his lips as he comprehends her question. "What you mean to ask is, will I disintegrate into dust immediately, or die a horrific death right before of you?"

"Yeah." She wrinkles her nose. "I really don't think I want to stick around to watch that."

He laughs, a deep rumble in his chest. She smiles at the sound, realising that she has grown to like this man, however brief their acquaintance may have been.

Charlie pauses for a moment, thoughtful, and when he speaks again his voice is more sober.

"Honestly, I do not know. But I am certain it will not be quite as dramatic as that. Frankly, I am not even sure if this plan will work. Naaya never gave me much detail, nor did she explain why she thought that taking the elixir again would reverse its effects. She really did not want to talk much about the elixir at all."

Georgia nods. "Well," she says, sighing with resignation. "I guess we should keep moving then."

They walk further up the hill and find the clearing of the old Badagang post. Lush forest surrounds them and everywhere she looks is a sea of shimmering green. The deafening sounds of cicadas rise to crescendos and drop away, repeating this pattern over and over again. Wild daisies grow where there used to be houses, and colourful butterflies dance amongst the blossoms. Georgia smiles as she is reminded of the Butterfly Valley in southern Taiwan, where her parents once took her as a child.

Home to over four hundred varieties of butterflies, the tiny island of Taiwan has one of the highest concentrations of butterfly species in the world. In the sixties, the country exported so many butterflies per year that it was dubbed the 'Butterfly Kingdom.' Georgia remembers a particular trip with her family, walking in the forest with her parents and seeing the tiny vibrant creatures flitting about. Brown and black wings highlighted with spots of iridescent purples, yellows, and blues, they glimmered in the summer sun through the dense forest foliage. Excited, she squealed with delight, and the sudden noise brought about an explosion of colour as thousands and thousands of butterflies fluttered into the air around her.

She smiles at the memory, one of the few times she remembers really connecting with her parents, and when they seemed to be happy in each other's company.

As Georgia and Charlie come to the end of the three-kilometre climb, she spots the Zhuilu Cliff up ahead. From this distance, she can see that the trail hugs the almost vertical cliff face at a height of some five or six hundred metres above the Liwu River.

"You know, this used to be the hunters' trail for the Truku people," she says, gesturing to the cliff. "They would travel to other villages this way, hugging the rocky cliff face on a tiny ledge. When the Japanese came, they forced the villagers to carve it out to about a metre wide so it could be easily accessed by Japanese soldiers. The native men had to suspend themselves with ropes from the top of the mountain and slowly chip the path out of the marble cliff face."

Charlie shakes his head. "Slave labour, huh?"

"Yeah," she says as she takes out her map. "It's sad that some of our greatest achievements were built by slaves. The Great Wall of China, for example," she refers to one of the things that Emperor Qin is most well-known for.

Studying the map, she checks their route, pointing to their location. "This is where we are right now. It's the highest point of the trail."

"And the cave should be just beyond the Zhuilu Cliff?" Charlie asks, leaning in to look at her markings on the map.

"I believe so," she replies. "Naaya wrote that there were two creeks that came from the northern peaks, intersecting with the east-bound Liwu River. We crossed the first one about ten minutes ago. The special mushrooms she collected were at a clearing near the second creek, and she was on her way to that creek before she fell into the cave. But it's hard to know the exact route she took back then. The location could be anywhere along the river."

As they continue their path and approach the Zhuilu Cliff, they are greeted with a spectacular bird's eye view of Taroko Gorge. Next to the track, there is an information sign erected by the national park administration, written in both Chinese and English:

> *The Zhuilu Cliff is over 500 metres long. The road is narrow, and rockfalls often injure tourists here. Please do not loiter here, walk as close to the wall as you can, watch out for rockfalls, and pass quickly.*

Georgia looks at the path ahead. It's covered by loose

gravel, barely a metre wide, with only a plastic-clad steel cable along the cliff wall to hold on to. There are no safety harnesses, and certainly nothing between her and the vast void of the chasm below.

Typical Asian country safety standards.

Charlie, of course, is already quite a few metres ahead of her, moving as if he is strolling along a spacious boulevard. She shakes her head, gripping the cable and following him.

As they progress on the path, she cannot help but admire the extreme beauty of it all. From here, she is rewarded with breathtaking views of the expansive Taroko Gorge beneath her, and looming mountain ranges all around. She feels grand and yet insignificant, all at the same time.

A lone mountain hawk-eagle glides gracefully through the air, looking for prey. It rises high above to land on the mountain above her.

She hears the sound of scree scattering from above, then Charlie yelling: "Look out!"

But it's too late. Georgia looks up just in time to see stones raining down on her, one of them hitting her on the shoulder and knocking her off balance. She loses her footing, feeling her body toppling to the side, and she barely has the time to gasp before she is over the ledge.

59

NOT EVEN A SINGLE damn paper clip.

Frustrated, Sarah starts to pace the room again. Grinding the ropes against a corner underneath the stairs, she managed to free herself from restraints some hours ago. Since then, she's been trying to figure out how to get the door open. Made of sturdy wood, it swings inwards, so even if she had enough strength it's impossible to break it down by force.

The good news, though, is that after studying the lock she's decided it appears to be a simple pin and tumbler mechanism. Sarah is pretty confident she can get it open if she finds some kind of thin wire.

She's done it plenty of times before, especially when her kids were still living at home and had a habit of locking their bedroom doors at night. Rather than forbidding them to do so, Sarah allowed them the illusion of privacy and sense of control, but would habitually pick their locks to make sure they hadn't snuck out of the house for the night.

No lock was going to keep mummy out. All it took was a couple of hair clips and five minutes of her time.

But now, having searched all over the basement, Sarah

cannot find a single thing that can help her unlock the door keeping her imprisoned.

She walks over to the desk again, getting on her hands and knees to crawl under, hoping she missed something the first time. Beneath the table, Sarah runs her fingers over every surface, through every crevice, looking for anything she can use. She comes up empty-handed.

Admitting defeat, Sarah lies on the cold floor, fighting the rising sense of despair. Squeezing her eyes shut, she takes a few deep breaths to will away the tears.

Pull yourself together, Sarah.

She opens her eyes again and stares at the incandescent light on the ceiling. It flickers as if to mock her. That's when the idea hits.

Hmmm. She remembers watching MacGyver pull this trick on his show once. It might just be the thing that saves her.

She rises to her feet and drags the heavy desk to position it under the light, climbing onto the table top. Her hands trembling with hunger, she pulls on the sleeve of her sweater to cover her skin, then stands on the tips of her toes, reaching for the incandescent bulb screwed to the ceiling. When she twists it, the room darkens a shade more, now lit by only the light across the room. Wincing from the scalding heat of the bulb penetrating the fabric, she quickly moves to release it from its socket. Prize in hand, Sarah jumps down, placing it on top of the desk to let it cool.

Years ago, when she was a stay-at-home mum looking after two toddlers, Sarah relished mid-day TV whenever her kids were down for a nap. It was the only moment in the day she had some time to herself, a brief interval of peace and quiet in her otherwise maddening life. It was during this that she became obsessed with re-runs of *MacGyver*.

Her fangirl crush on Richard Dean Anderson aside, it was a damn good TV show. Sarah had always held a keen interest in physics and the general way that the world worked around her, and this action-adventure show entertained and educated her at the same time. As a secret agent and trained scientist, the resourceful MacGyver would solve complex problems by making extraordinary things out of mundane objects. He constantly wowed Sarah with the ever-expanding applications of his Swiss Army knife and duct tape.

Now, MacGyver may just be the one who saves her life.

She looks down at the light bulb on the table, recalling a particular episode where he picked a door lock with filaments retrieved from a lamp.

Two bits of spring steel—perfect shape and size.

Grabbing the end of the bulb with her sleeve-covered hand, she smashes it against the edge of the table. The glass shatters easily, and she pulls on the two pieces of support wire, releasing them from the plastic base.

Bingo.

60

GEORGIA IS HANGING on for her life, her legs dangling off the precarious cliff.

Everything happened so fast that she struggles to recall the details, and she thought she was dead. Instead, she finds herself suspended over the rocky ledge with Charlie holding on to her wrist.

"I have you, Georgia!" he calls. "Hang on!"

Instinctively she looks down, and instantly regrets it. A rush of vertigo hits her and she kicks her legs in reflex.

"Do not look down!" Charlie cries. "Look here! Look at me."

She turns to look up at him, seeing that he is lying on his front, leaning over the edge of the path. He has a deep cut on his forehead and the wound is oozing blood.

"Hold on tight, I will pull you up." He grips her arm with both hands.

"I can't, I'm slipping!" She is bordering on hysteria.

"Just hang on to me, Georgia. Trust me. Take a deep breath," he coaxes. "I am going to pull you up, okay? But you have to stop waving your arms and legs like that."

"Okay." She stares into his green eyes, panic still gripping her heart.

"Good. Give me your other hand."

She does as he instructs, feeling lightheaded with the blood roaring in her ears.

"You see that shrub coming out of the rock there? To your right?"

Georgia looks over and sees the small bush not far from her. "Yes."

"I want you to put your foot on it, I think it is big enough to support you."

She reaches to place her right, then left foot on the thickest part of its trunk, distributing her weight.

"Good, Georgia," Charlie says with encouragement. "Now, I am going to pull you up slowly, okay?"

"Okay," she nods.

Gripping her forearms, Charlie slowly inches back from the ledge, pulling her with him. She grabs a boulder when he manages to lift her far enough, allowing him a brief pause before he grasps the top of her backpack to heave her all the way up on to the gravel path.

"Are you okay?" Charlie asks.

She nods, wide-eyed and breathless in her reply. "Thank you."

Loosening the straps of her pack, she shrugs it off, sitting on the path for a while to recover. Georgia watches as Charlie wipes the blood off his forehead with his long, slender fingers, the wound already healed. From this angle, his thin frame makes him look like a fragile waif. She is surprised at his physical strength.

"Is that one of the effects of the elixir?" she asks.

He turns to look at her, unsure of her question.

"Your strength, your speed—is that because the elixir?"

He exhales. "Yes. The elixir does not just make my cells heal faster; it improves the overall efficiency with which my whole body operates. The ratio of strength to muscle mass is greatly increased, too."

Georgia nods, suddenly feeling exhausted. She rises to her feet, pulling her backpack with her, anxious to keep moving.

"Let's get off this cliff," she suggests.

They move along the track quickly this time, Charlie trailing closely behind her. The end of the path opens up to a clearing amongst the trees. Georgia sits down on a log, exhaling a long sigh.

Charlie sits beside her, giving her a light pat on the back. "We made it, Georgia. That is the worst of it done. Are you feeling okay?"

She nods, giving him a weak smile. With shaky hands she reaches into her pack and pulls out two chocolate bars, offering one to Charlie. They munch on the sweets silently, Georgia slowly regaining her wits.

When she is feeling herself again, she pulls out the map from her backpack, spreading it on a rock beside them.

"Naaya mentioned a small flatland where she collected the mushrooms, and it's not far from the second stream. I think it may be near where we are right now. This clearing is another of the police station ruins left behind by the Japanese."

She points to a spot on the map, then traces a straight line to the brook as she says, "From here, we should make a direct path towards the water."

"Go off the trail?"

"Yes," she replies. "Naaya would have chosen the shortest way to the river. The trail that we're on, it veers northward before intersecting with the creek."

After a pause, she asks: "Did Naaya ever mention anything about how she concealed the entrance to the cave?"

Charlie shakes his head. "No. But I did get the sense that when she brought her people back to the cave, they eventually made a more accessible entrance to replace the hole that she fell into. They went to the cave frequently, performing all sorts of sacred rituals there."

She nods, biting her lower lip, wishing that she had Tanaka-san's Ground Penetrating Radar with her. Without access to more sophisticated equipment, she is left with rudimentary survey techniques.

"This could be a long search, huh?" Charlie asks, reading her mind.

"Yeah."

"What about this tree that she wrote of, the one she walked towards before falling into the cave?"

"I thought about that too." She shakes her head. "I searched for information, but I couldn't find anything about a tree with medicinal uses for the hair in these areas. Naaya did mention that the tree was very rare. In any case, I think it's probably irrelevant, since it's unlikely that it'd still be standing after all these years."

She brings out a pen from her pack and draws a grid over the area that she believes contains the cave, two hundred metres in length on each side. "We'll search this section in a systematic fashion. But I'm more concerned about unstable surfaces we could fall through, since we're going off the established trail."

"That is fine," Charlie says. "I will walk ahead, and you can follow a few metres behind."

She nods and reaches into her backpack again, taking out a compass, some climbing ropes, and a small machete knife. She hands the latter to Charlie.

"For cutting through any branches and foliage in our way," she explains. Looking at the compass, she points to a direction away from the trail. "The river is due west of here. We'll follow a straight line and see what we come across on the way."

61

GEORGIA SITS ON A ROCK, feeling utterly spent. They have been going back and forth between the clearing and the creek for hours now, scouring the area in a grid-like fashion. This would have been much easier if the terrain they are surveying were clear and flat. Instead, they are constantly clearing their paths, climbing over boulder and avoiding any snakes, spiders, and other forest-dwelling fiends in their way. Their search has been slow and tedious, and as the sun edges towards the horizon, she announces that she's calling it quits for the day.

She settles down to tend to the multitude of cuts, bruises, and mosquito bites all over her body. Pausing, she looks over at Charlie, who's busy setting up camp for the night. The exertions of their day haven't seemed to tire him one bit, and he still moves with the same graceful efficiency that Georgia envies. And of course, the skin on his shins and arms remains unblemished from their rigorous search in the forest.

Through a gap in the foliage, she gazes out to the gorge. The sun, now half-concealed behind a peak, casts warm light over the valley, and a faint breeze picks up, rustling the leaves. The sound of crickets begins as the light gradually wanes.

Reaching into her pack, Georgia finds the small laptop that Charlie bought during one of their supply runs. She powers up the little machine, which came with a solar-powered battery charger, and opens several high resolution satellite images of the region.

"What are you looking for?" Charlie asks, peering over her shoulder at the infrared images highlighted in false colour.

"I'm looking for some subtle differences on the ground of this area," Georgia explains. "It's a pretty effective technique to detect any structures built by man. You've mentioned that Naaya's people used the cave as a place of worship, so I'm hoping that they built some kind of structure or symbols of their gods near the entrance. If they did, I'd be able to tell with these satellite images."

"How does it work?" Charlie asks, curious.

"Well, let me show you an example." She brings up images of her recent dig in China. The first shows a satellite photograph of the site in the visible light spectrum, showing nothing but fields and vegetation. The second is a processed version of the same area, depicting clear patterns of circles and squares, an obvious indication of man-made structures underground.

"See, these patterns don't normally occur in nature." She points to the perfect shapes on the image. "They're what we're looking for. The infrared images detect subtle differences in chlorophyll, which indicates vegetation health. Plants growing on top of any stone or building material are usually less healthy, so they'll show up like this."

"The problem is," she continues, switching to the satellite photos of the Taroko area again, "I've gone through these images a few times and I haven't been able to find anything."

"What does that mean?"

"It probably means that they didn't build anything above ground. Everything must be inside the cave."

Charlie nods slowly, digesting this. "So we are back to relying on—what did you call this—surface survey technique?"

"Yeah, without more equipment, it's just you and me, walking up and down the river bank, hoping that we'll stumble on a discovery."

He scratches his head, then smiles at her cheerfully. "We have supplies for a whole week, Georgia. I am sure we will be able to find something."

MARK KNOWS he has been played.

To him, business is an art of war to be practised with finesse, but war cannot be won without loyal and capable servants. Decades of experience in the world of trade has endowed him with acute senses when it comes to subordinates, and right now he is convinced that he has grossly underestimated Georgia.

He is incensed. If she had done her job properly, he wouldn't be here right now, playing stake-out with Hank at a private cabin on the outskirts of Taroko. Mark hardly has the time or the patience for this charade.

"Sir," Hank says beside him, pointing to the red dot on the tablet screen. "I've tracked Professor Lee's movements. She's been hanging around this particular section of the valley for several days. It's quite exposed. I can send our men in there right now—"

"No, I want to see how this plays out."

"But sir," Hank protests, frowning. "I don't understand. Georgia has achieved her mission, she has found Hsu Fu and they are right there, within our grasp—"

Mark raises a finger for silence. He leans over the tablet,

staring at the blinking red dot to ponder on what Georgia's possible motives may be. Her behaviour makes no sense whatsoever. If Georgia doesn't want to bring Hsu Fu in, why isn't she on the plane right now, planning either to disappear or find the highest bidder for her discovery? Why hide here, in the middle of one of the most popular tourist destinations in Taiwan?

What could possibly be out there in the gorge?

She's up to something, and Mark has no idea what that is. If there's one thing he's learnt in business, it's to never make your move without knowing what your adversary may be planning.

A thought occurs to him, and he tells Hank, "Bring up a map of her movements over the past few days."

His assistant takes over the tablet, tapping various commands on the screen before handing it back. Mark leans in, studying the organised, linear lines that trace Georgia's path.

"She's looking for something." His revelation comes out at a whisper.

"But that makes no sense. What could she be searching for out there?"

Mark furrows his brows, considering this. Then it dawns on him. "The elixir. She must be searching for it with Hsu Fu. That's why they've been out there all this time."

Beside him, Hank inhales audibly.

Well, this is an interesting development. Instead of simply finding the immortal man in question, Georgia is aiming for something even better: the cure to mortality itself. Mark sits back in his chair, his mind roaming over the potential of this revelation.

"Sir," Hank pipes up again. "Let me at least set up a surveillance team in the area to watch her movements. Just in case."

"No," Mark replies, his voice sharp. "I don't want too

many people involved. The fewer people know about this, the better. Send the men home." He looks at his assistant pointedly. "I assume we can handle it ourselves."

Hank purses his lips, giving him a silent nod.

It is quite clear now that Mark has misjudged the professor's character, and that is something that rarely happens to him. He wonders what her true intentions are. Will she share the elixir with the rest of the world? Or will she sell it to whoever pays the highest sum?

No. Judging from her behaviour so far, he gets the feeling that Georgia wants to keep the elixir all to herself.

Mark works his jaw, feeling rage simmer in the depths of his stomach. *That is simply unacceptable.* He will make certain that she does not achieve her goal.

THEY ARE RUNNING low on supplies.

It has been five long days of searching, traversing back and forth from the riverbank in a methodical fashion, looking for any signs of an entrance. So far, they've found absolutely nothing.

Now, with the sun setting, they have returned to their camp by the river. Georgia examines their food supply and decides that if they don't make any progress in the next two days, they may have to consider going back. Expeditions like this usually take months to plan, and she knows they have been ill-prepared for it.

During dinner, they discussed their options, debating at length over what to do. Both of them are loath to give up on the search, but there doesn't seem to be any other alternative.

She glances over at Charlie, who is sitting on the tarp with his back against a rock. His eyes are closed, and she can tell that he is not asleep, but meditating. Once again, she's struck by the calm and tranquillity he exudes. The sense of stillness about him is so palpable that it makes her also close her eyes, basking in quietude. Even the entire valley seems to descend into silence.

A tremor begins to hum in the valley, building quickly into a shudder as the ground shakes beneath her. Then, as quickly as it started, it is gone. Georgia's eyes fly open, looking about her with momentary confusion. All of a sudden the birds in the trees explode into cacophony, flying into the pink sky. In the distance, bats surge high above the gorge. She realises at that moment why the animals went quiet only seconds before.

"Earthquake," she says.

"Yes." Charlie nods.

Taiwan is one of the most tectonically active regions in the world. Tremors like these happen almost daily, the majority of them originating just off the east coast. Most of the time the quakes are harmless: minor shudders that are barely detected by those who live on the island. Every few decades, though, a severe earthquake hits, causing widespread destruction and death.

Georgia stills as an idea crosses her mind. She reaches for the little laptop next to her, her fingers flying across the keyboard.

"Georgia?" Charlie watches her, moving closer to see what she is doing.

She studies the two topography maps that she down-loaded from NASA's archives before making this trip. Zooming in, she finds what she's looking for.

"Of course," she whispers.

"What is it?"

She tilts the computer towards Charlie to show him the images. "We've been looking in the wrong place all this time."

"We have?"

"These are the topography data of our location right now,"

Georgia explains as she points to the maps. "This one was taken before 1999, and this one was taken after."

Charlie squints at the images. After a few moments, he sees what she is getting at. "The river bed has moved."

"Yes!"

"What happened in 1999?"

"A major earthquake," she explains. "It was dubbed 'Quake of the Century' by the local media. Over two thousand people died, and tens of thousands more injured. There were billions of dollars of damage to all the buildings and infrastructure. Hundreds of landslides happened during the main quake and the aftershocks, altering much of Taiwan's landscape."

"The 921 Earthquake." Charlie nods, aware of the incident she is referring to.

"Yeah," she says, typing on the keyboard again to overlap the two images. Looking around them, it takes her a few moments to translate their exact location. She points to the distance when she's sure she's got the right spot.

"We should be looking over that ridge instead."

62

M*ACGYVER WAS FULL OF SHIT.*

Sarah glares at the piece of wire in her hand with disbelief. It's too damn big for the hole.

Unwilling to give up, she turns to look around the basement again. She really needs a hammer, but knows for sure there's no such thing in here. Her eyes fall on the desk across the room.

Striding down the stairs towards the table, Sarah examines its sturdy metal legs, and crouches down to lift one as she places the wire underneath. Then, with as much force as she can muster, she bashes the weight of the table down. She misses a few times, but with patience she repeats this awkward action again and again, then studies her results.

Perfect.

After doing the same for the other piece of the filament, Sarah walks back up the steps to the door. This time, the filaments fit exactly into the hole.

She bends both wires at the end, and inserts them into the lock at varying angles. It's been a while since she's had to do this, but revisiting the skill is like riding a bike for her. Feeling around the keyhole with one of the wires, she guesses there are at least five or six pins in the locking mechanism. It's a matter of locating the pins and pushing them up one by one.

Sarah fiddles with the wires for some time. Their size is not exactly ideal for this job, even after they've been flattened somewhat. She distinctly recalls it only took MacGyver under a minute to perform this trick on TV. But it's TV after all, and she's just happy to have gotten this far.

It takes her at least half an hour at the door, but when the faint, undeniable click issues from inside the lock, she feels on the verge of weeping with relief. Sweat beads at her brows, and she wipes her clammy hands on her dirty clothes, taking a few breaths before putting gentle pressure on the other wire to twist it to the right, praying it's in the correct direction.

The lock turns without resistance, and Sarah watches with disbelief as the door swings open after a gentle tug on the knob.

Holy shit. It actually works.

Relief sweeps over her and she suddenly bursts out in tears, laughing and sobbing at the same time. Then she clamps her hands firmly over her mouth, peering through the opening, trying to detect any movements on the other side.

Stepping through the doorway with heightened caution, she's half expecting to find herself in a derelict house, a creepy abode for a serial killer just like in the horror movies she likes to watch. Instead, she sees nothing but a small concrete shed. Like the basement downstairs, it's pretty much empty.

A cold draft hisses softly through the metal door to the left, and she walks over to open it, finding it locked.

Ugh.

Sarah turns to retrieve the wires from the door to the basement. It looks like this place will be keeping her a prisoner for a little while yet.

When Sarah finally manages to get the door open, it becomes apparent that the tiny shed which has kept her captive for god-knows-how-long is located somewhere in the Australian outback. The sun is high in the sky, so thankfully she won't have to navigate the bushes in the dark. After all the trouble she's gone through to break out, it would be the height of irony to die from a venomous snake or spider bite.

She shivers uncontrollably in the shade, the winter's breeze nipping through her thin sweater. Stepping into the sunlight, she rubs her arms, trying to warm up. There must be a road here somewhere, Sarah decides. Her kidnapper couldn't have carried her too far without a car, even if he is built like a bull.

She looks about her, but there are only trees beyond even more trees. Gazing down, Sarah searches for any hints of a track near the door of the shed. The man visited multiple times, and since the shed is empty, he must have walked here from his house or car. She observes the flattened vegetation on the ground, finding a very faint trail leading away from the door.

Her feet crunching on dead leaves, she follows the ill-defined path, but loses sight of it a few hundred metres away from the shed. Frustrated and looking all around her to regain her direction, the distinctive sound of an approaching vehicle makes her look up. She turns right, sprinting in the direction of the noise, and encounters the road not long after as a large truck thunders past.

"Hey!" Sarah runs after the lorry, waving her hands wildly in the air, hoping the driver will spot her in the rear view mirror. It continues on without slowing, throwing up dust in its wake.

Huffing, Sarah rests her hands on her knees, trying to

catch her breath from the run. She has no idea where she is, but sooner or later a car will come by again. When it does, it'll stop for her. She'll make sure it does.

She needs to get to a police station. She must warn Georgia.

63

AFTER ANOTHER DAY of fruitless search, they retire to their river-side camp.

According to the topography changes in the region, Georgia and Charlie have been searching just over a hundred metres off the mark, but that has been sufficient to throw them completely off course. Their supplies are now so low that they'll need to turn back if they don't find anything tomorrow.

The truth, though, is that Georgia has no idea if they're even looking in the right area. She needs more data: satellite images, geology analyses, and historical archives that she cannot access from here. Taiwan sits on the meeting point between two tectonic plates, and it would make sense that the terrain has changed significantly over the years. Without more information, she cannot possibly extrapolate where the river was flowing over two thousand years ago.

Realistically, they'll need to widen the radius of their search. But Georgia tries to not think about that, since there's no time for it. Charlie has been optimistic all this time, and she's determined to be the same for his sake.

"Rum?" Charlie offers her a metal flask with one hand as he stirs their food with the other.

She smiles gratefully and takes a long swig from the container, feeling the liquid burn a warm trail down to her belly. Her feet, swollen and sore from a week of vigorous hiking, are immersed in the cool stream.

"What's for dinner?" she asks. Her mouth is salivating as the aroma emanates from the pot on the small burner.

He chuckles. "According to the packet, it is Kung Pao chicken with rice. But it looks more like brown goo if you ask me."

Laughing, she says, "Don't worry, I'll eat anything you give me right now—"

Georgia stops mid-sentence as a tremor shakes the earth beneath them, quickly escalating into a violent quake accompanied by a deep, resonant boom. It barely lasts a second, but it is enough to send the entire valley into chaos.

"Another one," Charlie comments, raising his voice above the din of the frightened birds.

Not far from them, Georgia spots a swirl of black creatures emanating from the forest, flying high into the purpling sky.

The same sight also appeared yesterday when the tremor occurred, but now it triggers something that makes her rise to her feet. Georgia's sure she hasn't seen these bats sleeping in the trees during the day, which can only mean one thing.

"Charlie." Georgia points towards the nocturnal animals.

He turns to follow the direction of her finger, his body going still when he catches her meaning. "Bats live in caves," he says.

"Yeah." She is already crouched down, hurriedly putting her boots back on.

Charlie is a step before her, breaking into a sprint for the woods. Georgia runs after him once her shoes are on, making a swift ascent up the river bank and into the shadow of the trees. But as suddenly as the bats appeared, they are gone. Charlie runs without hindrance through the forest in the direction from which they appeared, and she struggles to keep up, weaving her way through the trees and rocks.

Up ahead, he stops in his pursuit, calling out to her, "I think they came from here somewhere!"

She is still catching up to him, hands out to protect her face from the leaves and branches in her way, when her foot catches on something. The obstruction sends her flying through the air, and the wind is knocked out of her as she lands on something hard at an awkward angle. Pain spreads across her side, and she fights to bring air back into her lungs.

Charlie is beside her before she even has time to roll over. "Georgia! Are you okay?"

Unable to speak, she nods her head. Every breath radiates pain through her entire chest, and she groans with agony as he helps her sit up. She puts her hand on the rock she landed on to support her weight. Lifting the side of her T-shirt to check for lacerations, she winces with pain as Charlie probes her ribs delicately with his fingers.

"You have bruised them, but there does not seem to be any fracture."

She nods gingerly, pushing up against the rock to stand.

"No, Georgia," Charlie protests. "Just rest. You have bruised your ribs. It will hurt like hell for quite a while."

Georgia shakes her head, uninterested in his suggestion. She asks breathily instead, "Did you find where the bats came from?"

"No, but I will keep looking. Stay here."

She nods as he walks away. Her fingers brush against something on the rock that is supporting her, and she looks down at it for the first time.

"Charlie, wait," she calls as she sweeps the dead leaves aside to get a better look at the stone. She can see that it's no ordinary boulder, for it's perfectly round in shape. Covered with moss, there is a deep carving on its surface. Georgia traces her fingers along the concentric circles:

"Oh my god," she whispers.

"What is it?" Charlie kneels next to her to get a better look.

"This symbol, it's been used by many cultures to represent a pool or a pond," she explains. "In some ancient civilisations, it also symbolises the past, present and future in one: the state of timelessness."

"Eternity," Charlie says, reading her thoughts.

She looks up to survey their surroundings, scanning frantically around her. The valley is now darkening as the sun slips behind the mountain peaks.

"The cave must be here," she says. "It must be here somewhere."

She begins to brush away the debris of leaves and soil surrounding the rock, encountering nothing but more soil. Widening her search, Georgia moves away from the stone and up the slope on her hands and knees, removing dead foliage as she goes.

"Charlie," she says without turning, focused on her search. "Can you please bring our gear over here? I need torches and digging equipment."

"Of course."

He leaves to go back to their camp, and she continues to remove the top layer of the forest bed with her bare hands.

The sharp pain in her side flares up whenever she makes any sudden movements, but she does her best to ignore it.

Five metres away from the rock, Georgia comes across a small hole in the ground.

"Help me," she says to Charlie, who has already returned with their rucksacks. He hands her a trowel.

Quickly skimming off the topsoil, they uncover an area of roughly two by two metres covered with flat stones. The soft whistle of airflow emerges from the hole where some of the rocks have fallen away.

"This must be where the bats came from," she says, wincing as she attempts to remove one of the stones.

"Rest, Georgia, let me do this," Charlie suggests.

She nods, taking shallow breaths as she watches him remove the obstructions one by one. Soon, a square opening is revealed. A cool draft wafts up to them, carrying the distinctive scent of bat guano. Georgia shines a torch down the cavity, the light hardly penetrating its palpable darkness, as she listens to the thunder of her own heart in her ears. The air smells damp, and the beam of light reveals a series of stone steps leading down into the darkness.

"I think this is it, Georgia." Charlie's voice comes out at barely a whisper.

She nods, at a loss for words as she gazes into the void. Suddenly, a lone bat surges out of the shadows, seeking escape. Georgia cries out with shock as she stumbles back, its wings fluttering in her face. The abrupt movement sends stabbing pain through her chest, drawing tears to her eyes as she groans.

Charlie tends to her, concern etched in his features. "Maybe we should go back," he suggests. "You are obviously in a lot of pain."

"No." She looks at him with disbelief. "We just found the cave. We have to go down there. I'm not walking away now."

Charlie begins to protest, but seeing the expression on her

face, he says, "You stay here and rest for a while. I will go down first to make sure it is safe."

"Okay," she agrees. "Be careful, the steps might be slippery."

Charlie pulls out his torch and, testing the first few steps tentatively, begins to slowly descend into the entrance. As his head disappears underground, Georgia leans over the opening, anxious as she watches him being swallowed up by the inky abyss.

64

"Charlie?" Georgia calls out, hearing her voice echoing through the darkness. She sees the faint beam of his torchlight swinging about in the distance. He looks to be a long way down. "What do you see?"

"A giant cavern," he replies, his voice barely audible. "It's… indescribable. Come down slowly, the steps are safe."

Georgia puts her legs through the hole, and begins to carefully descend the stony stairs with her torch in hand. Passing through the portal between light and darkness, she enters a subterranean world where damp, earthy scents and the din of squeaking bats envelop her in the eerie gloom. To the right and far below her, she can see Charlie switching on a small, battery-powered lantern. The light helps to illuminate some of the space, but is swallowed up by the deep dark further beyond.

Onward she descends, the perfectly carved-out steps continuing down a long way. She steadies herself with a hand against the rocky wall on her left. The treads are worn to a shiny patina from frequent use, and with the moisture lingering on every surface, she is careful to not slip on them.

When she finally reaches the bottom, Charlie calls to her, shining his light on the wall beside the stairs. She moves to him, gazing up at the myriad of carvings decorating the rock surface, depicting figures, faces, animals, and other abstract concepts.

Charlie lets out a soft whistle. "Beautiful, isn't it?"

She nods, her eyes unable to leave the intricate designs. "Looks like Naaya's people really venerated this cave."

She moves the torchlight along the wall and stops a few metres down. Looming high over her, a giant symbol, inlaid with jade, is carved deep into the surface:

Charlie inhales sharply at the sight of the carving. "Isn't this the same design as the one on that pendant from the Truku cultural centre?"

"Yeah," she says, bringing out the necklace tucked in her shirt. "The old woman who sold it to me said it's the symbol of the god, Zai."

"The mountain god to the north," Charlie mutters. "The giver of life."

Georgia turns, sweeping her torchlight across the cave, walking around to take it all in for the first time. The giant, natural chamber is about four storeys tall at its highest point, and at least a hundred metres across. She finds a large, round hearth in the centre of the cavern, and she imagines the rituals and ceremonies that would have been held here, celebrations of healing and eternal life. Long strands of fibrous tree roots extend down from the ceiling, seeking nourishment. Like the roots, though, she finds no presence of water here.

"I don't see any pools, Georgia," Charlie comments, walking up to join her beside the hearth.

She furrows her brow.

It must be here, she knows it in her bones. "Maybe there's another chamber," she suggests, tracing the distant walls of the cave with her torch. She squints in the dim light. "See if you can find another opening. I'll start from over there."

She walks to the farthest end of the cave and traces her path next to the rocky surface, encountering more carvings as she walks along. In her mind, Georgia pictures this cavern thriving with people, giving their tributes to the gods and paying their respects to this sacred site.

Some hundred metres down, the wall opens up into another chamber.

"Charlie, over here," she calls, her voice echoing through the space.

He quickly joins her as Georgia ventures a few paces into the secondary cave, encountering a pair of tunnels. Directing her torch down one of the openings, she sees in the distance that it divides into yet another three different pathways.

"There must be an entire cave system down here," Georgia says.

Charlie shakes his head. "How are we going to explore them all?"

She lowers her rucksack to the ground, rummaging through its contents to produce a handful of glow sticks. Handing some to Charlie and stuffing the rest into her pocket, she says, "Use these so that you don't get lost. I'll take the tunnel to the left, and you can take the other. Yell out if you find anything."

He nods in agreement as she straightens with the pack on

her back. Walking into the first tunnel, she sees that it splits into two. Instinctively, Georgia decide to take the left. She reaches into her pocket to retrieve a glow stick, snaps and shakes it to activate the chemicals, and drops it on the ground near the entrance.

65

SARAH SITS with her legs hanging outside the open doors of the ambulance, watching the scene unfold before her. The lights of the police cars flash red and blue, bathing the woods in alternating colours. The sun set only moments before, and in the absence of daylight, the shadowy forest has taken on a sinister aura.

She gives an involuntary shiver, the reverberations of her encounters now hitting her with full force. Suddenly, the evening air feels unbearably cold.

"You okay, Sarah?" Constable Benjamin Peterson hovers over her. "Would you like a blanket? Another sandwich and a hot drink, maybe?"

"Yes, please." Sarah's teeth chatter as she replies.

The young policeman opens the boot of a nearby sedan, returning with a thick woollen blanket, a thermos flask of hot tea, and sandwiches in plastic packaging. Sarah accepts all of them gratefully, devouring the food and drink, slowly feeling warmth seep back into her body.

Feeling somewhat herself again, she reaches for the phone that Constable Peterson has lent her, trying Georgia's number for the fifteenth time that day.

"Hi, this is Georgia," her familiar voice says on the line. "Please leave me a message and I'll get back to you as soon as I can."

Damn it. Sarah's brows crease with worry as she hangs up the phone. *Where are you, Georgia?*

The paramedic attending to her finishes his examination, speaking to the uniform close by. "It's just a minor case of malnourishment and dehydration; everything else seems okay. She's strong for her age. There's no external injuries, but I'd still like to do some blood tests at the hospital, just to make sure the drugs haven't done any internal damage."

Sarah shakes her head. She says loudly, "Not until I've spoken to the officer in charge."

Not when her kidnapper—that sick, perverted freak—is out there, probably going after Georgia right now.

Hours before, after she finally waved down a Canadian tourist driving through the country—who informed her that they were somewhere in the Blue Mountains—the authorities were alerted. Within an hour, the police from the local Katoomba station had sealed off a few hundred square metres around the shed. But after Constable Peterson took down her preliminary statement and her description of the crook, Sarah detected a palpable shift in all the uniforms' demeanour. Then, half an hour ago, a senior officer from the Australian Federal Police showed up, taking control of the entire investigation.

Shit is serious. From her limited knowledge of the way things work, the elite AFP unit only investigates important cases that involve terrorism or international crimes.

Looking up at the sound of footsteps, she sees the officer in question trudging through the bushes on his return from examining the crime scene. Decades older than Peterson, Sergeant Turner is a solid specimen of a man, in his bearing as well as physique. He is at least a head taller than the younger constable walking up to join him, and twice as wide. Just one of Turner's powerful thighs seems to be of the same girth as Peterson's entire torso. The junior policeman looks like a twig next to his superior.

"Sarah," Turner says as he reaches her, his voice a low rumble. He pulls out a small notebook from his back pocket. "I know you've told your story to Constable Peterson a few times, but I'd like to hear it in your own words. We'll do a full statement when we get back to the headquarters, but for now, can you describe to me again what your kidnapper looked like?"

She shakes her head at his question, voicing the more urgent concern on her mind. "I'm worried about Georgia. Have you had any luck tracking her down?"

"No. We'll contact the local officials in Taiwan to assist us, but it's going to take some time to locate her, since we don't have much to go on at all. Are there any family you can reach for Georgia—a husband, a next of kin, or a sibling?"

Sarah purses her lips. "I think the emergency contact she listed at the university is her grandmother, who lives in Taiwan. Georgia's an only child, and her parents live somewhere in Australia, but she never talks about either of them."

"Her grandmother or her parents—do you know their names?"

She shakes her head. "I can't remember. Georgia's always just refers to her grandmother as 'Amah.' I'll have to look it up at the office."

"I see." Turner jots down some notes. "Now, can you please describe to me what your kidnapper looked like?"

"He's stocky, built like an ox. About one sixty, one sixty-five centimetres. Asian... In his late twenties, maybe? His head is shaved clean, and he's got a goatee."

Turner writes everything down in his notebook. "Did he have any distinctive features at all?"

Sarah squints her eyes, trying to recall. Her memory seems very cloudy all of a sudden. When she spoke with the Canadian tourist, who was the only one kind enough to stop for her, she discovered she'd been in captivity for six days. During that time, she was in and out of consciousness, and everything now seems like a blur. She's been trying to piece together the chronology of events ever since.

"He has a scar," she says, suddenly remembering.

"A scar?"

"Yeah," she confirms. "It was long and nasty, and it ran all the way down the side of his face like this." Sarah gestures to her ear, then traces her finger to the chin.

Turner is silent as he absorbs this, the lines between his brows deepening.

"What?" Sarah asks at his troubled expression.

The sergeant stares at her, as if assessing how much to reveal. He exhales a long sigh. "I'm not going to sugar-coat it, Sarah. That basement you were kept in is a purpose-built bunker. Based on the MO, and the description you've just given me, I'm pretty sure the offender is experienced. He's probably been planning this for a while."

She narrows her eyes, reading his shuttered face to decipher his unspoken words. "Are you saying that the creep has done this before, but you haven't been able to catch him?"

Sergeant Turner lowers his gaze. "I'm saying I have reasons to believe that your case may be linked to others." He rakes a hand over his military crew cut. "I'd like to show you some surveillance footage from our other investigations to see if you can identify him."

She nods. "Okay."

"Good," Turner says, returning to his notes. "Now, you told Constable Peterson that the kidnapper left you alone for quite a while before you escaped."

"Yeah, I got real hungry," she complains.

"And you managed to unlock the door by...?"

Sarah sighs. Peterson has already made her repeat this

part of the story several times. It's pretty obvious he doesn't believe her at all. None of them do.

"*MacGyver*," she utters the single word, as if it would explain everything. Then she clarifies, "The light bulb episode."

Turner's serious face breaks into a grin, an expression that looks almost odd on his rough features. "I know that episode," he says, then shakes his head. "Never thought it was actually doable, 'til *MythBusters* tried it themselves. That's pretty impressive what you did there, Sarah."

She blinks, surprised at his reaction and at the unexpected compliment. Clearing her throat, she says, "Thanks."

Turner's smile fades as quickly as it appeared. He looks down at his notes again. Frowning, he asks, "You said that the suspect interrogated you. What were the interrogations about?"

She shakes her head. "I honestly can't remember. The drugs… they screwed with my head. But I know it had something to do with Georgia."

"Because of her photograph on the wall?"

"Yeah."

"Those photographs—do you know what they're for?"

"No." She shakes her head. "But it sure as hell gives me the creeps."

"And your kidnapper didn't return again after your last session with him," Turner confirms again.

She nods, watching him scribble quickly on his notepad. Frowning, she asks, "Do you think it's because he finally got the answer he was looking for?"

The sergeant looks up from his notes, fixing her with his gaze. "Maybe. Or maybe he just gave up because he couldn't find the answers he needed."

Next to Turner, Constable Peterson speaks up for the first time. "It's a miracle you managed to get out on your own. You're very lucky. In cases like these, often the suspect comes back to finish the victim off, or sometimes they just never return, to—" he breaks off as Turner throws him a sharp look.

"To leave me to die down there, alone." Sarah finishes Peterson's sentence for him. She shakes her head and grips the blanket around her tightly.

Turner's phone buzzes in his pocket. Taking it out and glancing at the screen, he says, "Excuse me a moment, I need to take this." He gives the constable a stern, pointed look before walking away.

Sarah watches Sergeant Turner with keen interest as he takes the call several metres away, trying to make out what's being said. When he finally returns, his expression has changed from grave to ashen.

"I don't like that look," she observes.

"Sarah." He crouches down next to her, looking at her intently. "I got my guys back at the office to run a search on the ownership of this land. I figured that'd be a helpful lead."

"And? Who does it belong to?"

"Mark Lambert, the billionaire."

66

GEORGIA MAKES ANOTHER TURN, walking several minutes into the narrowing shaft before reaching a dead end. It appears the tunnel has previously collapsed in on itself, and the passage is blocked with rubble. She spins around, retrieving the trail of glow sticks and returns to the last junction. Starting down the next entrance, she continues to explore the dark labyrinth whilst marking each turn with the little fluorescent tubes.

The glow sticks have been invaluable in helping her to explore this complex cave system. But they've been searching for almost an hour now in the maze of tunnels, and so far, they've found nothing.

She makes a right turn, and the passage opens up into a larger chamber, which splits off into even more tunnels. These myriad underground shafts must have been formed by water burrowing through the earth for over millions of years. At this rate, they'll never be able to find what they are looking for.

At that moment, the ground beneath her trembles, shifting abruptly from side to side, and she lunges for the nearest surface to keep her balance. The walls shudder, sending fine dust and sand down from the roof of the chamber. It lasts for several seconds, then settles again as if nothing had happened.

Heart racing, Georgia exhales a breath she didn't realise she was holding. Abandoning her search to retrace her way back to the main cavern, she runs into Charlie emerging out of the last tunnel.

"Did you feel that?" asks Charlie. "Are you okay?"

"Yeah, you?"

"Yes."

"I don't like this," Georgia says. "With all the recent seismic activity in the area, there's no telling if it's building up to an even bigger event. The last tunnel I came across had collapsed in on itself, probably from a previous quake."

Charlie nods in agreement. "We had better make this quick. Did you find anything?"

She shakes her head.

"Me neither. Just dead ends and then never-ending tunnels." Charlie sighs.

"I think we might be approaching it all wrong. The cave we're looking for must be connected to the main chamber. It can't be tucked too far from the ceremonial site," she speculates. "Let's go around the perimeter of the cavern properly this time, I'll head this way and you can go in the opposite direction. We'll meet at the steps."

"Okay," agrees Charlie.

They begin their slow search along the walls of the cave, careful to note all of the carvings and any other openings. Her movements are slow in the darkness, and she can hear the bats high above her, their high-pitched squeaks permeating the space. She avoids looking up at them, knowing from past experience that she would be rewarded with guano on her face.

"Georgia!" Charlie calls out, "I think I have found something!"

She turns and walks quickly towards the sound of his voice, finding him staring intently at the wall before him.

"Look." He points the beam of his torchlight at a large carving located at the height of his chest. "Here is that symbol again."

Georgia studies the three concentric circles engraved and inlaid with jade, then begins searching around them for an opening. She finds it low on the ground, barely high enough to crawl through on one's hands and knees. This entrance, like the one at the top of the stairs, has been obstructed by rocks. Within the darkness of the cave, if it were not for the symbol that Charlie found, she would have missed the low-lying opening entirely.

"It looks like Naaya blocked this one up too," Charlie says. He kneels down to start removing the stones.

They take several minutes to move the barriers out of the way. Then, crouching low, she shines her torch through the small cavity. Unlike the cave system they have just spent an hour exploring, this one seems to have been excavated by man. It is of a more regular shape, the surfaces are smoother, and the long, narrow tunnel leads straight into the deep black beyond.

"This must have been dug by Naaya's people to connect the two chambers," she surmises, squinting into the inky hole. "I can't see the other end."

"Let me go in first, just to be safe," Charlie offers. He pauses at the entrance, listening intently. "Do you hear that?"

She scrambles next to him, putting her head into the hole, straining to detect what he is referring to. Unable to block out the tweeting of the bats overhead, she crawls a couple of paces in, holds her breath, then finally hears what Charlie is talking about. A sound echoes in the distant void:

Drip. Drip. Drip.

Excited, she backs out of the tunnel. "I hear the sound of water."

Charlie's face is unreadable as he shrugs off his backpack to drop it on the ground, the controlled grace of his movements at odds with the strain in his shoulders. Abandoning his torch, he picks up the small lantern instead, taking a deep breath.

"Okay," he says when he is ready. "I will call out for you once I reach the end."

She nods in agreement, watching him disappear into the tunnel. Impatient, she looks into the entrance every now and then, seeing the movement of the obstructed light from his lamp.

Long moments pass, and fed up with waiting, she sticks her head into the tunnel.

"Charlie?"

"Yes," he answers, his voice subdued.

"Everything okay?"

"Yes. Come on through."

Georgia pulls out a glow stick, its fluorescence still radiating strong, and leaves it on the ground with her torch. She enters the oppressive darkness of the tunnel. The rocky surface under her is cool and damp, and the smell of moist earth and stagnant air fills her nostrils. Her backpack scrapes along the top surface of the shaft as she crawls on her hands and knees. She feels something skitter across the top of her hand and she withdraws it quickly, shaking the critter off.

She hates insects.

Georgia fights the rising sense of claustrophobia. The light from Charlie's lantern in the cave chamber before her motivates her to scurry along with haste.

"It is not too much farther, Georgia," Charlie says, as if sensing her anxiety. She can see the outline of his silhouette at the other end. "You are almost there."

Relief floods her when the walls of the tunnel finally fall away and open up into another cave.

Drip. Drip. Drip.

The reverberations of the slow dribble of water resonates through the space, and it's difficult to pinpoint its exact origin. Taking the lantern with him, Charlie searches for the source. Georgia sees that they are in a much smaller chamber this time. The ceiling is still quite high, but the cave only spans about ten metres. Unlike the larger cavern, this one remains undecorated, its walls bare.

Charlie slowly makes his way towards the far corner, sweeping the light of the lantern across the cave floor. Several metres down, he suddenly stops, standing at the edge of a small pool. The water glistens with a silver glow in the dim light.

Georgia rises to her feet and joins him. Charlie is staring intently at the water, and for the first time, he looks as if he is unsure of what to do.

Drip. Drip. Drip.

She sees a quivering of the lamplight, and realises that his hands are shaking.

"Charlie?"

He doesn't respond. He doesn't turn to look at her. He just stands there, gazing wordlessly at the water.

Then, without a word, he kneels down slowly and places the lamp beside him, his movements careful and deliberate. He cups his trembling hands into the water, and raises the liquid to his lips. Exhaling a long sigh, he takes a tentative sip.

Charlie remains very still, crouched down as if waiting for something monumental to occur. Georgia watches him and draws in a breath, taking a nervous step back. Superstition overcomes her for a brief moment, and images of horror movies spring to mind. She fears that he may start to disintegrate before her very eyes.

But he doesn't. He stands up instead, slowly turning towards her.

"Well?" asks Georgia.

Charlie shrugs, amusement in his eyes. "I am just as new to this as you are."

"How do you know if it's worked?"

"I guess there is only one way to find out." Charlie takes out a small knife from his pocket, and with one swift movement, he makes an incision on his open palm.

67

HANK SHINES his torch down the gaping hole in the forest floor, seeing the long descent of steps into the underground cave.

"I lost the signal from her phone here, sir," he says to Lambert, who is standing beside him. "They must have gone down there."

"Just as I suspected," Lambert utters, a look of undisguised scorn on his face. "Georgia has known the location of the elixir all this time."

Sitting down beside the large rectangular entrance, Hank swings his legs into the opening. He makes a few tentative steps before progressing down the stairs with more speed.

"Careful, sir," he warns. "It's a bit slippery."

Hank continues the descent, sensing his boss following closely behind him. Anticipation percolates through Hank's blood, and he feels as if he is on the precipice of something truly momentous. He can scarcely believe that he is finally here.

Nothing, after this, will ever be the same.

Reaching the bottom of the long flight of stairs, he surveys the huge cavern around them. His torchlight moves over the wall beside him, illuminating intricate carvings inlaid with jade.

"Jesus," he says in awe. "Just look at this place."

Lambert is quiet beside him, his eyes roaming over the cavern with unadulterated wonder, his usual calculated calm now completely dissolved. Over the past few weeks, Hank has noticed the slow unravelling in his employer's indomitable composure. It's obvious the whole matter has affected him on a personal level, something which Hank has never observed.

"She must be here somewhere," Lambert says after they have taken some time to assess the place. "You take the far end of the cave and I'll search around here."

"Yes, sir." Hank sets off, sweeping his torch about, looking for any signs of the professor.

After several minutes of search, he notices a green glow on the ground in the distance. Intrigued, he walks closer to investigate. As he approaches, Hank sees that the luminescence is emanating from a glow stick beside a low-lying hole in the cave wall. Close by, there is a pile of rocks, an abandoned backpack, and a couple of torches. He lowers to the floor, poking his head into the tunnel, and sees light at the other end of the long passage.

His grin grows impossibly wider as the sound of voices travel to his ears.

"Found something?"

Recomposing his face, Hank pulls back from the entrance to find Lambert standing beside him.

"Yes, I see a light, sir. Professor Lee must be in there." He rises to his feet. "You go on in, sir. Best you confront her first. I'll follow right behind you."

Lambert considers this, then gives him a terse nod, lowering onto his hands and knees to enter the small entrance. As Hank watches his boss crawl in hesitantly, he decides to give Lambert some time to reach the other end before following suit.

It'll provide himself with the brief repose to prepare for what's about to come.

Hank can barely contain his excitement. This is the exact moment he has been waiting for, something he's envisaged for as long as he can remember.

Crouching down to lift the left leg of his pants, Hank pulls out the .357 Magnum Colt Python strapped to his ankle. Checking that the pistol is fully loaded, he clips the holster behind him, securing it next to the Japanese *Kaiken* dagger tucked in his belt. Even though he rarely resorts to using a gun, he likes to bring it as backup for special occasions such as this.

The Kaiken, though, is something that has never failed him. Custom-made by one of Japan's most legendary sword-smiths, this trusty weapon has been with him for years, a true lucky charm.

Muffled voices emerge from the small ingress, and though Hank cannot make out what is being said, he can tell it's a heated discussion.

He chuckles in exultation.

Then he looks at his watch to count down the minutes, before leisurely crawling through the tunnel after Lambert.

68

BLOOD, thick and dark, oozes out of his palm.

Charlie stares intently at the cut on his hand, willing it to keep bleeding. But after a few seconds, he sees the all-too-familiar signs of his body beginning to repair itself. A minute passes, and then all evidences of the incision are gone. The only thing that lingers is the sticky red fluid, which he wipes on the side of his pants with bitter disappointment.

His heart drops.

Georgia places a hand on his arm. "Maybe it takes time?"

"Maybe." He sighs, turning to her to give a small smile. "Let me take some samples of the water anyway. I can study it once I get back home."

A blinding glare suddenly saturates them, and Charlie spins around, blinking at the light source next to the tunnel.

"Hello, Georgia." The voice, ominous and deep, resonates through the small cavern.

Alarmed, Charlie looks to his companion. Georgia has a hand in front of her face, shielding her eyes from the harsh beam of light. The momentary confusion in her features is quickly replaced by recollection as she processes the man's voice.

"Mark?" She squints. "What are you doing here?"

The intruder lowers his torch and strides towards them, stepping into the glow of the lantern. Charlie immediately recognises Mark Lambert from photographs on the internet, but this is not his usual cool, immaculate appearance. Instead of the pristine tailored suits he always seems to appear in, he is now dressed in worn hiking gear fit for purpose. His silver hair is tousled, there is a few days' of growth in his facial stubble, and the look in his eyes has Charlie's gut clenching with trepidation.

"The question is," Lambert replies, his face twisted in a scowl. "What are *you* doing here, without informing me first? You were instructed to keep me updated at all times. Clearly I should've kept you on a tighter leash. You haven't been doing what you were told."

Georgia's head jerks back at his condescending tone. "I'm not a dog for you to order around."

Lambert waves her off dismissively, his attention already directed past them. The beam of his torchlight drops to the pool, his eyes glinting in the darkness as they focus on his prize. His lips part, a reverent breath escaping him. As if entranced, he takes a step towards the water.

Georgia, at least a head shorter than the man, moves to block his advance. Lambert's eyes flicker back to her face, fury burning in his grey gaze.

"Get out of my way, Georgia," he hisses.

"No." The muscles of her jaw clamp down.

Lambert moves as if to strike her, and Charlie instinctively rushes to her aid, putting his body between them. In a blink of an eye, he seizes Lambert's outstretched hand, twisting his arm and spinning his body to immobilise his hand against his back. Lambert cries out in pain, scuffling to break free, and Charlie pushes him to the ground, grabbing both arms to pin them down with his knee.

"What the hell are you doing?! Let me go!"

"I am not doing that until you calm down," Charlie says. "We do not want anyone to get hurt here."

Lambert struggles beneath him, but the advantage of Charlie's position gives him easy control. His captive winces as he applies more pressure.

"Georgia—ah!" Lambert strains his head to look at her. "Why are you doing this?"

"Doing what? You're the one attacking us, and you're the one who lied to me, Mark," Georgia says, shaking her head with hurt in her eyes. "You're dying, and you want the elixir for yourself. All that lofty talk about wanting to cure untreatable diseases… It was all a lie, and I should've seen right through it from the beginning."

"What the hell are you talking about? I didn't lie! And I'm not dying. Where on earth did you get that idea from?"

Georgia's brows furrow. "Your sister—she had Huntington's Disease."

Lambert suddenly goes still at the mention of his sibling. He stops fighting against Charlie's grasp. A few moments pass, and his breathing slows.

"Yes, she did," he confirms, his voice almost a whisper. "And yes, it was also highly likely that I'd have it too. But I did all the tests when she was first diagnosed. I don't share the same gene that led to her illness."

Georgia flicks a quick glance at Charlie, uncertainty creeping into her large brown eyes.

"You want to know my medical status?" Lambert huffs. "I'm getting older, of course, and I've got rheumatoid arthritis. It gives me the worst aches and swelling in my hands, and when I try to grasp too hard, I can get pretty severe cramps. But it's not likely to kill me. I'll admit—if you give me something today that means it'll all go away, I'll gladly take it. But that's not why I'm doing this. That's not why I hired you to find Hsu Fu."

Charlie frowns as his eyes trail to Lambert's hands pinned

under his knee, seeing the telltale early signs of deformities in the fingers. It would appear that the billionaire is telling the truth.

"Then why are you doing this?" Georgia asks, her voice unsure.

Lambert blows out a sigh. "Look, can you just let me sit up so we can talk properly? This is not doing my joints any favours."

Charlie looks to Georgia, who gives him a slight nod of her head. He loosens his grip on Lambert, stepping back to let him stand. Mark rubs his shoulders and arms grudgingly, his stature somewhat diminished. He drops his hands to his sides, his gaze flickering between Charlie and Georgia as he speaks.

"I made a promise to Nola before she died. My sister… she was the kindest person I've ever known, and even when she was writhing with pain, all she could think about was other people." He shakes his head. "It was already too late for her, but she still begged me to invest my money in finding a cure for her illness, so that others like her would never suffer again. That was her one dying wish.

"Over the years, my pharmaceutical company has poured millions of dollars into the research, but we have made no progress. When I found out the legend of Hsu Fu could be true, even if it was just a minute possibility, I felt it had to be worth investigating. But really, this project has become much bigger than just fulfilling my sister's dying wish."

Charlie studies Lambert's face with scepticism, trying to ascertain the truth of his words. He has been so convinced of Lambert's ill-intent. The man's background and ruthless reputation has reminded him of countless tyrants throughout history, not excluding Emperor Qin himself.

"How did you find us?" asks Georgia.

Lambert replies with a wry smile. "I keep a close eye on all of my investments. It's business 101, and a habit I stick steadfastly to. Hank's been tracking your movements ever since the beginning. He's been my right-hand man for years, and he looks after all the projects that I'm most concerned about. We lost you for a while, but when you turned on your phone again, I had my team track it and install a Trojan on the device, so we'd know where you were even if your phone was turned off.

"When I saw you were deep in the mountains on the east coast of Taiwan, I figured you must be on the hunt for something. That was the only logical explanation, since you'd already found Hsu Fu." He flickers his gaze at Charlie. "So I told Hank to hang back and give you a little room, to see what you could find."

Lambert drops his gaze to the ground. When he raises his head again, Charlie sees he has regained his calm composure. The billionaire now fixes his steely gaze on Georgia. "But you, Georgia, I just don't get. Of all the people in the world, I'd never have expected you to do this. You're clearly aware that with all of my resources, we could synthesise the elixir for the whole world. You are a scientist. How can you be so selfish as to try to stifle a discovery as big as this?"

Georgia flinches as if he had slapped her. "I—"

Lambert throws up his hand, continuing, "You know, I had Hank do a background search on all the candidates I had in mind for the job. Out of all of them, you were the one I thought would share my views on this. You lost your daughter. Don't you wish that had never happened to you? If you were given a chance to make a difference, wouldn't you make sure other parents would never experience what you went through?

"Think about it, Georgia. We've just made the most significant scientific discovery in history." His eyes grow wide, his voice filled with fervour. "Think about what the elixir could mean for the world. The frailties of our bodies hold us back as a species. Imagine how much we could actually achieve, what we could evolve into, if we could live forever."

At this, Charlie shakes his head. He can see Georgia's resolve is already wavering, but he is unwilling to give in so easily. Something does not add up.

"If this is all true," he counters, "and your intentions are completely benign, then why did you send the mercenaries after us?"

Lambert's brows knit together. "What mercenaries?"

"The men who attacked us," Georgia exclaims, gesturing to Charlie, "when I first found him at the Grand Hotel in Taipei. They were armed."

Momentary confusion flashes across Lambert's eyes, but he swiftly reins it in. He casts a quick glance behind him, and Charlie follows his gaze, seeing nothing in the dull blackness of the cave.

"I never sent any armed men," Lambert says.

"I don't believe that," Georgia rebuffs. "Who else would know that I was searching for Hsu Fu?"

The billionaire utters an exasperated snort. "Look, Georgia, I've done a lot of despicable things in my lifetime. If I have my eyes on a goal, there's generally not much I'd let stand in my way of achieving it. But in this case, I actually believed in you, erroneous as that proved to be. I didn't send those men because I genuinely had confidence that you were on my side. At least, on the side of science. Plus, Hank was meant to keep an eye on you."

"If you did not send them, who did?" Charlie demands.

Lambert opens his mouth, but whatever he intends to say is silenced as a large knife is thrust through his throat from the back. Charlie recoils with shock as blood splatters his face. In the haze of the moment, he dimly registers Georgia's strangled scream.

He watches in stupefied silence as Lambert falls to his knees, holding his throat as he takes shallow, gasping breaths.

He coughs spasmodically as red foam bubbles and splutters from his open mouth. Blood gushes down the front of his T-shirt as his startled eyes fixate on Georgia. He lunges towards her.

She takes an instinctive step back, and Mark Lambert collapses face-first on the ground, his strangled, gurgling sounds reverberating through the heavy air.

Trembling, Charlie lifts his gaze to look at the figure standing behind Lambert, and his whole body goes cold as familiarity of the killer's face sinks in.

69

GEORGIA FINDS herself unable to move. The horror of the moment paralyses her, and she cannot seem to tear her eyes away from Mark's convulsing body. Within seconds, he is motionless and silent. The pungent scent of blood fills the air as it begins to pool around him.

Tears stream down her face as a wave of nausea hits her. With a thick swallow, she forces the taste of bile back down her throat. She looks up at the assailant, who is now crouched beside Mark's body, wiping his large blade on the back of the dead man's shirt. He smiles up at her as if to exchange pleasantries.

"Sorry you had to see that, Professor. But really, he was going on a bit," he says by way of explanation. He cocks his head to the side. "Admittedly, I've been itching to do that for the better half of the last ten years. There is nothing compared to that tactile feeling of sinking a blade into human flesh."

Something in the soft cadence of his British accent and the light timbre of his voice triggers a jolt of recognition in her. She gasps in disbelief, a sudden sense of vertigo overcoming her.

"Hank?"

His smile widens into a grin. He nods at her. "Smart girl, Georgia."

Astonished, she gapes at the man with whom she has developed a rapport through friendly phone calls over the past few months. There are so many things about Hank in person that surprise her, and topping that list is the fact that he's Chinese. Then she realises that his last name, Law, is used both as an English and a Chinese surname, though the latter is usually spelt as Lo or Lau. In their phone exchanges, his perfect Londoner's accent, soft-spoken voice, and congenial nature had her picturing him as a skinny, young gentleman with a mild disposition. But the person who is before her is the exact opposite of that.

Short and stocky, Hank's sturdy build and stance makes her think of a vicious bulldog. His head is cleanly shaven and his round face sports a goatee, the well-trimmed facial hair partially concealing a long, deep scar down the side of his right cheek. He is fully equipped in black tactical gear, just like the men who pursued her and Charlie at the Grand Hotel. But the most arresting thing about him is his dark eyes, aglow with a brutish glimmer.

Hank lets out an amused snort. "Now *this*, this is what I call a reunion, in the truest sense of the word." His glacial stare shifts to Charlie, and he gestures to Mark's corpse with a flick of his knife. "Does this scene remind you of something, Hsu Fu? Hm? I have to say, it's all a bit poetic, finishing just like the way we started all those years ago. Must feel like déjà vu, no?"

Georgia swivels to look at her friend, whose face is as impassive as ever. "You *know* this man?"

But Charlie does not move, does not utter a sound or even give away his emotions with a twitch of his eyebrows. Nor does he respond to her question as he fixes his gaze on the man before them.

It is Hank who answers her instead. "How rude of me.

Allow me to introduce myself, Professor Lee." He chuckles, spreading his palms. "Lambert introduced me to you as Hank, but the poor fool, he didn't even know who I really am. The name I was born with is known to you. It is Wang Jian."

She blinks. *Wang Jian? The general?*

She turns to Charlie. "You told me he was dead?"

"He was," his replies in a whisper. "I killed him."

Hank sniggers. "Correction. You *thought* you killed me. At least, you gave it a good try."

"How?" Charlie utters, his face unreadable.

Hank, or Wang Jian—whoever this man is—smirks at them with amusement. "That night, in your witch friend's hut, you slit my throat with a sword, yes. But you didn't cut me in the same way I did our billionaire here. And, unlike me, you aren't so skilled in the art of killing. I'm a man-at-arms—I've always been—and I've had eons to hone this single skill. I know exactly which arteries to go for to bleed a person out in seconds."

He taps at the base of his throat, in the hollow where his collar bones meet. "The fastest way to kill a man is to stab him right here, straight through to the spine. Or, you can go for the arteries just behind the windpipe. If you simply slice a person across the front of his throat, it takes him forever to die."

Still crouched down, Wang Jian looks up at Charlie as he makes a clicking sound with his tongue. "Now, unlike you, I tend to pride myself in my professionalism. When I set out to kill someone, I make sure they are well and truly dead. Leaving loose ends, my friend, is like forgetting to pay your taxes. Sooner or later, it always catches up to you."

He stands slowly, rising to his full height, and though the man is not tall at all, Georgia feels as if he is looming over her.

"And you, Hsu Fu," Wang Jian continues, "you left a lot of loose ends that night. You didn't stick around to watch me die, and that was a mistake. That's why you weren't there to realise you didn't quite cut me right, or to see me crawl over to the bloody head of your witch friend. I drank her blood, you know. Then I smeared it all over my wound. It was a long shot, I realised, but what did I have to lose by that point? I felt life slip from my body, and I closed my eyes, fearing it hadn't worked and I was sure to die that very night. But it *did* work. I woke up days after, caked with dried blood, two rotting corpses by my side."

"How—" Charlie finally speaks, shaking his head with disbelief. "How did you find me?"

"Well." Wang Jian rubs the back of his bare scalp playfully as he paces back and forth in the cave. "I must say, you were actually pretty difficult to track down. After I woke up in that witch's hut, I spent years sailing up and down and all around Okinawa, trying to find this damned island you went on about. I got there in the end—the Senkaku Islands. But what did I find? Nothing. Birds and rodents and rocks."

He stops his pacing, wagging his knife at Charlie. "That was a good one. You fooled me there. Imagine my rage when I scoured the entire place and found no signs of the Immortals." He lets out a soft laugh. "I swore I would hunt you down, however long it took me. I searched all over the world, but every time I believed I was close, I always ended up a few steps behind. You covered up your tracks pretty well, I'll give you that. But eventually, I asked myself: What is the one single weakness of an immortal man who is almost invisible?"

Charlie's expression is a mixture of realisation and fear. He throws a quick glance at Georgia, whispering, "Loneliness."

Wang Jian nods, exhaling as he closes his eyes briefly. "Loneliness. Yes. Believe me, I know it well. It creeps in over the years like a fungal growth that moulders and spreads until it has seeped into every crack of your soul."

He scratches his goatee, running a finger down the length

of his scar. Redirecting his icy stare at Georgia, his face twists with a menacing smile.

"So, I began to plan. It was an elaborate and carefully thought-out strategy that took years to perfect. First, I needed someone like Lambert. A conceited, power-hungry control freak rich and influential enough to pull this whole charade off. A billionaire with a keen interest in history and antiquities, and someone with the right amount of personal motivation to see it through. It took a little time, but I found a good fit.

"It took me years to work my way into his most trusted circles. That was what took the most time, and one of the more annoying tasks I had to carry out. All these years I had to call him 'sir', and carry out all the dirty work he threw my way. It was humiliating, how over-qualified I was for the job.

"Of course, the final piece of the puzzle," Wang Jian says, nodding at her, "was you."

"Me?" Georgia shrinks under his stare.

"Yeah," he says with a smug grin. "I am sorry to tell you this, Georgia, but you've been a pawn in my plan all this time. A vital part of the scheme, but a pawn, nonetheless."

Wang Jian begins pacing again, waving his knife about casually. "I spent years slowly feeding Lambert just enough information to pique his interest, but not so much that it made him suspicious. Who do you think 'discovered' the Oracle bone that held the information of Hsu Fu's whereabouts? Or told Lambert of the Hata scrolls? Or even convinced him you were the perfect person for the job? Who do you think orchestrated it so you were so desperate for money, you had no choice but to accept Lambert's offer? Every detail, every clue, it was all set up carefully so you couldn't say no. You are a clever girl, Georgia, but I know people. In the end, you were predictable."

Georgia feels her insides roil, the skin on the back of her neck prickling with intensity as she absorbs his revelation.

Wang Jian has been watching her every movement, understanding her weaknesses and strengths, figuring out exactly the right buttons to push. An icy, stinging wave washes over her as she imagines him waiting patiently in the shadows, plotting the right moment to strike.

"Do you see the beauty of this grand scheme?" Wang Jian stops his pacing to stand before her, his palms outstretched. "The perfection of it all?"

She shakes her head, finding her voice at last. "I don't understand. Why me?"

Wang Jian jerks his chin back, the look of surprise almost comical in his features. Then he cackles loudly, as if suddenly realising the joke she is not privy to. He looks to Charlie.

"*Seriously?* You mean you haven't told her yet?"

"Told me what?" She turns to watch the tall man beside her, who is still staring at Wang Jian wordlessly. "Charlie? Told me what?"

"Oh, *this*..." Wang Jian laughs, rubbing his scalp playfully. "This is just too much."

Georgia glares at him. "What are you talking about?"

"Georgia." Wang Jian shakes his head, grinning. He gestures to Charlie with a jerk of his head. "You think the fact that he lives just down the road from your grandmother is a coincidence? Or that he just *happened* to donate his most recent collection to your best friend and sweetheart? Did you honestly believe it would be so easy to track Hsu Fu down, all by yourself, within a matter of months? I've been searching for him for over two thousand years, and this is what I *do*. I hunt people."

He chuckles, the sound sending a chill down her spine.

"No, Georgia." He taps at his temple with a finger. "Use your professor brain. Hsu Fu *wanted* you to find him."

"Yes, because he needed my help to find this cave," she says, hearing the tremor in her voice.

"Maybe." Wang Jian shrugs, amusement gleaming in his dark eyes. "But trust me, that was not the only reason."

She turns to look at the man beside her. He has been awfully quiet since Wang Jian showed up.

"Charlie," she demands. "What's he talking about?"

Her friend, the man she has grown so fond of over the past few weeks, exhales a long sigh. He turns to gaze at her, a forlorn expression on his features.

"I did not tell you the full story, Georgia," he admits. "I am sorry."

70

CHARLIE SIGHS, feeling apprehensive. He looks intently at Georgia's face, noting every minute movement of her delicate features to gauge her reaction.

"Do you remember how I told you about Hsu Jen?" he begins.

Georgia knits her brows, confusion written all over her face. "Your daughter?"

"Yes," he confirms. "Hsu Jen was fifty-five when she died. As I told you, I was away on a voyage at the time, searching for the elixir. Even though my daughter had lived a happy, fulfilling life, leaving behind four children and six grandkids, I felt as if the centre of me had been gouged out. I lived like a hollow man for a long time. That was when I decided to distance myself from the family. Gradually, from being the grandfather that was forever young, to the green-eyed ancestor, I became family lore, a legend. Eventually, they forgot about me altogether.

"But from time to time, I checked in on my family without their knowledge. After all these years, all the centuries of living like a nomad with minimal possessions and emotional attachments, I still found myself insolubly drawn to kinship. Of course, I made a deal with myself: I would only ever observe, and never interfere with their lives. It was important that they did not know about me; I felt it would only put them in danger." He pauses, taking a deep breath before he imparts the next piece of information. "Your grandmother… it took me a long time to find her, what with all the chaos going on in China during that time."

"Amah?" Georgia asks, looking perplexed. "What's she got to do with this?"

Charlie observes her studiously as he says, "She was the last descendant of the Hsu lineage I could track down. Most of them died in the Sino-Japanese war, or the Second World War. The remaining few perished during the Great Famine in China, or were persecuted during Mao's Cultural Revolution a few years later. Your grandmother almost died herself during the Nanjing Massacre; and even though I had promised myself that I would never do it, I could not help but take her to the hospital when I found her unconscious and dying after being raped and stabbed by the Japanese soldiers. In the end, I am glad I did what I did, because otherwise I would not be standing here, with you."

Georgia does not speak. She blinks blankly at him, making Charlie doubt whether she will process the implications of what he is unveiling.

He lets out a long sigh. "Look, what I am trying to tell you, Georgia, is that I have been watching you since you were a little baby. That is how I also know of Ethan, and why I decided to make this donation to his museum—"

"Bloody hell, will you just get to the point already," Wang Jian interjects, shaking his head with a mixture of annoyance and amusement. The general turns to Georgia, who stares at him with wide eyes. "Want to know how I found you, Georgia? I mapped all of the Hsu descendants, one by one. You are the last of his clan. You should have seen this family tree, it was magnificent. I reckon your assistant probably thought so too."

"Sarah?" Georgia says, visibly alarmed.

Wang Jian nods, smiling. "You should know she is very loyal to you. Not many people can hold their ground during my interrogations. But Sarah, she never caved. Feisty woman if I've ever met one. And believe me, I've met a fair few in my lifetime." He chuckles.

"Where is she? What did you do to her?" Georgia demands, terror lacing her shaky voice.

"Oh, I only grabbed her to see if she knew where you were." Wang Jian waves his hand dismissively. "I've stashed her somewhere safe. But by the time anyone manages to find her, she'll be long dead. A shame really; she's got real spunk about her, and I admire that."

At Georgia's horrified expression, the general continues, "Look, if it's any consolation, she was lucky I located you from your phone, otherwise I might've had to use more *traditional* methods to extract information from her. Hsu Fu knows what I mean: he had his fair share of torture back in the day."

Charlie clenches his fists by his side, and all of the hatred he had ever felt for the general comes rushing back.

"Do you see now, Professor?" The general continues, looking awfully smug. "Do you see the grandeur of my scheme? Like I said before: what we have here is a reunion, in every sense of the word."

Grinning, he rubs the back of his shaved scalp, then runs a finger slowly down the scar on his face. Watching the general perform these distantly familiar quirks brings a surge of memories in Charlie. All of sudden, he is back in Japan again: tied to a tree, bloody and screaming, as Lu Hsing carves bits of flesh from his body. Wang Jian hovers somewhere in the background, rubbing his scalp with frustration, demanding: *Tell me. Tell me everything.*

Charlie shudders, shaking off the horrific images.

"You know, all that time I spent waiting, all the hard work I've put into this, and all those years of dealing with this arsehole—" The general kicks the corpse beside him, and an involuntary yelp escapes Georgia. "I must say, I am extremely pleased with the final result. I couldn't have wished for a better outcome.

"And now," Wang Jian declares, fixing his cold gaze on Charlie. "It looks like we've come full circle, and we'll end this where it all began. I'll get to finish what I started all those centuries ago, and you'll get to join your silver-haired witch friend. You have no idea how long I've been waiting for this moment."

Wang Jian licks his bottom lip, giving a playful twirl of his knife, and takes a step towards them.

71

"I DON'T GET IT," Georgia speaks up, trying to stall the inevitable. "Why did you bother to look for Hsu Fu all this time? Emperor Qin is long dead, and you're not bound by his mission anymore. Surely it can't be *professionalism?* Why would you go through all this trouble just to finish a job that you were charged to do two thousand years ago?"

Wang Jian pauses in his tracks. For the first time since he arrived in the cave, she sees fury making its ugly flush across his face.

"I guess he didn't tell you that, either, huh? Of course he didn't." He hisses with rancour. "I bet he's been portraying himself as the patron saint of mankind."

Georgia looks at Charlie, her heart sinking as she sees the obvious guilt in his face. "What's Wang Jian talking about?"

He closes his eyes, shaking his head slowly.

"Charlie."

He sighs. Turning to her, he finally says, "That night, when Wang Jian and one of his men came for us at Naaya's hut… The other man I killed was Wang Jian's son."

"My *only* son," Wang Jian adds, the wrath and pain in his voice palpable. "This'll resonate with you, Georgia, since you watched your own daughter die. Imagine what it would have been like, to wake up to eternal life, only to gag at the rotting scent of your son's body lying beside you. You shoo the rats away from gnawing at his remains, and you try to feed the dried, caked blood of the witch between his lifeless lips, praying to the gods it will work the way it worked for you. It doesn't, of course. Your son is gone. Forever. And you have an eternity to ponder on that."

Georgia swallows hard. She feels as if she's about to be sick. The crazed look in the general's glare only adds to the churning in her stomach.

"Hsu Fu took from me my only family, and left me with nothing," Wang Jian says. "So no, *nothing* would have stopped me from hunting him down. In fact, the only thing that has kept me going over the years is the thought of revenge."

"I am sorry—" Charlie begins remorsefully.

"You're sorry! You're *sorry?*" Wang Jian roars, the outburst resounding throughout the cave.

Georgia flinches, her eyes darting around the chamber, worried the explosion of sound will destabilise the structure. The echoes die without incident, and she watches Wang Jian as he tangibly reels in his rage, breath by breath. Slowly, the scowl on his face transforms into a triumphant smile.

"I don't want your apology, Hsu Fu," he says softly, shaking his head. "No. What I want is for you to suffer the way I have. I want you to feel the pain I felt the night you took away my only son. I want you to howl as you watch the last of your loved ones die in your arms."

Without warning, the general's movements are a blur as he strikes Hsu Fu on the temple with the hilt of his blade, rending the taller man senseless on the ground.

His eyes ablaze, Wang Jian shifts his gaze to Georgia.

She takes an instinctive step back, but hardly fast enough to dodge Wang Jian's rapid advance, and she feels the air knocked out of her as he brings her down, his full weight crushing her. She lands hard on her back, her head cracking against something solid.

The pain in her bruised ribs flares, and gasping for breath, she glimpses the flash of Wang Jian's knife. Georgia recoils, watching in slow motion as the weapon arcs towards her, expecting the inevitable blow. But just before it lands, Wang Jian's weight suddenly disappears. Hsu Fu lifts the general to his feet, then strikes Wang Jian's jaw with a rock in hand.

The general staggers back and drops into the shallow pool, blood oozing from his face, swiftly followed by Charlie, who throws his full weight on him. Grunts, muffled curses, and the sound of splashing water pervade the cave. Georgia struggles to sit up, a wave of dizziness hitting her as pain radiates through her skull. Her rib cage feels as if it is on fire as she fights to put air back into her lungs.

She squints at the two men wrestling in the water. Some time during the struggle, the small lantern has been knocked over and kicked to the far end of the cave. Georgia fumbles to retrieve Mark's torch, still alight and abandoned beside his lifeless body.

She points the torchlight at the men, trying to see what is happening. In the shallow water, Wang Jian straddles Charlie's chest, his hands clamped like a vice over the taller man's throat. The knife is nowhere to be seen, but there is a deep wound in Charlie's arm, gushing with blood.

He doesn't seem to be healing. And he is being choked to death.

Something glints in the beam of the torch and Georgia sees the unmistakable silver object clipped to the back of Wang Jian's belt. Before she can fully register her intentions, she is reaching to snatch the pistol from him.

"Stop!" she yells, pointing the gun at Wang Jian. "Let him go!"

The stocky man turns to look at her, seeing the weapon in

her hand. He releases his grip on Charlie and slowly stands up. Then he smiles, his mirth building into a gleeful chortle.

"What you gonna do, shoot me?"

"I will if I have to." She cocks the hammer to demonstrate the sincerity of her threat. By sheer will, she stops her hands from trembling.

Wang Jian's cocky smile fades.

"Georgia. No." Charlie chokes, his voice a hoarse strangle of a whisper. He frantically extends a hand out towards her. "The cave—"

Distracted, she sees Wang Jian pounce towards her, and reflexively she squeezes the trigger just as it's knocked out of her hand. The gun goes off, the bullet ricocheting thunderously across the chamber. There is a brief moment of deadly silence, before a deep, resonant rumble envelopes them.

"Oh my God," she whispers, as the ground beneath her starts to shake.

72

GEORGIA WATCHES in muted horror as the cave begins to crumble. Fine dust and sand fall in streams all around them, followed quickly by rocks of all sizes.

Then she hears Charlie yell out, "Run, Georgia!"

She turns to see him bring a large stone down on Wang Jian's head. The general falls to the ground, grunting as blood pours down his face. Charlie darts towards her and grabs her by the arm, pulling her to her feet.

"Run!"

His voice startles her out of stupor, and she follows him, racing towards the tunnel entrance. But as they crouch down to enter, the small passage caves in, issuing out a cloud of dust.

Georgia stumbles back just as a deep fissure splits the ground open, the jolt sending her tumbling across the cave floor. She sits up, scrambling backwards on her hands and feet as the crevice spreads, forcing her into the pool of water at the other end of the cave.

Several metres away, Wang Jian has recovered and throws himself at Charlie, bringing both of them to the ground. The two men once again lock in a deathly embrace. Wang Jian gains the upper hand, pummelling his fist savagely into the other man's face.

His opponent unconscious, the general rises to his feet, fixing his fiery stare on Georgia. He advances towards her, and at that moment, another violent quake disturbs the chamber around them, sending sections of the ceiling caving in on him.

She scurries back swiftly to avoid being struck, splashing about in the water that is almost reaching to her chest. Amidst the rubble she sees Wang Jian crushed under a giant boulder, his feet protruding at an awkward angle from underneath the rock.

He isn't moving.

Georgia's eyes search frantically through the dim cave. It doesn't take her long to find what she's looking for, the horrifying sight stilling her: Charlie's arm, limp and bleeding, also partially buried by the debris.

"Charlie?!" she calls out. With effort, she rises to her feet.

But her voice is drowned out in the deafening chaos, and she hears no reply. She only manages a couple of steps towards Charlie's body before the ground disappears from under her. As she falls through the floor, she reaches her hand out instinctively, grasping in vain for something to hold on to. Her fingers struggle to grip anything solid as she is washed down the chasm, crashing and tumbling until something strikes hard against the side of her skull.

She briefly registers the ringing in her ears and the darkening edges around her vision. Then, everything fades into pitch darkness.

73

Somewhere in the far distance, someone is calling her name.

Georgia tries to ignore it, to block it out and push it to the background, so she can go back to sleep. She is so very tired. But whoever it is, they are stubbornly and annoyingly persistent.

As she opens her eyes with the intention of telling the person to go away, she's greeted with an almighty headache. Squinting into the bright light, the face of her assistant swims into focus, so close to her own that Georgia shrinks away with surprise.

"Oh, thank God," Sarah says, relief all over her features. "How are you feeling?"

"Sarah?" Georgia frowns, blinking a few times to clear her vision. "What's going on? Where am I?"

"You're at a hospital," Sarah explains, standing up in her chair. "The NTU Hospital in Taipei. I'm gonna get the doctor for you."

Without another word, her assistant sprints through a doorway. Georgia props up on her elbows to look about her, seeing the large, whitewashed room she's sharing with five other patients, most of them with a loved one sitting close by, some of them with curtains drawn for privacy. She wrinkles her nose at the scent of disinfectant permeating the air. There is a window at the far end of the room, its venetian blinds filtering the sunlight into stripes across the vinyl flooring.

Georgia furrows her brows, trying to clear her thoughts as she attempts to recall how she ended up here. Then she sits up with a jolt, her heart racing and her breath coming on fast, as memories of Charlie, Wang Jian, and the cave come rushing back.

Sarah returns with the doctor and a nurse in tow. At the sight of Georgia's terrified expression, she exclaims, "What's wrong?!"

"Georgia." The doctor, an elderly man, walks over and places both hands on her shoulders. He coaxes gently, "You're having a panic attack. I need you to sit back. Take a few deep breaths for me."

The young nurse reaches for the electronic controls, raising the upper half of the bed. They ease Georgia back as she strives to inhale slowly.

"Good, very good," the doctor says soothingly in Chinese as she relaxes. "There. Feeling better?"

She nods, staring up to his creased face as he smiles.

"I'm Doctor Yang," he says. "Do you know where you are?"

"Yes," she replies, "at the NTU hospital in Taipei."

Nodding, Dr. Yang reaches into his pocket for a penlight to examine her eyes. "Can you tell me your full name and date of birth?"

"Georgia Lee. Seventh of December, 1982."

"Good," Dr. Yang says as he straightens up. "Are you experiencing any nausea or headaches? Any dizziness?"

"I had a headache earlier…" replies Georgia. "But it seems to be better now."

Dr. Yang nods. "Any ringing in your ears?"

She shakes her head.

"No other discomfort at all?"

"Just tired, I think." Her voice is hoarse.

"What is the last thing you remember?"

"I…" She pauses, darting a quick glance at Sarah. "I'm not sure. I think I must have hit my head on a rock."

"That's okay, it'll probably come back to you later." He nods at the nurse, who moves over to measure Georgia's temperature and blood pressure.

Dr. Yang looks through her charts, and jots down the latest readings. Then he looks up to smile at her. "You have recovered well. Everything seems to be back to normal. But I'd like to keep you for a couple more days for observation, just in case."

"Okay."

"In the meantime, try to get as much rest as you can. Your body has been through quite a lot these last few days."

She nods. "Thank you."

Dr. Yang and his nurse saunter out of the room, and Sarah moves forward, planting herself into the chair beside the bed.

"You feeling okay?" Her forehead is crinkled with worry.

"I think so," Georgia says. "What happened?"

"Oh, Georgia, I've been so worried." Sarah shakes her head, grasping Georgia's hand. "You've been out of it for almost a week, burning high fevers and delirious half of the time. The doctors believe you've contracted an infection from exposure."

"How did I get here? How are you in Taipei?"

"They found you downstream on the bank of the river in Taroko Gorge, unconscious. We had no idea how long you were out there. The doctors decided to move you to the hospital in Taipei for better treatment," Sarah says. "When you didn't report to the Park administration on the day you were expected to be back from your trek, they sent out a search party. There's been a few earthquakes in the area which caused some minor landslides, and several of the trails have been damaged. They've still not found Lambert and his assistant, and the other person on your trail permit… Charlie, was it? It's all made front page news: *Billionaire Missing after Earthquake in Taiwan*, blah blah blah."

Sarah starts to recount everything that happened since they last spoke on the phone: the kidnapping and interrogations, her rather clever prisonbreak from the basement, and the investigation Detective Turner has been carrying out. A mixture of shock, anger, and relief overwhelms Georgia as she listens.

"Turner reached out to the authorities here, that's how we were contacted when they found you. I hopped on the plane the very next day," Sarah explains. "Of course, when the news came out and they released photos of Lambert and his assistant as missing persons, I realised that Hank was the one who kidnapped me."

"I can't believe he did that to you. When he told me that he took you…" Georgia whispers, her lips trembling. "I feared for the worst. I am so sorry. It's all my fault."

"Nonsense." Sarah squeezes Georgia's hand. "I swear, though, if that man is still alive… When Turner captures him, I'll be petitioning to the government to bring back the death penalty."

"He's not." Georgia shakes her head. "I'm pretty certain he died at Taroko."

"What do you mean, *died?* What happened out there?"

Georgia takes in a deep breath. Speaking in English with a quiet voice so the other patients in the room can't listen in, she tells Sarah her story. She reveals everything about Naaya and the elixir, about Charlie, and about their search in Taroko. A violent mix of emotions roils in her gut as she describes in detail all that happened in the cave and Wang Jian's mad obsession, driven by the single goal of hunting one man down for the sake of revenge.

Her eyes began to fill with tears as she recalls that Charlie didn't make it out of the cave, but died saving her. She still can't fathom the truth of who he was, a distant ancestor who watched over her like a guardian spirit. Ironically, she realises, Charlie did get his wish in the end. Even if it wasn't exactly how he expected to reach his goal.

By the time Georgia finishes her tale, her voice has diminished to a muted whisper, and the light outside the window has faded into night.

A hospital employee pushes in a trolley, making the rounds to distribute dinner to patients. Georgia eyes the tray of hospital food, unable to conjure up an appetite. When the orderly leaves again, Sarah heaves a long sigh, shaking her head. She leans forward to rest her arms on the bed.

"That is some fucked up, crazy shit," she says, wringing her fingers uneasily.

Georgia can't help but give a wry smile as she wipes her tears away. Her assistant's potty mouth is comfortingly familiar.

After a long moment of silence, Sarah looks up at her. "Listen, Georgia, you simply can't tell anyone else this. Sergeant Turner will want a statement. The whole of Taiwan's gonna want a statement. They have three missing people on their hands, one of them a high-profile figure in the Forbes Billionaire List. If you tell them this story, they'll think you've gone mad. They'll say you hit your head harder than you thought. The cave is destroyed, so you can't even prove the elixir existed in the first place. It'll ruin your reputation as a scientist. It'll most likely wreck your career."

"I know," Georgia agrees. "What do I tell them, though?"

Sarah worries her hands some more, thinking on this. "Tell them everything, except the cave. Tell them that Lambert paid you a ridiculous sum because he had this crazy idea in his head. You didn't believe in the elixir for one second, but you had to secure the funding for the department. Tell them it was all a wild goose chase and you found nothing, and it all tragically ended when the earthquake brought rocks down on you on the trail."

"What about Charlie? How do I explain him?"

Sarah shrugs. "He was just another expert that Lambert hired. No one knows him or his real name. They couldn't even find a photo of him for the news release."

Georgia nods silently, considering Sarah's advice as she leans back against the raised bed, suddenly overcome with exhaustion. She lets out a yawn.

Sarah pats Georgia's hand. "Look, you're tired, I'll let you sleep. We can talk more tomorrow. I gotta make some phone calls anyway; your grandmother's gonna be so happy you're finally awake."

"Amah? Is she okay?"

"Yeah," Sarah replies. "She's been coming in every day to check on you. I sent her home earlier, I could tell she was getting tired."

Georgia nods. "Tell her I'll give her a call in the morning."

"Sure," Sarah smiles, rising to stand. She looks at Georgia's untouched food. "You want me to grab you something more decent?"

"No," Georgia shakes her head, smiling.

"Okay. I'll see you tomorrow."

"Thanks. See you tomorrow." Her voice is a whisper, and she's barely able to keep her eyes open.

Watching Sarah leave, Georgia pushes the tray of food away, reaching for the electronic controls to lower her bed. As she curls up on her side and hugs her knees to her chest, she feels an instant calm envelop her like a thin blanket. She closes her eyes.

As always in quiet moments like this, the thought of Jacqui surfaces in her mind. Ghosts of her daughter swirl all around her, appearing and disappearing into the dark recesses of her head. The days before Jacqui's death are replayed like a movie, and Georgia feels the presence of her baby girl in a powerfully physical way. She can almost hear her gurgling laughter, almost feel Jacqui's fine silky hair between her fingertips, almost detect her scent.

A deep sense of longing throbs within her chest.

As Georgia edges towards sleep, her mind roams over the possibilities of what could have been if she'd managed to salvage a sample of the elixir. It fills her with remorse to think she could have prevented all of this from happening to other parents—the pain she went through during Jacqui's illness and death, and the anguish she felt as she watched her marriage disintegrate. She could have spared others like Nola Lambert from her agonising fate.

But is humanity ready for it?

Then, just as her mind gives in to slumber, she remembers that contemplating any of it is futile.

Charlie's gone. The elixir is lost forever.

EPILOGUE

Two weeks later, Melbourne

GEORGIA TAKES A FORTIFYING BREATH.

"You can do this," she mutters to herself, raising her hand to knock on the door.

It's a rare, sunny winter's afternoon in Melbourne, and she's on Ethan's front porch in Collingwood, waiting for her best friend to open his door. The sun hangs low on the horizon, casting a golden glow over the quiet neighbourhood. Minutes pass, and Georgia fidgets, readjusting the shopping bags in her hand and wondering if it would've been better to call first before showing up unannounced.

Well. It's too late to think about that.

"Please be home," she whispers.

Georgia knows Ethan is probably mad at her for abandoning their plans to see each other again in Taipei after their tryst. She knows he must have seen her on the news too, judging from the recent messages he's sent. And yet, she has thwarted his every attempt to contact her. Until now.

Yeah, he's got to be furious.

It's better to talk to him face to face, she decides, and knocks louder this time.

"Coming!" A gruff voice issues from the other side of the door. At the familiar sound, a smile spreads across Georgia's face.

The door flies open, and she draws in a sharp breath as she looks up at Ethan's face. He is tugging at a crumpled shirt he's hurriedly put on, his darkened hair dripping with water. Seeing her before him, a startled look of incredulity flashes across his eyes as his hands fall still. Then, utter, undisguised relief replaces the shock on his face, and for a split second, it looks like he's about reach for her.

But he doesn't. Instead, he balls his fists, crossing his arms over his broad chest as if to prevent himself from touching her.

"George," he says, his voice full of strain. Then he frowns as he looks her over. "Are you okay?"

She nods, giving him a small, hesitant smile. "Hi."

They stare at each other silently.

"I can explain," says Georgia.

Ethan shakes his head, a seething look of dismay now settling in his features. His voice low, he says, "A phone call, a text, an email—hell, *anything* to let me know that you were okay would've been nice."

"I'm sorry…."

Ethan rakes a hand through his damp hair, blowing out a huff of frustration. Shaking his head again, he says, "We hadn't seen each other in six years, George. Then we had this one amazing—mind-blowing—night together, and you just walked out of my life again without even a note? And then, after a whole month of not knowing what happened, I see you on the news, *found unconscious in the jungles of Taiwan!* Do you know how worried I've been? Why didn't you pick up any of my calls or return my messages?"

When Georgia comes up with nothing, Ethan lets out a

sigh, his arms falling to his sides as if in defeat. She feels a lump lodge in her throat at the hurt in his soft blue eyes.

"After everything we've been through... after all that we've been to each other... you still don't trust me enough to come to me when you're in trouble." Ethan shakes his head. "I don't get it, George. What do you want from me?"

Panicked for words, she utters the first thing that comes to her mind. "You... you thought that night was mind-blowing, too?"

Ethan blinks, and a surprised sound escapes his lips, the staccato snort thick with frustration. Crossing his arms again, he narrows his eyes.

"I—" Georgia stutters, "I know. And I'm sorry. I'm soooooo sorry. There's a really good reason behind it all, I swear," she pleads. "It's a pretty long story, though. Can I please just come in for a bit, and we'll talk?"

But Ethan doesn't move. He stares at her mutely and maintains his stance, his broad frame filling the entire doorway. It appears he has no intention of letting her in without a decent amount of begging.

"Please? I'll cook you dinner," she adds, lifting the shopping bags to show him her peace offering.

He seems to consider this briefly. Then he lifts his chin, still not budging. "What if I already have plans? What if I've got someone coming over? You can't just show up, expecting me to always drop everything for you."

Her heart plummets. She should have called first. Of course he has plans. It's Saturday and Ethan's a hotblooded, attractive guy. Why did she assume that he'd be free?

Then Georgia remembers something Sarah said, and she grits her teeth. She didn't just fly seven thousand kilometres from Taiwan, after everything she has survived, to be sent home again. It's been hellish over the past two weeks, dealing with all the authorities in Taiwan, and then trying to fully recover her strength from everything she's been through.

No. Ethan's just going to have to cancel.

"Do you?" she presses. "Do you have plans?"

He stares at her, his nostrils flaring as he inhales audibly. After a long, agonising moment, she sees the familiar mischief flash in his eyes.

"No," he finally says.

Her spirits soar, and she has to purse her lips to stop from grinning. Standing on the tips of her toes, she rises to his height, jabbing a playful finger at his chest.

"Then. Let. Me. *In*." Georgia gives him her best doe eyes, sing-songing, "I'll be making your favourite. Chicken sandwich with lettuce and extra mayo."

She dangles the bag of food in front of Ethan's face, the scent of roast chicken filling the air. Georgia watches his Adam's apple bob up and down as he swallows, his stomach letting out a fierce growl.

With a grunt, he relents and moves aside to make room for her through the door. "Fine. But only 'cause I'm starving right now. Don't think you're forgiven," he warns. "We're eating and then we're talking this shit out."

She almost skips inside with triumph, heading straight down the hall into the sun-filled, open-plan living room. At the adjoining kitchen, Georgia places the groceries on the bench, moving around the familiar space to gather everything needed to prepare their meal.

Ethan ambles in, grabbing the TV remote to mute the news channel. He rests against the back of the couch opposite the kitchen counter, crossing his long legs before him as he watches her closely. Then he opens his mouth to ask something, only to be interrupted by Georgia's raised hand.

"Let me make these sandwiches first," she says, knowing what he's about to say. "I'll get into everything once we sit down to eat."

He purses his lips with a terse nod and says instead, "Careful with the knife, I only sharpened it yesterday."

"Okay."

As Georgia starts to slice the lettuce into thin shreds, she worries the edge of her lower lip, madly sorting through everything she needs to say.

On the way over here from the airport, she again debated inwardly over what to tell Ethan. In the end, Georgia decided that if they're ever to have a chance at being together, then the full story must be revealed. She needs to start with Lambert's offer over four months ago, and end with what happened in the cave. Ethan deserves the truth; it's the least she can give him.

"See, there you are again, on the news," Ethan says, breaking her out of her thoughts. "You have no idea how worried I was after I saw this."

Georgia looks up towards the TV in the lounge room as Ethan turns on the volume. Although she's seen the report a few times already, the images still make her cringe. On the screen, she sees herself strapped unconscious to a stretcher whilst being lifted into an ambulance. Dark, wet hair plastered around her ghostly pale face, she's dwarfed by the paramedics working around her. The video footage is replaced by a photograph of Lambert at a charity function, dressed in a tuxedo as he smiles dashingly into the camera.

"...one injured and three missing, the recent landslides as a result of earthquakes in Taiwan are causing further delays as authorities continue the search. Among the missing is the renowned billionaire, Mark Lambert. Mr. Lambert and his assistant, Hank Law, were hiking in the area when the catastrophic collapse..."

Her eyes glued to the screen, she continues to chop the vegetable before her, until the sharp edge of the blade sinks deep into her flesh. Hissing with pain, Georgia recoils her hand, grabbing a nearby tea towel to wrap around her forefinger.

"You okay?" Ethan is on his feet, striding towards her as she blinks back the tears.

"I cut my finger," she says.

"Here, let me see."

She shakes her head. "I think I might need stitches. I think I cut it pretty deep."

"Let's just wash it out first," he coaxes, gentle taking her hand to unravel the soaked, bloody towel. "Jesus."

She winces as he peels the fabric off. Ethan pulls them towards the sink, guiding her hand under the cold, running water. She turns away, the sight of blood making her woozy.

After a silent moment, Ethan lets go of her hand abruptly with a soft laugh. "Oh, very funny, George. Trying to get some sympathy points, eh?"

"What do you mean?" Georgia frowns, turning back towards the sink as the last traces of blood wash away. She blinks at the sight of her unmarred finger.

What the—

Georgia is certain she cut it. The memory of the knife carving into her skin is as clear as the water running over her hand right now.

A myriad of questions hits her all at once. There were no injuries on her body when she woke up in the hospital, not even a bruise, despite everything that happened in Taroko. How was that possible? And whilst she was unconscious, she burned a delirious, high fever for a whole week, just as Charlie had after he took the elixir. Could this be her body reacting to the virus Charlie described?

Then, fragmented, kaleidoscopic impressions resurfaces in her mind: the deafening roar of the walls crumbling around her, the pain of her fingernails splintering as she desperately grasped for purchase, the way she coughed and spluttered on the water as she was washed down the dark tunnel before being knocked unconscious.

She gasps, lifting her hand to study it closely. The elixir is not lost, after all.

Her mind as sharp and lucid as the light glinting off the water beads on her skin, a single thought arises from within.

Is humanity ready?

❋❋❋❋❋

ACKNOWLEDGMENTS

My deepest gratitude to family and friends, for your encouragement and support through the daunting task of completing this book. Thank you especially to mum and dad —as always you stand by me through all of my endeavours.

Thank you to my beta readers, for your invaluable feedback: Pamela Blackburn, Alicia Sometimes, Tara Wang, Shannon Murphy, and Katrina Wilson. A special thanks to Meagan Lipscombe for enduring my (rather awful) first draft, and Vanessa Lawless for accepting the cruel and unusual punishment of not only reading the first, but also the second version of this book. Thank you, also, to Joanne Turner for her guidance on the inner workings of the Australian Federal Police.

To my friends at the Taipei Writers Group: I am infinitely thankful for your guidance, critical input, and friendship throughout this entire process. I have learnt so much from all of you. Thank you especially to Mark Will, Jenny Green, and of course my editor, Pat Woods.

Last but most importantly, to my husband, Mark Blackburn: for being the cheerleader, the cook, the beta-reader of every single draft, the sounding board, the website guru, the marketing manager and publishing assistant, and all-round, mind-blowingly amazing guy. Without you, this book would simply not exist.

GEORGIA LEE SERIES, BOOK TWO

THE GOLDEN KHAN

The deadly race for the secrets of absolute power begins…

1227 CE, MONGOLIA. The greatest conqueror ever known is entombed with a terrifying weapon, a secret which can obliterate any enemy and bring the greatest nations to ruin.

NOW, dark forces are gathering to possess what is in his grave to create a new world order…

Just as archaeologist Georgia Lee begins to grapple with the earth-shattering consequences of her last expedition in Taiwan, her life is once again thrown into chaos when she is called to examine an artefact containing vital clues to the undiscovered tomb of Genghis Khan, founder of the largest contiguous land empire in human history.

What follows is a desperate race across the vast, infinite landscape of Mongolia to solve one of the greatest archaeological mysteries, and to thwart those who threaten to destroy the world as we know it.

But to find the tomb, Georgia must first untangle the truth from the lies of what has been told of the Mongols and expose the real Golden Khan – the legend behind the mighty Mongol Empire. She must also fight to protect her own secrets from those who would kill to possess them.

The Golden Khan is the sequel to A.H. Wang's best-selling debut novel, The Imperial Alchemist, and the second book in the Georgia Lee Series. A seamless blend of fact and fiction that will have you guessing at every turn of the pages, this is an intelligent, daring, fast-paced thriller that will keep you up all night.

Available now at all major book retailers!

Or get free sample chapters of The Golden Khan by signing up below:

www.AHWangAuthor.com/contact-me

ABOUT THE AUTHOR

A. H. Wang is a contemporary visual artist and author with a fascination for history and a passion for adventure. Born in Taiwan and raised in Australia, her travels have taken her across five continents and dozens of countries. Throughout her journey, she has developed a sincere appreciation for local cultures and the lore of ancient civilisations.

As well as making art and writing, you will find her deeply involved with her meditation practice. In a previous life, she was also a scientist, an engineer, a holistic counsellor, and a Reiki Master. She now lives in Taipei, Taiwan, with her husband.

www.ahwangauthor.com

facebook.com/ahwangauthor

instagram.com/ahwangauthor

goodreads.com/ahwangauthor

bookbub.com/authors/a-h-wang

Printed in Great Britain
by Amazon